TEMPEST

THE TERRAN CYCLE: BOOK TWO

PHILIP C. QUAINTRELL

Copyright © 2016 by Philip C. Quaintrell
First edition published 2016.
Second edition published 2021.

Cover Illustration by Tom Edwards
Book design by BodiDog Design
Edited by David Bradley

ISBN: 978-1-916610-25-5 (paperback)
ASIN: B08Y4L8TZB (ebook)

Published by Quaintrell Publishings

ALSO BY PHILIP C. QUAINTRELL

"The evil that men do lives after them. The good is oft interrèd with their bones."

William Shakespeare

PROLOGUE

With no sound at all, the *Tempest* was violently ripped from subspace and hurled back into the vacuum of reality. On every deck, alarms cut through the eerie silence of their long journey home. The Rem-stores automatically came to life, rousing their occupants with stimulants designed for such emergencies. Overhead spotlights illuminated the slumbering chamber in a soft glow, as the first of the Terran crew stepped out of their advanced sarcophagus.

Adanae put one foot on the cold polished floor, trying to make sense of her own thoughts. Her heart was racing in her chest as the stimulants worked to rouse her as fast as possible. Using her Terran abilities, she connected to her body's receptors and slowly began to take back control, slowing her heart rate to a steady sixty-five beats per minute. Pushing her awareness beyond the Rem-store, she felt the familiar presence of her fellow scientists and friends.

After a few seconds, Adanae's vision corrected the constant spinning, bringing back the clarity of the *Tempest*. She stepped out completely, allowing the connecting tubules to disconnect and the machine to close up behind her. The cold air was uncomfortable on her naked body. More of the Rem-stores began to open down the corridor with their internal green lights illuminating the walls. The gloomy corridor was filling with more naked bodies and a lot of confused expressions. The overhead lights flickered, telling Adanae the ship was diverting energy - never a good sign.

As she held out her hand, palm down, the ship produced an oval column of liquid-like nanocelium that rose up to meet her, where it coalesced into a solid object. Using anti-gravity projectors, a triangular device with the apex cut off was presented at the top of the column, floating end over end. Adanae quickly scooped it up and pressed it below her navel. The nanocelium contained within, immediately dispersed across her body like a second skin. Without thinking she opened her hand and used the emitters in her fingertips to create an orange holographic menu inside her palm. By flexing each finger, she manipulated the hologram into selecting the colour white for her armoured exo-suit. As a scientist, she had always preferred white, as opposed to the black typically worn by their warriors.

"ALF, turn that damned alarm off!" With no response from the AI, she remembered that he was no longer on board but, instead, entombed on a distant moon, light-years away. "*Tempest*, deactivate the alarm." At once the blaring signal stopped, bringing back the chatter of the others along the corridor as they suited up as she had. "Report."

"Light-drive engines have been manually taken offline," the ship's male voice stated. "In the unscheduled emergence into real space, the aft hull was breached. Life support systems are compromised."

As lead scientist, Adanae took charge and ordered the six nearest crew to leave and man the bridge, located two decks above them.

"*Tempest*, how could the drives be taken offline manually? Everyone was in Rem-storage."

"Incorrect. Prior to the alarm, one Rem-store was opened ahead of schedule. Life-support at fifty-seven percent. Estimated twenty-one hours before complete depletion of oxygen stores."

Adanae felt her stomach flip. She knew exactly whose Rem-store had opened; he was the only one who would do this.

"Where is he right now?"

"Please specify."

"Where is Malekk, *Tempest*?" Dealing with a sub-AI was frustrating.

"Engineering - deck three."

"You are to treat him as hostile, *Tempest*. Do you understand? You have to stop him before he does any more damage." She knew it had been a mistake to keep him alive, let alone keep him on the ship. She turned to Grif and Nalana, signalling them to follow her.

"Unable to comply," the *Tempest* AI replied. "Internal security measures have been shut down."

Adanae groaned in frustration as they exited the deck. She instructed everyone telepathically to man their stations and have teams ready to fix the drives and life support after they dealt with Malekk. She wouldn't normally use such an intimate form of communication on a large scale, but she needed everyone to receive their orders on the other decks as fast as possible. The grav tubes beyond the chamber allowed for a quick descent to the engineering deck.

She knew that the ship, shaped like the head of a spoon, was spinning out of control in the middle of space. If it wasn't for the grav plating, they would all be pummelled to death inside the giant centrifuge. She suddenly began to worry *where* they were. What if they were being pulled into the gravity well of a planet or a star?

"*Tempest*, what is our location at present?"

"Unknown. Sensors are currently offline while life-support is compromised."

She blamed the stimulants for not making the connection with the flickering lights earlier. The ship would automatically shut down nonessential automations to divert energy to life-support. She sent a quick telepathic message to Ryson on the bridge. She wanted sensors brought back online as soon as possible.

"How long have we been in storage?" Grif asked.

"Fifty-one days, eleven hours, twenty-eight minutes and thirty-four seconds."

"Is that it?" Nalana exclaimed. "Have we even left this arm of the galaxy yet?"

"Negative."

"We should have brought a bigger ship," Grif replied.

"Or a Starforge." Nalana joked. Without ALF it was impossible to use a Starforge. Only the AI could comprehend the mathematics required to fold space in such a way, and the individual components wouldn't even fit on board.

"Quit the jokes," Adanae ordered. "We have to stop him." They were approaching the doors to engineering.

"We brought him down the first time, we can do it again." Grif sounded confident, as an organic ball of plasma was birthed in his hand, wiping away the shadows.

"We should have killed him there and then." Nalana activated her suit's menu and reshaped the nanocelium. Her head and face were instantly encompassed in white plating that sloped down into her chin. Grif quickly followed suit, but Adanae didn't even think about it. She suffered from claustrophobia enough as it was on board the ship, without coating her face with a metal helmet. She had been meaning to go through her mind and erase the fear but had been too busy with the *Second Chance* project.

The console on the wall wasn't responding to their touch, and the door's sensors refused to recognise their presence. Adanae pushed out her awareness, feeling Malekk's position beyond the door in her mind. He wasn't hiding. It was playing out, exactly the same as the first time they caught him. While in orbit around the planet of the future Terran, Malekk had tried to sabotage the genetic manipulation of one of the local creatures. They later learned that he had been in the process of building a communicator array, powerful enough to transmit a message to Savrick and the rest of the Gomar. Adanae was already regretting being on the side of keeping him alive for trial when they finally returned.

The war had been black and white before people like Malekk came along, sympathisers to the Gomar cause, willing to kill their own on the orders of some madman. Savrick was only too willing to use the Terran against themselves; he probably thought it was poetic.

He had killed two of their crew in their first encounter. He may be a scientist but, like all Terran, he had been instructed in the ways of war when the first solar system had been wiped out by the Gommarian. Adanae knew he wouldn't just surrender at the sight of them and, if his actions were anything to go by, he was intent on killing them all. Nalana removed two hilts from the base of her back and activated the nanocelium to create short blades. Adanae on the other hand, welcomed the tingle in her spine and the resultant heat flowing into her hands as she connected to the universe.

They used telekinesis to slide open the door, breaking the internal servos. Speed and numbers were the only advantages they would have. Nalana dashed to the left, leaping up the wall to gain some height on Malekk. Grif slid to the floor, firing off a couple of plasma orbs in the traitor's direction, no doubt using his connection to the universe to guide his aim. Adanae stood her ground, cocooned in a thick shield of telekinetic energy. More proficient in her telepathic abilities, she poured her consciousness into Malekk's. His defences were good but she distracted him enough to give the others a chance. One of Grif's shots fizzled against Malekk's shield, creating a rainbow as the light refracted, but the second struck him across the thigh dropping him to one knee. Nalana came down at that same moment, her blades angled to plunge through his chest. In a last show of strength, Malekk held up his hand, telekinetically pushing her back into the wall. That use of energy was all Adanae needed to force her way past his defence and blanket his mind with her own suggestions.

Pain was the only thing she had in mind. They all felt his shield disintegrate as his mind exploded in agony. Grif took advantage and strode over to the kneeling man, his fists clenched. There was no hesitation as he punched Malekk square in the jaw, dropping him to the floor like a stone.

An hour later they regrouped on the bridge, having placed Malekk safely back inside a new Rem-store. How he had escaped his previous store was a mystery, but his proficiency with machines was no secret, much like his Gomar allies. Adanae watched him sleep on the holographic monitor, his short brown hair and cropped beard appearing green in the light.

"The drives should be back online within the hour," Ryson reported. "Life support's back up and running at full capacity, but we'll probably need to perform a full diagnostic across all the major systems. We don't know what else he tampered with."

"Where are we?" Adanae asked. The feed from outside showed a solar system with a small blue star. There were four planets orbiting it, each one a desolate rock with no hope of conceiving life in the cold system.

"We're approximately twelve thousand light-years from the new world and three thousand light-years from the moon where we left ALF." Ryson left his chair and joined Adanae and the others at the central station. Everyone on the bridge stopped and listened to them plan their next move.

"*Tempest*, how long until we reach the empire at maximum yield?"

"Twelve years, three months and nineteen days." It was a hard pill to swallow for everyone. They had already been away from the empire and all those they loved for ninety-seven years.

"Who knows what the empire will look like when we get back? Maybe we've already won and there's a big party to return to." Grif didn't sound convincing.

"Or maybe we're heading into a trap," Nalana offered, pessimistically.

"Then at least we've secured the Terran lineage." Ryson tied his blonde hair behind his head using telekinesis.

"I'm more concerned about our immediate problems." Adanae pushed the image of Malekk's sleeping form into the middle of the station. "Twelve years is a long time for something to go wrong. He's dangerous."

"What do you want to do, eject him into space?" Ryson was clearly against the idea.

"Why not?" Nalana spat. "He's a traitor and, more than that, he nearly killed us all in our sleep. I say we space his ass."

Grif stroked his goatee. "He's still a Terran. He deserves our burial rites at least. He should be given back to his star." Such rites were hardly used before the war since many Terran chose to live forever.

"He was born on Crychek," Adanae pointed out. "We can't keep him on board until we reach that system. Besides, he isn't actually dead yet. Until he's tried it would just be murder."

"Ejecting him into space is murder!" Ryson looked shocked at Adanae's words.

She tried to ignore it but coming from Ryson it was hard. They had been lovers for the majority of their time away, and she couldn't help being fond of him.

"Then we just send him out in his Rem-store," Nalana countered.

That gave Adanae a thought.

"He'd still die when the Rem-store loses power!" Ryson continued to protest.

"ALF designed those things to last thousands of years."

"Then he'll probably outlive us all." Adanae announced, "I'm making an executive decision. We won't kill Malekk, but he can't come with us either." She ignored the confused expressions and continued. "He is a killer and a traitor. I don't think he deserves a Terran burial, but I can't condone murder on my watch. So he gets to live, forever. We're dropping him off on the nearest planet, inside his Rem-store."

Grif wouldn't meet her eyes and Ryson simply walked off the bridge, shaking his head. Nalana was already setting the ship on course for the nearest planet.

Another hour passed by before the drives were fully operational again. Most of the crew were already getting back into their Rem-stores and handing the ship's functions over to the *Tempest*. AI Adanae took one last look at the monitor, seeing the abandoned capsule half buried in the planet's rocky, dead surface. At least he gets to sleep forever, she thought. Who knew what they were flying home to? Adanae turned off the monitor, knowing she would be the last person to ever lay eyes on Malekk of Crychek.

ONE

The first sun had set beyond the horizon, leaving Kaldor gleaming in the setting orange glow of Hadrok's second binary star. The golden spires and glittering pyramids reflected the beauty and harmonious culture that was all things Terran. The city created such a contrast with its bleak surroundings of slate-black rock and slow-rolling hills of white fog. The ground encompassing the circular perimeter was pocketed with ancient craters, and never-ending fields of colossal spikes, where the molten rock had been blasted from orbit and cooled before ever landing. Before the singularity was achieved, the planet had truly been hammered in the last great war of the Terran. Before the Criterion's creation and the emergence of ALF, Hadrok had borne witness to the last conflict between a race that could never be content.

Thousands of the pre-Criterion ships had thundered through the atmosphere to be entombed where they fell. The majority of Kaldor's population were here for scientific reasons, seeking out the old ruins in the hope of unlocking secrets to their ancestors' lives. The idea of war was just barbaric to the modern day Terran. At their current height of evolution, they saw no need for violence or weapons; ALF provided everything they needed, leaving them free to explore their natural abilities and push the boundaries of all scientific law. They created beauty and art and unimaginable pleasures, constantly reaching for the limits of them all. They had expanded into the galaxy and claimed the stars as their birthright. Thanks to the teaching of the Avatar, the first Terran to learn how to rejuvenate his cells, they had even conquered death.

Savrick would put that to the test.

He rose to his full height atop the giant arcing spike that overlooked Kaldor's high wall. He surveyed hundreds of vehicles, aesthetically designed, flying between the many buildings as they transported Terran at their leisure. Some he witnessed did not require the use of a vehicle and used unbelievable feats of telekinesis to move around the sprawling city. From his lofty vantage, they appeared as insects ready to be squashed under his boot. His hate for them had only grown over the years he had spent watching them.

He looked back to the base of the mountain behind him, narrowing his vision on a small ledge with a cave entrance. Esabelle was inside waiting for him to return; she had been so scared when he told her where he was going. But he had no choice. All his training and hard work over the last six years had been for this moment - he couldn't falter now.

Savrick looked down at himself, amazed at what he had accomplished in that time. He had forsaken the Terran rags he used to wear and now stood in what he imagined was a fierce sight. His armour covered his entire body exposing only his head, leaving his twin braids to flow in the high wind. He had spent years salvaging the hulls from various ships the Terran had yet to find. His instructions had been exact, detailing every size and measurement for its purpose. The cube had provided him with the necessary tools to construct the suit and implanted the designs into his mind. He gripped his right forearm at the memory of his first encounter with the alien cube. The pain had been intensely agonising to the point he lost consciousness. When he awoke it was with the faint memories of a conversation he had never had, like a dream he couldn't quite recall.

He knew then what he had to do though. The cube had given him clarity and purpose and the means with which to act. He had laboured for years making the armoured suit, consulting the alien entity more and more as the interactions became less painful. The designs had been hard to get to grips with, but he trusted the cube; it had knowledge beyond ALF. Savrick had spent days at a time permanently connected to the cube, allowing it to download fighting techniques he hadn't even thought possible into his brain. It taught him strategy with the subtlety of stealth and the chaos of surprise, but most of all it gave him power.

The suit interlocked perfectly with the Harness that had controlled him for so long. The armour simultaneously disabled the Harness while supplying the brain with genetically purposed stimulants, designed to enable the user control of their Terran abilities. To a Gomar it was freedom. He had spent the last two years learning about the universe, seeing it the way a Terran did. All matter was connected and yet disconnected as every particle constantly vibrated on a subatomic level. And that was a level he could manipulate.

The cube had instructed him to concentrate on destructive abilities. That was how the Terran could be beaten. No generation of Terran had been in a conflict for a million years, let alone the scale of war Savrick now had in mind. But the AI was not to be underestimated. He felt that particular comment had come from the cube but it had become hard to discern individual thoughts.

The Criterion would adapt to war and eventually so would the population under its care. It seemed ALF already had a better understanding of Terran abilities than any actual Terran. Savrick would need an army and a weapon they wouldn't see coming. The cube had known all this and already had plans.

He looked down on Kaldor and knew this would be the beginning of the end. His instructions had been clear - retrieve a single canister of nanocelium and return it directly to the cube. After that, he would have his weapon and the next phase could begin. There were Gomar on every planet being oppressed, and he was wearing the answer. The plan was simple enough but the cube had emphasised the time pressures. After this attack, ALF would respond with contingencies they couldn't even fathom, so he had to be fast. Savrick pushed out his awareness feeling the complex glow with every being below. He recoiled momentarily, still coming to grips with his extra senses. Their arrogance made his blood boil with rage. They had taken everything from him and he would make them pay for it. His newfound power made him feel bold and invincible. He was about to change the face of the galaxy, and he felt exhilarated at the thought of a Gomar at the heart of that change.

He felt the warm breeze wash over his face with a scent of sulphur. He looked over the tip of the curving spike and knew there were just over two kilometres from its tip to the floor of Kaldor. With a smirk of wicked glee, he crouched like a stalking predator, burying his armoured fingers into the rock.

"We are forever..." Savrick mockingly whispered the Terran motto as he launched himself off the great spike. His feet kicked up plumes of black rock before the momentum ran out, leaving him to plummet vertically head first. Twisting spires and hovering platforms passed him by at a blurring speed until a single glass dome was all he could see. He cocooned himself inside an impenetrable bubble of telekinesis, using it to increase his speed as well.

The dome's covering shattered under his impact, blowing away the metal frames and raining shards of glass down on the inhabitants. At the last second, Savrick twisted his body bringing his full force down on his bent knee. The stone floor cracked like a spider's web around him while he remained crouched in the crater. There were screams from all around as unsuspecting Terran were cut down by the larger shards and debris.

Savrick slowly stood up, impressed with the exoskeleton he had made. Combined with the telekinesis, he hadn't felt a thing as he punched through the building. Everyone was staring at him in shock and disbelief. A woman directly in front of him quickly grabbed her daughter and protectively placed herself between them. There were others who had reacted quicker with their hands over their head as they maintained the broken glass in suspended animation.

Kill them all!

The thought had come from nowhere but it was his voice he heard. He looked out over the sea of faces and saw the people who had forced him to love T'lea in secret. The people who had forbidden them from having a child, the people who had tried to take their child. They would all pay the price.

The crowd was filling up, but not with people. In between the faces, hard light holograms were appearing in flashes of light. Every hologram bore the face of ALF wearing his usual floor length robe. They slowly moved through the crowd edging closer to Savrick. He clenched his armoured fists at the sight of the ancient AI. Everything that had ever happened to him, to the Gomar, could be laid at the feet of the Criterion.

It was an infuriating thought that the AI could not feel pain. Pain was the only thing ALF deserved. It was an injustice that it could not be made to suffer as he had. Savrick looked around at the scared faces of his Terran cousins and knew that there was another way to make the machine feel pain.

He would take his time.

From within the crowd, a single figure became clearer than the rest as she made her way to the front.

"Kalian..." Esabelle was looking at him with disappointment on her face. Reality flickered and his head split with pain as two lives collided in a tangled web of memories. "Kalian!" his daughter shouted. The Terran environment fell apart, giving way to his true surroundings, his identity coming back.

"It happened again, didn't it?" Esabelle's question brought Kalian back to reality.

They were running side by side along one of the *Gommarian's* many miles of corridor. This had become part of his training routine over the last five and a half months. Esabelle had taken it upon herself to continue Kalian's training after the Outpost had been buried under a hundred thousand tons of the Conclave vessel, *Helion.*

"Who was it this time?" she pressed.

"Savrick..."

Ever since his mind had been invaded by Esabelle's father, he had struggled to separate their thoughts and memories. Of course, he now had the issue of separating Li'ara's mind as well, since saving her life on Naveen. It was becoming awfully crowded in his head. Esabelle had been teaching him to compartmentalise his mind and file the different memories like a computer program. After compiling them he could then choose to save or delete. Most of Savrick's he was more than happy to destroy, but Li'ara's were harder to part with.

"I was on Hadrok, *he* was on Hadrok," Kalian corrected himself. "You were only a child." Having run almost twenty miles, he was finding it hard to articulate through his laboured breaths. "He had already found the cube and was about to attack Kaldor." He was continuously amazed at the feats his body was capable of. He had never run so far and so fast in his life, and yet he had only begun to sweat five miles back.

"You need to focus. When you feel your mind going there, pull back, but keep hold of the memory. You need to contain the memory without becoming a part of it."

She barely sounded out of breath. In fairness, he thought, Esabelle had been training herself for thousands of years inside Elandar's virtuality. In a way, she was the most amazing of all the Terran. Born of two Gomar, she should have been so uncontrollable as to be dangerous. But instead, she had done what no other Gomar had achieved and mastered her mind, utilising her abilities without ever wearing a harness or one of Savrick's armoured exoskeletons.

She was perhaps better than ALF when it came to teaching control. He thought of the ancient AI for a moment. There had been no word from him since they left Naveen, and they all wondered if he could have survived the *Helion's* impact.

They continued their run down the numerous corridors, having run almost the entire length of the ship. In comparison to the Conclave ships, the *Gommarian* had a very human feel to its design. In place of the cathedral-sized walkways, they ran through corridors with four flat edges. The overhead spotlights gave it an ominous gloom that never felt quite bright enough. Of course, there is more to the great ship than meets the eye.

Using systems set up by Esabelle, the bridge crew had the power to alter the internal and external structure, allowing for different rooms in every size depending on the need. The six factories, however, were larger than a lot of Conclave ships, ready for the capture and breakdown of raw materials. Kalian was also aware of the changes made to the ship's engine in terms of propulsion. With no interactive pilot to power the many systems, using Terran abilities, Esabelle had created a massive port at the rear of the ship. This port was connected to the Starillium, an engine capable of faster-than-light travel since they needed to use a more common form of transport. Kalian still found it mind-boggling that, with the right amount of energy supply, a Terran could actually generate a subspace wormhole and push a ship through it. That was an ability he knew he would never unlock without a power-source the size of a star at his disposal.

Kalian mentally controlled every cell in his body, commanding them to replenish his energy supplies to prevent any fatiguing poisons. He could feel his muscles rapidly breaking down the lactic acid and filtering it through various organs. He tasked his bone marrow to produce extra red blood cells, in order to carry the required oxygen to his starving lungs. Small adjustments such as these made compartmentalisation harder.

Rounding the next corner, Kalian could again feel reality blending into the surreal memories. He had no choice but to stop running and concentrate on neurological control. Esabelle shot past him as he re-filed the memory belonging to Li'ara. He had glimpsed a red-headed girl wandering the halls of a museum on Earth, before pulling back from the moment that wasn't his. He tried not to dwell on the images of Earth; he had convinced himself that looking to the future was the only way to cope with the loss of his homeworld.

He stood, doubled over with his hands resting on his knees, his breath laboured. Kalian saw the judging feet of Esabelle step into view before him.

"This is why we train." It was not the voice of a woman who had just run twenty miles. "You must learn control over your mind *and* body while performing low-level tasks."

Kalian couldn't help but crack a sarcastic smile at her notion of low-level tasks. He was still struggling with his mind/body connection when it came to the finer things. He was happy with his progress during their sparring matches though. By opening up a virtuality inside his mind he could retreat and assess new threats and possibilities in a fraction of time. It was also the only thing he could beat Esabelle at. However, once their abilities came into play, Esabelle would always gain the advantage.

Kalian managed to stand up straight as his respiratory rate decreased. Different gauges and receptors in his blood informed him of a steady heart rate, as well as new stores of Adenosine Triphosphate from converted lactic acid. The only thing he craved now was a drink and something to eat. The *Gommarian* was capable of replicating almost any food or drink from its memory banks though, Kalian had come to prefer some of the Novaarian delicacies Telarrek brought onboard. Thinking of food gave him a particular taste in his mouth, and somehow he just knew it was Rorstack, a six-legged creature native to Hadrok. It was the first time one of Savrick's memories had imprinted into a sense, rather than remaining firmly in his head. He decided to keep it to himself.

"We should head to the bridge." Kalian attempted to change the subject, "Li'ara said there was another ship arriving today." He could tell from her look that his training could not be overlooked for long.

"Fine, but we're sprinting there." Kalian grimaced at the prospect of running another three miles. "And we're going to use telekinesis to increase our speed." He threw his head back in mock disgust. When they ran at such speeds he was forced to continually expand his awareness into the surrounding space. If either of them collided with another person they were likely to break bones.

Before setting off again, Kalian noticed the large circular door that sat forebodingly at the end of a branching corridor. The door concealed a containment bay filled with twelve Rem-stores, and twelve sleeping Gomar.

Kalian pushed his awareness into the chamber and registered the feedback of a dozen unconscious beings. Just feeling their presence made his spine tighten with the build-up of energy. Any one of them could tear a Conclave vessel apart with their mind.

"You don't like them being onboard." Esabelle wasn't asking; she knew Kalian's position on the subject.

"They're dangerous." Kalian had survived his encounter with Lilander and the beast by the skin of his teeth. If ALF hadn't obliterated the beast with a Novaarian orbital cannon, he would have certainly died at the old Avatar's hand. And to his luck, Lilander had followed Li'ara onto the *Helion* where she met a similar fate to Savrick. Kalian tried not to think about it, but he knew Savrick would have killed him had ALF not dropped the Nexus-class ship onto Naveen. Really, he had done nothing but distract the Gomar until ALF and Li'ara could spring the trap. Against any other being he was a force to be reckoned with, but a Gomar?

He needed to train.

"You still think the Highclave suspect?" Esabelle asked.

The council had been informed by the Laronian prisoners, taken along with the humans, that some of the Gomar had remained on the *Gommarian* when the *Valoran's* Starrillium went supernova. With Telarrek's help, they had managed to conceal the fact that the Gomar were still alive. Thankfully, the last thing the Laronians saw before their rescue was the armoured bodies of their captors fall to the floor. Esabelle had overloaded their cerebral links but hadn't actually killed them. Telarrek and Ilyseal agreed that the Gomar were too powerful to be handed over to the Conclave. If they ever lost control of them, it could be disastrous without either Kalian or Esabelle around to even the odds.

"I think if I were them, I'd be pretty paranoid. There's too much they don't understand about us. We're two halves of the same species, but all they see are the Terran, not the human. There are only fourteen people in the *whole* galaxy that are technically Terran now, and twelve of them should have been *ejected* into the nearest star." Kalian had never agreed with keeping them alive, not after the genocide they wrought.

"We have to plan for all eventualities, Kalian. They may still prove useful." Esabelle placed her leg high on to the wall while she leaned into it, stretching the muscle.

Kalian knew she didn't need to physically stretch the muscle, but it was typical of Esabelle. She could mentally command her muscles the same way any Terran could, she just preferred the human way. He had questioned her about it only once; her answer had been explanation enough.

"Do you know why the Terran lost against Savrick?" she had asked. "Hubris. They believed themselves to be untouchable, that death was a myth. They took their abilities for granted, and in their arrogance they became soft. They were too reliant on their artificial god and their own ability to manipulate the universe. The way we are right now is what we need to be to maintain our existence. There's still enough human in you to make you appreciate what you have. Don't always rely on the Terran way of doing things."

Kalian had agreed with her point of view. With the things he could do, it was easy to think of himself as more than human.

"Do you think they ever recovered any of the bodies?"

Esabelle appeared doubtful at Kalian's question. "Not this again. They were pulverised under all that weight, along with the beast. There would be nothing left to find. Our genetic secrets are safe, for now."

"What about, Sef?" Telarrek had been the last one to see him alive.

"He's gone..." Esabelle looked almost sad.

Kalian could empathise in a way; she had cared for them and kept each of them alive for millennia when she piloted the ship. It wouldn't be so unusual for her to still feel some connection to them, even if she did hate Elandar and her father especially.

He eyed the touch pad next to the circular door. They had keyed the lock so it could only be accessed with either Esabelle or himself present. It didn't offer much comfort. He connected to the room one last time, ensuring their captivity, before racing Esabelle to the bridge.

THE COMMAND BRIDGE was a buzz of activity with over a dozen UDC personnel overseeing the numerous diagnostics. Some sat at their station, while others were forced to stand and move from one place to another as data was transferred between holographic charts. The *Gommarian* was fairly self-sufficient, requiring little input from the makeshift crew.

The room was lit by a rainbow of colours from the various hard light holograms and touch consoles. Perhaps the most impressive feature was the panoramic viewport that encompassed the forward section of the bridge, as well as half of the ceiling. Li'ara wasn't fooled by the image, however; she was well aware of the bridge's location within the mammoth ship and knew the image was generated from external cameras. In the belly of the *Gommarian,* they were surrounded by miles of internal walls and an incredibly thick hull.

Li'ara took stock of the crew before her and appreciated their diligence. They had each lost something or someone from Earth and Century and were dealing with that loss in their own way. The fact that they continued to perform their duty admirably was a testament to their strong character. The UDC will do that to you, she thought.

Discounting the scientists onboard, she knew there were only one thousand four hundred and seventy-six UDC soldiers and crew personnel. It wasn't much but they were getting by, for now. There had been talks surrounding the future of their race among the higher ranking scientists, as well as Captain Fey's ranking officers. So far the only thing they could all agree on was that the *Gommarian* was not the right place to start again, as it were.

Trying to stay positive, Li'ara focused on the new arrival. She came to stand behind Lieutenant Rodriguez who was monitoring the escorted human vessel. The Conclave continued to send out their beacon of hope into the Orion Arm, awaiting any response from survivors that were out-system when Savrick attacked. In the last five and half months, three ships had made the trip to Conclave space and transferred to the *Gommarian*. Unfortunately, High Charge Uthor had personally informed them of a ship found floating in between the two galactic arms. The ship had insufficient life-support systems to bridge the galactic gap. All crew were dead.

Li'ara stooped over the Lieutenant's shoulder to examine the specs on the new arrival. It was apparently a deep space explorer in search of more precious Solarcite, or Intrinium as the Conclave called it. With a crew of only sixteen, it was relatively small in terms of adding to the population, but every human being was a win.

"This is the *Gommarian* to the *Columbus*, do you copy?" Lieutenant Rodriguez checked the shield strength on the hangar entrance as she waited for their reply. After an affirmative, she sent a command alerting the hangar crew before replying, "You are free to pass through the hangar shield *Columbus*. Your landing platform is being highlighted for you now." After another affirmative, she opened the comm to the escorting Novaarian craft. "You guys know the drill."

Li'ara smiled at the familiarity that had grown between the Novaarians and the humans. Telarrek was a familiar face with his frequent visits to help install everyone's translators. He explained that Ilyseal had been reassigned but he wasn't allowed to divulge any more than that, though privately he had admitted that he was unaware of her new role. Captain Fey had extended an invitation to the Novaarian Highclave councillor, Elondrasa, though she was yet to accept. It seemed Conclave politics was even more complicated than Central Parliament's had been.

Li'ara was about to turn and leave for the hangar when Kalian walked onto the bridge. She hadn't actually seen him, but she *knew* he was behind her. Ever since the events on Naveen, she couldn't deny the connection they now had. He had entered her mind and taken control of her body in order to save her life. In doing so, they had shared a single mind, sharing their thoughts, feelings and memories. Esabelle had been teaching him to deal with the after-effects, especially since he also had some of Savrick stuck in his head.

For Li'ara's human brain, there was no way to deal with it. In her own typical Li'ara way, she had been shrugging the effects off. She revealed to Kalian that some of his mind had transferred over but she kept the true extent to herself. In a way though, Li'ara liked the bond she felt and, with the connection, she knew he did as well.

She turned to see Kalian and Esabelle. Seeing the Terran gave Li'ara mixed feelings but she couldn't narrow them down. Becoming the soldier once again, she pushed the feelings aside, along with the feeling she knew Kalian would be experiencing at seeing her.

Li'ara walked over, resisting the urge to embrace him. She had purposefully avoided the subject of the two of them for months. She rationalised that too much was going on, and that they were both respectively needed in their own roles, though Kalian's had yet to be defined. Captain Fey was happy for Esabelle to continue his training, for now, obviously seeing Kalian as a potential asset. Li'ara didn't agree with that, but she knew Kalian wouldn't let anyone tell him what to do, not anymore. He was a different man from the one she had met on Earth six months ago. Besides that, she knew he was too powerful to control now anyway.

Just like everywhere else he went on the ship, Kalian was the centre of interest for those around him. Li'ara noticed every head turn to watch him enter the bridge, their gaze lingering longer than their duties allowed. She understood their fascination of course; had they still been on Earth, Kalian would be a subject of great debate and cause for celebrity. Most had seen the images from Naveen and knew what he was capable of, but to know that he was the next step in evolution was profound. The captain had ensured that all onboard were in possession of the facts given to them by ALF, to ensure complete transparency. Kalian had tried to keep to himself after that, uncomfortable with the attention it gained him.

Once within arms' reach, Kalian pulled Li'ara in and hugged her, clearly unable to push his own feelings aside. Aware of the eyes on them, Li'ara awkwardly pulled back as they caught Captain Fey's attention. Kalian gave Li'ara an apologetic look and stood before the captain.

The captain's auburn hair was showing a sign of grey as it was pulled into a tight bun. Being over a century in age, however, she was doing well. Li'ara admired her for the weight she carried as the highest ranking UDC officer, and the burden of leadership she was forced to carry. A small group of the higher ranking scientists had been voted in as a temporary council, so as to keep the population out of military control. Captain Fey was more than happy about this as it reduced her responsibility for seven thousand people.

"Ah, Mr. Gaines, perhaps *you* could help me to convince Professor Jones here that the *basement* is off limits." The captain looked almost pleading with her question.

Li'ara watched Kalian take in the sight of the young professor. This wasn't the first time he had come to the captain asking for permission. As part of the original terraforming team, Professor Garrett Jones had been a leading geologist tasked with studying the topography of Alpha NL- 2204. His fascination with the cube had been evident from the moment he saw it during their first and only visit to the basement.

ONLY A HANDFUL of key personnel was aware of the basement and its significance. Li'ara knew it was the chamber beneath the Starrillium where the cube was housed. She wasn't sure what to think when it came to the ancient artefact. Esabelle had described it as a living thing with a mind and motives, but the one time they had all examined the box it looked like, well, a box. Granted it was a bit bigger and had an alien language imprinted on the side, but this wasn't the first time they had come across an alien language with a mystery behind it.

Thinking of the Outpost reminded her of the conversation she had with ALF. He had warned of a potential threat from some unknown enemy, with potential designs on the galaxy and a particular hatred towards all things Terran. At the time she had assumed the AI was constructing elaborate tales to balm his own conscience regarding past failures. The cube's presence, as well as Esabelle's recounting of her own experiences, was hard to ignore, however. She told of the cube's influence over Savrick and its own urges to wipe out the Terran Empire. With no more to go on than a *potential* threat, which could have died out hundreds of thousands of years ago, the matter concerning the cube had been put aside. Instead, they had focused on relations with the Conclave and setting up a way of life onboard the expansive ship.

In Li'ara's eyes, the professor had always looked somewhat dishevelled in appearance. His black frizzy hair was never under control and his dark complexion was never without two or three days of stubble. He had a single mechanical augmentation to his right temple in the form of a silver diamond. Li'ara knew it was connected to his optic nerve and allowed him to see in the different spectrums, as well as different magnifications. His eyes had a purple tint but she was never sure if that was a side effect of the augmentation or an aesthetic alteration.

"We've talked about this Garrett. The cube is too dangerous, and it has too many unknowns. We need to focus our efforts on what's happening now." Kalian replied in what Li'ara knew to be his diplomatic tone.

"I am a geologist... on a spaceship!" Garrett left his words hanging as an explanation unto themselves.

Li'ara was mildly amused at the usefulness of a man who studied rocks to be stuck in space. "That cube could hold answers to the universe! We are obligated as scientists to investigate. If it does pose a threat shouldn't we take steps to understand it?"

"The cube is a security matter," Commander Astill countered, "and so falls under our jurisdiction, Professor." The commander was an intimidating size on the captain's platform. Astill descended from aboriginal ancestry and had a shoulder-width that left you wondering if he had undergone augmentation. He emanated authority over Garrett with an iron expression. With that Li'ara could tell the conversation had been shut down. It was the authority he carried that gave him his promotion to second officer. Many had thought the role should have gone to Li'ara but she knew the captain trusted Astill from their time on the *Hammer*.

"Very well," Garrett replied sharply. "I will be taking this to the council for further debate."

"As you like, Professor Jones." The captain's reply was non-committal, caring little about the whims of a single geologist with nothing to do. Garrett stormed off the bridge clutching his Datapad tightly as he walked into a cadet.

"He is a strange man," Kalian commented.

"He is becoming *obsessive*," Esabelle replied with a look of concern.

The captain casually waved her hand, "He's just bored like so many others. This ship provides everything we need." Having devoured the Laronian warship, the *Gommarian* was still converting its raw materials for essential resources. They had another month before they would have to look for new sources, such as an asteroid. "I'm currently trying to negotiate some planet-side R&R with the Novaarians. I think people will feel better having a real gravity-well under their feet." As they were only allowed to travel through Novaarian territory it would have to be one of their planets. However, if that planet had other Conclave species co-inhabiting it, the negotiations would become far more complex.

"Captain, Ambassador Telarrek is on the observation deck, level *thirteen*." Lieutenant Rodriguez emphasized the number. Li'ara knew it to be more code; in this case, it meant Telarrek wanted to speak specifically with Kalian and herself, as well as the captain.

"Restrict access and inform the ambassador we will be there shortly," Captain Fey ordered.

THE WALK to the observation deck had been awkward for Kalian. He wanted to talk to Li'ara about everything and apologise for hugging her in front of the bridge crew. He thought about asking her to have dinner with him in his cabin, but he already knew how she would reply. Kalian could see her reasoning behind not taking their relationship further, but it didn't mean he had to like it. He wanted to know if she had a part of him inside her head like he did of her. She had been particularly guarded around the subject, but that was typical Li'ara.

The observation deck was wall-to-wall holograms of real-time space outside the ship. The projection was so seamless, that Kalian felt he could enter space with a single step. Telarrek stood as a thin silhouette to the distant red star that illuminated the wide square room. The closest Novaarian planet was Bendosa, a jungle planet currently resting on the other side of the sun. Kalian agreed with the captain, it had been too long since any of them had set foot on natural ground.

"Greetings of peace, my friends." Telarrek stepped away from the view, filling his lean figure out. Coming to his side was another Novaarian Kalian had never seen before. With his memory now up to Terran standards, he found it easier telling their almost identical features apart.

"It's good to see you, Telarrek." Kalian reached out as the two gripped one another's forearm. At nearly seven feet, Kalian had to look up to see those golden eyes that swirled like a miniature galaxy.

After greeting the others, Telarrek introduced his companion. "This is Naydaalan, my eldest hatchling."

Kalian looked at Telarrek's son, knowing he was probably older than any human on the *Gommarian*. He had the same blue freckles around his cheeks, like his father, though his frame appeared bulkier. His translucent tendrils fell short at his back rather than running down to the top of his legs. Naydaalan stood proudly next to his father wearing the golden armour that plated his muscle groups.

Respectfully, the Novaarian bowed his head at the introduction. "It is an honour." His voice was softer than his father's.

"He has been appointed my personal guard." Telarrek placed a hand on his chest to signify himself.

"An honourable job." Kalian gave Li'ara a sideways glance, knowing Naydaalan's job wasn't dissimilar to her own. She looked back but gave no emotion away. She didn't need to anymore, Kalian already knew how she would feel under the circumstances. On the inside, she was smiling at the compliment.

"You wanted to speak with us, Ambassador?" Captain Fey interjected.

Telarrek took a moment to consider his words, "The Highclave has requested a private meeting with Kalian." The captain's face switched off like a light. How often was he at the centre of events? Kalian sympathised with her, knowing she had been hoping it was a response to any number of requests on the humans' behalf.

"And the nature of this meeting?" the captain enquired dryly.

"In truth, I do not know, Captain Fey. It is rare that the Highclave request such meetings; they are usually more public, as a sign of trust to the people."

Kalian doubted that last part. From his encounters with the alien council, it was clear they had a lot of *private* meetings. They made most decisions before the meeting even took place.

Kalian saw the concern on Li'ara's face and understood her emotion. The last time they had seen the Highclave they had demanded the *Gommarian* and himself be handed over. Apparently, he was dangerous.

"Will they be coming here?" the captain continued her questioning.

"No, the meeting will take place in orbit around Ch'ket. I will escort you," Telarrek replied with a short bow.

"I'm coming too." Li'ara wasn't asking.

"It was expected," the Novaarian replied.

Kalian knew well enough when Telarrek was smiling. The captain walked away as if she could step into the starry backdrop. Kalian could tell she wasn't happy about the situation. Once again she had been excluded from a potentially important meeting, and her relationship with Kalian was undefined. She had never ordered him to do anything but, if she did, Kalian would respect her authority; they had to remain united.

"We stand on the edge, Kalian," the captain began. "I do not care for our origins or our makers. We must make our peace with what has been taken from us. But I do not have the luxury of time to dwell on that. I must look to our future, to our *survival*. I am not arrogant enough to believe we can survive on our own out here, and a ship is no place to live forever. Take it from someone who has spent most of her life on one." She paused for a moment taking Kalian in. "You are a *unique* individual, we all know that. But you are, time and time again, placed into a situation of great importance for our race. I pray that you are up to the task."

"I'll do my best, Captain." It was the only reply he could think of under the weight of his burden.

"See to it that he does." Captain Fey gave Li'ara a knowing look. Kalian knew the captain trusted him, but Li'ara's presence would make her feel better.

"There is one other matter that I must bring to your attention." Telarrek removed a small disk from his belt and held it out to the group. It went on to emit a three-dimensional image of the *Rackham*.

Roland...

Kalian hadn't seen that ship since the agent left, just over five months ago. The craft was of unique design with an intricate pattern of swirls across the bronze hull. The engine was a cylinder, attached to the port side with a curving point at the head. The main body was closer in shape to an ancient shield with a rounded aft section that curved into a point at the bow. The starboard side was concave as if a giant bite had been taken out of it. Placed centrally on top was the arcing viewport of the cockpit raised against the hull.

Esabelle, who had remained quiet as usual, had explained to Kalian and Li'ara months ago why she had given the ship to Roland.

"He would have been a caged animal if he remained onboard," Esabelle had stated. "I know all too well the feeling of being trapped on this ship. He would have caused more trouble in the long run." They had agreed with her assessment of the man. He would only have caused more work for the medical staff.

Telarrek elaborated, "There have been confirmed sightings of an unknown human male, using *this* ship, and breaking Conclave laws."

27

"What's he doing?" Li'ara asked. She had never particularly liked the scoundrel. Back within Central Parliament, his particular role had been distasteful. It was the missions that Roland accepted that gave the UDC a bad reputation. It didn't help that he was a drinker, either.

"The reports are inconclusive, but the initial assessment suggests that he is *bounty hunting*." Telarrek's expression was grave.

"Of course he is..." Li'ara replied.

"Bounty hunting is illegal under Conclave law. We have made efforts to root out their source but the Bounty Clave, as they are so named, have made equal measures to elude us. How Roland North has become part of this organisation I do not know. I have tried to calm the various parties involved in this investigation but it is becoming harder. I am afraid I must now break the law myself in order to bring about a peaceful end."

What was Telarrek suggesting? Kalian knew this wasn't the first time the old Novaarian had broken his mandate for a human. Before the events on Naveen, Telarrek chose to reveal the Conclave's interest surrounding Kalian, deliberately going against the Highclave.

"You want us to track him down, don't you?" Li'ara got there first.

Telarrek sighed before making a slow bow in acknowledgement. "I have a small craft at my disposal; it would allow for unchecked access into Conclave space. It would have to be a small manned team; you are too easily recognised now. I do not know what would happen to any of you should you be caught off this ship. Having witnessed the advantages to your evolution, the Highclave will no doubt have an interest in studying you. They are not sure how many of you have supernatural abilities and, for now, your existence remains a secret, Esabelle.

"Also, it should be noted that the Highclave are not the only power in the Conclave. There are many organisations and powerful individuals, not to mention the criminal factions. I worry that Roland may antagonise the wrong people if he is left to his own devices."

Kalian was slightly amused at the worry Telarrek had for the renegade agent. It was also entirely possible that Roland could cause such damage, given the time.

"We'll bring him back before he goes too far," Kalian reassured him.

"*I'll* bring him back." Everyone turned to Esabelle, who had remained silent until now.

Kalian assumed she was quite accustomed to listening rather than fully participating, having spent thousands of years plugged into the *Gommarian* with nothing to do but listen.

"I gave him the means to leave this ship; it should be me who brings him back." Kalian was about to protest before Esabelle continued, "There are many skilled individuals onboard, but let's face the facts, the only people who stand a chance of reining Roland in are standing in this room, and you two are going to Ch'ket."

Kalian didn't like it. His feelings for Esabelle were mixed thanks to having fragments of Savrick rolling around in his head. In their time together over the last five months, he had come to enjoy her company, both as a friend and a mentor. But he also felt a closer attachment that, he decided, came from the knowledge that she was the only person like him. In that regard, they had a lot in common. All that emotion was complicated by Savrick's love for his daughter and the need to keep her safe.

At the same time, he couldn't deny her logic regarding Roland. He had decades of experience in the field and would no doubt have more than a few tricks up his sleeve. The fact that he had succeeded in evading Conclave security for so long was impressive enough. Esabelle was a force of nature, however, and that particular nature had been evolving and growing stronger for thousands of years. With that in mind, Kalian reasoned that she was definitely the right choice to go out into the Conclave and bring back the reckless drunk.

After a moment's contemplation, Captain Fey said, "Then it's settled; the two of you will go to Ch'ket and Esabelle will find Roland." She turned to Telarrek. "Bring my people back to me, Ambassador." There was no missing the weight behind her words. Should this be some kind of trap set by the Highclave, he could easily imagine Captain Fey arriving on the doorstep of the Conclave's capital planet, with a battle-ready *Gommarian*.

"Any ideas on where I should start?" Esabelle was referring to her search.

"The nearest bar?" Li'ara offered with a wry smile.

The group shared a laugh at the reasonable assessment. Kalian couldn't help but feel Li'ara's sarcastic wit had arisen after his mental intrusion on Naveen. Perhaps there was more of him imprinted on her than he first thought? Hopefully, he would have a chance to talk to her on their way to Ch'ket.

"Our spies believe he has accepted the bounty on a high ranking Shay within Protocorps. I can redirect the flow of that information, giving you some time," Telarrek said.

"Protocorps? What's that?" Kalian asked.

"They are the corporation behind the creation and maintenance of the Conclave AI. It was this contribution to the Conclave that put them on the Highclave. That said, they are very powerful with far-reaching influence. I believe it unwise to cross them," the Novaarian explained.

Kalian had read several data files on the Conclave AI since meeting the Terran version, ALF. Situated on the Conclave capital world, it was responsible for communication across the multitude of planets, as well as coordinating planetary defences and mapping the constant changes in galactic geography. It monitored all economic flow between the different species and maintained local traffic on every world. Over the millennia, since its creation, the AI had become the keystone of this advanced civilisation.

Kalian wondered if the other species chose to overlook the fact that the Shay had majority control of this keystone. It was easy to see how it could be missed since the AI offered a much easier life to every species. Having met ALF however, Kalian was well aware of how manipulating and powerful an artificial intelligence could be. Or in the Conclave's case, how powerful its masters could be. ALF had described the AI as a stunted child after examining it himself. In comparison to ALF, it was an infant, at least in age if not intelligence, but ALF had been referring to its stunted growth. The Shay kept the AI within the limits set by the Highclave, never allowing it to learn beyond what they wanted.

"So he's actually on the capital. Is he mad?" Captain Fey asked.

"No, this particular Shay is currently on their home planet, Shandar. I believe this would be the best place to begin your search, Esabelle."

With Telarrek's last comment Esabelle gave a curt nod and made for the exit, only turning back to Kalian's call.

"Be safe..." It was all he could think to say.

Who could stop me?

Esabelle's words were only heard in Kalian's mind, though he recoiled for a second, not expecting the mental reply. They had only conversed this way once before and he found it to be too personal and intrusive. She had explained that it was common among friends and family within Terran culture, but it was still too alien for him.

Shrugging it off, Kalian faced Li'ara and Telarrek again, "I take it we will be leaving immediately?" Telarrek bowed in acknowledgement of his question. "I just need to stop by my quarters and pick something up, before we go." There was a small Terran device, given to him by ALF, which he felt safer having on him.

Kalian was certainly intrigued as to the reason for this secret meeting, but he couldn't help but feel a worrying itch in the back of his mind for Esabelle. She was going off into the Conclave on her own and, thanks to Roland, who knows what situation. He impressed reason upon himself and focused on the individual he was concerned for. She was right in so far as assuming there was no force available to the Conclave that could stop her, but Roland had an air of chaos that stuck to him like glue. Again, Kalian tried to look at the situation logically, how much trouble could one man really create?

TWO

Krono Towers wasn't so much an apartment block as a fortress, with its own private security firm, automated defences and an alarm system connected to local planetary security. The latter was rarely required, however, with the first being the worst kind of mercenary and the second having no stun setting. Such were the steps taken by Protocorps to secure their fat-cat board members.

Like all the buildings of worth, the Krono Towers were situated in high orbit around Shandar, each floating complex connected to the next via extensive bridges, encompassing the entire planet like a world-size net of floating buildings. With each descending level, the inhabitants were gradually held in lower regard until, finally, the poorest occupied the structures within the atmosphere itself.

The planet's appearance was a constant swirl of thick white clouds in a never-ending global storm. The surface had never been seen since the planet's natural habitat had been abandoned before the Shay entered the Conclave. They told of an older generation who had poisoned their world under an unhealthy industry, devoted to their love of all things artificial. Having now corrected their industry - by using planets they considered to be of little worth - they refused to leave their homeworld. The only way to navigate through the atmospheric level was by allowing the AI to take control, ensuring all local traffic avoided mid-air collisions with one another and the multitude of floating buildings.

The Krono occupied the planet's top tier in the shape of an upright tuning fork, four miles from top to bottom. Like every other complex, the exterior was matte black giving the planet a uniform appearance against the white backdrop. In a way, Shandar's impression was the perfect reflection of the Shay, with its combination of an organic world coupled with the exterior technology. Almost every Shay, regardless of wealth, had some form of robotic augmentation, whether interior or exterior - so obsessed were they with the advancements and possibilities offered to them by physical and neurological alteration.

Such were the reasons for Roland North's first visit to Shandar three months ago. Using every backdoor deal, he had finally found a surgeon willing to operate on his unique human physiology. He now possessed reinforced joints around his knees, shoulders and every rib on his right side. After a painful encounter with an angry Gomar, he had been forced to seek out the augments. The new parts, made from Callic-diamond plating, were the same materials used for bolstering the hull on all Conclave security ships. The neurological implant, however, had taken a little longer to become accustomed to. Situated in the Cerebrum, the sophisticated webbing was dispersed across all four lobes with a wireless connection specific to the *Rackham's* navigational frequencies. With this, he could control the ship from anywhere for backup, or in most cases an escape route.

That was three months ago. Now he was back for a very different reason. Roland sat back in the grubby throne-like chair of the cargo vessel, scrolling through the holograms pertaining to the stubby ship's recent additions. The ship had been stolen a week ago when he first had the hair-brain idea to accomplish the current job.

He really needed to stop making plans when he was off his face.

Ch'len had seen to the vessel's enhancements for him, using one of the many questionable connections the little Ch'kara had. Roland had to admit, the fat little shit had his uses; he seemed to know someone in every dark corner of the Conclave. His main reason for keeping the sarcastic alien around was his connections with the Bounty Clave. Roland had been rejected from becoming a member due to the simple reason of not being a Conclave citizen - that and being a human made him too high profile for such a secretive organisation. With Ch'len he could receive all the bounties he needed, though the alien had insisted on accompanying him everywhere to ensure his cut.

"Len!" Roland shouted down the comm in his ear.

He didn't like the look of the port side shielding; if this was going to work, and he wasn't going to die in the process, everything had to be right.

"Don't call me that!" The Ch'kara's voice yelled back angrily. It wasn't that Roland refused to use his full name; it was just that he couldn't be bothered to pronounce the 'Ch'.

"You said everything was in place. Why does the port side manifold have less armour? If I die you don't get paid you little gas cloud!"

"We didn't have enough units to pay for it all!" Ch'len was sitting in the pilot's chair in the *Rackham's* substantial cockpit. Every word was just audible over the loud music Ch'len was playing through the *Rackham's* internal speakers. "I've run the calculations - you'll be fine. Just push it to starboard more."

The way he added the last part didn't fill Roland with confidence. Taking his mind off the flying death trap, he changed the hologram to the Krono building schematics. Whoever was paying the units for this bounty had to be someone on the inside, they knew too much. The miniature towers floated in a red light where the top left tower became highlighted in blue, specifically apartment 21-LB on the nine hundred and first floor. Roland's backer knew exactly where and when his target would be, and had access to the schematics he was now looking at.

"Has there been any movement in or out?" Roland asked.

"You *could* say that. An unidentified female Shay came and left two hours ago. Ral-vet hasn't left though." Ch'len was watching the real-time footage of the security cameras outside Ral-vet's apartment.

The *Rackham*, being Terran in design, had the most sophisticated software, capable of cracking most Conclave forms of communication and monitoring equipment.

Roland let out a dirty chuckle, "So Mr. Tanek's gettin' himself some action, huh?"

Ral-vet Tanek was apparently some overpaid bureaucrat who sat on the Protocorps board. Roland didn't much care who or what he was, he had obviously pissed off the wrong people and now he had to die - it was that simple. It wouldn't be surprising if it was someone else within Protocorps that had put out the hit. Unfortunately, there was an addition to the contract, one of a technical nature. As well as killing the Shay, Roland also had to access his personal, and some-what secure, mainframe housed within the apartment. Of course, all of this was dependent on actually getting into Krono Towers.

The structure's inhabitants had biometric scans before entering. Since Roland didn't possess either the retinas, DNA, hand print, voice verification or a Novattoo imprint that every Conclave member had on the inside of their wrist, he had been forced to think of another way in.

"Is the hangar clear?" Roland didn't want a massive amount of collateral damage.

"Security just made a sweep through, but there are no civvies," Ch'len replied.

Roland took a breath and one last swig from his cantina. "Closing the canopy now. See you on the other side."

Rising from the dirty chair, he made his way into the storage bay at the back of the ship. On his way, he checked over his armaments attached to the different points on his body. He inspected each Tri-roller holstered either side of his thigh. The handles were translucent amber with a thick rectangular barrel containing two ports, one below the other, with a mid-section that reminded him of an ancient Earth revolver. The weapon held three Intrinium cores, each capable of a hundred shots. He spun them on his index fingers, thinking of himself as an old cowboy, before slotting them back into the holsters.

Placing his hand on the small of his back, he felt the hilt of the

Terran blade lying horizontally across his waist. He had configured the nanocelium to replicate a short blade for when things got up close and personal. The two grenades on his belt were set to the maximum setting for the most damage. The strap across his chest, was fully stocked with Intrinium clips and various gadgets for hacking stubborn terminals and generally blowing shit up. He knocked his fist against his chest, feeling the Callic-diamond armour under his shirt, before throwing on his long hide coat.

Roland checked the black band around his left bicep, feeling the tiny spheres contained within. He had rigged the device so that after pulling the cord it would detonate all the gravity bombs at once, firing them in every direction. Finally, he examined the soles of his Laronian boots making certain the propulsion inserts were clipped securely.

Standing flat against the storage bay wall, he fitted a breather to his face since there would be a brief window of time where the hangar re-sealed the breach after entry. Using one of the storage harnesses he tied himself in; it was about to get bumpy.

Having already placed the ship on auto-pilot and overridden the security protocols, the cargo vessel would continue its predetermined flight straight into the hangar. The hangar was the weakest point on Krono Towers as the door wasn't made to the same safety standards as the outer wall. With no access codes, the door would refuse to open, but that's where the extra armour came into play. Ch'len had used his 'friends' to retrofit the ship with overlaying plates of armour to take the impact of the hangar door. The new canopy was the thickest since that would take the brunt, but the port side was not so thick, apparently.

The ship made a whine as everything not secured down immediately floated towards the back of the storage bay. The grav enforcers had gone offline as power was redirected to the thrusters. As well as being the best way to penetrate the building, it would also create a certain amount of chaos, and chaos he could work with.

With no warning, the calm surroundings exploded violently as the lights cracked and shattered, the ship slammed into the door and

Roland was shaken vigorously in his harness. Everything crashed into something while the outer walls of the vessel scraped through the hangar like a bullet passing through a sheet of metal. One last shudder told Roland the ship had reached the end of the hangar before his head whipped back, knocking him unconscious.

Ten seconds later he opened his eyes - it was always ten seconds. The human Rem-plant, though less sophisticated, was always reliable when he was in trouble.

He opened the hatch to see that the emergency shielding had already covered the jagged hole. The floor had been shredded to splinters along the crash trail. The only sound came from his breathing as it filtered through the mask. Bringing up his right arm, he activated the touch-pad built into the sleeve of his coat. It told him the oxygen levels were already rising back to breathable levels, that and security had been alerted.

"Their forces are splitting as expected," Ch'len said over the comm. "Half are deploying to protect the apartment, and the other half is coming for you."

"I'm fine by the way..." Roland replied sarcastically.

"You're just a child, you'll bounce back." Roland knew Ch'len would be smiling to himself. The Ch'kara insisted Roland was only a child since he hadn't even reached a hundred years old, and he knew it pissed the human off.

"Thank you for your concern, *Len*." He muted the comm for a moment to avoid hearing the tirade of abuse.

Moving to the exit he ripped off the breather and lifted both Tri-rollers until they were either side of his head.

Let's skip to the good bit.

The door opened before he could reach it, allowing three mercenaries to burst through, each wielding a two-handed repeater capable of firing a high explosive Intrinium round. One of them was easily recognisable as a Shay with completely robotic legs in the shape of a bird's. The other two, concealed within their helmets, he guessed to be Laronian from their size and shape. Distracted by the converted cargo ship buried in the wall, they had no time to realise

37

they were already dead. Each shot struck the aliens in the head, reducing their visors into vapour - there was nothing left of their faces.

Roland looked back at the broken ship, a smug grin on his stubbled face. Its original shape had already been hard to make out due to the reinforced armour welded onto every available space but now, with a shattered cockpit and smoke rising from various cracks and tears it was unrecognisable. He didn't care how banged up it was - it wasn't his ship after all - he was just smug about being alive.

Leaving the hangar behind, he entered the plush corridor on Krono Towers' eight hundred and sixty-third floor. Terrified faces looked back at him from multiple doorways along the corridor, before quickly disappearing inside to the safety of their homes. Decorated in red and gold, the floors were polished wood and the walls were lined with tall mirrors and hanging chandeliers. Roland admired the style of living for a moment with a long whistle.

"So this is how the other half lives..." His old job had kept him from putting down roots and experiencing anything other than being a ghost. In truth, the *Rackham* was the first real home he ever had, and now he was forced to share it with that chubby little gas cloud. The methane contraption that kept the Ch'kara alive might not have a smell, but Ch'len definitely did.

"Stop daydreaming and get your pasty human ass up there. Oh, and you've got incoming..."

His last words were just audible as explosive rounds obliterated the wall next to Roland's head. Fragments blew in every direction, showering him with debris as he ran down one side of the L-shaped corridor. He calculated less than ten seconds before they rounded the corner and continued their assault. These corridors made the perfect space for gravity bombs, and he was more than willing to oblige. Midsprint, Roland thrust his arm back, letting off a quick shot down the corridor and proving his timing to be accurate as the super-heated matter struck the first mercenary to round the corner. The Raalak took it straight in its thick neck, melting the rocky surface in less than a second until its head rolled from its giant body.

"Don't take the Translift." Ch'len's only warning before it pinged to signify its arrival. Roland would never tell him but it was moments like this he was happy to keep the Ch'kara around. Without waiting to see the half-dozen mercenaries pile out, he unstrapped the gravity bomb from his bicep. He was forced to duck and weave in an attempt to avoid the pot shots that continued to blow the walls and floor to cinders. There was no hesitation as he pulled the cord from the strap activating the release mechanism. There was no more finesse required than simply dropping it at his feet. As expected the bomb did what any bomb did, it exploded. The ball bearings shot out in every direction, sticking to whatever surface they came into contact with.

As always, Roland found the reaction hilarious. Every ball bearing created a new gravity well that stretched for three metres in every direction. One second the mercenaries were running on the floor, the next they were being flung into the wall as if they had tripped. It wasn't long after they regained their new sense of up and down before a new ball bearing dropped them into a different gravity-well. The frequency of shots decreased along with their accuracy, often shooting each other by accident. Roland turned just in time to see a Tularon launch into the air slamming its furry head through the ceiling. It didn't get back up.

"There's a private grav pillar coming up on your left," Ch'len continued. "You're going to have to hack it. Use your-"

"I know what to use, Len!" It was times like this when Roland hated having the Ch'kara in his ear. The door he was looking for had a simple universal touch terminal fitted into the adjacent wall. He removed a rusty looking cylinder from the strap that ran diagonally across his chest. After a particularly close shot nearly took his head off, Roland flattened himself into a small alcove while jamming the cylinder directly into the terminal. Tentatively, he raised his left arm out, remaining as flat as possible, and twisted the end of the cylinder to begin the decoding. He estimated the bombs only had enough charge for another two minutes. With that in mind, he quickly leaned out and shot two mercenaries. He chuckled sadistically as their bodies dropped into the wall and ceiling as if it was the floor.

Roland glanced at the cylinder, annoyed at how long it was taking to hack a simple terminal. There were more advanced devices available for such an illegal act of course, but he simply couldn't afford them. A quick succession of chirps told him the terminal was now under his control. The door parted down the middle to reveal an empty shaft that ran the entire four miles of Krono Towers. Roland had used a similar form of transportation during his first time on the Conclave capital, only those were commercial size grav pillars that could take hundreds of people at a time. Before stepping in he said the number of the floor he needed, otherwise he would just float.

The timing was perfect; as a Novaarian mercenary reached the door, Roland shot up the grav pillar narrowly avoiding the weapons fire. The shaft was dark with intermittent neon lights on each floor he flew past. Eventually, his speed began to lose momentum as the designated floor approached. After a gentle ping, he stepped out onto another well-decorated hallway with a single chandelier in the centre. Before continuing, he pulled a grenade from his belt and dropped it into the shaft while verbally commanding the previous floor. The drop was so far he didn't even hear the explosion; at least they couldn't follow him now.

To cover all exits, he moved to the Translift and removed a metallic square, the size of his hand, from his belt. Using the magnetic seal, he stuck the square to one side of the Translift and activated the invisible laser that ran across the entrance. When the mercenaries arrived they would pass through the laser and trigger the explosive.

On the other side of a pointless central ornamental table was a set of double doors made from some alien tree. The plaque read: 21-LB.

"Emergency services are responding; Conclave security is swarming the bridge to Krono Towers and patrol ships are diverting to your location." Ch'len always had the best news.

"What about merc activity? I'm outside the apartment and there's not even an automated defence." Roland was suspicious.

"They've been forced to deactivate automated defences due to the hysteria your little accident caused. Inhabitants are running wild in the corridors; they probably think the big bad humans are invading," Ch'len said mockingly. "As for the mercenaries, I can't say. Comm chatter indicated they were moving to protect Ral-vet. Don't forget though, his apartment is extensive. It's more like a mansion up there."

"So they're probably all inside..." That suited Roland, close quarters just made it easier. He regretted not paying for the retina upgrades now. At the time he had the option of getting optical implants to see heartbeats through walls. Instead, he had gone for reinforcing his joints since they took most of the damage in his line of work.

"They're coming up the Translift. Unless you want to get caught up in your own explosive I suggest you move." Ch'len was definitely eating something as every word was slightly garbled.

With a flair for all things vintage, Ral-vet had an ancient form of door that used hinges and a handle. Roland quietly entered the apartment, Tri-rollers at the ready. Moving to the side of the old doors, he waited to see if he had tripped any alarms. Then the hallway beyond exploded. The wood cracked as it took some of the force but remained in place.

That had done it.

Shouting came from inside the apartment, followed by several running footsteps. The footfalls of the Raalak were unmistakable as all four of its feet pounded the staircase above Roland. The view as he came in was majestic with a well-lit foyer decorated with expensive ornaments and fittings of every precious rock. On the far side was a panoramic window giving view to Shandar's top hemisphere, dotted with thousands of structures much like Krono Towers. Above Roland was a set of twin staircases that descended into the middle of the foyer. It was a shame it was all going to get shot to shit.

His first action was to prime a grenade before flicking it towards the point at which the staircases met. The timing was perfect as the mercenaries converged on that same spot just as the explosive unleashed its payload. To protect himself, Roland ran around the left-hand staircase as the grenade blew. The disconnected arm of a Raalak flew over the bannister nearly colliding with his head, along with the helmet and leg of what he assumed to be a Shay. Thanks to human ageing and Conclave medicine, Roland, a man in his mid-sixties, had the agility of a twenty-year-old. He kicked off the wall and hopped over the bannister until he was face-to-face with a stunned Laronian. He wasn't sure if the alien was shocked by the grenade or the fact that he was seeing a specimen of the rare species known as human. Either way, Roland shoved his Tri-roller under the scaly blue chin and blew the top of his head off.

Smoke filled the area, the smell of charred flesh rising with it. Body parts were strewn across the stairs and foyer with debris from every ornament. Roland continued his climb up the stairs letting off a couple of shots, killing the Novaarian on the opposite side. He looked back a moment to check it wasn't a certain Novaarian bounty hunter he had crossed a month or so back. That was not someone he wanted to meet again. Unfortunately, it wasn't him; the lack of facial scarring gave it away.

"There are no cameras inside. I'm blind," Ch'len stated.

"This isn't my first rodeo, Len." Roland stood on the landing between the stairs.

"What's a rodeo?" the Ch'kara asked confused.

"Never mind," he replied flatly.

"Knock knock..." Roland regretted teaching the Ch'kara this particular type of joke.

"Who's there?" the bounty hunter entertained the chubby moron if only to see if he finally said the right lines. It was just then he heard the soft ping of the Translift outside. Moments after the doors parted the apartment was shaken by the blast of his little gift.

"I guess we'll never know." The comm erupted in laughter as Ch'len howled down the microphone. Roland had to hand it to him; that was pretty funny. Shaking his head in mock disgust, Roland continued to stride down the corridor decorated in pixel-paintings of various worlds and ships of grand design. It was this distraction that caused him to miss the Laronian and the Shay emerging from the room to his left. They crashed into him knocking the Tri-rollers from his hands and forcing him through the door to his back. All three crashed into the pool room in a struggle of limbs, the combined weight coming down on Roland.

The myopallic armour took the majority of the force from their bulk, but he still felt the air evacuate his lungs in a painful gasp. Giving over to muscle-memory, he immediately used their momentum against them, rolling backwards, flipping the Laronian into the oval shaped pool. Roland felt the vice-like grip around the back of his neck, as the Shay's robotic hand pulled him back to rest on his knees. His boots slipped on the wet floor stopping him from gaining a foothold and rising to his attacker's height. In his peripheral vision, Roland glimpsed the Shay's organic arm swing down towards his head with something shiny between its four pale fingers. Instinctively his left arm shot up connecting with the descending wrist and blocking the knife centimetres before it cut into his flesh. He felt the sharp sting as the blade sliced down his cheekbone drawing blood.

The Laronian was recovering from his impromptu swim and beginning to climb out of the pool. Thanks to the reinforced joint around his shoulder, Roland could keep his arm locked above his head with little effort and keep the blade at bay. The Laronian complicated matters somewhat. He loved a good fight when the opportunity presented itself, but he had a job to get on with and the Laronian was about to alter his chances of winning. Roland thought it best to end things a little quicker.

Before the Shay knew what Roland was doing, he had removed the Terran hilt from the small of his back and activated the nanocelium within. The hide coat concealed most of his actions before he plunged the blade into the gap between his raised arm and the Shay's own blade. He pushed through until the mercenary's armour was touching his hand and the robotic grip loosened. His next move was a blur of motion as he launched off his knees, pulling free his Terran blade and relinquishing the Shay's knife in his other hand as he did. The approaching Laronian had no time to react as Roland threw both weapons into the alien's head. Blood poured out of both wounds, mixing with the pool water as the liquid flowed in every direction.

After retrieving his blade and Tri-rollers he turned back and shot the still breathing Shay. The side of his head blew off in a combination of brain-matter and a sophisticated web of circuitry. Roland stood at the door, admiring his work so far, as he rotated his left shoulder. As entrances go, his was damn good. Sometimes the slow and quiet option was preferable, depending on the circumstances, but quick and loud had a shock factor that was just plain fun.

"How's it looking out there?" The apartment was so isolated it was impossible to get a feel for the rest of Krono Towers. Chaos would work for him; he had planned on chaos.

"Local security has entered the building. They're coordinating with some Protocorps representative who looks mighty pissed at how long it took them to react. Another team of mercs are on their way up but..." Ch'len sounded distracted.

"What is it?" Roland asked impatiently.

"There's something wrong with the feed, the monitors keep dropping out one-by-one in short bursts," Ch'len continued. "From what I can tell, it started at the base of the bridge and is slowly working up towards you. It could be nothing though."

Roland had a bad feeling.

"What could cause that kind of interference?" he dipped his head into one of the numerous rooms only to find yet another lounge.

"I don't know. Some kind of hack into Krono's main systems, or a portable EMP maybe?" Ch'len offered.

Shit...

Roland didn't like the sound of that last part. There was a particular type of individual that could emit an electromagnetic pulse at will, and he didn't fancy bumping into any of them. It couldn't possibly be who he was thinking it was, could it? Had he finally caused enough trouble that one of them had come for him? In a way, he had always known they would come, especially the kid, with his floppy emotions and ridiculous moral code. Roland just wished it wasn't in the middle of making a hundred thousand units.

"Keep me updated." He continued the hunt for his prey. If it really was one of them or even both, he would deal with them when the time came. After a small firefight in the next hallway, he finally discovered another staircase leading to a sparse looking office. A desktop of thick black glass hovered at one end of the room with no structural support. Every corner of the room had a single sculpture of a different looking Shay with unique augmentations made to their stretched faces. The entire wall to the left was glass, giving an over-view of the apartment below in all its blown-to-hell glory.

The office was dark, the only light from the apartment below. He approached the hover desk and peered into its crystalline surface. Like most Conclave tech, it was operated by hand movement or verbal command. Since he didn't possess Ral-vet's voice he waved his hand over the top, bringing up the turquoise holographic display. He moved around the desk, shoving the equally hovering chair aside, in order to see the display. Thanks to a fully integrated translator, he could now fully comprehend every Conclave language, spoken or written. Unfortunately, the words were not to his liking.

"We have a password problem," he said out loud for Ch'len's benefit. Before his partner in crime could respond, Roland heard the unmistakable sound of a repeater reaching full charge.

"You have bigger problems than that I'm afraid..."

Roland looked over the display to see the fat barrel of the repeater staring back at him, but perhaps most embarrassingly, it was being held by Ral-vet Tanek. He missed the Ch'kara's response; too busy being pissed at himself for holstering the Tri-rollers. "Keep your hands flat on the table, *human*." The Shay said the word like it was an insult. "Who hired you?" The right side of his face was completely robotic with a bright blue eye in the pit of metallic plating and gold tubes. Both arms were robotic below the elbow, revealing a contor-tion of engineered tendons and extra rotation spheres for dislocated movement. The layered robe concealed his body but Roland heard the sound of servo motors, most likely from another augmentation to the legs. "I said, who *hired* you?" his voice had a machine-like echo to it as he became irate.

"Your mother!" Roland felt the heat from the blast that shot past his head, cratering the wall. He calculated the next few seconds would be precious as far as his survival was concerned. In his experience, people didn't give a second warning shot. Before he could spin some lie, to keep him alive a few seconds longer, Ral-vet's weapon flew from his hand, continuing through the glass wall and raining shards into the apartment below. The Shay's look of shock only lasted a second until it turned to one of pain. He rose into the air, arms spread apart not quite under his control, as he was slammed into the wall by an unseen force. The metal plating around his face crumpled, cutting into his pale flesh and drawing thick globules of red blood. His cries of agony faltered as the augmentation around his voice box fluttered through the different octaves.

Then he saw *her*.

"Esabelle, I almost didn't recognise you with all your clothes on." In comparison to the naked form he had originally met, the Terran now wore a black floor-length cloak with the hood pulled down. She strode into the centre of the office with her right arm stretched out towards Ral-vet, who continued to struggle against the wall.

"Hilarious as always, Roland," she replied dryly. With that, she lowered her arm and dropped the Shay into a heap on the floor, leaving him struggling to breathe.

"I thought for sure it would be the kid, but I suppose *this* isn't quite his style." Roland walked round the hover desk, never taking his eyes off the tall brunette. She was far more attractive than he remembered from their first encounter on the *Gommarian*. Her dark hair flowed halfway down her back, set against a strong angular face with deep blue eyes. Her skin had gained some colour but was still paler than most, in an angelic way, he thought. It occurred to Roland that this exact scenario had played out the first time they met, only it was Savrick's best bud Elandar standing over him.

"What the hell is going on in there?" Ch'len screamed down the comm.

"Just keep the engine runnin'." Roland didn't trust him to fly the *Rackham* but he was pretty good with all the technical maintenance.

With that, he touched his ear, cutting the communication between them.

"I gave you freedom, Roland. Our species is entering a new phase in its existence, and we are *trying* to make allies with the biggest power-house this side of the galaxy. So putting it plainly - you need to stop fucking it up." There was definitely something about this woman that turned him on.

"And which species is that exactly? I was under the impression you and I weren't actually in the same gene pool." All he had was words, there was no way he could beat her in any kind of fight. He decided to let it play out a little longer, find her angle before making his move.

"As much as it pains me, we are the same species. I'm just a little further along than you." She was cocky, but then again she could be.

"So what's the plan; you haul me back to Kalian and he throws me over his knee and gives me a spanking?" If that really was the plan he was sure as shit going to give her hell trying. Esabelle looked as if she were about to reply when she froze as if hearing something he couldn't.

"There are more coming." She was doing that weird thing they did. He wasn't sure how it worked but he wouldn't mind having the ability. "Of all the bounties you had to take this one? A highly valued member of one of the Conclave's biggest corporations? What were you thinking?" Esabelle moved to the shattered window peering down into the broken remains.

"The job was simple: kill him and retrieve some data-file from his private terminal. In return, I get a hundred thousand units. So if you don't mind, that's what I'm going to do." Roland returned to the hover desk and reactivated the holographic display. He slammed the desk, realising his error in leaving the hacker in the Translift wall almost two miles below. Esabelle quickly turned on him, approaching the desk.

"We need to leave, *now*." With her final word, the sound of a dozen boots storming the apartment came from the broken window.

There was a lot of shouting, leading Roland to believe it was corrupted local security in the pocket of Protocorps.

"Not until I get what I came for." He had no idea where to start with the password. His only option would be to torture Ral-vet into telling him, and from the increasing sound of heavy boots, there wouldn't be time for that. Esabelle audibly sighed before marching to his side at the desk.

"Keep them busy - you seem to be good at that." She shoved him aside while placing her right hand flat against the polished surface. The display flickered before turning into a waterfall of Conclave symbols forever in flux. Roland had no idea what she was doing but it was definitely affecting the terminal. He had a fanciful image in his head of the things they could accomplish if they worked together. He knew that would never happen though; she was all about the cause, and Roland just wanted to live.

"Make no mistake," she continued. "When we're done here, you *are* coming back with me to the *Gommarian*." That was a bridge he wasn't looking forward to crossing. He removed his last grenade and threw it like a bowling ball down the corridor - there was a brief scream before the explosion drowned everything out. His Tri-rollers chirped like children eager to play. Ral-vet was struggling to sit up while he tentatively explored his damaged face and throat.

"I'm in." Esabelle removed her hand from the desk and examined the new display. Roland tried not to look impressed but wasn't sure if he succeeded. "What's the name of the file you need?" Using the touch-pad on his jacket he brought up the relevant information sent to him by the anonymous client. The subsequent hologram showed a series of numbers and letters the file would be found under. Esabelle continued her search as a Nix scuttled out of the smoky corridor wielding two repeaters. Of all the aliens Roland had encountered, the Nix was the most nightmarish looking. He didn't hesitate in raising his own weapon and blowing a hole through the weird looking head, with all its eyes.

The turquoise display changed as the appropriate file opened up. After a stream of information, the picture changed to a holographic blueprint. There was something familiar about it that he couldn't put his finger on. The structure was tall with a large dome at each end and a multitude of connections and machine parts in between. The centre of the construct was a simple cube, apparently attached to everything via a countless amount of thin and thick cables. What was it?

"It can't be..." Esabelle stood back from the desk as if she had seen a ghost, her pale face reflecting the turquoise display. To answer his questioning look she adjusted the image with a hand movement. The structure vanished as the central cube magnified, filling the entire picture. The details along its surface were unmistakable, and Roland knew where he had seen it.

Now he had questions.

"What is this, what are we looking at?" He knew the cube was identical to the one sitting under the *Gommarian's* Starrillium, but how did Protocorps have one, and what was it attached to?

"The Conclave's central AI," Esabelle stated flatly. Roland was very rarely fazed by anything, the drink and violence usually saw to that, but this was worrying even to him. From the discussions he had been privy to before leaving, he knew the cube was partially responsible for the Terran war, as well as Savrick's mad search for any human life. The cube was supposedly alive, in some way, and harboured strong feelings towards Terran life, in all its forms. They had decided that anything willing to play such a long game in exterminating an entire species, by such intelligent and deceptive means, was not a force they could easily contend with. If one cube could do all that damage with a single species and one ship, what could this one do?

Quicker than Roland thought possible, Esabelle was standing in front of Ral-vet. She lifted her hand, mirroring the rising form of the broken Shay. Once level with her she flipped her hand palm out and Roland knew his mark was telekinetically pinned to the wall.

"I can't get inside your head." She physically grabbed him by the throat and closed the gap between them. "But that doesn't mean you won't tell me everything you know."

Roland had mixed feelings about why this was still turning him on.

Ral-vet's organic eye stared back at her with no hint of fear. Through the pain, he was obviously feeling, the Shay managed to twist his mangled face into a crooked smile. At that moment Roland knew they didn't have enough time to break him. Backing up his revelation, the lobby below filled up with more mercenaries who cautiously surveyed the mayhem.

"We haven't got time for this." Roland directed his words at Esabelle who stepped away from the pinned bureaucrat. She did that thing again where she appeared to absorb information with a faraway look.

"Where's the *Rackham*?" Esabelle asked.

"I've got her parked in the cloud bank." Roland had planned on using the thick atmosphere as an escape plan to lose any tails. Esabelle paced the room stopping at the broken window to evaluate the security between the staircases.

"How quickly can you have it outside this building, specifically that wall?" She pointed to the far wall with the panoramic view of the planet beyond. He didn't like where this was going. Roland had a plan and they needed to stick to it.

"I've already got an exit strategy, okay?" He lifted both Tri-rollers to head level, indicating his well thought-out plan.

"That's not a plan." She said the words as if they rhymed with *dickhead*. Esabelle turned back to the scene below. "Trust me on this one, I can protect you." Now he knew what she was planning and he definitely didn't like it. But he couldn't deny everything he had seen her kind do. This is why he hated being sober; logic was just annoying.

"Why should I even help you escape? You want to drag my ass back to human *uncivilisation*." Roland looked over and counted seven security personnel.

"Oh I will take you back, but first we need to make a stop at the Conclave capital," Esabelle replied coolly. This new cube had got under her skin, she needed answers. He could use that to his advantage. The Conclave capital was a big enough place to lose her and get back to business. The cube intrigued him as well but Esabelle and Kalian were more than equipped to handle it.

Using the link in his cerebrum, Roland connected to the *Rackham* and commanded it to leave the atmosphere and fly directly up Krono Towers. He felt the unusual response that presented itself as a green light in his mind's eye in affirmation to his order. No doubt Ch'len was going crazy wondering why the ship was moving ahead of schedule. Roland tried not to laugh out loud at the thought.

"Fine, we do it your way. The *Rackham's* en-route." With that, he turned to Ral-vet and severed his head with a shot to the neck. Now he would get paid.

"After you..." Esabelle gestured for him to drop out of the office window.

"Oh, I insist," he replied with as much mock chivalry as he could muster. "Psychopathic bitches first." A sarcastic smile was all she gave before stepping out, to fall the three floors into the lobby. Roland quickly followed her movement and stepped out himself, activating the Laronian boots as he did. During his fast descent, he watched Esabelle dramatically throw off her cloak to reveal a tight combat suit beneath.

She had already dispatched two of the seven with hand to hand combat before his boots' repulsers kicked in to control his landing. Roland willingly joined the melee, breaking bones and disabling a Trillik and an Atari in the process. He killed the third with a flick of his Terran blade as Esabelle broke the neck of a Laronian with her bare hands. The last, a Shay, she telekinetically pushed into the glass wall. The impact was so strong the reinforced glass cracked in a spider web pattern around the body. This entire fight had probably been planned out in her head before they even started.

The hallway outside filled with more security - a bigger team from the sound of it. They both looked at one another in the moments they had left. Roland was sure he heard Esabelle's voice in his head.

Ready?

Thinking it to be his own imagination, he simply nodded as they both ran flat out towards the expansive view. Blue energy shot past them as the guards flooded the lobby and fired on them. It must have been a strange sight to see the suspects running to a dead end. That was until Esabelle threw out her arm and unleashed a flash of energy that momentarily blinded them all, Roland included. Whatever the energy was, it hurled into the glass and atomised everything in a colossal explosion, exposing the apartment to hard vacuum.

This ushered in a new kind of chaos that even Roland was unaccustomed to. As they were violently sucked out he was pulled into Esabelle's personal space, leaving behind sound and warmth and more importantly, oxygen. Immediately after being dragged out they changed trajectory, thanks to Esabelle, and plummeted down the many miles of Krono Towers at a frightening speed. Only then did it occur to Roland that he wasn't suffering from the deadly exposure. He knew Esabelle would do *something* weird to keep them alive, but this was incredible. They were both encompassed in some kind of telekinetic cocoon that contained the warmth of the apartment as well as a limited amount of oxygen. The bounty hunter did his best to keep his breathing as shallow as possible.

Looking down meant he was actually looking back at the expelling apartment, viewed between their feet. Dozens of guards were dying or already dead as they continued along their momentum into space. He was informed through his link that his proximity to the *Rackham* was imminent, a fact that was evident from the fast approaching ship that seemed to be above them but was, in fact, flying up the tower. Using a finer control, only available to him, Roland commanded every aspect of the *Rackham's* flight. He was working fast, unsure of how long Esabelle could keep up this god-like feat.

This was either going to be the coolest getaway of all time or the craziest death of all time...

THE *BLADE* HUNG in space outside the quarantine zone, using its forward and aft thrusters to keep it from crossing the virtual line. With a holographic display overlaying the triangular viewport, Krono Towers had been enveloped inside a yellow sphere, put there by local security. Any vessel without authorised clearance would face immediate grounding if it was connected to the AI hub on Shandar. Since the *Blade* wasn't, it would in all likelihood be shot down or disabled and boarded. Neither was a viable option, but the latter would certainly result in a life sentence on a Raalakian prison planet once they found all the illegal hardware.

With all four hands dancing across the cockpit console, Kubrackk quickly calibrated the ship's array to intercept the security laser comm, as well as piggy-backing it back to Krono Towers to relay the internal feed. He was furious with his timing. Once again, his prey had swept through like a hurricane on Arakesh and avoided the retribution he had coming his way.

"Is it him, Boss?"

Kubrackk loathed the presence of his two companions, but they were a necessary evil if a stupid one. Asking the latest infuriating question was the Trillik, Spelnar. It was his technical skills that allowed the *Blade* to hack most Conclave encrypted operating systems, bypassing the AI's first few layers of firewall. Kubrackk turned to see the Trillik's four black eyes staring at him intently. Like the rest of his race, Spelnar had a skin combination of green and blue with two lanky arms and a muscular frame closely resembling his own Novaarian features, purely coincidental considering their cohabitation within Novaarian space. His smooth head was round with sharp elfish features fitted around the four oval eyes. It was his tail that always pissed Kubrackk off. He was forever tripping over the multitude of tendrils that split off half way down.

Like most people who spoke to him, Spelnar's gaze lingered on the scar that ran over Kubrackk's left eye and down his long face, ending at his mouth. Most wondered why he had never had it removed but, the truth was, he liked it. He thought it was well suited to someone in his line of work. It said he wasn't afraid to do what was needed when the bounty called for it.

"Of course it's *him!*" Kubrackk spat. Spelnar shot back into his seat and looked anywhere but at the Novaarian. The console chirped as it received the feedback from the security channels, before raising several holographic displays of the internal carnage. The Novaarian took a breath at the sight of such destruction.

Like everyone else in the Conclave, he had seen the footage from the battle on Naveen half a cycle ago. It had been hard to believe such beings existed, but no one could deny the damage they had wrought to the Conclave as well as their own planets. There were so many tales and varying stories about the humans it was hard to know what was real and what was fiction. There were stories about Earth and some place called Century, but there were also whispers of an identical race called the Terran. This was where it became blurry and hard to define. Instead, the whole lot of them had been categorised as dangerous with tendencies towards mass-destruction.

With that in mind, Roland North was something of an enigma. Kubrackk had seen first hand what the bounty hunter was capable of, and though he was not to be underestimated, North did not appear to be in the same league as the individual seen on Naveen. That particular human had been brought before the Highclave but Kubrackk couldn't remember his name. It didn't matter really; North was his target, his own personal bounty. Looking at the monitors gave him second thoughts. He was looking at the hangar inside Krono Towers with its giant scar across the floor leading to a bulbous cargo ship half buried in the wall. It had crushed other parked vessels and reduced most of the hangar to a smouldering wreck. The corridors were filled with smoke from hundreds of pot-shots between North and Proto-corps mercenaries. One particular stretch of corridor had a dense pile of bodies where they had obviously been caught in a kill box with gravity mine bombs.

Translifts and grav pillars had been disabled with explosive effect a mile long. His mark had clearly been Ral-vet since it was his executive suite that had been assaulted and, from the looks of it, ejected into space. The apartment looked as if a hundred war bred Raalakians had charged through it. Most of its contents and occupants, Ral-vet included, had been sucked into space, though his cause of death was yet to be determined according to the intercepted laser comm. Most intriguing of all was the footage from the external cameras, specifically the ones Protocorps had aimed at their board member's apartment.

"There's two of them?" This time it was Spelnar's idiot partner in crime, Lole, who pointed out the obvious. He was an overweight Tularon with too much fur around the eyes and head to even be attractive amongst his own kind. Kubrackk noted the fear in his voice and clamped down on the urge to shoot Lole in his leathery face.

"Apparently so..." Kubrackk said through gritted teeth. He replayed the image of their escape expecting to see a file corruption message pop up. What he was seeing couldn't be possible; it had to be the female. North usually operated alone, using the technical skills of that useless Ch'kara from the safety of his unique ship. The image defied the laws of physics but the escape was certainly impressive, and Kubrackk hated the fact. He would make the human suffer for his betrayal, even if he had to chase him to the end of the galaxy.

"I'm not so sure of this plan boss!" Lole continued. "These humans ain't right. They can do stuff that ain't natural..." He stopped speaking when Kubrackk wrapped his lower fingers around the hilt of the Quad-roller strapped to his chest.

"He forgot to engage that nifty stealthware of his," Kubrackk explained. "The *Rackham* is on course for the capital, so that's where we're going." It was mistakes like this that he needed. North wasn't perfect and he certainly wasn't some super-powered being like the others. Kubrackk was confident he could deal with the girl when the time came.

He set a course for Shandar's star; unlike the *Rackham,* the *Blade* relied on the magnetic waves from a star spot to charge the Intrinium and power the Solar Drive. When he was done having his fun with North, Kubrackk decided he would make the *Rackham* his own.

THREE

Telarrek's ship had emerged into real space four hundred thousand kilometres away from Ch'ket's sun. Having traversed the remaining distance to reach the fourth planet, where it entered a geosynchronous orbit, the crew were patiently awaiting further orders. Kalian stood on the observation platform on the port side taking in the new planet. He had seen holo-images and read about Ch'ket in data files, but it couldn't prepare him for the incredible view.

Using his memory like a terminal, he pulled up all the information he had ever seen or heard regarding the planet. He instantly knew it was three times the size of what Earth had been with a diameter of thirty-seven thousand kilometres. Before entering the Conclave, many millennia ago, Ch'ket had possessed two moons rich in myopallic ore. Kalian looked out knowing he would see no trace of either since the Ch'kara had mined both orbiting bodies to their core.

Of course, the size and history of the planet were not what it was famous for, and it was clear from the observation platform why. The entire planet was haloed in colossal shipyards, each in a different orbit, while others interlinked and connected via bridges. Kalian counted five in total but it was hard to see all the rings through thousands of cargo ships arriving and departing; the sight reminded him of a beehive. The giant shipyards were made to mirror Ch'ket's orbit so Translifts could be built from the surface, through the atmosphere, and connect to the many rings. To Kalian it looked as if the planet was encompassed in a massive head-brace.

Everywhere the eye could see, ships of every kind were in various stages of construction across the enormous ports. Separate from the planet, Kalian could see other ringed shipyards in the distance where the Ch'kara had run out of space to encircle their homeworld. As a species, they were obsessed with building and engineering, but to actually turn their whole world into a shipyard felt a little over the top. The latest figures reported that eighty-five percent of their population were engineers in some form or other. From the images he had stored in his head, Kalian knew the surface was actually a stunning place with grand architecture and works of beauty and art like a lot of other Conclave cultures. Regrettably, the surface could only be appreciated through the visor of a breather, since the atmosphere was toxic to all except the Ch'kara.

"Incredible isn't it?" Li'ara appeared at his side, though Kalian had always known where she was on the ship. He knew where everyone was onboard. Esabelle had taught him to find the nuances that made individuals unique, allowing him to tell the difference between every Novaarian and human. He had yet to try it on the other races since their isolation on the *Gommarian*.

"To think they were building ships like this before we even discovered electricity..." Kalian tried not to let his thoughts dwell on the fact that the entire human race was engineered, and that Terran culture, his true ancestors, were far older than those before him. He looked at Li'ara and found his thoughts easily distracted. She really was bewitching to him, even more so since Naveen. He concentrated on the construction of a nearby ship, its internal structure more visible than its external, in an attempt to resist the urge to say everything he thought about her.

There was a palpable tension between them and he wanted nothing more than to cut through it and get to the heart of their situation.

"Li'ara..."

"Kalian..." She cut him off but looked away, her hair covering any expression. She didn't know what to say, as much as he didn't. A silent conversation took place, one they had verbalised before, in which they both agreed there was too much going on around them. Kalian agreed to a point but it became harder every day. Before he could speak again they were interrupted by a life-size hologram of Naydaalan.

"Greetings of peace," he began. "We have received the Highclave's coordinates on the edge of the solar system. Ambassador Telarrek will meet you in the hangar as we proceed with security clearance." With that, his image quickly faded away.

"We should go." Li'ara hardened again. "Whatever this meeting is, we're representing our whole race. We need to be ready."

He knew what she was really saying; there were more important things to think about than the way they felt for each other.

NAYDAALAN PILOTED, with Telarrek as his co-pilot, while Kalian and Li'ara sat behind. It had taken over an hour to reach on thrusters alone, Ch'ket now a distant speck outshone by the system's main star. Their destination appeared to be the gas giant easily seen in the viewport. The planet was twice the size of Jupiter, with turbulent storms visible as they raged across the surface in streaks of yellow.

"Are we meeting *inside* it?" Kalian asked.

Naydaalan turned in his seat without making eye contact, "No. The coordinates lie just beyond Cerula."

The shuttle angled towards the planet's northern hemisphere with the intention of flying over it. After scaling Cerula, the horizon gave way to an immense shipyard hiding in the planet's shadow. Both humans slowly rose from their seats, unable to take their eyes off the lone ship in the centre of three humongous construction rings. It wasn't finished yet but, from the shape and size, Kalian guessed it to be in a similar vein to the *Gommarian*.

There were thousands of crafts and engineering teams working in every section with sparks ejecting from the innumerable welding bots. New materials were being transported to and from the great ship by the ton. What was more impressive was how small it made the *Marillion* look, as the golden sphere's hulking mass overlooked the project from close by.

"What is this?" Li'ara asked.

"I believe this is the reason you were summoned to these specific coordinates," Telarrek explained. "It is no doubt the Highclave's way of showing you their resolve against the threat of your ancient ship." Telarrek was hard to read and Kalian couldn't tell if the Novaarian had already known about the construction.

"So they're building something to take on the *Gommarian*..." Li'ara was giving the ship a scrutinising eye.

Kalian looked over the ship himself as he thought about the unusual layout to the Conclave's military. He knew that each of the five core species possessed their own navy, as such, and that they protected the other races within their territory. The Conclave had its own security force that held jurisdiction over the capital world and all boundaries between the different territories, essentially taking control if a dispute ever broke out. The local security on every planet was formed from that particular species, with the races only mixing onboard the Conclave ships.

Was this ship the start of a new type of security, or a new navy? Along with the *Marillion*, the Conclave would wield a formidable force. In Kalian's opinion, they would be better forming an organisation that defended every aspect of the Conclave and combined all the races. A navy not unlike the UDC, where the funds and resources could be pooled into one force for the good of the wider populace, especially when your populace was stretched over seven hundred and twenty worlds with a combined population of just over six trillion. But what did a history lecturer know about protecting an entire civilisation that had lasted longer than Earth ever did?

"I am sure it is only precautionary." Telarrek sounded as if he was trying to convince himself more than them.

Kalian knew this was a response to their earlier meeting after the events on Naveen. The Highclave had demanded that the *Gommarian* and himself be handed over due to the threat they posed. His refusal had been a little dramatic.

More security checks sprang up across the holographic field demanding access codes and authorised verification. Naydaalan deftly responded to several requests at once with all four arms dancing over the console. The view shifted, leaving the construction site to disappear off to the port side and the *Marillion* swelled as they closed the gap.

"They will not allow you to board the flagship." Naydaalan faced them. "They will meet us halfway." The same procedure as last time, Kalian thought. The Highclave considered the ship's interior to be too sensitive for their prying human eyes.

After another agonising hour of waiting, they were finally given the go-ahead from the *Marillion's* crew to board the council's domed vessel. A familiar Nix was waiting for them inside the miniature hangar outside the central dome. It scuttled over on clawed feet, hidden beneath its flowing blue and silver robe, its chevron head regarding them with an unreadable expression.

"Ambassador Telarrek..." Its voice rasped every syllable as it greeted the Novaarian.

"Greetings of peace, Xydrandil." Telarrek bowed respectfully at the Highclave's gatekeeper.

"Your hatchling is not permitted to enter, Ambassador, only you three."

Naydaalan visibly bristled at the rejection. As his father's personal guardian, he probably didn't like the idea of being too far away. Then again, they were standing in the shadow of the Conclave's flagship as well as its most secure project; it was fair to assume they would be safe here. With a sharp grunt, the young Novaarian retreated to the ship without looking back.

Xydrandil led them through the connecting corridor where they were scanned by the last security check. Both humans had been instructed to leave their weapons on the shuttle, much to Li'ara's irritation. Once again they found themselves standing before a raised platform in an arcing hemisphere around the dome. The space above the councillors was fitted with subdued white lights while the floor under Kalian's feet was lit with stark spotlights.

Elondrasa was situated in the centre with Lordina and Brokk to her right, and Ch'lac and Nu-marn to her left. As always they were regally dressed in the finest garments, jewellery and accessories available to their races. Elondrasa and Lordina wore beautiful head-dresses coated in exquisite gems and crystal that best suited their skin tones. Brokk's tall, flat head was haloed by a floating golden crown that never touched his stony surface. As always, the Ch'kara was surrounded by a cloud of atmosphere from his home planet, with several technical accessories attaching his breather-gear to his clothing. Nu-marn, like his entire race, was almost indistinguishable from a machine. Kalian noted extra augmentations to his face that had been surgically applied since their last meeting.

"Greetings of peace, Kalian Gaines, Commander Ducarté." Elondrasa acknowledged them both before waving for Telarrek to stand aside. Kalian always got the feeling the Highclave were not completely comfortable with Telarrek's familiarity with the humans. After four hundred years of studying and observing a species, it would be hard not to grow fond of them, especially after watching their worlds burn.

They both bowed their heads and waited for the Highclave to explain their reason for being summoned. Kalian didn't hold much respect for the council members, but it would be stupid not to show respect to the five most powerful beings in the Conclave. With that thought in mind, Kalian pushed his awareness into the surrounding structure, assessing any threats the Highclave possessed. In an instant, he knew the floor was connected to a separate generator, that when activated would unleash an electrical charge incapacitating or killing any who stood before the Highclave. The walls and ceiling were lined with hidden cannons that would attack at a moment's notice to protect their masters. Kalian could feel the complex arrangement of particles that formed the organic life behind the concealed doors. He counted two teams of security personnel, a dozen in each, ready to burst into the room should they try anything untoward. There was another power source within the podium itself. Kalian assumed it would be a micro force-field, designed to protect the Highclave from a direct assault.

"You really think that bucket of bolts is going to rival the *Gommarian*?" Li'ara being as tactful as ever. The question made the Highclave visibly uncomfortable. Kalian was formulating a diplomatic response to smooth over the break in etiquette. They probably weren't expecting a response to the massive ship's construction - it was meant as a visual warning.

"Since you have refused to hand over the Terran vessel, we have been forced to react accordingly." It was Nu-marn from Shandar that replied with a sharp tongue.

"The *Sentinel* will be operational by the end of the cycle." Lordina's comment felt like more of a threat than a comment.

"You couldn't handle the *Gommarian*." Li'ara could argue with the politicians until the universe collapsed. Lordina was clearly posturing to make a more hostile response. Kalian heard Captain Fey's voice in his head and remembered her speech about the importance of survival.

"If I may, councillors?" Kalian interjected before it became too heated. "We have already discussed this matter. The *Gommarian* is too advanced and too dangerous to be handed over. Those of us living onboard do so ignorantly of our precursors' secrets. We do not possess the tools or instruments to investigate its inner workings." He was careful to leave out Esabelle and the fact that they knew a fair few of the ship's secrets, including the technologically advanced nanocelium.

"And you think that such an advanced ship belongs in the hands of those who cannot operate it effectively? We saw what that ship did to your home planet." Ch'lac sat forward in his seat, the atmospheric gases contained inside the micro force-field.

"Honestly?" Kalian continued. "If we had a planet to call our own, somewhere we could start again, I would send the *Gommarian* into the heart of the nearest star and leave it there." From the expressions before him, Kalian could see that was not the option the Highclave were looking for. Lordina looked hungry for a fight until Li'ara waded in again.

"It belongs to us. It was made by our ancestors and designed for our use," Li'ara stated.

"Your *engineers*..." Nu-marn corrected her choice of words.

"Same difference." She gave him a defiant look.

"Your history is an unusual one and in need of further debate and study," the Raalakian broke in. "But this discussion is for another time and is not the reason for this meeting." Brokk straightened his back, exhuming his superior height over the others. For what had historically proven to have been a violent race, Kalian always found Brokk to be one of the most diplomatic members of the council.

A change in subject was not what either of them was expecting. Kalian was sure it would be another tireless argument over the fate of the *Gommarian*. Why else would they have been summoned? It couldn't just be to show off the *Sentinel*. In truth Kalian found their intentions to be more of a threat than the actual ship. It had only ever been discussed in small groups, and among the most trusted on the *Gommarian*, that if it ever came to conflict the ship possessed more than enough capabilities to fend off almost every attack, not to mention the three Eclipse missiles sitting around with nothing to do. Those weapons alone could wipe out three solar systems with the press of a button. Like all scenarios of this nature, it came down to a question of morality; who had the conviction to end so many lives? Kalian was confident it would never come to that, providing Li'ara didn't take the lead on negotiations.

The council's eyes fell on Elondrasa. "Since the arrival of your people and the attack by Savrick, we have taken a great interest in all things Terran. We have science teams watching the Norma Arm, as you call it, for any indication of life. Being so far, there appear to be no changes in the current star field. Our best astrophysicists calculate that we will not see any supernovas in that cluster for another two hundred thousand cycles. There are serious talks about whether to send an exploratory expedition to see what remains of the Terran Empire..." She let her words hang, gauging any reaction.

Kalian and Li'ara kept their best poker faces on, giving nothing away.

This particular idea had in fact been bounced around the *Gommarian* once or twice as well. Esabelle informed them the ship could easily take them back since Albadar, the Terran capital world, was still logged in the navigation system along with hundreds of other Terran worlds. She also told of the devastation her father wrought on every planet, the Gomar had left only ruin in their wake. It was decided that going there would be futile when they still had a chance of joining the Conclave and thriving here.

"Our interest in a new race would normally be scientific," Elondrasa continued. "But the Terran and the Gomar pose a very serious threat. Savrick was proof of that. But we understand that however similar, you are not from the same civilisation as them, and that you yourselves have many questions about the people that made you." Lordina didn't look convinced of that fact. "So we have decided that as a bridge between our races, we might work together to discover the secrets of the Terran."

Kalian couldn't help but smile at the prospect. It was an olive branch they could take advantage of with their own superior knowledge of the Terran/Gomar history. This was the connection the Captain had been talking about, something that would start the process of integration.

"We would be honoured to unravel these mysteries together." Kalian feared there would come a time when they had to inform the Highclave about Esabelle and ALF. They were the two greatest fonts of information and it would be hard to explain where they learned so much without credible sources. Right now, however, all things Terran were considered too big a threat. If the Conclave got their hands on either of them there would be consequences; both Esabelle and ALF were not easily beaten. Kalian decided it would be better if the Conclave learned more about the relationship between the Terran and the Gomar. After that, they would easily distinguish between a race devoted to exploration, beauty and art - if a little misguided - and a race driven by anger, revenge and social injustice.

"We are glad to hear it," Ch'lac replied coolly.

"There is such a mystery that has given us cause for this partnership," Elondrasa continued. "An ancient relic has been unearthed on Trantax IV, in Raalakian territory." The space between them was instantly filled with a green hologram the size of Brokk.

It was a cube.

Kalian took a deep breath steadying his reaction to the familiar object. He didn't dare look at Li'ara; any interaction may give them away. It was definitely an identical cube to the one housed under the *Gommarian's* Starrillium. The image was clear enough to show the intersecting circles and lines of unintelligible writing. It didn't look as battered and damaged as the one on the ship, but Kalian only assumed that made it more dangerous.

"There are six hieroglyphs that correspond to the text found on The Wall," Elondrasa explained. "We believe it to be connected to the Terran, though the surrounding isotopes show the relic has been on Trantax IV for just over a hundred thousand cycles."

Kalian made some quick calculations in a fraction of time. He knew the Conclave had been around for a hundred and ninety thousand cycles, which wasn't far off the equivalent in human years, and the Terran Empire was just under three million years old...

His mind was trying to make the connection but he couldn't see the answer. He knew someone who could though.

"It's not Terran," Kalian said. Li'ara turned to him but he ignored her shocked appearance - she needed to trust him.

"And you know this how?" Lordina asked raising the scales above her right eye.

"Savrick told me..." he lied. "Before he died he told me about *them*." Nu-marn shifted in his seat uncomfortably. The Highclave hadn't believed this the first time Kalian tried to warn them. Li'ara saw the lie and visibly relaxed. "He found a cube identical to that one, on a Terran planet called Hadrok. It twisted his anger and directed him towards starting the war that ended an empire that lasted over two million cycles. I don't know who *they* are or what their goal is, but they are dangerous."

The council looked to one another for a moment, mixed expressions of concern and disbelief. A silent conversation took place between the veteran councillors as they judged his words.

"There is a vessel transporting the next rotation of supplies to the dig site," Brokk's voice sounded like he had swallowed a handful of stones. "It will dock at Ch'ket and await your arrival. We would like for you, along with the Ambassador here, to accompany them to Trantax IV. You do seem to have better luck with ancient relics than most, Kalian Gaines."

He was referring to Naveen. Conclave scientists and philosophers had studied The Wall for thousands of years and never made any progress with it. They had assigned it to a precursor race that no longer existed. Kalian hadn't even been on Naveen for more than a day when he unlocked its true purpose. He had a few genetic advancements the Conclave scientists lacked, however.

"We will leave immediately." Kalian didn't really know what they could learn from the cube. They hadn't applied many resources to discovering the secrets of their own cube, let alone one in such good condition. Either way, they had to go, if only to ensure the Conclave didn't meet the same fate as the Terran. "Could you inform Captain Fey on the *Gommarian* that we will not be returning for the time being?"

"They will be so informed." It was Telarrek who answered from the back of the room. He had obediently remained silent throughout the meeting and Kalian was eager to learn how much the Novaarian already knew regarding current events.

"Then this council is adjourned." Elondrasa rose to her full height, reaching over seven feet with the golden headdress.

"Thank you for your time. I hope this will be the beginning of a new dialogue between our people," Kalian said before bowing as he nudged Li'ara to do the same.

Xydrandil scuttled ahead leading them back to the shuttle with Telarrek following behind.

"Thank you for your time?" Li'ara repeated mockingly.

Kalian smiled at the jest as the doors sealed the Highclave away behind them. "This could be a good thing, for all of us." He kept his voice low.

"Nothing is ever good where a cube is involved," she replied in an equally hushed tone.

They entered the hangar to see Naydaalan practising combat manoeuvres with his staff before he realised they had returned. He quickly stood to attention as his father passed him boarding the craft, his staff planted next to him. Xydrandil remained behind watching silently as Naydaalan prepped the ship and engaged the thrusters, his robes flapping from the engine's output.

They departed the domed platform while Telarrek ordered his son to set a course for Ch'ket. Kalian looked out of the viewport, stealing a last glance at the sizeable shipyard housing the Conclave's newest and largest vessel. It was quickly eclipsed by Cerula which eventually became a bright speck on the monitors as they arrived back in orbit around Ch'ket. Telarrek informed Naydaalan of everything that had transpired with the Highclave before joining Kalian and Li'ara in the main cabin.

"Naydaalan is docking the ship in the Cyphon ring," Telarrek offered. Kalian easily recalled the information he had on the enveloping rings of Ch'ket and knew the Cyphon ring paralleled the planet's equator. "The cargo transport is already in the port and awaiting our arrival."

"Did you know about the cube?" Kalian asked outright.

Telarrek raised his long head looking back down on him. "I knew Trantax IV had been recently quarantined and that there was a potential Terran connection. I did not, however, know they had found a cube. The discovery is troubling." The Novaarian looked to his left as the Cyphon ring encompassed the entire screen of view. Hundreds of vessels could be seen unloading materials and crew while others were transporting various parts for ships on the other rings. From this distance, they could easily make out the details on the Translifts that connected the many rings to the planet's surface. They were thicker than any Conclave ship Kalian had ever seen. The end was concealed within a dense cloud cover, but he could see the giant shaft filled with multiple Translifts, big and small, as they continuously shot up and down.

"Why did you never tell them about our cube?" Li'ara asked.

"They would use it as an excuse to take the *Gommarian* by force," Telarrek explained. "There would most certainly be casualties, on both sides. I believe that both of us working together is the best scenario. Besides, we know the cube on the *Gommarian* was responsible for the Terran war, but this cube has remained dormant for a hundred thousand cycles. We may learn valuable information from this cube; it may have some answers regarding its makers and their reasoning for targeting your race."

"I would worry about why they're targeting the Conclave," Kalian commented.

Telarrek whipped his head back from the view. "Explain."

"Well a cube was found on a Terran planet; look what happened to them - to *us*. Let's just hope history isn't repeating itself."

Telarrek seemed to look through Kalian as he weighed those words. No doubt they would sit heavy in his mind.

Soon after departing the craft, Naydaalan led them to the designated hangar. They passed every kind of species the Conclave contained. Some slithered and crawled while others had footfalls that could be felt through the thick flooring. The clothing on all varied wildly in design and colour or, in some cases, there was a lack of clothing. It was an enjoyable difference from life on the *Gommarian* where every encounter was a human one. There was no divide between the species as all interacted with the other, no thought to their different biology and culture. Being the Ch'kara homeworld it was easy to understand the increased number of their species. Some were working as others were meeting friends and family while their ships were upgraded or fixed. The rings were kept oxygenated since they were widely used by all the races; it was only the planet itself that required visitors to wear breathers.

Kalian was impressed by how clean and sterile they kept what was essentially a giant workshop. Hover bots whizzed around cleaning spillages and picking up fallen tools, all the time avoiding the constant flow of people. One hover bot floated behind its owner as it tightened a bolt in the Ch'kara's breather equipment. Kalian couldn't be sure if it was fixing the gas cylinders or the micro force-field emitters; either way, the Ch'kara appeared oblivious.

They didn't go unnoticed as they passed by. Every individual that saw them stopped whatever they were doing to gawp at the humans. Some quickly disappeared, hoping not to be noticed by the dangerous species, while others moved closer for a better look. Naydaalan subtly removed his staff, reacting to the unwanted attention.

They eventually found themselves standing in the right hangar with the cargo transport, *Dawnlighter*, waiting for them, along with an old friend.

"Greetings of peace..." Ilyseal stood at the ship's side entrance.

Telarrek failed to hide his surprise and joy at seeing his old second-in-command. They had worked side-by-side for over six hundred years while they observed and studied the human race. He couldn't help the high pitched grunt as he launched forward, embracing her, "Greetings of peace, old friend."

The Ambassador stood back allowing Kalian and Li'ara to greet her as well; Naydaalan remained to the side, impartial to it all. Instead of the expected Novaarian garb, Ilyseal wore a red, tight-fitted flight suit, as seen on most Conclave personnel.

Noticing his look of confusion, Ilyseal elaborated. "I am afraid my actions in the Corvus system required an example to be made."

Kalian was shocked to hear that such heroic actions could be reprimanded. Ilyseal had led the mission to separate Savrick's forces, giving Kalian and the others more time to uncover The Wall's secrets. In so doing, she had permitted Roland's crazy idea to defeat the Gomar by destabilising the *Valoran's* Starrillium. The supernova obliterated the attacking crew and reduced the number of Gomar to double digits.

"Despite the effectiveness of our counter-attack," Ilyseal continued, "the *Valoran's* supernova had an interaction with Corvus's main sequence causing an unprecedented solar flare. Thankfully our early warning to the planet prevented any subspace travel from being interrupted. Unfortunately, the flare disrupted almost every satellite and communication array in the Corvus system. Some had backup systems but many had their silicon software fried. Along with the disruption to the AI hub, it cost billions of units to repair."

"So what have you been doing?" Li'ara inquired.

Ilyseal's red tendrils swished from side to side as she took in the sight of the cargo vessel behind her. "I have been assigned to the Trantax IV project..."

Telarrek's visage mirrored his anger and disbelief at her answer. "I shall look into the matter; you deserve better for your service. You helped keep the Conclave safe where so many others would have failed."

Ilyseal appeared almost embarrassed at the praise from her old charge.

"And you still might..." Kalian added knowingly. "I know you're supposed to transport us to Trantax IV, but we need to make a short detour."

Li'ara gave him a questioning look before a realisation of dread spread across her fair features. "This is not going to end well."

WAS this what it felt like to be a god? To stand and look down on a planet beneath you, and know it was yours. It was fair to say that Protocorps controlled almost everything Shay. Anything it didn't openly own it possessed via shell companies and blackmailed puppets. Their reach stretched as far as the capital with influence on every world and political arena. They had sole rights to maintenance and software protection for the Conclave AI in every hub. The Shay government didn't even make decisions, without first consulting the very board members that currently sat behind the head of this galactic conglomerate.

Kel-var Tionis stood with his hands clasped behind his back as he looked down on the northern pole of Shandar. The view from the top of Protocorps Headquarters was a three hundred and sixty degree panoramic image of the planet below, and the thousands of super-structures that blanketed it. The great storm below was becoming rivalled by the storm brewing among his board members. For all their power they had failed to protect one of their most prestigious members from a lowly bounty hunter. Further still, they had been unable to locate the backer behind the bounty.

Before turning from the beautiful vista, Kel-var lingered on the distant horizon - from his vantage above the planet's equator. There was still a buzz of activity surrounding Krono Towers, with the many machines and cranes mending the exterior damage. Squads of secu-rity vessels hovered at designated zones coordinated by the AI ensuring a safe perimeter. Kel-var's office had been flooded with questions from the media surrounding the attack, but he had left the replies to the PR teams while his own assistants drafted an appro-priate speech. He was set to give the heartfelt eulogy at the capital tomorrow before the usual gaggle of reporters.

"What is the point of all that security if they cannot fend off one bounty hunter?" Sel-gar Verenes exclaimed with some notable fear behind his anger. As the head of CalNet, Sel-gar was well placed for exporting the precious crystals, used for storage memory in almost every piece of Conclave hardware, from the Noonatril system deeper in Shay territory. He spent most of his time lounging in his luxurious housing complex, while he personally observed the Noonatril in the mining colonies. His round frame was concealed beneath layers of white and gold robes, his robotic hands clenched into fists on the tabletop.

"Haven't you seen the footage? It was a *human*..." Bal-son Narek said the word as if it was diseased. Bal-son was the living heir to one of the oldest family dynasties and wielded a hefty amount of sway in Shay politics. His family had backed the presidential candidate for thousands of years, running their campaign to victory every time. If you wanted the vote for a seat on the Highclave you had to be willing to sit in the pocket of a Narek.

Arguments broke out across the table regarding the validity of the footage. It was public knowledge that all the humans were in one place under the watchful eye of the Novaarians. What the public didn't know, that Kel-var and his board members were privy to, was that the humans were living onboard the monstrous ship that attacked the capital planet.

"What kind of message does this send about us?" Sel-gar continued. "We are supposed to be responsible for the safety and well-being of every world operating under an AI hub. How are we supposed to convince the people that we can maintain the Intelligence if we cannot repel a simple bounty hunter's attack against one of our own?"

"Why should we fear these humans? There are so few of them left to pose any real threat." It was Nal-mev Nargeen that spoke up. Far too often he was concerned with the newest profit margin allowing his sight to drift from their true goals. The slender Shay reclined in his chair appearing bored with the current topic. He was only just within the limits of Conclave law regarding augmentation, with all four robotic limbs and extensive neurological adjustments and organ replacement. Kel-var didn't give Nal-mev much attention outside of these private meetings; he was efficient enough when it came to controlling Nemtech industries, the sole company responsible for programming the software that bridges the gap for neurological control of all electronic augmentation.

"*They* didn't spend all that time reducing their population to mere thousands if they weren't considered a threat!" Sel-gar spat back. After the mention of their masters, a tension filled the room.

"We shall have to find a new way to market Krono Towers," Balson remarked. "The internal devastation is worse than the exterior."

Kel-var didn't care about real estate; they had entire companies who could handle that.

"What about the external satellites?" Tu-garn Davorn's augmented voice boomed over the rest. As always Tu-garn adorned one of his expensive tight fitted suits equal in cost to a small

Intrinium-rich planet. Unlike most Shay, Tu-garn preferred his external physical form, opting for internal augmentation. Kel-var knew his entire skeleton had been replaced with Callic-diamond, enhancing his physical strength. "It clearly shows *two* humans escaping in a manner that should have been certain death. No being could survive that kind of exposure!"

"I have had the footage verified." Kel-var decided to wade in and take some control. "There is no trickery, the images are confirmed." No one talked over him; his presence alone often commanded attention. "There are two humans, one male, and one female. We are still collating all the data, but we do know the two individuals are not those who stood before the Highclave." After seeing the images from Naveen, Kel-var had created a whole division devoted just to Kalian Gaines. Any current information was scarce since the humans were being kept isolated deep inside Novaarian territory. With the resources at his disposal, it had been simple to retrieve the data stored in the Novaarian archives. They had spent centuries observing them on their own planet, Earth, and had apparently paid close attention to Kalian Gaines. He was the next step in the humans' engineered evolution, making him the first Terran of his kind.

That made him dangerous.

Kel-var thought about the information the Highclave, and even the humans themselves, were in possession of and knew it was sketchy at best. There were only ten individuals in the whole galaxy that had access to the greater truth and they were in this very room, bar one.

"We need to focus on Ral-vet's death," Kel-var continued. "His private terminal was hacked using an untraceable device, but the search data was scrambled. We have to assume they know everything Ral-vet had access to."

The board members shared a look of concern. They were the seventh generation to inherit the knowledge of the cube, their prophet, and it was their duty to keep it secret until the appointed time.

Thinking of the prophet was the only thing that increased the rate of both Kel-var's hearts. Using his neurological augmentations, he decreased the rate allowing him to keep his calm composure in front of his peers.

"Do you think they know about the AI?" Sel-gar asked with frantic looks to his fellow members.

Kel-var had never enjoyed the company of the fat Shay. Sel-gar was ruled by his fear and his appetite for Noonatine cuisine. He was weak in the opinion of most but Kel-var had no choice in who sat on the board; their ancestors had found the cube and so it was the lineage of those ten who would continue the great mission.

"Ral-vet was directly responsible for the central hub on the capital," Kel-var replied with some impatience for Sel-gar's obvious question. "I want to know how two humans are travelling freely through the Conclave, and what they want with that information. Who is paying them to target us and why?" he looked over them as they avoided his gaze; they had no answers. In his virtual vision, he brought up the most recent report from the division responsible for tracking and studying Kalian Gaines. Their spies had informed the team that both Kalian and Li'ara Ducarté had been transported to the Ch'ket system, for a secret meeting with the Highclave. Of course, he already had this information due to Bal-son's closer sources and Protocorps' own involvement with the new ship they were building out there.

"I have it on good authority that the bounty hunter is called Roland North." The words came from the end of the room where Gor-van Tanar sat. His face was partially hidden by the red hood that drooped over his head and shoulders, only allowing his augmented eyes to shine fluorescent blue in the dark. Gor-van was a valuable member of their organisation, with a finger in every dark corner of the Conclave. Most of his assets worked for him off the books via a trail that would never lead back to Protocorps. He was the legitimate head of multiple transport businesses, but he was also in control of the biggest crime family on Shandar. "He was responsible for the counter-attack in the Corvus system. He planned the demise of eight hundred Gomar in a single strike. I also have reason to believe he encountered a Gomar in combat and not only survived but won."

"How do you know this?" Tu-garn asked skeptically.

"He visited Shandar not long after the events on Naveen. He sought out a surgeon willing to replace several bones as well as strengthen damaged joints. And there was drink involved." Kel-var had stopped being surprised at Gor-van's sources. "He is just a human, he has no Terran abilities."

"And yet he has left nothing but death and destruction behind him!" Sel-gar let his chair take his full weight as he slumped back.

"It would seem the humans are not to be underestimated..." Gor-van replied.

Kel-var had never underestimated an enemy. Arrogance only led to death; that's what his father had said. He considered his own position at the top of the Protocorps chain and knew he hadn't obtained the role by underestimating his rivals. Over seven thousand potential Terran was not something he took lightly. Ideally, they needed a human of their own to study, to truly understand their enemy.

He gave Gor-van a knowing look and received a nod in reply. Gor-van could be trusted to take care of the bounty hunter problem, while he concentrated on more pressing matters.

"We are going to have to push the timetable on the Trantax project," Kel-var stated. "I will consult the prophet on the capital before proceeding. What security is watching over the project?"

"The *Nova*, a Nebula-class," Gor-van replied.

"Do we have anyone onboard?"

"Of course."

A redundant question Kel-var supposed. "Notify them of our extraction teams and have them on standby."

The cube had been found and made public before Protocorps could get directly involved. They had been content to go through official channels to take control since the Conclave had no idea what they had found, but the Highclave had decided to keep it on Trantax IV for now. Should the matter require it, however, Kel-var had organised several specialist teams to remain on standby for retrieval. For reasons he couldn't fathom, they had brought the humans in on the ancient relic, and Kel-var did not want any interaction between the two.

"Why not consult *them*?" Bal-son enquired.

"Because I know what they will say," Kel-var replied sharply. From the beginning, *they* had always trusted the prophet with carrying out their will, and Protocorps was an extension of that will. "If there is no further business, this meeting is over." No more topics were offered forward. "Then I shall say this; if any of you are as stupid as Ral-vet Tanek, I suggest you transfer any sensitive data to a secure offsite location rather than storing it on your home terminal. Ral-vet is *lucky* to have died the way he did after such an oversight. If any of you are responsible for future transgressions of this nature, the consequences will be far worse than an Intrinium round to the head." With that, he swept his cloak behind him and made for the door. He sent a message to his personal aide and instructed her to ready a vessel for immediate departure; he would be in the capital by day's end.

The prophet would know what to do...

FOUR

Travelling with an Ambassador had its advantages, Kalian thought. After the *Helion* nose-dived into Naveen's surface, the central console showed the moon's lower hemisphere had been quarantined. No ship could pass through the virtual barrier without authorisation; thankfully Telarrek was a walking authority, especially in Novaarian territory. Ilyseal helmed the *Dawnlighter* as it passed through the atmosphere to fly over the dry desert below.

The moon would forever hold a special place in Kalian's memories. It was here that he learned humanity's origin, a question that had been pondered for thousands of years. It was also the place he unravelled the mystery of his own life and discovered his relevance in the universe. There were darker memories here as well. He had almost lost Li'ara to this moon as well as nearly dying himself.

The *Dawnlighter* continued to sail over the desert passing through the virtual yellow wall that flashed up on the viewport. The quarantine bubble had a diameter of three thousand kilometres with the Novaarian battleship, *Pillar,* parked in low orbit above. After a brief exchange with the *Pillar's* charge, Telarrek had secured their passage until sunset. Kalian just hoped that would be long enough to find what he was looking for.

"Now that's a big hole." Li'ara had risen to stand by Ilyseal in the pilot's seat. The viewport gave the perfect image of the titanic wreckage left by the *Helion*. The crater stretched for two and half thousand kilometres in every direction with a depth of over a thousand feet. Hundreds of cranes and retrieval bots were busy at work removing every individual piece of debris. The Wall had been at the centre of the crater before the impact, though there would be nothing left of it now; even the nanocelium couldn't withstand that kind of attack.

The ground was charred on the edges of the crater with smoke still rising from electrical components that continued to catch fire in the heat. With the main bulk of the *Helion* already removed Kalian could see the shining interior. Having burned at well over two thousand three hundred degrees Celsius, the sand had turned to glass giving the appearance of a giant concave mirror in the midday sun.

As they drew closer they could see the various teams of Conclave personnel dotted around the massive excavation site. Many were directing the cranes through the use of portable virtual stimulators while their superiors looked on from their podiums surrounded in holographic spheres.

"This isn't just a cleanup job, is it?" Kalian looked to Telarrek. "They're looking for any remains of the outpost aren't they?"

"Yes. We are a society that craves knowledge. The Highclave see you as not only a mystery but also as a threat. They will go to every length to uncover your secrets."

"You know as well we do Telarrek, the Conclave is not ready for Terran technology. We agreed that the Conclave must continue along its own evolutionary path. No interference." Kalian wanted to reiterate the conversation they had shortly after the death of Savrick. He knew Telarrek would be under immense pressure from his superiors to give over everything he learned from his time with the humans. He wasn't losing faith in his alien friend, he just wanted to hear Telarrek echo his thoughts, and they had to be on the same page about this.

"It is your people who have a habit of playing God, not ours." It was Naydaalan who replied. It wasn't hard to miss the underlying contempt he held against humanity.

"Naydaalan!" Telarrek quickly silenced his son. "Forgive him, he is young and forgets his place."

"No, *I'm* sorry." Kalian could sympathise with Naydaalan's point of view. "We have placed you in a difficult position, Telarrek. Because of us, you have been forced to keep secrets from your own people. It can't be easy." Kalian truly felt bad for putting Telarrek in that position; if it wasn't for the old Novaarian they would have died many times over by now. Even though they didn't know it, what was left of mankind owed Telarrek a great debt and, being as honourable as he was, Telarrek would never call it in.

"You need no forgiveness. I have seen first hand what the Gomar are capable of, and I have no intention of allowing the machinations of this *cube* to come to fruition. I have faith in you, Kalian Gaines. I have seen what *you* are capable of, and together I believe we can save the Conclave from Earth's fate."

Kalian felt a pang of guilt for doubting Telarrek's resolve. It was easy to forget how old he was; at nearly a thousand years he had more willpower than all of them combined. Kalian was proud to call him a friend.

Ilyseal brought the ship to land on a designated pad close to the central pavilion on the edge of the crater. The giant white tent was surrounded by several large generators that were connected by tubes, big and small, to the different equipment as well as the floodlights that encompassed the impact site. Every living worker stopped to watch the craft touchdown as sand was kicked into the air from the manoeuvring thrusters. Kalian could feel the complex structure of eighty-three beings outside the ship, every one of them waiting to lay their eyes on a real human. They had no doubt been alerted by the *Pillar* of the unusual visitors.

They descended the ramp into the dry heat of the cloudless Naveen desert. Kalian felt his breath fall short at the sudden change in atmosphere. Telarrek led the way with Naydaalan still visibly bristling from his recent reprimand. Li'ara came up on his right, adjusting the armoured plating around her shoulder.

"I hope you're right about this." They stood side by side, partially concealed from the crowd behind the towering height of the Novaarians. Li'ara activated the display on her gauntlet and brought up climate control. She dragged her finger down the display dropping the suit's internal temperature to imitate that of the ship.

Watching Li'ara control her own temperature gave Kalian an idea he had been wanting to put to the test. Pushing his awareness beyond his own physical body, he reached out feeling the atmospheric molecules around his own body. It was as if the world had stopped. He viewed everything at once in only the way a Terran could. It was easy to see how the whole universe was connected through the different densities of molecules. In the heat of Nova Prime's star, the air particles were vibrating at incredible speeds creating the thermal energy of the desert. He slowed the vibrations down with a single thought before applying that same thought to the particle constituents of his own matter. He then assigned this use of power to a subconscious part of his mind, allowing him to function on a higher level with no thought to it.

The world returned in a flood of noise and solid matter that took the form of his Naveen surroundings. Kalian couldn't help but smile at the difference he felt in temperature under what he knew was a blazing sun.

Looking out, they could both see the many alien faces trying to glimpse the humans between their Novaarian companions. Amid the noise of all the construction, Kalian could still hear the whispers that passed between them. Some were fearful, while others wanted to come up to them and feel their pink alien skin.

"Return to your duties! This mess isn't going to clean itself up!" A single Laronian made his way out of the crowd as they dispersed. He wore an all-in-one black suit that fitted his every contour with electronic components attached to every limb and across his chest. They each projected a new hologram feeding back information on the various projects around the crater, as well as an inbuilt virtual stimulator for override options. His blue scales glistened in the sunlight, though Kalian knew the shine came from the transparent skin that ran over the scales. As he approached he was soon accompanied by a Raalak and a Shay, both in the red security uniform of the Conclave.

"Greetings of peace..." Telarrek let his words linger, unsure of the Laronian's name.

"I am Commander Lanakdar of house Trintell." It annoyed Kalian that he didn't respond with the polite greetings of peace. It was rude, even a human knew that.

"Commander Lanakdar of house Trintell, I am-"

"I know who you are, Ambassador. The entire Conclave knows who you are." Lanakdar's gaze quickly flickered to Kalian and Li'ara. "You are aware that this is a Conclave project, *not* a Novaarian project, despite its locale."

"I have already spoken with Charge Tyrek on the *Pillar*. He has granted us-"

"I am aware of your conversation with the Novaarian captain."

Naydaalan made a low pitched growl at the Laronian's continual rudeness.

Lanakdar ignored the young Novaarian, "You may have until sunset, but you will be accompanied by Conclave security at all times."

"As you wish Commander. We will comply." Telarrek maintained the diplomatic demeanour required of his stature.

Kalian couldn't be sure but it looked as if the Raalak was squaring up to Naydaalan. Their eyes were locked together, both of them puffing their chest out while they clenched their multitude of fists.

"I'm not sure what you expect to find here," Lanakdar continued. "We have removed most of the *Helion* and have already begun excavating underground, though so far nothing remains of the alien outpost." The Laronian let his eyes linger on the humans a little longer. "Why are they here? I was under the impression all the humans were confined to that death ship."

"We're burning daylight." Li'ara broke through the Novaarian blockade and strode towards the crater's edge. Lanakdar took a step back - as did his security detail - while Kalian just smiled at Li'ara's unique way of cutting through the crap.

The size of the impact was hard to appreciate from the cargo transport; standing on the edge now, Kalian felt an unusual sensation in his gut. It was quite the drop. To think he had been at the epicentre of this. He suddenly felt better about the likelihood of the Conclave finding any Gomar remains. It also made him doubt his own chances of finding ALF.

A recovery bot flew out of the crater, forcing Kalian to duck his head from the proximity of its propulsers. It continued past them with a twisted piece of charred framing in its mechanical arms and Kalian resisted the urge to short-circuit its motors. The glass covering the crater was cracked in almost every section from the constant activity over the surface. There were twenty-one holes that had been mined into the site. Each one had a team of six-legged mechs, clearly designed for dangerous exploration and extreme mobility. With as many arms as there were legs, the mechs moved in and out of the caves carting new samples and potential fragments for testing.

The nearest hole was only a hundred metres away on their left. A mech scurried out using the top of the tunnel, while its powerful pincer legs moved unhindered by gravity. Kalian followed its path as the exploratory mech continued along one of the circular paths dug into the crater. There were twelve rings in total, each one crossed with a vertical path that led up to the ridge. Being so steep the vertical paths had been fitted with massive platforms to help transport any of the recovery team or larger equipment.

"Kalian..." Li'ara moved closer, away from the prying security team. "I hate to say it but, how could anything in the outpost have survived this? It's just so deep."

"We don't know how extensive it was. For all we know, it went right through to the other side." He couldn't help but doubt his own words. They couldn't even use conventional technology since the nanocelium was undetectable to any Conclave scans.

"So where do we start?" she asked.

"Give me a minute." Kalian stepped away from the group, heading closer to the edge.

What would Esabelle do?

"Put aside everything you know about the universe, Kalian," Esabelle had instructed during their meditative sessions. "Forget distance and size. Everything is connected. There is no difference between you and the air, the ground spread out beneath you or the mountain before you. You are just as much a part of the universe as the elements or even the stars. Do not be bound by the constructs of the human mind - you can perceive beyond that."

Kalian closed his eyes, shutting out the sight of the glassy crater, as he knelt on one knee, placing his hand palm-down on the cracked surface. He opened his mind to all the input he could handle. He was instantly flooded with Naveen's secrets. He felt the size of the moon in his mind as if it was just another part of his body. The sheer mass nearly overwhelmed him as he struggled to comprehend the idea that the moon and he were one and the same. He could feel every grain of sand stretching all the way to Naveen's northern hemisphere where the Novaarian city, Alavaarn, rested. He tasted salt as the artificial ocean next to Alavaarn was consumed by his awareness. Compared to the size of the moon, the ocean's tonnage felt like a pebble in his mind. Mountainous caves sat beneath the surface with ancient estuaries scattered like a cobweb across the moon. There were different kinds of minerals and rock that changed density as he looked deeper towards the molten core.

He narrowed his awareness to a ten thousand kilometre radius. Digging through thousands of years of sediment, he quickly found what he was looking for. There was no trace of the outpost's remains; the impact had completely obliterated it - but that wasn't what caught his attention. Leading off from where the outpost should have been was a single tunnel, about halfway up from the bottom of the crater. The nanocelium was easy to detect with its unusual level of intelligence from the individual nanites.

"What's he doing?" The Raalak took two thunderous steps on his quadruped feet. Naydaalan gracefully stepped between him and

Kalian before Li'ara even had the chance. Kalian pushed the distraction away, concentrating on the new tunnel. Tracking it to its source he knew the length of the tunnel continued for another three kilometres, heading away from the crater. At the end, Kalian could feel the cold nanocelium surface of a sphere, two metres in diameter as if he were touching it with his bare hand.

With that he opened his eyes, adjusting his retinas for the change in brightness, and stood up to examine the crater. To the left of their position, he could see one of the many caves dug halfway up the impact site. It wasn't perfectly in line with the tunnel, but it would do.

"We need to go inside that cave." Kalian pointed to it for the benefit of the group. They would need the use of the platforms to reach it.

After deflecting Commander Lanakdar's questions, with regards to the reason for the specific cave, they eventually walked around the track having departed the platform. The cave entrance was twenty feet in diameter allowing the whole group to walk through comfortably. Everything beyond the first forty-feet of the cave was pitch black until the Shay activated the white lights that ran along the ceiling. One by one they lit up revealing the incredible length the diggers had travelled. At over a mile away they could all see the great machine parked at the end of its journey, awaiting further orders to dig.

"What now then? We just walk?" the Laronian asked sarcastically.

Li'ara gave Kalian a look that suggested she would be happy to shoot the commander.

"Play nice..." Kalian whispered to her as he headed further into the cave. "We need to go down here," he announced to the group.

"And what happens when we get to the end, we just turn around? This tunnel has been thoroughly scanned and rescanned. There's nothing here but dirt and rock." Lanakdar was checking the holographic reports on the tunnel as he spoke.

Kalian and the others ignored him as they continued to traverse the distance. Pushing his awareness out like sonar, Kalian eventually discovered the parallel tunnel coated in nanocelium. The group stopped with him while he reached out for the muddy wall. He drew in a breath, focusing his awareness to a point. The nanocelium was fifteen feet away, lying as dormant as The Wall had been before Kalian activated them. It was just bad luck on behalf of the recovery team that they hadn't decided to dig the tunnel fifteen feet to the right.

"Time to wake up..." He released a small pulse of electrical static through the wall giving it just enough power to reach the nanocelium. Following their original coding, the nanites reacted to their maker's call, contracting as they changed shaped to reach him.

"What did you say?" Lanakdar asked.

"Time to go to sleep." Kalian couldn't see into their minds since they emitted a different frequency, but he could still reach inside. Since their alien brains were unique, he didn't have the time to shut down the correct section in case he actually killed them. He, instead, opted for just blanketing their whole mind with darkness. Kalian made sure their synapses were still firing with signs of life before coming back into his own mind.

Now in front of them were two prone forms, happily sleeping. Lanakdar would wake up with a headache after the Raalak's heavy arm landed on his face. Stubbornly the Shay began to stir as he stumbled to his knees. Kalian reasoned he must have had an artificial backup system to wake him up. It wouldn't be surprising if all Shay had to shut their brains down like a computer, rather than rely on the organic part of the mind. Naydaalan quickly stepped in, with his staff extended, and whipped the Shay across the top of his head. Now there were three prone forms.

"How did you do that?" Ilyseal inquired as she checked over their sleeping bodies.

"A trick Esabelle taught me."

"You have learned a lot since the last time we were here," Telarrek observed.

"Well, they have been spending a *lot* of time together," Li'ara quipped while she absently checked over her own weapon in its thigh holster.

Kalian chose to ignore the comment. She could hardly complain about the time Esabelle and he spent together if she was happy to stay away. As a welcome distraction, the muddy wall started to move with large chunks of dirt being pushed out. The overhead lights briefly flickered from the new stress until a clear rectangle had been cut out from the wall.

There was no door, just a pitch black rectangular hole. Kalian easily adjusted his eyes to compensate for the dark while Naydaalan produced two spherical lights. After squeezing them in his hand, the orbs lit up and floated free into the tunnel behind Kalian. It reminded him of the first time they discovered the outpost's hidden depths.

The nanocelium door opened into a corridor that seemed completely out of place, buried within the bedrock. They walked silently for half an hour along the featureless corridor until eventually, they reached the one and only room. The two lights hovered into the circular room illuminating the suspended sphere at its centre. Kalian readjusted his eyes for the light, slowly edging round the great ball to allow room for the others. The room was tall enough to fit the Novaarians, who had been cramped in the human-sized tunnel.

"What is this, Kalian?" Telarrek's upper hand moved over the sphere without actually touching it. The Novaarian's sense of wonder reminded Kalian that before his post as ambassador, Telarrek had lived for centuries as a scientist.

Taking in the dark sphere, Kalian felt an image rise out of his subconscious. He had seen something similar during his training in the outpost, while ALF downloaded raw information using the subconducer. During his lessons on all things Terran he had been shown an image of the Criterion, the planet-sized sphere that housed ALF's physical hardware. Looking at the sphere made him see the similarity.

"I think this is ALF."

Telarrek's gaping sleeve slid down his upper arm revealing the Novaarian bracer within. Its metallic surface lit up with multiple scans feeding the information directly into his vision - one of the many upgrades available to a Conclave ambassador.

Kalian didn't need technology anymore. He placed his hand on the curved surface, allowing the nanocelium to read his DNA. The reaction was visibly instantaneous. The sleek surface rippled out from Kalian's hand creating a tidal wave effect across the entire shell as the nanocelium changed matter. Naydaalan took a step closer to his father, with his lower right hand reaching around his back to rest on his spear. Ilyseal bowed her head to human height in order to get a better look around Kalian's hand, inquisitive as always. Her demotion to cargo transport was perhaps the worst punishment the Highclave could have conceived for her.

"Hello, Kalian." ALF's voice came from all around them. "I see you still keep the entourage, plus one." With every word the sphere rippled, emanating from the spot Kalian had touched. "Though I'm betting from his genes there's a relation to the Ambassador here."

Naydaalan looked disturbed at the silent genetic scan.

"I see you're still a smart ass," Kalian replied.

The ripple effect became exaggerated as ALF let out a hearty laugh. "I don't even have an ass, but I can't disagree with the first part."

"Consider yourself lucky you don't have a physical body, robot..." Li'ara gave the sphere a look that could melt nanocelium.

"Still haven't forgiven me then? I assure you I calculated the odds of your survival to the highest decimal."

ALF had no chance of winning her over. Kalian could feel the anger Li'ara had for the AI and knew it wasn't a grudge that would easily go away. Kalian would never admit it to Li'ara, but he had come to see the reasoning behind ALF's plan to dump the *Helion* on top of his head. Had the AI not manipulated Li'ara into boarding the great ship, Kalian may never have found the strength to overcome Savrick and save both Li'ara and him. Though saving Li'ara was probably not even entered into ALF's plan.

"Well the next time you feel like playing the odds, don't do it with my life in the balance," she retorted sharply.

"How did *you* survive, ancient one?" Telarrek asked.

"I was never in danger," ALF explained. "Since the *Tempest* landed here, my physical housing has remained apart from the outpost. I felt it a safety precaution in case it was ever discovered by someone other than a human."

"Thank you for helping me to escape." Telarrek bowed his long face in respect.

"You are a friend to humanity, and therefore a friend to me, Ambassador Telarrek."

Kalian suspected that ALF saw humans as his children, much the same way he did with the Terran.

"You seem to be aware of current events?" Kalian had noticed ALF refer to Telarrek as ambassador twice now.

"Thanks to the proximity of the recovery team above, I have been able to access the subspace hub on Nova Prime and therefore the Conclave at large. There is nowhere I cannot go." ALF's omniscience never failed to make Kalian second-guess its intentions. Nothing should be that powerful.

"Can you physically leave this room? The Conclave will inevitably find you here." Kalian knew he could levitate the sphere all the way back to the ship, but he couldn't conceal it from the recovery team.

There was a pause before ALF replied, "You didn't come just to see if I survived did you?" The AI was already working things out.

"No," Li'ara stated flatly. "Personally I would have been happy to have never found out, and I'm still not sure this is the best plan." She looked at Kalian with pleading eyes.

He wondered if her inherent distrust for the machine came from him or the other way around. Of course, it was possible that neither of them trusted ALF.

"In the Conclave, knowledge is power." Kalian turned back to the sphere. "Well, we have access to the greatest power source in the galaxy."

"You're going to make my nanocelium blush. Why are you really here?" ALF pressed.

"You had a few theories on the *cube*; do you have any actual information, facts?"

There was another pause before ALF responded. "Where is it?"

Kalian hesitated at ALF's abrupt question. "It's still onboard the *Gommarian*, but it's safe, it can't harm-"

"Not that one - though you should have fired it into the nearest star - the other one, the one that has brought *all* of you here." ALF's ability to calculate all possible outcomes, combined with his intense physical scans of body language, gave the appearance of a telepathic being.

"It is on Trantax IV, on the outer edges of Conclave space, in Raalak territory," Telarrek answered.

ALF paused for what could have been a century to an AI "Fascinating..."

"Explain," Telarrek said.

"Apparently whatever targeted the Terran Empire also considers the Conclave to be a threat. From my own findings, the cube was sent after the probes came across the Empire. Have any such probes been located in the Conclave?"

"Nothing, this is the first discovery of its kind," Telarrek explained.

"What did you derive from the probes?" Ilyseal asked eagerly.

"That task was assigned to my other self, shortly before I left on the *Tempest*. The last information I received before disconnecting from the Criterion concerned the probe's final resting place inside the Vault."

"What's the Vault?" Li'ara asked.

"We all have our secrets, Li'ara Ducarté. The Vault's contents are mine. Sadly it lies on the other side of the galaxy, beyond all our reach."

"The Highclave has asked us to help in their investigation." Kalian tried to bring the conversation back on track, he wasn't sure how long Lanakdar and the others would remain asleep. "With your experience, we might actually get some answers. If you can come with us..."

"Did you bring your armour?" ALF inquired.

Kalian removed the flat device from his belt, holding it out in his palm.

"Place it on the shell."

The moment the device touched the sphere it was completely absorbed by the nanocelium, disappearing from sight. Ripples continued to emanate from somewhere inside despite ALF's silence. Kalian felt the build-up of static electricity in the air as the particles became charged. Random sparks of lightning ejected from the sphere's surface harmlessly connecting with the surrounding walls with deafening cracks. Naydaalan protectively stood in front of his father, battle ready.

All at once the ripples stopped and the lightning ceased as the sphere dropped to the floor in a rain of powder. Kalian bent down and wiped away a small pile of inert nanocelium to reveal the black triangle with the top sliced off.

Three points of light appeared on the surface in a multitude of colour, bringing a full-size hologram of ALF to stand before them. He wore his usual white and grey robe with a neatly trimmed beard and shoulder-length hair. He stretched his arms, imitating a man waking to a new day having been cramped in the same position for too long. "Anyone fancy a road trip?"

GARRETT COULDN'T REMEMBER how long he had been sitting listening to the makeshift council go on and on. He didn't care about how many women were pregnant or how many attempted suicides had been averted. Earth was gone, Century was gone and the human race stood on the brink of extinction with an extra-terrestrial threat hanging over their heads. So what if a few more people were being born and few more were dying. It made no difference to the bigger picture. Why was he the only one that could see that?

"When we prepared for Alpha we couldn't have anticipated this kind of strain." Laurence Wynter sat opposite Garrett at the circular table, a man who appeared to be in his mid-forties but was closer to a hundred and twenty. Laurence had been head of the oversight committee for the hiring of all key personnel that would run their separate divisions during the terraforming process. In essence, he was the reason everyone around this table had been selected in the first place. Garrett didn't like him. Before the attack, he had been one of the many sons in the Wynter dynasty, just another rich brat who didn't have to play by Central Parliament's rules. Even now, on a ship that provided everything, making money obsolete, he continued to lord himself over everyone.

"I know Laurence, but the councillors just can't cope with the load," Jim Landale explained. "Eighty percent of the people onboard lost family and friends, including some of the councillors! They were hired to deal with seclusion and isolation from civilisation."

Garrett didn't mind Jim, on the odd occasion they spoke, but noticed that most people avoided him, including his own staff. Jim had been the head of human relations in the Arc, the central hub for the terraforming project.

"Well isn't that what we're dealing with?" Laurence countered.

"What we're dealing with isn't even close to what they were trained for on Alpha."

"Counselling is one thing, but I'm hearing a lot of complaints about Novaarians walking around freely. People are finding it unnerving." It was Joseph Barns who changed the subject. Joseph was in charge of the astronomy contingent responsible for Alpha's discovery in the first place. Their role within the terraformation had been minimal and was mostly an honorary position.

Garrett rubbed his eyes in an effort to stay awake. His opinion was never sought after by the other team leaders. With a specialist field in geology, he wasn't considered the most valuable member.

"I have spoken to Captain Fey," Laurence held up his hands while looking to Commander Astill. "She assures me our concerns are being raised with the Highclave itself."

"The Highclave? I thought we could only deal with Ambassador, what's his name?" Jim asked.

"Telarrek," Commander Astill answered. "His most recent visit brought word from the Highclave. Our representatives are meeting with them right now."

The commander's statement changed the atmosphere of the

room. Everyone looked at each other in confusion and some annoyance. Garrett knew what their problem was. They were all wondering why the table was full if a representative was meeting with the Highclave.

"Is Captain Fey meeting with them?" Sharon Booth asked.

Garrett gave her a fleeting glance not wanting to make eye contact. Ever since she had rebuked his advances, it had become very awkward around the xenobiologist. Laurence Wynter hesitantly looked to the commander who explained what Garrett already suspected.

"The Highclave specifically asked for Kalian Gaines." Astill's words came as no shock to Garrett; Gaines was at the centre of everything. From what they knew of the history lecturer he wasn't technically human. So why was he representing the human race? He was sure Kalian knew a whole host of alien secrets that he wasn't sharing with them. He couldn't be trusted.

The mention of the extraordinary being gave everyone pause. Kalian Gaines was a mixed subject among the various heads. Some viewed him as a hero after it was told of his victory over Savrick, the one responsible for humanity's demise. Most of the scientists wanted to study him, though Garrett got the feeling Sharon wanted to do more than study him.

"The captain has impressed upon him all our concerns and issues to be raised. Commander Ducarté has accompanied Mr. Gaines as well so..." It was a typical Laurence Wynter response to an order from Captain Fey. He didn't have the spine to stand up to her and enforce the will of the council, of the people. At this rate, the future of the human race would be a militaristic society.

"We need to discuss expansion into the next quadrant," Samuel Vock, head of project management, added with a change of topic. "There's enough room in this ship for each person to have a cabin to themselves. We've only explored around twenty percent of the entire thing."

"What we *need* to discuss is the one thing we never talk about!"

Garrett burst out. He couldn't help it; they continued to waffle about matters and resources that the *Gommarian* took care of.

"Not this again Garrett," Laurence said.

"Yes, *this* again. There is an artefact, or an entity, or something on this very ship that may well be the reason for our near extinction. And all you ever talk about is trivial shit that doesn't matter! We need to examine the cube, properly. I bet the ship could replicate the equipment we need using the nanocelium. It would be as simple as entering the requirements into the *Gommarian's* systems. Esabelle did it when she made a ship for that North man. It's possible." He looked at them desperately, pleading. Why wouldn't they see reason?

"Garrett, we've gone over this. The cube is-"

"No Jim, that's the point, we haven't gone over this! We were all briefed by Captain Fey on the Terran and Esabelle's account. She said it was a threat and that *they* are coming. And yet here we are discussing where we're all going to sleep on this giant ship! If just one of those cubes caused the destruction of an entire species, twice over, then don't you think we should learn about it if more are coming?" He couldn't make his point any clearer.

"You're right Professor Jones, the cube is a threat," Commander Astill continued. "That is why it is a UDC matter. We will handle it." The commander's tone was enough to broadcast his confidence and authority.

Garrett looked away like a sulking child. Everyone was looking at him as if he was some paranoid freak. It infuriated him.

Laurence Wynter clasped his hands together and cleared his throat as he straightened in his chair. "We can put together a small exploratory team to investigate the next quadrant." He continued as if Garrett had never spoken. He looked up but no one would make eye contact with him.

"Idiots..." Garrett muttered as he stood up, abruptly. His chair dragged across the floor with a loud screech, dramatising his exit. He marched out of the room so fast he almost fell down the steps into the throng of people milling around the cargo bay.

The expansive bay may well have been designed for cargo on the

Gommarian but, on any other ship, it would have been a colossal waste of space. The last count had over three thousand people still living in the central space where the Gomar had kept them hostage.

Tents had been erected in every space available, with larger pavilions dotted at random intervals for social gatherings and storage. Esabelle had shown them how to use the nanocelium ports to replicate almost anything they desired. It had taken a while at first for people to even touch the fabric, having seen how it was made from microscopic machines. Thankfully, the majority of the population had been willing to try out the spacious rooms already built into the ship after Esabelle's re-design.

Garrett regained his composure after narrowly avoiding a group of children playing by the steps. He had never agreed with Central Parliament allowing the scientists and even some of the soldiers to bring their families along. The terraforming project was a very long process granted, but children just got underfoot. Garrett had lost his mother on Titan when Savrick attacked. She was his only family, having never married or conceived children himself. He was content with his goodbyes before he left with the Arc fleet. He had never been close to his mother, but he took solace in knowing her death would have been instantaneous when the sun went supernova. It wasn't that he was numb to her passing like some of those who had lost loved ones onboard; he was just impartial to her death. He tried not to dwell on the psychological implications of that thought process.

He gripped his satchel a little tighter as he moved through the crowds, subconsciously avoiding any contact. He felt through the bag, searching for the latest tool he had engineered from the nanocelium ports. If the council wouldn't act, he would. He passed by one of the pavilions, taking in the strong smell of cooking meat, as he removed his hand-held Datapad provided by Esabelle. He had already planned out his route, locating the appropriate vents in the more secluded areas of the ship.

He made a bee-line for the exit, breaking free from the muggy humidity and constant foot traffic. It took half an hour before he reached his chosen destination, a corridor labelled M-II on his Datapad. The corridor lit up as he entered, exposing the bronze tinted walls and complete lack of aesthetic design. The vent was a simple three-foot square grid at the base of the wall to his left with six bolts securing it. He checked the surroundings before proceeding. He had chosen this corridor because of the absence of any adjoining rooms giving him more opportunity for secrecy.

Garrett looked over the schematics one more time. He could see the location of the Starrillium was half a kilometre in front of him if he faced the vent. That meant the cube was in the chamber below. He noted that specific chamber was absent from the blueprints, but he had seen it for himself. Placing his satchel on the floor he retrieved the flashlight that attached to his wrist. His info-band projected the time in blue numbers against his forearm. He knew it was 21:05 Earth time and wondered why he even checked. He had no reason to keep to any time, he had no job onboard and measuring time by a star that no longer existed seemed redundant.

As he crouched by the grate, a side-panel the size of his palm slid across to reveal the vent's control menu. Garrett ordered the grate to open with the push of a button; forcing the nanocelium in the bars to retract back into the wall - the effect was like watching metal melt. He crawled in head first, shoving his bag in ahead of him. The tight space was no bother to him; he had racked up hundreds of hours crawling through caves and narrow rock passages on the multitude of excavations he had taken part in. He lost count of how many hours he had spent crawling through the caverns on Proteus, Neptune's second largest moon.

Crawling on his belly through the hot vent he continued to consult the map; any wrong turn would make backtracking very uncomfortable in such a tight space. He estimated at least forty minutes before he reached his prize.

COMMANDER ASTILL ENTERED the bridge after what had to be the longest council meeting yet. He was actually relieved to dismiss Lieutenant Commander John Matthews.

Matthews rose from the captain's chair as his commanding officer approached. "Commander on deck." The bridge crew rose to salute their commander until Astill told them otherwise.

"At ease, carry on. Lieutenant Commander, how's everything looking up here?" Astill asked, surveying the bridge crew. They were eleven hours into their shift by now; even he was due to be relieved by Captain Fey in an hour for the night shift.

"Rodriguez is overseeing inspection of the *Columbus*, sir. Worth is liaising with the Novaarians trying to sort out translators for the new sixteen. Apart from that, all systems are operating at optimal levels..."

Astill knew what Matthews was getting at - there was never much for them to do with the *Gommarian* being so self-efficient. "How are the newbie's getting on?" the commander asked.

"The captain sat down with them personally before she started her shift yesterday, sir. Worth assigned a couple of our guys and liaised with Wynter to have a couple of civvies accompany them for the translators. Even though they were escorted here by the Conclave it turns out they never actually met one face-to-face. The captain thought some extra human faces would help them with the transition. Long meeting?" Matthews checked his info-band and Astill glimpsed the time as well; 21:34 - it had been a long day.

"Just the usual. They want to put together another exploratory team to check out quadrant three. We're gonna need to assign them a security detail. Inform Lieutenant Hiroshi that he's going to have to volunteer a couple from his squad."

"Yes, sir." Matthews headed for the nearest console to complete his duties. Astill assumed the role of captain and placed himself in the padded chair, letting his head sink into the cushion. He closed his eyes momentarily, shutting out the rainbow of holographic colours. He tried not to think about his brother and sister and their families. From his last message through the relays, he knew they had been vacationing together on Hawaii World, a smaller planet twice the size of Earth's moon. It resided in the Century system, where half of the surface had been encapsulated in a habitat dome to recreate a Hawaiian paradise. He had wanted to visit the popular holiday resort himself when his current tour finished.

He opened his eyes again, allowing the visual information to flood his mind in the hope of distraction. He looked on as Lieutenant Commander Ramone called Matthews over to review some new data flashing on the wall-length hologram, to the left of the bridge. He saw them pointing at different readouts with puzzled expressions and decided it would be a welcome distraction from his dark thoughts.

"Is there a problem, Lieutenant Commander?" Astill crossed the bridge, passing the consoles and even walking through a transferring hologram that Rodriguez was sending to Worth.

"Sir, internal sensors have flagged an unknown heat source just outside the Starrillium," Ramone explained as a more intense scan was being made of the area. "It appears to be in the vents themselves. A refined scan confirms it to be human."

The wall hologram presented them with an image of a human outline crawling through the vents before shimmying down a vertical shaft. It clearly showed the person's position in relation to the Starrillium above.

"Who the hell would be crazy enough to crawl through the vents?" Matthews asked.

That was when it clicked into place for Astill. The Starrillium wasn't the intended destination for this particular crazy person.

"Who's on duty in that sector?" Astill looked to Matthews who quickly checked on a sub panel on the wall hologram.

"Esposito and Clark are the closest to the Starrillium, sir."

"Re-direct them to the basement and inform them I'll be there shortly. Matthews, you have the Conn." Astill made for the exit removing his sidearm to inspect the gauge. The nanocelium ports had security protocols embedded into the programming to only allow certain personnel to request weapons. Every request had to go through the captain first for her specific requisition code. His weapon was set to stun with the nanocelium ammunition designed to attack the target's nervous system. For this individual, however, he was tempted to change the settings.

———

GARRETT DROPPED down the final shaft, hoping the grate wouldn't melt away until he was standing on it. It didn't. He half slid, half fell, continuing into the abyss below as the grate melted into the wall before he touched it. He shouted out in pain, lying in the foetal position as he nursed his right ankle. It was definitely twisted if not broken.

The adrenaline began to wear off and Garrett remembered where he was as he caught his breath. He was immersed in complete darkness. The chamber had been disconnected from the ship's systems, even the lighting and heat. He fumbled with the flashlight on his wrist searching for the button at the back. The beam cut through the black, illuminating the entire room in a dim glow around the column of light.

The torch had come on over the top left corner of the cube a few metres away. Garrett could see the golden bronze reflected from the intricate pattern of hieroglyphs that ran in circles across the surface. He scrambled to his feet, using his good leg to push himself up; he could only apply the smallest amount of pressure to his right leg. In the torchlight, he could see his breath in front of him and felt the cold in his lungs.

Looking around the chamber, he could see the multitude of wires and tubes draped on the floor. Tracking them back he found they were all connected to the cube at random places on every side. He shone the torch to see the ports in the ceiling and walls where the tubes had once attached to the *Gommarian*. It was through these connections that it must have integrated with the massive ship and Esabelle herself. It was hard to believe that there was any kind of entity inside, Garrett decided; it must be some kind of intelligent machine.

He limped closer to the cube, flinching in pain with every step. It was six feet in width and depth with sharp corners and edges. At this distance, Garrett could see the damage it had taken before Savrick found it. The straight edges had cracks running off them with small craters pitted into the faces of the cube itself. The corner at the bottom to his right was completely missing with a jagged outline.

He counted six interlacing circles of hieroglyphs on the side he was facing. He didn't understand any of it. Some of the symbols didn't even appear as if they came from the same alphabet; they were so different. He took a moment to examine the other sides, stepping over the many wires and tubes. The other three sides were similar in that they were adorned in hieroglyphic circles, though he noted not the same pattern. Some of the circles were wrapped around the thick cables as if they represented potential entry points into the cube.

He felt that very human urge to touch it. To feel it would reveal more of its secrets, surely. He turned back hesitantly, shining his torch on the locked door behind him. He would have to figure a way out of here later, after he had some answers. He focused his attention on the side facing the door - it had fewer cables than the others, making the surface easier to study. Garrett delayed touching it, deciding to use his visual augmentation first. He only used it sparingly now, since the components needed to recharge the control panel on his temple had been lost when the human civilisation fell. Wynter had already put together a team of cyberbiologists, to retrofit some kind of Terran technology that would interface with the various augmentations in their population.

He switched to infrared vision first, viewing the world in thermal imaging. His hand had an intense orange glow in front of his face as he wriggled his fingers to see the dark blue trace they left in the air. The cube was a dull blue against the black backdrop; it was colder than everything else. Garrett's only conclusion was that the cube was either dead, if that term applied, or it was inactive. Captain Fey had relayed Esabelle's account of how it had been disconnected from everything; it was possible that without any external connection, the cube was simply inert.

He switched through several visions, checking for any radioactive or electrical output. There were no signs of activity on any level. Leaning in closer he magnified his inserts to examine the material of the cube itself.

"What the hell...?" He had seen this type of metal before. At this magnification, Garrett could see the individual nanites tightly fitted together like bricks in a wall. "You're made of nanocelium."

His breath created condensation against the golden surface. He stopped his examination and turned off his inserts. He could hear something. There was a quiet tapping noise coming from inside the room. He stepped back, looking around the room for any activity but saw nothing. The sound became louder and he realised it was coming from inside the cube.

Garrett took another step back, suddenly regretting his unsanctioned investigation. The noises changed with heavy clunks and metal on metal. The hieroglyphic circles began to spin independently like the cogs in a time-piece, each stopping at different intervals until the cube changed shape. There was now a hand-sized hole in the centre. It revealed nothing but darkness inside.

Garrett took a breath for the first time since the noises began. He was frozen in place with his wrist stretched out to shine the torch. It was five minutes before he moved again, edging towards the cube. He bent down to look inside, but the torch couldn't pierce the shadowed interior. Just before giving up, something glistened in the light. He looked again but couldn't see it. There was something in there. He licked his lips considering his options; he couldn't leave here without answers. Commander Astill would throw him in the brig for the rest of his life.

Keeping the torch on the cube, he used his other hand and slowly inserted it into the circular hole. He could feel his heart pounding in his chest as he hesitantly reached out with his fingers. The silent atmosphere was instantly broken by Garrett's agonising screams. Something had shot through the flesh on his arm and hand, right up to his elbow. He immediately attempted to pull it out but was, instead, dragged into his shoulder. Black tendrils wormed out of the hole and forced themselves into the skin around his shoulder and digging into his back. Garrett's screams intensified as he felt the muscles and bones tear and crack under the assault.

The cube changed shape again, this time opening up from the hole, with the sides folding into each other. More tendrils shot out of the new openings, plunging into his legs and abdomen. He tried to pull away but slipped on the blood pooling beneath his feet. He screamed until he had no more air in his lungs. He was slowly dragged into the cube. His flashlight went out with the sound of shattering glass as a tendril wrapped around it and squeezed. The last thing he saw was the cube coming back together around him, entombing him in darkness and pain.

ROLAND SAT SLUMPED in his command chair, his head resting against his hand. The blackness of subspace stared back at him from the panoramic viewport of the *Rackham*. He stared back trying to contemplate the events that had occurred only a few hours ago. He had been stuck with his back to a corner more times than he cared to admit, but his training had prepared him to be resourceful and think on his feet. He relied on that training to get him through anything and everything. He wasn't even unaccustomed to the occasional unorthodox escape or infiltration. But even for him, the escape from Krono Towers was remarkably hard to fathom.

"That wasn't part of the plan, Roland!" Ch'len waddled onto the bridge to stand in front of him. After the string of curses the Ch'kara had launched at him, this was the first thing he had said since Roland came back onboard. The little alien had spent the last few hours cleaning his clothes and washing off the food and drink. When Roland took control of the ship, changing its trajectory at high Gee, the buffet Ch'len had laid out collided with him on the incline. At high speeds the artificial gravity couldn't compensate, a fact Roland found highly amusing.

"Well, it was either that or burn up in atmo. What would you have done you fat, little chupachup?"

"It's Ch'kara! And I wouldn't have jumped out into space with some crazy woman! I'm still not sure how you survived!" Ch'len pulled out a strip of dry Dak meat from his overalls and devoured it.

"You and me both..." Roland knew that Esabelle had cocooned them in some telekinetic field; it was the only way they could have survived the harshness of space. It was still the strangest memory, to actually fly through space without a suit or ship to protect them. Using his remote control he flew the *Rackham* up Krono Towers, passing them by as they plummeted towards Shandar. He then turned the ship around mid-flight and re-directed it back to the planet. The ship easily caught up with them, where it appeared to swallow the pair as the bay door opened at the mouth of the *Rackham*. Roland had been careful to match their speed so they didn't both slam into the back of the cargo bay. It had been quite elegant really, apart from diving out of the luxury apartment in the first place.

"Are we really going to the capital world?" Ch'len pulled out another strip of Dak meat.

"Yep." Roland brought up a small holographic display showing him Esabelle's position in the ship. She was still in the temporary quarters on the port side of the vessel.

"I thought we agreed we wouldn't go there. There's too much security for a human to just go walking around." Ch'len went to his own station in front of Roland.

"There's something I have to check out, so we're going. Can you get us some faces like we did on Vallara?" Roland put his feet up on the console, not wanting to dwell too much on the Laronian home-world. That job had its consequences.

"Of course I can, that's not the point," Ch'len spat back.

"And the point is...?"

"We're bounty hunters, Roland! Not adventurers! Whatever you've got mixed up in with your human friend, I strongly suggest you drop it and we get back to making units. Speaking of which, we need to send that information you got from Ral-vet's terminal to our client. We're still owed fifty thousand units!"

"You're telling me there isn't a place on the capital that we can transmit the data from?" Roland countered.

"Of course there is, but..." Ch'len had nothing to argue with.

"Then it's settled. We'll go to the capital and get our units, and Esabelle and I can investigate the AI at Protocorps headquarters." Roland smiled at the shock mixed with horror on Ch'len's face.

FIVE

The *Dawnlighter* was a simple ship in design with only one berth for the pilot, including kitchen and washroom, and a cargo bay that made up most of the ship. The three Novaarians had chosen to remain at the helm, catching up on recent events from the last five months. Li'ara, the only human onboard that couldn't accumulate a day's sleep with an hour's meditation, had no choice but to borrow Ilyseal's long bed for a few hours.

Suitably refreshed, she left Ilyseal's berth with a hot mug of blendar, the closest thing to coffee she could find in an alien kitchen. She sipped it lightly on her way to the cargo bay in search of Kalian - it had a sweet aftertaste once she got past the sour lemon flavour. The heavy, yellow striped doors parted as she entered the cargo bay. The *Dawnlighter* was a solid ship but Li'ara felt it could do with a paint job and a good clean here and there; certain components appeared to have even rusted.

The bay was stacked from floor to ceiling with crates of varying sizes and colour. She imagined they were filled with equipment and food stores for what would likely be an army of excavation workers. The Conclave never did anything small. She stopped halfway down the central walkway when some kind of rodent ran out between the crates, a piece of meat lodged in its jaws. Li'ara continued on, trying not to think about how many heads it had.

As always, she found Kalian doing the extraordinary at the end of the bay, standing at the top of the ramp. His arms were slightly raised at his sides with his palms facing outwards, his eyes closed. Spinning around him was a miniature tornado of tools and equipment while several crates danced around each other in the air, creating an infinity symbol with their constant movement. Li'ara paused for a minute to appreciate the spectacle. Watching him perform feats like this reminded her of what Kalian had become. He had given up so much of himself to become stronger, to fight Savrick, to protect her. And she loved him for it.

She caught herself at the thought of such an emotion. She had to be strong for him. The crates slowed down and the torrent of equipment and tools drifted back to their appropriate homes.

"Good sleep?" Kalian opened his eyes as the crates rested back into their housing. Li'ara nodded as she sipped some more of her blendar, enjoying its heat in the cold bay. Kalian looked past her with that far-away stare she knew all too well.

"What are you worried about?" she asked.

Kalian paused, making eye contact, "Esabelle..." Of course, she thought. "Being out of communication for so long, and her being on another planet. Who knows what shit Roland's got into. I wonder if I did the right thing letting her go."

"You didn't let her go, she made that choice. Besides, if anyone can kick Roland's arse across the galaxy it's Esabelle." Li'ara hated to admit, but the Terran was probably the most powerful being alive right now. In truth, she hadn't given Esabelle's mission much thought, especially since they had acquired a new passenger on their own journey. She could feel Kalian studying her own features.

"What are *you* worried about?" he asked.

The question made Li'ara realise how long it had been since anyone cared about her the way Kalian did. He genuinely wanted to know her fears and worries in the hope of making them go away. She hated how he softened her.

"I'm worried about the sociopathic robot we've brought along with us. And the fact that he now seems to be integrated into your armour, permanently." She eyed the pouch on Kalian's belt where the AI was stored.

"Well, look on the bright side," Kalian continued. "If he pisses us off we can just throw him under a rock and leave him there."

He was wearing that cheeky smile Li'ara found hard not to reciprocate. Before she could reply, he gave an audible sigh as the hum of the Solar Drive powered down. It was only after it stopped that they realised the constant drone had always been there.

"I'll keep him under control," Kalian continued with a more serious tone.

They both went up to the cockpit to find the three Novaarians sitting in relative darkness. The room was only illuminated by the glow of the main console's holograms, casting them in a rainbow of colours.

"We have arrived in the Trantax system," Telarrek announced.

Ilyseal appeared busy poring over data from the various holographic sources. "Intrinium cells charged for return journey. Releasing solar shields now." Ilyseal's words were followed by movement from the viewport. The canopy slid away, out of sight, as the star field took its place.

Li'ara wondered just how close the star was behind them. It couldn't have been as close as the *Fathom* was when they escaped the supernova at Century.

"There are six planets in this system." It was Kalian who offered the information. Li'ara knew he was accessing the data from his bizarre computer-like memory. "It's systems like this one that gave the Raalak their position on the Highclave."

"How so?" she asked.

"Raalak territory is littered with planets rich in Callic-diamond. Without their help, the Conclave wouldn't be able to build their ships to resist the temperature of a star's corona. No Callic-diamond hull means no Solar Drive." Kalian looked out to the stars with wonder on his face. It was as if he was made to live amongst the stars.

"So that's how they found it then?" Li'ara took her seat behind Naydaalan.

"Yes, the moment the mining team could not understand the writing on the cube it was quarantined," Telarrek explained.

"*Nova*, this is the *Dawnlighter* requesting permission to land on Trantax IV," Ilyseal spoke into the console. "I repeat, *Nova*, this is the *Dawnlighter*. I have cargo and VIPs onboard. Request permission to land."

"This is the *Nova*, *Dawnlighter*. We're processing your security code now." From the sound of all the clicking, Li'ara assumed it was a Nix responding to their hail. "You are clear to proceed, *Dawnlighter*. Sending coordinates now."

After a short journey across the solar system, Trantax IV came into view as a dark foreboding planet, haloed by five broken moons in the process of being mined. It wasn't the most inviting planet Li'ara had ever seen. A great storm was visible on the eastern hemisphere, slowly pushing its way across the globe with flashes of lightning throughout. Their flight path took them over the top of the shining hull of the *Nova*, its quad engine ports flaring brilliant blue. The Nebula-class vessel stood watch over the planet, ensuring the security of the Conclave's newest secret.

"I thought they'd have more ships standing guard," Li'ara commented.

"They don't know what they've found," Kalian replied.

"The *Nova* alone has enough world-breakers to wipe out every planet in this system. The planet is quite secure." Naydaalan kept his eyes on the Conclave vessel.

Li'ara turned to Kalian in her seat and whispered, "Obviously he didn't see the one Savrick rammed through outside the capital." That particular explosion had killed thousands of people. She was thankful in that respect that the *Gommarian* was under their control.

It wasn't long before the *Dawnlighter* pierced the atmosphere and descended to fly over the dark rocky terrain. From the surface, the sky was a murky purple with thick clouds setting in from the direction of the approaching storm. The site was easy to see, even amidst the dust clouds being kicked up over the black rock. The perimeter was lined with beacons that flashed from blue to red stretching over a mile in circumference. The sprawling landscape was covered in spiky black mountains. The surface looked to Li'ara like a piece of cheese with cavernous holes everywhere.

The site was dominated by a small mountain in the far corner. Most of the ground activity appeared to be situated around a cave entrance at its base. The *Dawnlighter* settled down on a platform close by that had most likely been erected during the first mining operation. They departed the craft via the ramp in the cargo bay to find yet another committee waiting for them.

"It's like Hadrok..." Kalian was looking around past the group. She recognised the name instantly but didn't make anything of it with so many curious onlookers. She made a point to ask about it later though; she worried about how much of that psychopath was stuck in his head.

The Trantax site had a stronger security feel to it than the recovery team on Naveen. For one, the majority of the personnel remained at their post attending to their duties. There were several rows of the same six-legged machines used for exploration on Naveen; however, these models were all deactivated as they sat in neat lines with their mechanical legs tucked into their bodies. Conclave security was visibly dotted around the perimeter, dressed in their usual red and black armour. Li'ara noticed the addition of a hood and facemask on all of them, something she wouldn't have minded for herself with the strong gusts of wind.

"Greetings of peace, Ambassador Telarrek." The welcome came from a Trillik, easily recognisable from their unique tails. Li'ara knew this to be a female of their species from the distinct horns above her top set of eyes, each one slanted back to match the sleek curvature of her elfin head. Her tight fitted undersuit was easy to see through the transparent overalls she wore, obviously some kind of decontamination garb. Perhaps the strangest addition to her outfit was the metallic backpack strapped around her lanky arms. Six mechanical arms protruded from the pack. Each one had a different tip designed for its own unique examination.

"Greetings of peace. You must be Doctor Taeril." Telarrek bowed in respect and introduced the others. "Doctor Taeril here is the Conclave's leading expert on all projects relating to Terran activities," the Novaarian explained.

"I only wish there was more to investigate." Taeril turned to Kalian and Li'ara. "Your ancestors didn't leave much behind in this quadrant of the galaxy." Surprisingly, the Trillik didn't seem too perturbed by the humans. Li'ara was used to aliens making a fuss of their presence.

"Is there more to investigate besides the cube?" Kalian asked with a hint of concern in his expression.

"No." Taeril's answer was a little too immediate and rehearsed for Li'ara's liking. "Come, the Highclave has briefed me on your reason for being here; though I am not sure what light you will be able to shed on our little mystery. The cube is very different from The Wall." She turned from the *Dawnlighter,* heading for the mountain to their right.

A Raalak, in head-to-toe security armour, stopped Ilyseal from advancing to discuss the cargo and its distribution. She gave them a look that told them to go on without her; as a cargo pilot, she probably wouldn't have been allowed any further, anyway.

They followed Doctor Taeril with an escort of four security personnel from a mixture of species. Looking around, there were still pieces of mining equipment lying on the ground, dropped when the miners were evacuated. Giant spotlights targeted several stacks of crates and tools being stored by the excavation team, mostly on converted landing platforms. There was a constant stream of activity, with workers driving by on uni-bikes trailing containers and samples. The giant bikes only had one thick wheel, wider than Kalian was tall, with a rider on top of the curving frame situating them directly above the wheel. They were careful to give the party a wide berth to prevent them from being covered in dust.

They soon began to descend down a long dirt ramp, dug out by the mining team for better access to the mountain. The landscape was incredible as they dropped below the surface. Li'ara looked out on the maze of a world that made up Trantax's underground. The current surface had clearly formed over the top of the old, leaving a thirty-feet gap between the two. The only difference in the two layers was the orange membranes that stretched between the rocks like the wings of a bat. It was possible the same organic membranes grew on the surface above but were destroyed by the storms.

"As you know, Callic-diamond is notoriously difficult to mine," Taeril said, on their way to the mouth of the mountain base. "The miners were digging here for two cycles before they breached the interior of the mountain. When we took over half a cycle ago, we concentrated our efforts on exposing the rest of the cube. It took some very expensive equipment to free the artefact from the surrounding Callic minerals without damaging it."

A single path had been dug through the maze to give a line of sight on the cave entrance. Li'ara counted ten guards along the route.

"Are there any plans to move the relic?" Telarrek inquired.

"There were in the beginning after we removed all the debris, but the orders came from the Highclave itself to leave it be."

"Why would they want that?" Li'ara asked. "Surely there are better places to run all your tests."

"Indeed there are. I believe they made the decision after my preliminary report, shortly after I arrived," Taeril said.

"And what was that exactly?" Kalian was fiddling with the pouch that contained ALF.

"I do not believe the artefact to be Terran in origin."

With that, all four of them looked at each other, though Taeril appeared not to notice. They eventually arrived at the cave entrance, where all six of Taeril's extra arms adjusted, so one could retrieve a pair of light-spheres from within her pack. The spheres floated on ahead, adding their glow to the fixtures already bolted into the rock. The light created twisted shadows and large silhouettes through the orange membranes as they passed by; there were definitely more of them inside the cave complex.

They found two more guards standing at the entrance to the final cave, each wielding a rather delicious looking rifle. Li'ara felt for her own sidearm and reassured herself that it was there if she needed it. They stood aside, giving view to the tarnished golden cube in the centre.

The cave had been well excavated, allowing plenty of room to fit a plethora of scanning equipment inside. The walls were lined with crates and hover-bots, with several shelves of alien looking tools. There were two deactivated exploration drones in the corner, their legs tucked away. One hover-bot was currently floating around the cube with miniature arms extended, performing extensive scans. A green laser fanned out from one arm and scanned up and down, covering the nearest circle of hieroglyphs.

There was no mistaking its likeness to the one imprisoned on the *Gommarian*. It didn't appear as damaged as their cube; there were no cracks or scorch marks. Kalian moved past them to circle the cube. Li'ara knew he wasn't just using his eyes to probe the relic.

"What makes you think it isn't Terran?" Li'ara took a step closer, to better examine it.

"Alien languages are all unique, Commander Ducarté. Though our translators allow our occipital lobe to understand each other's written word, the writing itself is very different. If you were to put all of the Conclave alphabets in a jumbled row, you would still be able to pick out the letters that belong to each species, since we each write in our way. The same can be said for the hieroglyphics on the cube. They may appear one after the other like any written word, but I do not believe they are from the same language. Since my translator cannot identify the individual words and letters, we know that these languages do not originate from any Conclave world." Taeril approached the cube, walking round to the side, opposite Kalian. "However, we found symbols on one side that we did recognise, though we still cannot translate them."

"The Terran language." Kalian joined her where he crouched down to inspect that particular circle of writing. None of it made any sense to Li'ara.

"Can you understand it, Kalian?" Telarrek and Naydaalan just fit into the cave without having to duck.

"I can read it but I don't understand it." He reached out but faltered before touching it, choosing, instead, to retract his arm and stand back. "Has anyone touched it?" he asked with some alarm, gripping his right forearm.

"No, we only allow the droids to physically interact with it. Why?" Taeril took a step back as well.

"I don't know, just a feeling. I don't think it should be touched by anything that's alive."

Taeril looked at Li'ara and the others but they could offer no explanation for Kalian's hunch.

"What does it say?" Li'ara stood by Kalian, meeting his dark brown eyes.

"It doesn't say anything. It's just one word... Evalan." They shared a confused look for a second while Taeril simply observed Kalian with fascination. "I have no idea what it means, and I have the whole Terran language in here." He put a finger to his temple. Li'ara knew the look he was giving her - it was time to consult ALF. She blinked slowly, knowing Kalian would pick up on her reluctance to turn to the artificial intelligence.

"How did you come by such knowledge?" Taeril was now looking at Kalian like a new relic to investigate.

"There was a machine in the outpost on Naveen. It downloaded the language and history of the Terran." He left out the part about ALF. "Is there any way we can have some privacy in here, just...?" Kalian gestured to Li'ara and the Novaarians.

Taeril hesitated, "I am afraid not. You have been given clearance to observe the artefact, but this cave is at the heart of a Conclave quarantine zone and, as such, you must be accompanied at all times."

Li'ara could see Kalian was tempted to use his powers to render the doctor and the guards unconscious. They had only just managed to get away with it on Naveen. Lanakdar and the others had come running out of the tunnel just as the *Dawnlighter* lifted off. No doubt that would come back to haunt them the next time they met the Highclave.

She caught his eye and shook her head to discourage him. His powers made him too bold sometimes, in her opinion. There was a greater security presence here and they could potentially start a conflict they couldn't end.

"Then it is a good thing they are accompanied by a high ranking Conclave official," Telarrek announced with some authority. Taeril looked to argue his point but the old Novaarian cut her off. "Have you ever met the Highclave, Doctor Taeril?"

She shook her head, beginning to grasp Telarrek's influence.

"I carry with me the full authority of the Highclave as a person-ally appointed Ambassador," Telarrek continued. I will oversee their inspection myself so that I might more accurately report back to the Highclave."

Taeril's mouth moved but no words followed.

"Now we shall have some privacy. I will call on you should we need your assistance, Doctor."

With a last look at Kalian and Li'ara, Taeril left the cave taking the guards with her. In their place, Naydaalan stood watch like a silent guardian.

"That was very cool," Kalian said, admiringly.

"What is the point of having such power and not using it? Had she been part of the security force, like Commander Lanakdar, I am afraid my influence would not have gone so far."

Kalian removed the Terran amour device from his belt and placed it on the floor. Three lights switched on giving life to ALF's image.

"I do not like being stuck inside that," he exclaimed. "I'm completely isolated from Conclave communications; I can't even travel through the AI hubs. Imagine being stuck in a room with no windows or doors and not even so much as a book to read!"

"If you prefer we can hook you up to the *Gommarian* when we get back?" Kalian was smirking.

"Very funny. I'm not going anywhere near *that* software." He gave the cube an ominous look. "I'm fairly certain it was made by one of these."

Li'ara could think of some better places to put the robot. The device allowed ALF to walk anywhere within a line of sight of the emitters. Kalian updated him on their conversation with Taeril, and the unusual word imprinted in the cube.

"I know every Terran word, but not that one. What does it mean?" Li'ara was watching for ALF's reaction to Kalian's question. He crouched down, shifting his holographic head to one side. His reaction was annoyingly neutral.

"Hmm..." He stood up stroking his old beard. "I have no idea."

Li'ara held her tongue to what she suspected was a lie. He was too manipulative to trust.

Kalian looked confused, "But didn't you invent this language?"

"Yes, after the last Terran war. The idea was to break down some of the barriers between the different cultures, bring them together." He gave the word another look. "But that word has no meaning, Evalan..." ALF tested the word out loud as if he were tasting a new food.

"How does a Terran word get imprinted on a cube in Conclave territory?" Li'ara asked. "The one on the *Gommarian* I would understand, but this cube hasn't been in Terran space, has it?"

"Judging from the sediments and local isotopes, this cube has been here for just over a hundred thousand years," ALF stated. Li'ara eyed the Terran device wondering how sophisticated it really was. "The cube on the *Gommarian* would have been travelling across the galaxy in search of humanity at the time. It's a logical assumption that both cubes never met."

"Do you think this one was sent here to broaden the search for humans?" Telarrek asked.

"Either that or the Conclave has been designated a threat," ALF replied.

Li'ara met Kalian's eyes, knowing that had been one of his assumptions as well.

"If that were the case, then why has it remained dormant here for so long while the Conclave has thrived?" The Novaarian moved around the cube to get a better look.

"I don't know." The AI began to pace. "I never got to examine the *Gommarian's* cube, so a comparison is impossible. I don't even know how long it had been on Hadrok before Savrick found it. The probes I found had been in Terran space for two hundred years before Savrick attacked. Have any probes been located?"

Everyone looked to Telarrek. "No, not that I am aware."

Li'ara had a feeling the ambassador was deliberately being kept in the dark by the Highclave. He could be trusted but his information was potentially inaccurate.

"This word suggests that the sender already knew of the Terran language, or it's evidence that both cubes are in contact. Though I cannot fathom why it would have that word, or any word, for either possibility. And I certainly don't recognise any of the other words. Though it is exciting to know there are so many other alien species out there. So many more mysteries." His reaction to the unknown was very human; it unnerved Li'ara.

"It's the sender part that troubles me," Kalian looked worried.

"They are an enigma wrapped in a conundrum." ALF was far too excited about this new challenge. Perhaps they shouldn't keep him locked in the device.

Better to drop him in a black hole.

"Does the *Gommarian* cube have any Conclave writing on it?" Telarrek asked. "If there is, it would be highly likely that both cubes are connected somehow, a form of communication we are not aware of perhaps?"

"True Ambassador, you *are* right. The Conclave didn't exist when the *Gommarian* cube was busy wreaking havoc in Terran space. I need to examine the other one to make an accurate assessment. Please tell me you've kept it safe." He turned on Kalian.

"It's locked away in the heart of the *Gommarian*," Kalian explained. "It can only be accessed with Esabelle or myself present."

ALF raised his virtual eyebrow. "And who is Esabelle?"

GARRETT COULDN'T BE sure if he was floating in liquid or a vacuum. When the pain had finally ceased, after the tortuous machines had finished cutting into his flesh, his body became visible in the abyss. He had no concept of time or space in the dark. The pain had been agonisingly intense, but his brain had refused to pass out, saving him from it. He didn't know if he had been in the cube for minutes or days. Reaching out into the dark, there were no walls or boundaries to confine him but he couldn't find the light that revealed his body. There was no evidence of any struggle or attack. His clothes were intact and there wasn't a drop of blood.

"Hello!" he shouted into the void. Gravity returned with the drop of his legs and arms and the full weight of his body resting on a floor as black as his surroundings. He looked around frantically, terrified that the pain might return. In the blink of an eye, he was no longer alone.

Garrett Jones, human.

Garrett's mother was standing three metres away. She was just as he remembered her before leaving for the Alpha project. At a hundred and three years old she had the complexion and body of a woman in her early fifties. She wore a turquoise dress and matching shoes with a small cream clutch under one arm. Her nails were as immaculate as he remembered in a shiny yellow polish, highlighted by her dark skin, to go with the necklace hanging over her dress. Her greying hair was cut short at the shoulders in a perfect line.

"Mother..." Was this death? Was he in some kind of limbo? Garrett had never believed in the afterlife, but he was seeing his dead mother as clear as day. "Am I dead?"

No.

The answer was terrifying. If he wasn't dead then he was still inside the cube, and if he was still inside the cube then the thing in front of him was definitely not his mother.

"What are you?" He took a step back but the distance between them never changed.

We are what came before. We are all that will remain.

"I don't understand."

Of course you don't. The ant never sees the boot until it's too late.

His mother continued to smile as if they were enjoying a pleasant conversation. Hearing it speak with her voice was not pleasant. There were noises in the distance, beyond the never-ending blackout. Everything was muffled from wherever he was.

"What's happening? What are you doing to me?" It wasn't a massive stretch to assume that what he was experiencing was some form of virtuality; his unharmed body was evident to that.

Preparing you for what needs to be done. Our task is not over yet.

"You didn't answer my question." The noises grew louder.

And you think you deserve one?

"Why are you talking to me at all then?"

Your species is fascinating. Even now we are taking control of your every synapse, infiltrating your body at every level. And yet we cannot isolate you.

Garrett's arms and legs felt cold and he realised it was the first real thing he had felt.

This... consciousness, it is beyond our reach, ethereal. Your elusiveness will prove to be your ultimate torment, however. You will be witness to the end of your kind, once and for all.

"I won't help you!"

You have no choice.

With that, the image of his mother disappeared along with his own body. He now saw through his own physical eyes again as the world opened up before him. The dark chamber that housed the cube was now as bright as day, though the lights were still off. As well as seeing it, he could also feel the power surging through the walls around him. There was no end of electricity being funnelled into the great sphere above him, the Starrillium. The nanocelium that coated every surface hummed with energy that made him feel physically connected to it.

He stepped out of the cube; it was nothing but an empty shell now, its purpose fulfilled. That thought was a strange one; it wasn't his but he knew it to be true somehow. Looking back it could no longer be called a cube. Like a Rubik's cube separated into its individual sections, the alien relic lay inert with dozens of tendrils lying dead in a tangle of tubes. A thick translucent liquid covered everything and continued to pour out across the cold floor. Seeing the fluid, Garrett realised it was dripping off him as well.

His clothes were shredded from head to foot, stained in blood; his shoes were missing exposing his bare feet. He looked over his new body expecting to see the multiple holes and gashes from the attack but found none. In their place he found hardened clumps of a metallic substance filling in the gaps. Dark tendrils spread out from them under the skin, embedded into the muscle and bone, completely integrated into his circulatory system.

A paralysing reality settled over Garrett. He had not consciously made any of these physical actions. His vision changed as his head turned, showing him the heavy-set door. He gasped out loud but the physical reaction never happened. He was trapped inside his own mind.

He heard sounds coming from the other side of the doors and his body reacted with deadly intent. He could do nothing but watch, as arms that were not his launched into the divide between the doors. His fingers were impossibly strong as they dug into the nanocelium metal. The door crumpled under the pressure, giving his hands room to separate the two halves. His new-found strength made the feat look effortless with the internal mechanisms, either side of the door, screeching and snapping under the strain. Various sections of the wall were bulging as the internal conveyors tried to push through.

His exit must have looked far more dramatic from the point of view of the three men standing on the other side.

Run!

They couldn't hear him. Garrett recognised Commander Astill in the middle of the three, his expression of total horror. He knew the faces of the other men but couldn't place their names. He could feel the intentions of the imposing mind occupying his own and felt bad that he didn't even know their names.

"Open fire!" Commander Astill blurted before the gunfire started. All three of them raised their weapons and unleashed a barrage of radioactive hell. They might as well have been shooting a mountain for all the effect it had. Garrett lunged forward with supernatural speed, catching the soldier on the end with a lethal grip around the neck. Using his left hand he quickly raised the soldier off the ground, flicking his arm at the wall. The soldier hurtled into the wall with a bone-crunching effect - it didn't matter though, his neck had already been broken before he left Garrett's grip.

Flesh and clothes continued to be torn away by the photonic spray of blue energy. Every scorch mark and hole soon sealed up closing the wound, as if it had never been there. With a quick slice across the commander's chest, Astill was knocked back several metres, taking the air out of his lungs. The last soldier shouted his war cry over the sound of the rifle. Garrett's movements were a blur as he deftly whipped the gun away before planting his foot firmly in the soldier's chest. He bounced off the wall, slumping into a heap on the floor. But Garrett wasn't finished. A part of him he couldn't control knew that humans were annoyingly hard to exterminate. The job had to be finished properly. He reached down, grabbing the soldier by his boot and pulling him across the floor until he was between Garrett's feet. There was no hesitation in the piston-like movement that drove his fist through the man's face and into the floor.

The labouring breaths of Commander Astill could be heard across the corridor. Garrett turned to his next victim as the man crawled on his belly across the floor, desperately reaching for his gun. He strode over to the commander, coming at him from behind. He quickly swept up Astill's arms and placed his bare foot squarely in his back.

Garrett tried to turn away from what he knew was about to be a horrific death, but could only look on as his grip tightened around the commander's wrists. In one smooth motion, he pulled the arms while pushing his foot. The reaction was worse than the professor imagined. Commander Astill's arms came clean off their joints, tearing the flesh away as they did. Blood spurted in every direction, covering Garrett as well as the walls and floor. Astill's screams were cut short when his face impacted the floor under the force of Garrett's kick. His broken facial bones were the least of his worries; he would be dead from blood loss in moments.

Leaving the bodies behind, Garrett strode off down the corridor creating bloody footprints in his wake. The cube was right; this was like torture. He was helpless to do anything but watch as his own body made its way across the ship with a purpose he couldn't understand. It was only five minutes before the next group of soldiers intercepted him, four of them this time.

Please, just run!

He wanted to scream and cry; he couldn't even close his eyes as he tore through the men. His new strength made him brutal in combat. Bloodthirsty arms lashed out in savagery ripping through armour and bone as if it were paper. The last soldier made a desperate attack with his knife, plunging it into Garrett's heart. He watched helplessly as his fingers launched into the soldier's face, digging through cartilage and tendons. His fingers shot through the man's eyes, dropping him to his knees in agony - it was a slow death. Garrett removed the knife from his chest and sliced the soldier's throat until the trachea split in half, gargling his screams. Only then did he retract his hand to leave the man bleeding out on the floor.

With a quick glance back, Garrett was sure the alien was tormenting him with the sight on purpose, he walked away leaving another tangled mess of bodies and severed limbs. After another ten minutes of walking, he had slaughtered two civilians passing by in the corridor, removing their heads in the process. He could hear the general din of the cargo bay with its constant commotion of foot traffic and inhabitants. The sound of children laughing up ahead made Garrett scream in his mind. He pleaded with the alien to go a different way; he had the sense now that he was heading for the bridge.

The dim corridor gave way to the brightness of the busy bay. Gasps and screams greeted him as he entered the crowded space. But his keen ears detected another sound above the pandemonium erupting around him - heavy boots at full sprint.

No more, please!

The crowds parted giving the squad of armed guards room to line up their sights on the target. There were twelve of them now, but Garrett wished they'd brought more; they were going to need it. What happened next was worse than what he thought his new body was capable of. As the soldiers opened fire he dashed to the side, covering several metres in a single bound, where he snatched a mother away from her cowering child and threw her into the line of photonic hell. It all happened so fast they didn't have time to stop firing before the woman was shot to death. Garrett knocked the son over before he could cry out, continuing his momentum to run behind the nearest pavilion.

His agility was incredible, allowing him to jump and slide through the throng of terror-stricken on-lookers. Any who got in his way he simply threw aside as if they were no heavier than a stone. He leapt from one crate to another before jumping over three tents in a row. While in the air the soldiers clipped him multiple times along his arm and leg, but it didn't hinder his landing. It was easy to get lost amongst the market-like rows until he was able to double back. The screams that followed him made it harder to evade his hunters. But Garrett realised this wasn't evasion.

In moments he found himself slipping between two pavilions and colliding with the group of soldiers. He shoulder-barged the closest of them, driving her into the group to create chaos. An instant back-hand broke the neck of the soldier to his right. He didn't stop. His motion was a blur of powerful kinetic energy as he dispatched every one of them, often with a single blow to a vital organ. In just over ten seconds he was standing in the middle of a bloodbath, surrounded by twelve savaged corpses.

With movements closer to an animal, Garrett made his way across the cargo bay swatting people aside. The two guards that had just arrived at the access corridor were dead before they knew what was happening. He jumped out of the crowd, catching the two soldiers by the side of their heads, smashing them together until they shared one. There was nothing between him and the bridge now.

CAPTAIN FEY STOOD with Lieutenant Commander Ramone and Worth as they looked on in horror at the cargo bay monitors. The late shift had refused to leave the bridge while they were in an emergency, leaving their replacements to take up the extra monitors. She took one last look at the portal relaying the image of Commander Astill lying dead outside the basement with Esposito and Clark. He was a good man and an even better soldier, she would miss him, she would grieve them all, but first. "Rodriguez, status report."

"He's making his way through the bay, Captain. His movements make him easy to track."

"But not so easy to kill," Matthews commented from the wall hologram.

"How can this be the same Professor Jones?" Worth asked as he double-checked the sensor feedback. There was no mistaking the hideous killing machine, even through the blood and tattered clothing.

"How did he even get access to the basement?" Ramone countered.

"Questions come later," Captain Fey interrupted. "Right now we need to put him down. Suggestions?" The bridge crew looked to one another with the same expression of hopelessness. The Captain shared the sentiment; how could they stop something capable of taking that kind of punishment?

"I've sent a priority alert to all UDC personnel off and on duty," Matthews offered. "Several patrols are converging on the bay as we speak but it's going take time to get there. All civilians are receiving orders via their handhelds to stay in their quarters."

"We need to evacuate the cargo bay as well. Tell the crew to go to the nearest nanocelium port," the Captain ordered. "I'm inputting the master code now so they can replicate weapons." She accessed the terminal built into the Captain's chair and typed in the code.

"Shit! He just killed Gardiner and Pitt!" Rodriguez reported from her station. The wall hologram showed the two soldiers moments before their heads were slammed together, ending their lives.

"Where's the closest Novaarian vessel?" Worth asked the cadet sitting at navigations.

"Twelve light-years away, sir." The captain could see the fear on the cadet's face.

"We still have a team of Novaarians in the hangar bay," Rodriguez continued. "They've just finished installing the latest batch of translators."

"Keep them where they are," Captain Fey ordered. "We have to contain him on this ship. If he tries to escape, we might need them to secure the hangar. Send them a warning and keep them updated."

"He's accessing the lift to the bridge!" another cadet yelled.

"Shut it down, keep him locked inside." She kept her composure in the midst of the crew. She had to be fearless and in total control if the bridge was to be maintained. Seeing the pile of dead bodies in the cargo bay made that task a lot harder.

"I can't Captain, he's doing something..." Matthews walked up behind the cadet to see for himself.

"He's overriding the servos somehow," Matthews reported in a panicked voice.

The Captain looked at the nanocelium port to the left of her chair. "Everyone pick up a weapon and aim it at the door," she ordered. "That son of a bitch has killed our brothers and sisters, now we end him." She was glad to see most of them nodding with hardened expressions. She needed them tough for what came next.

GARRETT HAD LOST all hope when the micro-tubules bored through the palm of his hand and into the lift menu controls. When the lights went out he hoped they had found a way to stop him, but he was wrong. Moments after the tubules interacted with the control, the lift came back to life, resuming its previous course. He didn't know why he was going to the bridge but he had the strongest urge to get off the ship and go somewhere specific.

The lift gave a soft *ping* before the doors were blown in by the photonic blasts of over a dozen weapons. He felt every shot impact his body, taking chunks of him with them. It was hard to miss a fully grown man in a confined space. When the assault finally ended everything was dark to Garrett, but he knew he wasn't dead, at least not any more dead than he already was. But what was the alien doing? From his surroundings, he could tell that he was slumped on the floor resting against what was left of the lift wall. He could smell the ozone from the discharge of so many weapons in such a small area.

"Is he dead?" It sounded like a woman but he couldn't identify her. The floor crackled as light footsteps made their way across the debris, drawing closer. Garrett felt the jolt of that same someone kicking his foot, looking for any response. His body didn't move.

"I think so!" There was hope in her voice and he knew it was the same woman that operated the communications, but he couldn't recall her name. He heard her swivel round to the bridge crew at the same time Garrett's body reacted with furious precision. He rose behind her, relying on their hesitation to shoot him through her, and wrapped his forearm around her neck, lifting her as he did. In the same motion, he tore the sidearm from her other hand and proceeded to shoot the bridge crew. She wriggled and squirmed in his grip, her toes reaching for the floor, but he kept her in place.

Six of the crew were dead in the first five seconds, photonic scorch marks staining their bodies. He counted fifteen more as they jumped for cover behind various stations and chairs, the captain among them. They fired back with less enthusiasm, desperately trying to miss the woman he held in front of him. A few lucky shots found their mark, knocking him back slightly, but he found his targets much quicker. Another ten seconds and six more were dead.

In what must have been a last-ditch effort, Garrett's hostage pushed his firing arm into the door frame of the lift. One of the remaining soldiers took advantage and shot the pistol, sending it spinning from Garrett's hand. He almost felt the alien shrug, as if it was no real inconvenience. With a quick squeeze, the woman's neck snapped in his headlock. Before her body hit the floor, he had already snatched up the nearest soldier and put his fist through his chest.

The next ten seconds was a blur of photonic light and sparks with splashes of blood throughout. There was so much blood he could smell it above the ozone. A few were left crippled as they scampered away with broken bones and internal damage. They were of no concern now; there was nothing between him and his goal. Garrett tried to shake off the thought, knowing it wasn't his. He stepped over the bodies and pulled a young cadet off the station he required. Garrett had no idea what he was looking at or how to use the bridge controls, but it didn't matter to the alien.

Like the lift controls, he simply placed his hand over the monitor screen and watched as dark tendrils slithered within the nanocelium machine. The screen flickered as the internal emitters faltered under the invasive intrusion. A hologram appeared above the station, showing the schematics for a ship in the shape of a spoon-head.

"Replication sequence has begun. Completion time: seventeen minutes," the computer announced. The feeling he had was right; the alien was trying to get off the ship. But to go where? The hologram changed from the image of the ship to local star charts. The hologram flicked through the images until one system remained with the sun in the middle and six orbital rings with planets at different points along them. The top left corner read: Trantax System. Through some internal control that Garrett couldn't fathom, the planet on the fourth ring became highlighted taking up the entire hologram.

"Course laid in. The ship will be ready to depart in fifteen minutes and thirty-two seconds." After its final announcement, Garrett removed his hand and the tendrils within.

The hangar bay was a thirty-minute walk away; Garrett made it there in under fifteen, after stopping to kill eight soldiers too stupid to run away. He didn't even slow his momentum when he arrived at the hangar double doors. Continuing his sprint, he charged through the doors blowing them off their servos like a grenade. The first technician he came across didn't have enough time to even look startled as he shoulder-barged him out of the way. He felt and heard the man's bones crack and pop as he was flung aside.

Three nimble bounds put him twenty feet in the air, directly above the team of Novaarians. With the exception of two, they were mostly the Conclave equivalent of civilians. Despite their extra limbs and height advantage, Garrett sliced and punched through their flesh and bone as easily as any human. Pulling the long arm off one, he used it to beat two of the others to death. He left the warriors for last.

They twirled and spun their staffs until they were easily longer than Garrett's five foot eleven frame. The first came at him with a jump, angling to bring the spear-like tip down into his chest. He made no move to evade. The spear cut clean through his body until it pierced the ground behind him. This brought the warrior's throat within arms' length, where Garrett whipped his hand out and squeezed. Everything inside the slender neck was pulverised, instantly killing the Novaarian. The second warrior made his play, dashing in from the side. Garrett gripped the spear, penetrating his torso in both hands and snapped it in half like a twig. Using one half he deflected the attacking spear with ease while swinging the other half round at lightning speed. The resulting collision ended up with the Novaarian gasping for air on his knees, half a broken spear lodged between his ribs and protruding out of his right shoulder.

Garrett released the spear, allowing the Novaarian to drop on to the floor and die. The usual screams followed him as technicians ran in the opposite direction. The furthest platform was octagonal in shape and fifty metres in length and width. The last details to the ship were being applied by the ever-building nanocelium that moved across the surface like living liquid. There was no beauty in its design; it was purely functional, though its intended destination was still a mystery to Garrett.

He entered the ship via a ramp on the starboard side as if he owned it. There was only one chair on the bridge and Garrett got the sense that it was the only room on the ship. Two columns rose up on either side, where he placed both his hands to spread the evil he carried inside. He was now one with the ship, the alien controlling its every action.

"Course set." The ship had already been programmed with its destination in mind.

"Launch!" It was the first time he had heard his voice. It was twisted and deeper with an almost robotic undertone.

It was... alien.

SIX

The *Rackham* entered the capital system seven million kilometres out from the main sequence. Shortly before emerging into real space, the stealthware was deactivated to make their arrival legitimate. After Savrick's attack, there was no stealth technology capable of breaking through the capital's defences. Ch'len had explained that they could have reached as far as the planet undetected, but nothing physical could pass through the atmospheric barrier unnoticed.

The Ch'kara had also insisted on charging the Intrinium cells before they approached the Conclave itself; it was the only way to ensure a quick getaway, something he had apparently become accustomed to with Roland around.

Extra lighting came on as the outer shielding closed off the ports on their approach to the M-class star. Roland kept a close eye on the sensor feedback regarding hull integrity. Sitting in a star spot was not the safest pastime when you didn't have shields like a Nebula-class vessel. The *Rackham* was special in that it could charge its Intrinium cells without having to immediately release the energy like other ships its size, but the nanocelium could only take so much battering. Conclave citizens, who didn't have their own Starrillium, had the luxury of parking their ship behind the protective shields of the fuel stations. These stations were situated over the star-spots behind powerful force-fields designed only to allow magnetic fields to pass through. Since the *Rackham* wasn't legally registered, they couldn't use the stations.

The bank of holograms to his right informed him the temperature outside was just over two million degrees Celsius. From inside the ship, the sounds of the outer hull were unnerving as the exotic metal expanded and contracted under the immense heat. If this was the price he paid for true freedom, he was happy to pay it.

"Hull integrity: eighty-four percent." Roland had programmed the internal computer to mimic the voice of a seducing woman. Ch'len said it was the only voice he would listen to.

"Alright, we've got enough juice to reach Raalakian space if we need to, we can go now." Ch'len was looking around at the creaking framework, not entirely trusting of the alien ship.

Roland waited until they were five million kilometres away before pulling back the outer shielding. Nobody wanted that kind of suntan. It wasn't long before they could visibly see other ships congregating around the entry point to capital space. The *Rackham's* sensors showed seventeen Nebula-class security ships and two Nexus-class destroyers forming a uniformed line over two million kilometres. Ever since the *Gommarian* caused the nova, new parameters had been set on all vessels carrying Starrilliums. Without express permission from all five Highclave members, the ships could not fly within a million kilometres of any inhabited planet.

They may have been spread over a great distance, but even having two of the Nebula-class ships could be considered overkill. The only real threat was the *Gommarian* and they had that under control in Novaarian territory. Roland had seen this kind of thing before however; it was a simple knee-jerk reaction to being attacked in the first place. The Conclave hadn't fought over anything for over a hundred and fifty thousand years. For the capital to be attacked and so many to die in the assault, it was only natural to see such a show of force.

Checking the internal feed, as he periodically did, Roland found

Esabelle sitting cross-legged in the engine room. He liked to keep an eye on her inside his ship, not just because she was easy on the eyes, but because her knowledge of the *Rackham* definitely surpassed his own.

And God knows I'm sick of looking at that ugly little bastard.

"And who are we gonna be today?" Roland asked.

"Well, with your disguises in mind," Ch'len continued, "I was thinking a Laronian couple, newly bonded, on the start of their round-the-galaxy trip. You're here to see the big city before heading to Nova Prime to see the famous ocean of jewels..."

"Is the backstory really necessary?" Roland asked dryly.

"It is *now*, thanks to your genocide loving cousins! The AI doesn't just want to know who and what we are anymore; it wants to know why we're here in the first place!"

While Ch'len uploaded the new identities, Roland slotted the ship into the nearest queue. The flow never stopped, so he entered the platform coordinates and let the ship fly itself. Smaller security ships hailed the occasional vessel pulling them out of the queue for physical inspection. This wasn't the first time they had been scrutinized by an AI hub entering a new system and, despite Ch'len's many flaws, Roland couldn't deny his expertise in this area.

He waited until the *Rackham* had passed through the atmospheric barrier before getting up from his chair. He kicked the empty bottles of alcohol aside, making his way to the exit with a head rush. He told himself he definitely wasn't drunk, but it had taken an hour to reach the planet and he had inevitably started drinking.

"Whatever you're doing at Protocorps, I suggest you get in and out as fast as possible," Ch'len warned. "Those are not the kind of people you mess with, Roland. They're powerful with far-reaching arms. Taking out one of their board members was bad enough, but actually breaking into their HQ is suicide, even with *her* at your side. We're supposed to be making money, remember?" Roland had already walked beyond the bridge door as Ch'len shouted after him, "And if this is just some ridiculous scheme to mate with that female, then you deserve what's coming!" Roland gave him the finger from behind.

There had been a few translation problems the day he explained that one. "Oh, very mature, child…"

"Fuck you, Len!" Roland made his way to the living space below the bridge, a smile strapped to his face at the thought of Ch'len's outrage. The living area was a combination of the kitchen and lounge with a circular table in the corner. He hadn't bothered to decorate it yet. He was so used to moving on all the time he had never stopped to decorate anything before. Unless you could call a complete mess a form of decoration. Empty bottles were left lying around with half-eaten pieces of food and dirty wrappers. The lights came on as he entered but he still tripped over his jacket on the floor.

"Len, you need to clean this shit up!" he shouted in the direction of the bridge. He picked his jacket up and made for the far wall between the adjoining rooms. With a knock, the wall parted in half, revealing its hidden wares.

"You keep your weapons in the *kitchen*?" Esabelle appeared from nowhere. Even Roland couldn't be that quiet.

"Help yourself." Roland stood aside having already retrieved his Tri-rollers and a handful of explosives and gadgets, cobbled together by Ch'len. Seeing the beautiful woman, he realised he was only wearing his trousers and a tight vest. He did his best to flex every muscle and remain tensed while he took a little longer to sort out his gear.

"Thanks, but I'll be fine." The air crackled and sparked around her raised hand before a miniature sun was born in her palm.

"Point taken." He reached back in and pulled out his body armour. "You know what this is?" He gave the dark vest a slap, presenting it to Esabelle. "Callic-diamond armour. This is the same stuff the Conclave plaster across their hulls to keep out the sun." It was one of his favourite possessions. It would have cost a small fortune if the Laronian he was hunting hadn't offered it to him as a bribe. Of course, he took the vest and captured the bounty anyway, but he didn't kill him so it seemed fair to Roland.

"Want to test that theory?" Esabelle raised her hand again.

"Trust me, it works. I once got hit square in the chest at six feet by a Quad-roller." He really hoped not to see that particular weapon again.

"What's a Quad-roller?"

"A big fucking gun with an angry Novaarian attached to it." He shrugged at her raised eyebrow. "Long story..." The armoured vest was lighter than the fabric one he was already wearing. After a couple of minutes, he was wearing his long jacket, concealing his arsenal within.

Esabelle held her hand out, activating a column in the floor. It rose up to her fingers, where she used the control panel to activate a room-sized hologram of the outside view. Roland tried to keep his mouth shut; he didn't know the ship could do any of that.

I really need to read that manual.

The image relayed the immensity of the city they were entering. The central tower was two thousand miles wide at its thinnest in the middle, with a height of just over four thousand miles, wiping out the view of anything else. Millions of ships, of every description, came and went from the various ports and landing platforms, while others diverted towards the connecting towers that looked like structural beams for the cracked planet. There were construction zones scattered across the tower, still repairing the damage from the micro-nova five months ago. Roland also noticed a higher number of red patrol ships in the area.

"You're going to need these if you want to blend in." Ch'len's voice came from beyond the hologram as he walked straight through the image. He was carrying a small case that he placed on the kitchen table. Inside were six dark bands of a material Roland could never figure out. It was somewhere between metal and rubber as the bands wrapped around the neck and wrists. He put his on first to demonstrate to Esabelle. A grid of yellow lines tracked across his face and hands as the profiler calculated the necessary features. To the user, there was no difference, except for the illusion surrounding their hands, but to Esabelle, Roland now appeared to be a Laronian.

"It's mostly used within the same species, not much use across the different races," Ch'len explained. "You're lucky your physiology is so close to the scaly ones."

Esabelle fitted her own bands and became a female Laronian - Roland decided she was still pretty hot. It always took him a while to get used to having one less finger, he could still feel it, just not see it.

"Why are we descending?" Esabelle looked to the holographic display as the *Rackham* angled towards the lower half of the central tower. "The Protocorps Headquarters is located at the top of the tower."

Roland looked to Ch'len for help, but he simply shrugged.

"We need to make a transfer and it has to be one of the Clave terminals." He said it as nonchalantly as he could.

"You mean you have to send the data we mined from Ral-vet's array to your client so you can get paid?" Roland tried to avoid her gaze. "You realise that all communications between planets go through the AI hubs. The same AI we are here to investigate, Roland."

"Hey, this ship is great and all, but it doesn't produce its own Intrinium cells. Those I have to actually *buy*. No transfer - no moolah - no moolah - no fly." He made childish gestures imitating the ship taking off.

Esabelle gave him an exasperated look. "Where is the Bounty Clave terminal, exactly?" she asked.

"Well the Clave isn't strictly legal," Ch'len continued. "There are lots of trans-communication hubs all over the place, but the bounty clave only uses one in the lower levels, outside Clave Tower."

"It's in a bar," Roland added to the Ch'kara's long-winded explanation.

Esabelle raised her scaly eye with a look of judgment over Roland. "Of course it is..."

KEL-VAR TIONIS MADE his way through the lobby and into the deeper and far more secretive parts of Protocorps HQ. The building itself was the central hanging spire from the very top of Clave Tower. The entrance was located at the bottom, only accessible via craft on the landing platform. The lower half was a legitimate business with all the trappings and personnel expected of such an enterprise. Everything past level one hundred and one of the two hundred and twenty-seven floors was a different matter, as Kel-var well knew. The only employees to be found past this level were those loyal to the cause. Kel-var's predecessors had been very specific about keeping the secret within a selected few of the species.

The Conclave offered its own security, which Protocorps happily accepted with such precious technology housed inside. But past level sixty-one, all guards and security measures were Kel-var's private army. The core AI was situated at the top of the spire, secured halfway between the planet and the artificial structure. Ral-vet's ancestors had been the ones to install the prophet here, thinking it to be the safest place on the capital. The Gomar had challenged that fact.

"I take it all repairs have been made." Kel-var stood in front of the white circular door that led to the prophet's chamber. He was talking to Sav-del Tanek, a high ranking descendant of the Tanek dynasty. Ral-vet had placed him personally for the job of maintaining the prophet's requirements and integration to the AI network.

"The micro-nova created a lot of radiation that fried some of the internal systems. We lost contact with half of the lower city and the connection hub to Corvus was disrupted when the *Valoran* exploded." Sav-del's explanation of the damage was not what Kel-var wanted to know, he had read the reports from Ral-vet the same day the Gomar attacked. Sav-del was just looking for praise on having such severe repairs made so quickly. Kel-var didn't hand out pats on the head; his look expressed such a notion.

"Levels are optimal now, sir," Tanek quickly went on to say. "All relays are connected and the generators are completely submerged in the tanks. The prophet itself sustained no damage."

"You will wait here," Kel-var ordered his entourage of security and PAs. Sav-del placed his hand over the scanner while positioning his organic eye into the retinal socket. The scanner took his biometric readings taking his DNA, finger-print and cross-referencing his Novattoo. The floor beneath his feet was also weighing him while a separate, hidden probe was measuring his height. He said his name out loud for the voice recognition before entering the new code that changed every two hours. The heavy door was three feet thick and designed by one of Protocorps' many science divisions. They had taken the raw material of Callic-diamond and altered its structure on an atomic level. The door could be fired into the photosphere of an A-class star and still survive.

Kel-var entered the expansive chamber, his dark blue robe flowing behind him as the door resealed, locking him in. The room was half a kilometre wide with a ceiling of rock and ancient stalactites. There was a single walkway that led from the door to the prophet in the centre of the chamber. Walking across, Kel-var looked down into the four great tanks of liquid nitrogen that kept the enormous generators cool. It was from here that all AI hubs were connected; stretching their influence across the galaxy required a certain amount of energy.

The generators were connected to the prophet via a multitude of cables that inserted into its various ports. The cube sat on a platform that dropped down between the generator tanks, and into the CPU for Protocorps to assume a small measure of responsibility, allowing them to keep up appearances of running the AI.

The walkway only allowed Kel-var to access one side of the prophet's cube-shaped body. The centre of the square had opened up centuries ago for bio-connection reasons. It was for that reason that Kel-var pulled back the sleeve of his robe, revealing the six circular ports implanted into the skin between his wrist and elbow. The ports were at different angles all the way around the pale flesh. He rested his arm on the shelf that supported his hand and elbow, exposing his forearm.

"I humbly beg an audience." Black tendrils snaked out of the hole, slowly at first, like an animal assessing its surroundings. The cables danced around his arm, slithering over the skin between the ports. All at once they found a socket and inserted themselves with an audible *click*. Unlike the earlier generations, Kel-var felt no pain when the connection was made. It had been his grandfather that designed the bio-connections a few hundred cycles earlier.

Speak...

The voice came from all around but Kel-var knew it was inside his head. He tried not to flinch at the imposing power he felt under every syllable.

"The Highclave has included the humans on the Trantax project. The Terran is on the planet already."

We are aware.

"I have teams on standby. I can deploy them to retrieve the artefact immediately and have it transferred to a secure location." Being as high up in their organisation as he was, Kel-var had the privilege of being privy to some of the prophet's secrets. He was well aware that the second cube had been around just as long as the one in front of him - it was simply redundant. Should the primary prophet become too damaged to achieve its goals, the second would activate taking its place. He could only assume it was aware of events on Trantax because of the data intercepted through the AI hubs, coming out of the Highclave's secure array.

Send your teams. I have an agent of my own in play.

An agent of its own? Kel-var was confused. The only agents of the prophet should be within Protocorps, and he had knowledge of them all.

"Are they to work together?"

Order your people to target and eliminate the Terran. My agent will retrieve the cube. Have the Helteron Cluster secured and ready for our arrival.

Kel-var tried to hide his reaction. The Helteron cluster was located between the borders of Shay and Ch'kara territory, but its secrets were highly guarded by Protocorps. That particular project had remained dormant since the discovery of the prophet itself, but its importance was not lost on him. And what did it mean by arrival? The cube had never left this chamber. Kel-var reasoned that it was referring to the other cube as itself. Protocorps' long-range sensors would have alerted him if *They* were actually arriving.

"What about the Terran vessel, the *Gommarian*? It would be an honour to assist in your great mission. I have resources available that could help to take the ship and wipe out its inhabitants."

No, you do not. You will proceed as planned. The humans and their ship will be dealt with by us. The timetable is being accelerated. I want you and your board members to personally oversee the Helteron project as soon as we arrive. You will go there immediately.

"Has *their* timetable been accelerated?" he asked hesitantly. He knew what was coming; he just never thought he would be alive to see its magnificence. Kel-var would never admit it, but half of him was afraid of what was coming, while the other half couldn't wait. It was no doubt due to the teachings and excitement of the generations before.

We are inevitable. You must be ready.

As always, the prophet only gave him enough to carry out his orders. He had so many questions, but he reasoned that he had been privileged enough to be told about the Terran and their past, a mystery the Conclave did not fully understand.

The thick door sealed shut behind him, where he met a sea of expectant faces. Even his security detail appeared interested.

"Ready my ship, we're leaving for the Helteron Cluster immediately." One of his PAs reacted to the order with a far-away stare as she used her virtual vision to inform the pilot.

"But sir, you have the address regarding the death of Ral-vet Tanek," another PA offered.

"I'm sure Sal-dev here can handle it, just tweak the speech." Sal-dev puffed out his chest with pride at being given such a high profile job, even if it was the death of his uncle. "I need to use a secure transterminal before I leave."

"You can use my office, sir." Sal-dev gestured for them to follow him.

Kel-var tried to focus on the immediate things he needed to do. He didn't want to dwell on the ominous predictions of the prophet. If the timetable really had been accelerated then his existence as he knew it now would soon come to an end, and he wasn't sure he was entirely ready for that. Then again, what choice did mortals have in a game of the gods?

THE VIEW from outside Clave Tower was awe-inspiring. Roland remembered the first time he had looked out on the prepossessing vista, after escaping the Laronian warship. It was truly the most alien view he had ever seen, even throughout his travels across the Conclave. From the lower city, they could see the never-ending ocean of towers and beautiful structures stretching out to the crack in the planet. Beyond that, the distant sun shone like a beacon in the dark, surrounded by glittering stars. It was easy to feel small when you could see half a planet laid out in front of you.

The expanse slipped from sight as the grav pillar dropped them below the nearest buildings. With a Novattoo imprinted on the side of the holo-bands they could easily navigate the many grav pillars used to traverse the vast city.

They stepped off at sublevel 131, where Roland guided them along the busy walkways of the lower city streets. Holographic neon signs illuminated the shops and bars with different beats flowing out of the various clubs. Every colour of the spectrum highlighted the available wares the sub-level denizens craved. Roland loved it down here; you could get drink, food, drugs and every kind of virtual stimulator. The one colour he was happy not to see was Conclave security red. He side-stepped the drunks and junkies stumbling through the streets looking for their next high. Even through the holo-band, he could see Esabelle's look of disgust.

They were forced to stop as the crowd ahead dispersed to avoid the Ch'kara being thrown out of the adjacent bar window. The organic pane burst as the little alien flew into the crowd, knocking over a Shay and a couple of Nix.

"Don't show your gassy little face around here again!" The

booming voice came from a Raalak on the other side of the broken window. The organic pane began to reseal as the Ch'kara crawled away into the shadows of an alley-way.

"A charming place you've found," Esabelle remarked. "Why doesn't Ch'len ever leave the ship?"

"He suffers from agoraphobia; he hates open spaces and crowds." He chuckled to himself, "Can you imagine that, in the biggest society in the galaxy?" They turned down another street where Roland pushed a Brenine out of the way, trying to sell them Glow. The bounty hunter had never touched the fluorescent drug but he had seen its effects on others and decided to stick with the poison he knew. The Brenine caught sight of his dual Tri-rollers and didn't press the matter. Covering his pure white skin with a tattered hood, the Brenine slinked off into the night.

"You don't see many of their kind away from their own planets," Esabelle commented.

Roland raised a scaly eyebrow at the woman. "How the hell do you know that? You've been cooped up in that ship your entire life."

They continued to push on through the streets.

"When I was integrated with the Gommarian, I scanned the Conclave archives for information on every species. It's all locked in here." She tapped her temple.

"Well, I've actually met a few. They tend to stick together. I don't ask too many questions, especially around here."

"They're light sensitive. On their homeworlds, eighty percent of all the cities are located underground. I imagine that's why they don't travel a lot."

Roland had once met a female of the species and had been surprised at how attractive he found her. As humanoids their shape was identical, even their facial features were similar with two eyes and a mouth. Their ears were small holes that ran down from the side of the head and along the jaw-line. Her eyes had been a beautiful blue, more brilliant than Esabelle's. The sockets themselves were bigger than a human's on a small slant that angled towards the smooth skin where a nose should have been. Their hair was closer to that of a porcupine, with small spikes sloping across the back of the head and down the neck.

"Well, I'm glad you find them so fascinating because the guy who owns the bar is a Brenine. And you *really* don't want to get on his bad side." Roland walked out of the alley onto the next street, narrowly avoiding a cargo truck hovering down the road. "We're here."

The truck rolled by revealing the neon green sign above a two-storey bar.

"The Abyss?"

"Kinda fitting ain't it?" Roland marched across the street pushing a drunken Trillik out of his path. Inside, the bar was exactly as he remembered it. The back was fitted with a dance floor while the front was one long bar with booths and tables. The upstairs was for a different kind of leisure activity, and not one Roland had got round to using. He wasn't a hundred percent certain that humans were biologically compatible like some of the others were with each other. It was dark and noisy with the music from the dance floor packed with the youth of every species. It always took him days to get rid of the smell of sweat and ammonia, mixed with alcohol and drugs, out of his nose.

"You must feel right at home," Esabelle said as she took in the sight.

"I like a drink or four, but even this isn't my scene!" They had to shout over the music. "Speaking of, go get us a couple of drinks while I send the data. Make sure you ask for the blue one, not the yellow!"

"We're going to Protocorps after this, we can't drink!" she argued.

"I work better with a drink, trust me! Besides, if we don't buy something we'll look suspicious!" Roland walked away leaving Esabelle to deal with the Novaarian tending the bar. The transterminal was located in a room off the dance floor. He quickly uploaded the data and sent it to the address given by his anonymous client. The screen froze as a message appeared informing him the address no longer existed.

"What?" he tried shaking the machine before resorting to hitting the monitor. "Give me a break!" he yelled in rage as he exited the room, shoving his way through the dancing throng to reach his drink. He found Esabelle sitting in a booth in the corner of the bar with low lighting over the table. He took a seat, being careful not to touch the disgusting table top.

"What's up with you?" Esabelle leaned in to ask over the music.

"I just got screwed is what!" Roland removed a small sphere from his belt and placed it on the table. Four metallic legs detached from the body propping it above the surface when a red LED came to life on the apex of the ball. Turning in his seat he depressed the button behind the booth. The music instantly dulled beyond the table, while the view distorted as if fumes were rising from the floor.

"Neat trick. What's the ball for?" Esabelle half shouted the question before adjusting to the new environment.

"These privacy booths aren't so private." He pointed to the ceiling. "The Brenine I mentioned, Revus, he likes to have his finger in every pie. Nothing goes through here without him knowing about it. Ch'len made the... I forget what he calls it, for this exact situation. That little ball keeps our business our own."

"So what happened with the data transfer?"

"The address doesn't exist anymore. Goodbye, fifty thousand units!" Roland downed his drink in one, allowing his head to slump into the cushion behind.

"I would very much like to know who wanted that data. Did they know what was on Ral-vet's array?"

"Well if you find them, you let them know they owe me."

"It's possible we aren't the only ones investigating this," Esabelle said with caution.

Roland's right arm vibrated as the flexi-screen around his jacket sleeve alerted him of an incoming call; there was only one person who had his details.

"Where's the money?" Ch'len's voice came from the inbuilt speakers in the corners of the screen as his face spread across the screen. "I'm checking the account and there's no money dropping into it. Where is it, Roland?"

"There's been a slight hitch," Roland continued. "We're not

getting paid the rest of the bounty." He immediately turned the volume down as Ch'len unleashed a string of obscenities.

"So we're out fifty thousand units and you are just sat there drinking?"

"We're going into Protocorps Headquarters, Len. There's bound to be something valuable in there." Roland retrieved the schematics from his belt and placed the holo-projector on the sticky table.

"There better be, or we're both eating Raalakian food for the next cycle! And put your earpieces in, I can't hear you."

Handing Esabelle hers, they both placed the two-way devices in their ears. Roland cancelled the call to Ch'len and activated the hologram of the hanging spires at the top of Clave Tower. The image cast them in red light with the hologram reaching two feet in the air. Roland double checked Ch'len's invention, making sure they maintained their privacy.

"You see those five towers clustered in the middle?" Ch'len asked. There were hundreds of towers suspended like great stalactites in the holographic image, each, in reality, a few miles in length. With Ch'len's words, the towers on the outside began to disappear as the emitters shrank to the five central towers. The image expanded making the towers two feet tall, giving them an accurate picture of Protocorps Headquarters. "The big tower in the middle is where everything goes on. The outer buildings are administration and parking only. It's important to note there aren't any grav-pillars. The only way to gain access is with a vehicle; before you ask, the *Rackham* is too big. It could only fit on the main platform at the bottom of the central tower." The image shifted to focus on an expansive platform attached to the very bottom. It was clearly for guests and executives only.

"It'll be heavily guarded anyway." Esabelle manipulated the projector to get a better look at the outer towers. Each one was connected to the larger building via bridges that extended all the way up. "This is our way in. We go through like any other employee."

"Speaking of employees," Ch'len added, "the contract between the Conclave and Protocorps is available to the public because of the responsibility they hold maintaining the AI core. They clearly state that all Conclave security is restricted to the first hundred and one floors. That means that you've got a hundred and twenty-six floors of non-Conclave security."

"Mercenaries, then." Roland smiled at the thought. Killing mercenaries was probably the closest thing he had to a hobby; that and drinking.

"More likely some kind of Protocorps private army. I'm surprised the Highclave would be happy with that arrangement. I can't believe they would leave something so sensitive to all the races in the hands of just one," Esabelle remarked.

"It was a deal they made centuries ago, apparently. I guess the Highclave at the time couldn't say no with what the Shay was offering." Ch'len had already started eating something.

It's no wonder we're always running out of food...

"Do we even know where the actual AI is housed inside?" Roland was starting to rethink his newest adventure. That was an awfully large army to fight, and for what? Who knows what they'll find in there. In fact, the only thing he knew they would find was a lot of guards eager to put holes in them. Still, there was that feeling of actually doing something, something important like he used to do. It had been a long time since he had done something worth dying for, a cause he knew was right. Fighting the Gomar had given him that feeling.

"No, its location has never been revealed. It could be anywhere inside," Ch'len said.

"Not anywhere..." Esabelle looked hopeful. "You couldn't send the data from Ral-vet's array, so let's take a closer look."

They heard Ch'len's constant munching stop. "I'm mining the files as we speak."

Roland looked at Esabelle's untouched drink, asking her a silent question with his eyes. She sighed and relinquished the blue nectar to him. It didn't last long.

Ch'len audibly squealed down the line, "Even if we can't send it to the client, there are enough corporate secrets on here to keep us filthy rich for centuries! Aside from that, it's bad news though. According to this, the AI is located at the very apex of the central tower."

Roland tried to hide his exasperation at the increasingly bad situation. He might never get to make those units if he entered that building. Even Esabelle looked to be re-evaluating their situation.

"It gets worse," Ch'len continued. "Let's say you do somehow manage to reach the top. The AI itself is locked behind a three-feet thick, Callic-diamond door. There's a whole file on the door's retrofit! There's no way you're getting through it without clearance."

"Is that gonna be a problem for you?" Roland directed his question to Esabelle.

She looked away for a moment, no doubt weighing up her own abilities. "I probably could, but it might take a while."

That wasn't what he wanted to hear. Time would not be on their side. Even if they were able to get through the private army, the second the AI core was considered compromised, the Conclave would send every soldier they had to help.

"There's another option," Ch'len thankfully offered. "It's ironic actually; we might get help from another Tanek. Ral-vet put one of his own in charge of the core's safety - Sal-dev Tanek. He has an office on the two hundred and second floor. I would bet my second stomach that rich shit can get you in."

"So we have to break in, reach the two hundred and second floor, grab Sal-dev, take him to the top where we 'convince' him to open the door to Protocorps' biggest asset, and then what? Are we blowing the cube up or are you gonna levitate it out of there?" Roland was definitely going to need another drink.

"I don't know yet. It depends what we find in there." Esabelle was opening up more of the hologram to inspect the outer towers' interior.

"What cube?" Ch'len butted in.

"I'll tell you about it later, just concentrate on getting us in and out of there," Roland countered.

"I have no *idea* how to get you out of there!"

"That's something else we'll have to figure out when we get in there," Esabelle said. "It's more important that we actually get *in* there, everything else is secondary."

"That sound's a lot like suicide..." Ch'len muttered in their ears.

"Then let's get on with it. Revus won't be happy with our level of privacy; it's only a matter of time before they look in on us." Roland deactivated the holo-projector and Ch'len's device, packing them into his belt before switching off the booth's privacy bubble. They slid out and made their way to the exit. Roland gave the bar a longing look as Esabelle linked his arm, pulling him towards the door.

"Won't you stay for another drink?"

Roland knew that voice. They stopped to look at the Brenine and his entourage walking down the staircase. Revus wore a well-tailored white suit to blend with his pale skin, accentuating his short dark spikes that flowed over his head. Those typical blue Brenine eyes stared back at them with hungry fascination. Roland stopped himself from checking the holo-bands around his neck and wrists.

"Sorry, we're meeting friends," was Esabelle's only reply. She didn't need to drag Roland with her this time, he was happy to leave before Revus complicated things. He didn't like the lingering gaze the Brenine gave them.

They left the bar, becoming lost in the crowds as they made their way to nearest grav-pillars. It was interesting to move through the alien throng and have no one take notice of them. In his human guise he received attention everywhere he went, making certain jobs harder than others.

After a quick ascent, they soon found themselves inside the base of Clave Tower. Its width never ceased to amaze him. From one side of the tower, the casual observer couldn't make out the other side it was so far. Esabelle proved her worth yet again with another incredible feat of Terran power. Placing her hand on the roof of a nearby vehicle, she disabled the alarms and the AI's control. She hesitated as the door opened. Roland followed her gaze into the crowd but couldn't find whatever caught her attention.

"What is it?"

"Nothing. So, are you ready to start a war?" Esabelle asked, starting up the drive.

"I don't start wars, sweetheart, I end 'em."

THE *BLADE* CUT THROUGH REALITY, emerging at the specific coordinates pre-determined by the Conclave AI, Kubrackk slammed one of his many fists into the main console, frustration getting the better of him. It took too long to get through the security checks to enter the capital planet. His prey was no doubt walking around those streets, breathing air he didn't deserve. Spelnar had already uploaded the fake licence and identity giving his ship a new name. As far as the Conclave was concerned, they were a young Novaarian family flying the *Twin Tail*.

"It was my turn to name the ship, Spelnar!" Lole whined.

"If you had my technical skills, you could name the ship furball!" Spelnar spat back, his twin-tail swishing side to side, hypnotically.

"I swear to all your gods and my own, if you don't shut up I'm going to use my Quad-roller as a suppository!" Kubrackk relaxed back in his chair with the usual silence that followed his threats. He wanted to stop and recharge the Intrinium cells before continuing on to the planet, but he needed to catch up with North.

They all held their breath at the sight of the vessel in front of them. Two security ships hovered over the top of it before commanding the occupants to follow them out of the queue. These random checks were becoming costly to people in Kubrackk's line of work. He had already heard of other members in the Bounty Clave who had tried to bribe the wrong guards and been severely punished for it. He reasoned that if the ship in front had been pulled aside, then it was unlikely to happen to them.

"Did you upload the information correctly?" Kubrackk had no reason to doubt Spelnar's abilities, but the armaments on those patrol ships were enough to make him second guess.

"Of course, boss!" Spelnar re-checked the monitor at his station to confirm. A few moments later the main console flashed with the appropriate visiting pass for the *Twin Tail*. Kubrackk's shoulders visibly dropped with a sigh of relief. Now there was nothing between him and his prey.

After clearing the checkpoints, the traffic moved at a quicker pace with the capital now taking up the entire viewport. It wasn't long before the AI requested a destination in order to take control of the ship. Kubrackk could see the benefits of having so much traffic controlled by one entity, but it didn't make him feel any better about having something else control his ship. He hesitantly placed his hand over the holographic handle to maintain manual control before thinking better of it. That was the sort of thing the patrols would be looking for, he thought.

"Boss?" Lole transmitted an incoming call to Kubrackk's console. "The I.D. is registered to the Abyss. It's Revus..."

"I know who it is, you idiot!" Kubrackk accepted the call bringing it up on the glass monitor to his left. "What do you want, Revus?" He instantly regretted talking to the Brenine so harshly. It had been a while since he had taken on a new bounty. He had forgotten how powerful Revus was in that world, not to mention the Brenine's boss. That was a man Kubrackk wanted to avoid at all costs.

"I see your time away from the game has done wonders for your anger issues." He looked back at Kubrackk from behind the desk, above his club.

It occurred to him how strange it was that Revus was even contacting him at all, it was usually the other way around.

"I was sorry to hear about Torvrackk, he was a good bounty hunter. Good drinker too."

Hearing his brother's name was like a knife in the back. They had hunted together for over three centuries, sharing everything as they enjoyed the spoils of their bounties.

"What can I do for you, Revus?" His voice cracked under the strain of feigning politeness.

"It's what I can do for you, actually. I take it you're still hunting the human, Roland North?"

Kubrackk tried to keep a blank face, his business was his own and the less the Brenine had to do with it the better.

At his silent response, Revus began to laugh as if mocking the Novaarian.

All four of Kubrackk's hands clenched together, cracking multiple knuckles.

"I know you are, Kubrackk. Lole has kept me up to date on your little blood feud."

He turned in the pilot's seat to stare holes into Lole's quivering form. The Tularon looked utterly shocked. Kubrackk could feel the rage bubbling inside with the need to spill the blood of the traitor in his midst.

"Thank you for your services, Lole," Revus continued over the monitor, "but I'm afraid your talents are no longer required."

With that Kubrackk removed his Quad-roller and blew Lole's head off in an explosion that knocked his whole body out of the chair. The contents of the Tularon's head decorated the surrounding walls and monitors, along with Spelnar.

"Clean that up!" he barked at the Trillik.

"Well, now that we've got that out of the way..." Revus relaxed back in his comfortable looking throne. "I know where he is right now." Those words caught Kubrackk's undivided attention. The console flashed again informing him of a new data file sitting in his inbox. The sender was Revus. "As you can see, he has recently crossed my path." The message revealed an image from inside the Abyss of two Laronians standing by the bar. He had seen this trick before when he had worked alongside North.

"Are you sure it is him?"

"I would recognise the smell of a human anywhere. So unique." A Brenine's sense of smell was nothing to doubt. "My people are following them as we speak. This information can be yours, for a price."

Of course.

"And what is this price?" Kubrackk ignored the grunts and sighs of Spelnar as he struggled to drag Lole's heavy corpse off the bridge.

He tried not to smile as he heard the Trillik slip in the blood and land in an even greater mess.

"I want his ship."

Now Kubrackk couldn't hide his reaction. The *Rackham* was going to be his prize after he was finished killing the human, "No deal!"

"Then you'll never find him."

Kubrackk sat back, contemplating his situation. He was honour bound to revenge his brother, it was the Novaarian way. Right now he was in no place to make the terms of this deal, he had no leverage. But once he had North, he would have access to the *Rackham*, and then he would be in a position to re-negotiate. Revus was simply a means to an end.

"Fine. I get North and you get the ship. Now, where is he?"

SAL-DEV'S office was perfectly placed to give one the feeling of superiority. With a wall of glass, it allowed Kel-var to look out from the Protocorps Headquarters and view the entirety of Clave Tower. Being truly massive in size, he was unable to glimpse the lower levels due to sheer distance. He turned from the dazzling view and activated the desk terminal while checking on his own devices for secure lines and total privacy within the office. He found several hidden cameras and microphones, which he quickly disabled before making the necessary calls.

He set up a collective call to contact the entire board at once; the word of the prophet was for all of them. The smooth tabletop emitted the faces of every member as they answered the call.

"I have spoken with the prophet," he began. "The Helteron project is being activated ahead of schedule. We are to all oversee it in person." There was visible distress across some of their faces, especially on Sel-gar's over-stuffed face.

"The Helteron project?" Sel-gar lost his words beyond the name.

"All of us? Why in person?" Bal-son's head floated directly in front of Kel-var.

"Because the prophet demands it, Bal-son. And we are its humble servants, yes?" There was silence from the floating heads, each nervously glancing at the other.

"I shall re-direct some of my resources immediately," Gor-van promised from under his hood. "Security will not be an issue."

"Security has never been an issue in the Helteron cluster," Nal-mev added. He wore distress like a mask. "That facility has more protection than the Highclave. It's what's inside that worries me..."

"What is happening here, Kel-var?" Tu-garn tried to move the conversation along from Nal-mev's comments. "Is the Terran such a threat that we turn to this?"

"Turn to what?" Sel-gar sounded more alarmed than ever. "Have any of you even been to the facility? Have any of you seen what it holds? The security doesn't even know what it's guarding. All we have are the original accounts from the first of us. There are no records of it, only what they passed on through the generations!"

"They wouldn't have organised so much protection and secrecy if they were lying about it, Sel-gar," Gor-van opined.

"I have seen it," Kel-var announced. There was silence again from the board members as all eyes fell on their chairman. "My grandfather took me when I was only a child."

"You had clearance to get in?" Nal-mev asked.

Kel-var had always believed his grandfather had taken him because it would be the last time either of them would be allowed inside. Only days after, the current board at the time changed the security system so that the facility could only be accessed by all the members at once. It was widely believed that the project's activation would not be for centuries, if not millennia. It had been a privilege and an honour to see such secrets at his young age, however unbelievable they were.

"I did. And I assure you, what lies inside is very real. You will stop whatever you are doing and travel to the facility immediately." With that he disconnected the array, ending the call. To his irritation, Sal-dev burst into the room a moment later. If it wasn't so costly, he would end the Tanek line altogether and be done with them.

"Sir!" He ran over to the desk with Kel-var's entourage of security piling in after him, almost trampling him as they did. "There's been a breach in the lower levels!"

"Of Clave Tower?" he replied condescendingly. "That is nothing for us to worry about, Sal-dev."

"No, sir. The *headquarters* has been breached. Two humans posing as Laronians, their holo devices set off the alarms when they crossed one of the bridges."

Kel-var was sure he had heard it wrong; Sal-dev couldn't have said humans. His bio-inserts connected to the tabletop and brought up the relevant feeds from the areas where the alarm was going off. He couldn't believe his eyes. There were two actual humans inside *his* building. He breathed a sigh of relief when he realised the Terran was not one of them; his features had been committed to memory.

"Why would they be here?" one of his assistants asked.

Kel-var froze the image of both humans and expanded the hologram. It was the same two who broke into Krono Towers and killed Ral-vet Tanek. This confirmed it; they had found the data on his terminal and made the connection to the AI. It was the only reason they would be stupid enough to actually come here.

"Activate every security procedure we have. Do not underestimate them." Kel-var gave the order to Sal-dev while sending a message to one of his assistants to continue with prepping the ship. "If you have to stand in front of that door yourself, Sal-dev," he pointed in the general direction of the prophet's chamber, "you *will* die before anyone steps foot in that chamber."

SEVEN

Captain Fey looked out on her bridge in dismay and shock. The sparks had finally stopped and the smoke cleared as the nanocelium had already begun to repair the ruined systems. Her dead crew lay motionless, strewn over various stations and left where they fell by the monster that slaughtered them. UDC personnel flooded the bridge searching for survivors among the bloody mess. They had only found two others and herself.

The captain wanted to get out of her chair and rally the soldiers before her, to reassure them that this crime would not go unpunished. The medic by her side had confirmed what she already suspected; her leg was broken along with three ribs and her collarbone. Right now, she couldn't get up if she wanted to.

She looked down to see the metallic cylinder in the medic's hand and hesitated about stopping him. Her nervous glance hadn't gone unnoticed.

"Don't worry, Captain, we've used the Terran medicine on others around the ship," the medic explained. "It's a damn miracle if I'm honest. The nanocelium have been specifically programmed to heal human physiology. When they're finished you'll just sweat them out in your sleep. And best of all, they work fast." She wasn't convinced of the alien medicine but, in her condition, there was no other choice. She still had a job to do.

The pain was brief as the medic injected the microscopic healers into her leg. The reaction she felt was profound. The pain in her wounds dissipated almost immediately, allowing her to breathe easier with the alleviation around her ribs. Her broken leg jerked of its own accord as the bones were realigned and fused back together before the broken skin sealed up. Cautiously, the captain rotated her arm to check the broken collarbone and was amazed to see its full range of motion.

Two soldiers passed her by with a dead crewman between them. The guilt began to set in like an anchor in her gut. How had so many young died and yet she remained? There was no justice in that. Not only had she survived, but she had been brought back to full health in minutes. If only it could heal them, she wished. The two other survivors stood up to check their own wounds had healed properly. Lieutenant Worth and Lieutenant Commander Ramone put an arm on each other with a mournful look to their fallen friends.

"Thank you." Captain Fey touched the medic's arm before standing up, gaining the attention of every crewman. "This will not stand. I assure you our friends will not have died in vain. We will discover the truth behind Professor Jones and confront it with the full force of this ship. There will be time to mourn our fallen and pay them the respect they deserve, but right now we all have a job to do. Find somewhere quiet to put their bodies and those of the civilians who died as well. I need a new bridge crew to take over. Lieutenant Commander, I assume you can find the suitable crew?" He gave a sharp nod. "I want a casualty report ASAP, including civilians. I want six men posted outside the basement doors at all times. Under no circumstances are they to enter. I also want a permanent guard post outside the Gomar."

"But Captain, it can only be accessed with either Kalian or Esabelle present," Ramone stated.

"That's what we thought about the basement..." That was all she had to say.

"Captain?" Lieutenant Hiroshi entered the bridge. "It's confirmed that Professor Jones has left the ship. He killed the Novaarian contingent and had the *Gommarian* build him a new ship. From the specs, it looks like he used stealthware. The Conclave won't even know something left the ship."

After the first few months, the Novaarians had given them some space to move around their territory without being followed so closely. They may have given them a twelve light-year gap but they were always monitoring the *Gommarian's* status from afar. She had a feeling that gap would be closed after today.

Lieutenant Worth brought up the nearest holographic monitor and started to furiously type in commands.

"What is it, Lieutenant?" the captain inquired.

"If he had the *Gommarian* build the ship then it should have logged in the intended destination." The crew crowded around the lieutenant and his monitor.

"Where the hell is the Trantax system?" Ramone asked.

"Raalak space..." Worth had brought up the relevant star chart. Everyone turned to the captain for guidance.

"Somebody get onto communications; I need a secure link to the nearest Conclave vessel." She looked at the bloodied communications chair where Lieutenant Rodriguez had been stationed for so long. They were going to catch this bastard.

KALIAN KNEW it wasn't a good thing when the AI didn't say anything for a while. With his computing power, ALF could comprehend a billion thoughts in a second. It had been nearly a minute now since Kalian had informed him of Esabelle and filled him in on the last five months of training together.

"Do you trust her?" he asked finally.

"Yes, she's done nothing but help us. She taught us how to use the *Gommarian* and use Terran technology. Not to mention the surviving Gomar she locked up."

"She kept them alive?"

"Yes, we have to think of the future, ALF." He knew he was only echoing Esabelle's words, but he was starting to come around to her way of thinking. "Who knows what's really out there, hunting us *and* the Conclave? We might need twelve all powerful beings on our side."

"They're animals, Kalian!" ALF looked almost angry. "Each and every one of them is capable of mass genocide and Savrick's daughter is chief among them! She killed the most in control of that ship!"

"She had no choice." Kalian was surprised to hear Li'ara come to Esabelle's defence. Perhaps it was more to do with her dislike for ALF. "They disconnected her consciousness from reality and handed her mind over to the cube."

"It's true," Kalian continued. "She fought against the cube's influence and gave what's left of our species a home. I think you're just upset because the offspring of two Gomar didn't grow up to be a disaster. She's just as powerful as any Terran and she taught *herself*."

"It took her two hundred thousand years to learn control, in a *virtual reality*," ALF countered. "The Gomar were walking bombs *before* I implemented the Harnesses. Their children were even worse. I didn't have two hundred thousand years to just wait and see - people were dying."

"Either way," Telarrek stepped in, "the *Gommarian* cube is safe in the hands of the humans. The Highclave have not been made aware of its existence. After we have inspected this one we can return to the *Gommarian* for comparison. ALF continued to pace the cube, his artificial eyes taking every detail in. In reality, Kalian knew the armour device was scanning the cube while the hologram imitated life.

"And this, Esabelle, she told you the cube was influencing Savrick? How? I saw him on the battlefield; he was no different from the other Gomar, save his bloodlust, perhaps."

"When he found the cube on Hadrok," Kalian explained, "he cut his finger on the rock. I think that woke it up somehow." He reviewed the shared memory in his mind like stepping into a virtual reality. "After it activated, there was a hole in the middle. He put his arm inside and felt excruciating pain. I know that pain always stayed with him. Whenever the cube wanted something he could feel it."

"How do you know this?" ALF ignored the artefact completely as he approached Kalian.

"After Naveen..." ALF's expression told Kalian he understood.

"I was afraid of that. I bet you have some of hers after saving her life?" The artificial intelligence regarded Li'ara briefly. Both humans shared an awkward glance before Kalian continued.

"I have some of his memories, but they're not whole, they're fractured and displaced."

"So you think the *Gommarian* cube manipulated Savrick into starting the war?" ALF pondered his own question. "I suspected the involvement of a third party for a long time. The things Savrick knew, his armour, the *Gommarian*, the Eclipse missiles. Well, that explains why he stole the nanocelium..."

Something about that description jumped out at Kalian. "That was his first attack, wasn't it? On Hadrok when he was on his own, before the war."

"You have seen this memory?" ALF inquired.

"Not all of it. The cube tasked him with retrieving a canister of nanocelium. I remember his feelings; he knew it wasn't his own thoughts. Savrick *knew* he was being manipulated by it."

"He stole a container of un-programmed nanocelium, but not enough to make the *Gommarian* or even a single suit of armour." ALF looked back at the cube. "Unless these things are powerful enough to replicate and actually reproduce any technology they come into contact with..."

"If these cubes are so powerful and ancient," Li'ara pondered, "why did it only influence Savrick? Why not take him over completely? Or just use the *Gommarian* to wipe out every Terran without the need for the Gomar?"

"These are questions we can try to answer after examining the other cube," Telarrek replied. "The Highclave will be expecting a report soon. Should we perhaps consider revealing all the facts and work together, especially since a cube has been found within Conclave borders?"

"We can't risk it yet, Telarrek." Kalian rubbed his eyes, wondering how long it had been since he slept like a human. "They would take the *Gommarian* and who knows how they would react to ALF's existence."

Before anyone could reply, the cave shook from a distant explosion. Powdered rock fell from the ceiling like rain as cracks became visible in the walls.

"What was that?" Li'ara looked to Naydaalan standing guard at the entrance. Moments later the cave was rocked by another tremor, closer to their location. The sound of screams and gunfire echoed through the tunnels as Dr Taeril came running around the bend.

"We are under attack!" She burst into the cave, pushing past Naydaalan who disappeared into the connecting tunnel, staff at the ready. Her gaze quickly settled on ALF before Telarrek's towering form stepped between them. Kalian used the opportunity to scoop up the Terran device and deactivate the hologram.

"Who is attacking us?" the Novaarian demanded.

The doctor hesitated, trying to look past Telarrek at the unknown bearded man. "Who...?"

The rest of her question was drowned out by weapons fire only metres away from the entrance. Naydaalan rushed into the cave, blood dripping down his blue speckled face.

"Mercenaries!" he announced. "We have to get back to the *Dawnlighter*, now!"

"How did they get past the *Nova*?" Telarrek asked.

"I don't know but they have. We must leave!" Naydaalan swung back to the entrance, firing a bolt of Intrinium into a Laronian mercenary.

"Can't the *Nova* take them out from orbit?" Li'ara removed her own weapon, instinctively taking a step closer to Kalian.

"They won't risk destroying the artefact," Doctor Taeril explained, looking around for the mysterious bearded man. "But they will send down reinforcements," she added hopefully.

"Ilyseal..." Telarrek made for the entrance holding a weapon, removed from the depths of his robe. The group ran from the cave, returning to the maze of Trantax IV. Water dripped down through the pitted cavern as the storm swelled overhead. They moved through the rocky corridors, stopping every time to check the corners and peer through holes in the rock. Shadows dashed across the surface of the orange membranes with the promise of conflict all around them. Intrinium bolts flew overhead, filling the cavern with the smell of ozone and cries of death from both sides.

Naydaalan held up both of his right hands as the group was forced to stop. The corridor ahead was being blown to pieces by weapons fire from the left. They could hear the deep voice of a Raalak on the other side as he bellowed orders to his men.

"Find the human!"

"The Callic minerals are interfering with our scanners!" That was unmistakably the voice of a Nix.

"Then use your eyes!" The Raalak's heavy footfalls carried on down the parallel corridor. Naydaalan waved the group on, quieter now, creeping through the winding maze. Li'ara was never more than two feet away from Kalian, often holding him back to assess the path ahead. He caught her eye and gave her a look that questioned her protective role. She shrugged off the silent question and continued to stick to him like glue.

"Old habits, huh?" he whispered.

"Someone's got to keep you alive." They shared a smile before more gunfire broke out in an adjacent cavern. Stray bolts flew overhead knocking free the needle-like stalactites. Kalian pushed out his awareness becoming instantly aware of the group around him and the exact measurements between them. He could feel every molecule move as the broken stalactites plummeted towards them. In that moment, he knew one was on course to impale Dr Taeril in front of him. Kalian reacted instinctively with a telekinetic push, slamming the doctor with enough force to push her into Telarrek. As the two tumbled on together, Li'ara yanked Kalian's jacket, pulling him away from the falling rock.

The wall to their right collapsed completely under the barrage from above. Both humans were cast in darkness after the light fixtures were crushed between the crumbling rocks. There was too much debris to see their companions now. Kalian could still feel the steady glow of their molecules on the other side as they picked themselves up.

"Kalian?" Telarrek shouted.

"We're ok. Head for the entrance, we'll meet you at the *Dawnlighter!*" The air crackled as the distortion around Kalian's hand coalesced until the darkness was banished by the blazing ball of plasma. He was careful to keep a telekinetic field around it to prevent the heat from burning Li'ara and himself. The stark light revealed a fresh cut above her right eye. He stepped closer, keeping the plasma at arm's reach, while tenderly wiping the blood away from her eye. The frequencies her brain constantly gave out fluttered under the proximity, but he made no comment.

"I'm ok..." She stepped away looking for her weapon on the floor. He held back from saying everything he wanted to, again. He wondered if there would ever be time. "Come on, we need to find another way out of this hell hole."

"Hold on, I want to try something." Kalian had got the idea from the glowing orbs. He held out the plasma, with his palm open, pointing it down the darkened corridor. Confident the miniature sun was confined to his field, he released the orb into the darkness using the telekinetic bubble to control its path.

"Nice trick," Li'ara commented. "You know I've got two orbs on me, right?" She indicated the two devices hanging from her belt.

"Right..." Kalian closed his mind around the super-heated matter and dissolved it. In the darkness that followed they both heard the footsteps ahead. Kalian could feel Li'ara hesitate as she retrieved an orb from its clip. Before he could push out and feel his surroundings, the entire maze was illuminated by a flash of lightning. Everything happened at once after that. The thunder covered the sound of the barrage of Intrinium that cut through the dark. Kalian half picked Li'ara up as he ran them both through the nearest wall, his telekinesis blowing the rock away as well as cocooning them.

Kalian picked himself up first, ripping his burning jacket off, torn by the stray bolts. They both reacted without speaking and simply fired their weapons into the dark, hoping to catch the attackers through the rock. Each enemy lit up in Kalian's mind giving him their location in the abyss. He concentrated his fire on each one, disintegrating the rock between them to find his mark. With every hit, their light went out in his mind.

The lightning increased overhead as the storm settled over the entire quarantine site. The thunder was deafening, with the rain picking up and the wind howling through the cracks above. The water was beginning to pool at their feet as the lightning hammered the ceiling. Kalian could feel more of the mercenaries converging on their location.

"Get down!" It was Li'ara's turn to save Kalian now. They both dived to the ground as the largest Intrinium bolt Kalian had ever seen flew over their heads. The explosion drowned out the storm, its destructive energies obliterating the wall behind them. The Raalak's heavy footfalls splashed through the water as every one of his four feet brought them closer together. This particular Raalak was a sight to behold. The top corner of his flat head was broken away like a rock that had been cracked open. His hard exterior was closer to gold than the usual pale grey Kalian was accustomed to. The armour seemed superfluous on top of what was already considered an impenetrable hide. More terrifying than his appearance was his weaponry. Either side of his head was a kinetic cannon attached to the armour plating running along his spine. The weapon he carried looked too heavy for any other species to lift, with a barrel the size of Kalian's head.

"Let's see what you humans are capable of!" His voice could easily match the pitch of the thunder.

"Run!" Li'ara dashed down the adjoining tunnel. Kalian stood his ground, firing every round of Intrinium he had. The bolts pinged off the armour, to the Raalak's amusement who simply took the hit, laughing as he did.

"Kalian, run!" Li'ara tugged his arm, pulling him to safety. They ran, firing blindly behind them as they ducked and weaved through the weapons fire that chased them. In a blur of movement, Li'ara disabled a Laronian mercenary that had the misfortune to run into them. After breaking his arm, she swiftly retrieved her Terran hilt from the base of her back and activated the nanocelium within. The blade shot up through the alien's rib cage and burst out of his collar bone.

Kalian leant against the wall and checked his gun; the holographic display on the side told him he only had ten rounds left. "I'm nearly out."

Li'ara put her boot on the dead Laronian and leveraged the blade out. With a quick adjustment to the settings, the blade reduced in size, making it more suitable for close combat. They were both drenched in soaking wet clothes, stained with blood and dirt.

"Maybe you should think about changing clothes." Li'ara eyed the pocket on Kalian's thigh. He chastised himself for not thinking of it sooner. Esabelle would have hit him around the back of the head by now. He was thinking like a human with the weapon in his hand.

I am the weapon...

The reaction was hard to see if you blinked. After slapping the device below his navel, the nanocelium erupted spreading across his body and converting his clothes like raw materials. Kalian felt the bold over-confidence that came with the exoskeleton. It clung to his body like a second skin with the thin plates overlapping one another down his arms and over his chest. The intricacy of the design was beautiful in the typical Terran way.

The weapon in his hand now had a very different purpose. He levitated it above his open palm before blasting it with a wave of electromagnetism. He felt the Intrinium become instantly charged like the engine of a star-ship.

"Time to run?" Li'ara had seen this effect before.

"Time to fight." Kalian flicked his wrist down the tunnel, sending the makeshift bomb into a cluster of incoming mercenaries. The explosion was a spectacular display of colours that removed eight lives from existence. It suddenly dawned on him that these were the first lives he had ever taken. He had been involved in the deaths of Savrick and Lilander but he hadn't actually been the one to kill them. Was this the consequence of having these abilities? Could he kill so easily without a care? To be evolutionarily superior was not to be God.

But it was so easy...

With a telekinetic field, he protected them both from the shock wave and flying body parts. Kalian closed his eyes, using his extra sense to build the surroundings in his mind. An increased sense of smell and hearing added to his outward awareness that detected every particle within the maze. He could feel the air pressure change on his skin as the mercenaries dispersed the air molecules with their movement. The maze was now mapped out in his mind's eye with every being inside it.

"Wait here." Kalian knew Li'ara wouldn't react well to that order. To avoid her stubbornness he sprinted through the rain with a speed she couldn't hope to match. In one smooth motion, he jumped into the wall to his right, stepping off with the agility of a cat before deftly hopping over the adjacent wall. With his increased strength the height was no problem, neither was the twenty foot plummet to the ground on the other side.

Every step had been calculated perfectly in his mind, leading to the surprise he gave the two mercenaries below. Using his own weight, Kalian gripped the back of their heads, driving them face first into the hard ground. Both Trillik were dead before they knew what had landed on them. He could feel the life-force of eleven more mercenaries in the maze, including the Raalak.

Being able to see them all meant the lightning flashes only served to his disadvantage now. The thunder could no longer mask their splashing steps from his heightened hearing. Two more came running around the corner without looking, too confident in their abilities to kill a primitive human. The air crackled and fractured around both of Kalian's open palms. He had already started to convert energy, drawing it into himself like a black hole until his hands glowed brilliant blue. Organic plasma swirled in a torrent of raw energy like a god holding a star in his hands.

The mercenaries got off two shots that were easily absorbed by the Terran armour across his chest. Using telekinesis to guide the super-heated matter, Kalian fired them at his attackers with the same velocity as any artificial weapon. The kinetic force propelled both mercenaries deep into the rock behind them. Their chest plates smouldered with an orange glow encircling the impact site. Kalian didn't stop to see the effects of his power but, instead, rushed off further into the maze. He jumped over walls and slid through cracks with deadly intent as he hunted his prey.

He decided to use speed instead of stealth in his next attack. A Laronian and two Shay were heading up the corridor away from him. With his speed, he knew he could get to them before they heard his footsteps over the thunder. Kalian relished the thrill of running so fast and feeling the rain against his skin. In moments he was on his prey.

Keeping in time with the thunder, Kalian jumped on the wall, hopping over the Laronian. In the same motion, he brought his body down in front of them, using his grip on the Laronian's head for balance. There was no time to react as he twisted the mercenary's neck, killing him instantly. Without stopping, he spun on the spot bringing his extended arm to bear down on the throat of the closest Shay. The wind-pipe was sent into spasm, shutting off the airway and sending the alien into shock. The Shay staggered back and dropped its gun in favour of gripping its throat in the hope of some relief that would never come.

The last mercenary had just enough time to aim its rifle at Kalian. Having already seen this scenario play out in his mind, it was a simple matter putting it into practice. Using one hand, he grabbed the end of the rifle and pointed at the choking Shay, just in time for the Intrinium bolt to end his suffering. To end it all, Kalian side kicked the remaining Shay square in the chest. He flew through the orange membrane and cracked his head on the spiky rock.

After some more acrobatics, Kalian found himself perched on top of a wall as he stalked a group of five mercenaries too scared to split up. They had obviously heard the deaths of their comrades and decided that sticking together would ensure their survival.

They were wrong.

Kalian looked at them and didn't just feel superior, he knew he was superior. There were a number of ways he could dispatch the group without even leaving the top of the wall, but he wanted to feel bones break on his armour. He told himself it was because they were threatening Li'ara's life and that he would do anything to protect her. But a voice deeper down told him it was because he liked it, the power. He tried to ignore the fact that it sounded like Savrick's voice.

With the flash of lightning, he jumped high into the air, with the perfect execution of strength. He landed in the middle of the five aliens and unleashed every combination he knew. He was able to hit three at any given time as he twisted around his opponents, using them as weapons and shields against their own. Blood soon mixed with the falling rain, turning the puddles red. He felt bones dislodge under the force of his attacks as he sent each of them flying into the dark.

"You are adept at fighting, human!" The Raalak stepped out of the darkened corridor, examining the dead bodies. "But you are no match for this..." He hefted the giant cannon, bringing it up to waist height.

"Alright, let's see whose is faster. Yours or mine." Kalian eyed the cannon while bringing up his hand in a representation of a gun, using his index finger and thumb as he had done, playing as a child.

The Raalak looked at the hand in disbelief. "I think you knocked your head, human. But have it your way."

They both raised their hands at the same time but no weapon was fired. With a speed no gun could match, Kalian flicked his thumb sending a narrow, concentrated surge of telekinesis between the Raalak's eyes. The hole through his head was clear to see as his incredible weight crumpled to the floor. Thick golden blood flowed out into the water.

Kalian looked around at the dead bodies, taking special note of the Raalak with a hole in his head. He closed his fist, the revelation of his power hitting him like an Intrinium bolt. It was survival, he told himself. Kill or be killed. Kalian rationalised that these were the only choices left to him, a position others had put him in. He was angry for a moment that he had been forced into using his abilities to this end. Esabelle had been teaching him how to use his powers, but she hadn't taught him why he should use them.

It didn't take him long to find Li'ara again, though she was typically not where he asked her to stay.

"Will you ever do as I ask?"

"Probably not. Did you find a way out?" She was carrying a bulky rifle taken from one of the dead mercenaries.

"Follow me." Kalian ignored her looks when they passed the bodies surrounding the dead Raalak. He was impressed and ashamed of himself all at once.

They soon found themselves on the surface, battling the elements. Flashes of Intrinium fire were visible in the distance in between the sporadic lightning strikes. The mercenary vessel had landed in the centre of the strip that led to the cave entrance. It had no markings or name stamped across the hull; it probably wasn't even registered with the local AI hub. But how had it got past the *Nova*? He looked up to see Conclave ships breaking through the thick storm. They were too late. The ground was littered with the bodies of security personnel and scientists. None had survived the attack. Kalian's keen ears picked up the sound of a cry from behind the ship, a Novaarian cry.

"Telarrek!" He set off at a run, only half noticing Li'ara dispatch a stray mercenary with her rifle. His worst fears were confirmed when he rounded the ship's protruding engine. Ilyseal crouched over the still form of Telarrek in the hammering rain.

THE HOLOGRAPHIC IMAGE of High Charge Uthor dominated the central space on the *Gommarian* Bridge. Captain Fey had never met a

Raalak in person and was quietly hoping the emitters were exaggerating his size.

"There must be something wrong with the comm, Captain, because I just heard you say that three Conclave citizens have been killed by a human and that this same human has left your ship using stealthware technology." Every syllable was like a rock-slide.

The captain tried not fidget in her seat, but she was aware of the dried blood on the armrest that hadn't been cleaned yet. "I'm afraid there's nothing wrong with the comm, High Charge. We're sending you the data now so you can see for yourself." She gave Worth the nod to transmit.

The Raalak appeared distracted for a minute while he reviewed the feed on his end. "How is this possible, Captain?"

Having seen Garrett first hand she knew just how unbelievable it was. She looked around at the bridge crew and realised there were some present who didn't even know what she was about to divulge. At this point, she saw no other option. Garrett was loose in the Conclave and they had no idea what the cube had done to him. If only Kalian or Esabelle had been onboard, they might have stood a chance.

"It's time to lay all our cards out on the table, High Charge." Uthor gave a puzzled expression at her terminology. "Something very dangerous has escaped this ship and we don't have the freedom to track it down and make things right. There is a device on this ship that is not Terran in origin. In fact, we don't know its origin or its true purpose. But we do know it's capable of influencing any who come into contact with it. I believe this is what has happened to Professor Garrett Jones. The thing you see in that feed is not Professor Jones, but something monstrous and very old." She gave Worth another nod and he transmitted all the data they had on the cube. "You should be receiving the information on it now." Uthor's stony expression gave nothing away. "There's more..."

She had thought long and hard about this while efforts were made to make contact with the High Charge. The Conclave was heavily based on trust, with every species divulging all their knowledge and history into a shared library. Captain Fey needed her people to have Conclave membership; it was the only viable future for their race. Perhaps now she could lay everything out and a real trust could be forged.

She went on to explain how Esabelle had saved them from the remaining Gomar and her own history with Savrick. She left nothing out, detailing the Rem-stores that housed the last of the Gomar onboard. Uthor stood patiently through the whole confession as she tried to clarify the role ALF had played in the creation of mankind and his presence at the Outpost. Even her knowledge of the Outpost was sketchy, but she knew enough.

"This cube, it is on the *Gommarian* right now?" Uthor finally asked.

The captain thought it was strange that this was his first question, but perhaps he was just prioritising immediate threats. "Yes. I've placed extra guards on it. No one will be getting near it, I assure you."

"You should have told us these facts a long time ago, Captain. I will speak to the Highclave as soon as possible."

"There's one other thing, High Charge. Our navigation system informs us that Garrett is heading to the Trantax system, but I have no idea why."

Uthor froze for a second before reacting. He turned away, looking at someone on his end. "What is the closest vessel to Trantax IV?" they didn't hear the reply. "Send a priority one. Use my array. They are to abandon whatever course they are on and rendezvous with the *Nova*." He turned back to Captain Fey. "Captain Fey, you will be receiving new coordinates momentarily. The *Gommarian* will travel to this location immediately without delay." That was an order. Before she could reply the image blinked from existence.

"They're gone, Captain," Lieutenant Worth said.

"Where do the coordinates take us?"

"Deep into the Ch'kara system from the looks of it." Worth expanded the data. "Ch'ket. We're going to the homeworld." There was some excitement in his voice before he remembered their circumstances. The captain could see the thrill of leaving Novaarian space and seeing a new alien civilisation, but she couldn't take her eyes off her blood-soaked chair.

"Set course, maximum yield."

NAYDAALAN PLACED his foot on the chest of the last dead mercenary and pulled his spear free. He dropped to his knees at Telarrek's side.

"I have failed you, father..."

Kalian was scanning the Novaarian's body with his Terran senses. Telarrek had taken a shot to the right of his chest and another to his left leg, but he was still alive. Even the rain couldn't keep the wounds from glowing with the heat of the Intrinium. Blood trickled onto his charred skin and down his robes.

"You could never fail me, Naydaalan." His voice was laboured, each word giving him pain. "Protect him," Telarrek gripped his son's hand. "Protect them all..." He lost consciousness after that. Kalian could still feel the life in him, or what was left of it.

"We need to get him to a Medder, now!" Kalian was already using his abilities to open the cargo bay on the *Dawnlighter*. He met Li'ara's eyes and told her it wasn't good with a look.

Ilyseal stayed with Telarrek in the med bay while Naydaalan piloted the ship at high yield, narrowly avoiding the incoming security ships. It wasn't long before the shining red hull of the *Nova* was in view.

"*Dawnlighter* to *Nova*, requesting emergency landing, we have injured onboard. I repeat we have injured onboard." Naydaalan's hands smeared his father's blood across the console.

"This is *Nova*, *Dawnlighter*. You have permission to land. Med team standing by. We're sending security teams down to the surface as we speak. From the looks of it, you're lucky to have even survived."

"How did they even get past you in the first place?" Naydaalan sounded pissed.

"We don't know, *Dawnlighter*. The Charge is kicking up a storm trying to find out. Your landing bay has been highlighted for you. You can't miss it; it's next to the human vessel."

The three of them exchanged curious glances.

"What human vessel, *Nova*?"

"It landed a few minutes ago. Distress signal. We weren't even aware they could leave that monster of a ship."

"I'm sending over our diplomatic codes, *Nova*. Let your Charge know we have humans onboard. They travel with the authorisation of the Highclave."

There was a long pause on the other end.

"Acknowledged, *Dawnlighter*." The comm went dead after that.

"Why do I get the feeling we're not welcome?" Li'ara said.

The cargo ship rotated on its thrusters, bringing into view the human vessel. It was unmistakably Terran in design with a structure made entirely from nanocelium.

"What the hell...?" Li'ara stood up to see over Naydaalan's tall frame.

Kalian followed her look of distress and found himself standing as well. There was a trail of bodies leading from the Terran ship to the Translift, all of them Conclave security in full shock armour and rifles.

"What could have done this?" Naydaalan asked.

There was no sign of any other bodies among the soldiers. Whoever attacked them did so with no casualties. A horrible thought crept into Kalian's mind. But there was no way this could be Esabelle. She wouldn't do this, she had no reason.

Then they saw *him*.

At first, he had blended in with the console in the distance, but now he made for the Translift. He was definitely human, but something wasn't right.

Kalian pushed his awareness out as well as improving his optic nerves. He couldn't believe what he was seeing, let alone perceiving the dense bundles of nanocelium that made up his body. "Garrett..."

Li'ara whipped her head back to look at him. "As in, Professor Garrett Jones?"

They both shared the same expression of dread.

"The cube." They ran out of the cockpit and made for the cargo bay. On the way past the med bay, Naydaalan told Ilyseal to get his father to the Medder. Kalian got the feeling that Naydaalan was replacing Li'ara as his new guardian.

The terminal at the Translift informed them that it had stopped at level 101 in the aft section of the *Nova*. They didn't wait for any entourage to appear or backup from another security team. They bundled into the Translift and set a repeat destination.

"What's on level 101 in a Nebula-class ship, Naydaalan?" Kalian asked.

The Novaarian hesitated while he thought over the internal plans of the ship. His golden eyes lit up when he remembered. "The Starrillium."

This was becoming a day for worst fears.

"What would he want with that?" Li'ara checked her rifle over.

"He could not do anything," Naydaalan explained. "The Starrillium has strict access; authorisation must come directly from the Charge."

"If he's been affected by the cube he shouldn't be underestimated." Kalian had a bad feeling about Garrett's intentions. The doors opened to more bodies strewn across the corridor. Not all of them security personnel, some were scientists or engineers. The level of violence actually shocked Kalian. One guard was permanently stuck with his back lodged in the ceiling, disrupting the lighting. Blood smeared the walls where Garrett had clearly put his hand through them. Necks were broken with some barely attached anymore.

"This is... primal almost." Li'ara carefully stepped over a Nix that had been torn in half.

"Savagery..." Naydaalan checked the pulse on a Novaarian sitting against the wall. His touch caused the body to slide down, leaving a blood trail from the back of her head across the wall. A scream in the distance gave them speed, Kalian easily taking the lead. The chamber that housed the Starrillium door was cathedral in size, and Kalian knew how big it was *inside*. To his dismay, the thick circular door was already open. It had only opened enough to let a person through though, as if the servos were acting against their will. One look at the control panel gave some explanation.

"What is that?" Naydaalan approached the infected screen. Black tendrils had penetrated the glass and interlaced across the surface like the roots of a plant.

"Don't touch it!" Kalian warned. They could hear rushing footsteps coming from the Translift now. "Naydaalan, you have to warn them about this stuff. They can't be allowed to touch it."

"I am coming with you," he replied defiantly. He had taken his father's words seriously.

"If you don't keep them out, more people will die. You've seen what he's capable of."

Naydaalan hesitated, looking back at the approaching troops. He turned to face the soldiers giving Kalian his answer.

"Don't even think about it." Li'ara was already walking into the Starrillium chamber, her rifle raised.

"As if you'd listen to me."

The Starrillium was identical to the one he had seen on the *Valoran*. The sphere was easily the size of any stadium with thousands of raised circles lining its metallic surface. Most of these circular holes were connected to massive tubes and wires that attached to the chamber walls. It was eerily silent for something that contained the most powerful force in the universe. It was hard to believe that he was only metres away from a blazing artificial star.

"Where is he?"

Li'ara's question was answered by Garrett himself. He dropped down from above the door, landing with a hand on each of them. He was quick and strong. Without pausing, he launched both of them to opposite sides of the chamber. Kalian's armour took the brunt of the impact but he knew Li'ara would not be so lucky. Garrett was on him before he could even get to his feet. Kalian was picked up by the throat and thrust into the console against the wall. His grip was reminiscent of the Beast.

Kalian instinctively tried to pry his fingers away but Garrett unleashed a barrage of punches to his gut. His attacks never paused. As Kalian dropped to the ground Garrett placed a hand on his face and pushed him into the wall again. He dropped to his knees and spat blood, his vision blurring. The next attack was halted by a series of Intrinium bolts slamming into Garrett's back. Li'ara was using her sidearm. Her right arm looked dislocated. Flesh and clothes exploded from his body, but the effect seemed to only irritate him.

Kalian's vision cleared up in time for him to see Garrett approaching Li'ara. The threat to her awoke something in him. The organic plasma flew from his hand, catching Garrett in the back and the leg. It dropped him to one knee but didn't kill him. Instead, the holes in his body began to knit back together with fine strands of nanocelium. The smile he gave Kalian was one of wicked malevolence. It was unnerving.

His speed was hard to track as Garrett fled the chamber leaving them to live. They both heard the soldiers cry out as he pushed his way past with brute force.

"Are you alright?" Kalian's voice was hoarse from Garrett's grip.

"My arm's in a bad way. What about you?"

"I'll survive. Why did he leave?" Kalian walked over to her, concern showing for her arm.

"Why was he even here in the first place?" Kalian looked around realising that was the better question. It was answered by the sounds coming from the Starrillium. The sphere began to hum for the first time as flashes of lightning shot across the surface. The hair on Kalian and Li'ara's skin stood on end from the charging static electricity in the air.

"What's happening?" Kalian looked to the console on their right and saw the cause. More of the dark tendrils had infected the terminal, digging deeper into the internal systems. The pangs of electricity increased, striking the walls around the sphere and showering them with sparks. The metal coating strained under some new pressure as the structure began to expand and contract. One by one the giant cables violently disconnected from the cube, thrashing like dead snakes. A viscous multicoloured liquid poured out of the end, covering the floor.

"He's overloading the Starrillium!" Li'ara grabbed Kalian's arm and pulled him to the opening in the door. "We need to get out of here, Kalian! If the shell breaks..."

"It'll vaporise the ship from the inside." Kalian knew then that running was futile. He could feel the energy soaring through the technology around him. The internal force-fields had been tampered with; it was only a matter of time. He looked at Li'ara and knew she would never agree to what he knew needed to be done. "We need to get back to the *Dawnlighter*, now!" The second she passed through the door Kalian took a step back.

"Kalian?" Li'ara turned and dashed back for him.

"I'm sorry..." He held up his hand and clenched his fist, causing the door to fit back together with a resounding *boom*. He placed a hand on the door, knowing he would never see her again.

But she will live.

He turned on the Starrillium, summoning as much courage as he had in him. He had to do this; he had to give it his all. Whole sections of the sphere were crumpling as the internal gravity of the star began to eat its way out. An unusual pressure formed in his ear before he heard ALF's voice.

"Are you ready for this?" The nanocelium in the exoskeleton had formed a new structure behind his head and curved into his ear.

"I have to be. It'll kill every life onboard." Kalian centred himself in the middle of the chamber, directly in front of the Starrillium. All the cables had disconnected now, their liquid contents flowing past his feet.

"You're going to need to find somewhere inside your mind where you can stay. You need to switch everything else off; you can't afford to feel pain. This is going to be the most exhausting thing you've ever done, Kalian. Remember, when you feel like giving up - *she* dies." It wasn't the first time the artificial intelligence had tried this tack to help him survive.

"Get out of my head." With that, the nanocelium withdrew back into his collar. He expanded his awareness one last time and felt Li'ara banging on the door as security personnel pulled her away.

At once the noise stopped for a second as the miniature lightning storm came to a halt. In that same moment, Kalian brought up the strongest telekinetic field he could muster. It simultaneously surrounded him while also grounding him to the spot. He would have to contend not only with the unfettered heat and blinding light but also the gravity.

Once he was secure he immediately threw a field around the sphere before the ferocious implosion. The sound was sucked out of the room in the same instant the light wiped out every shadow. Like an unshackled god the star blazed with raw energy. He almost lost it in that first second alone. The light instantly burned out his eyes leaving burnt craters of searing agony. The exposed skin on his face and hands were at the mercy of the heat. He realised then that the radiance of the star could never have been prepared for. A moment too late he disconnected his pain receptors and pushed into his defences. The heat was kept at bay but the receptors in his skin told him that he was still burning, just slowly. He would be lucky if his suit didn't cook him from the inside.

In those faltering seconds, the star had burst beyond his field and lashed out at the chamber with solar flares. The room was becoming a giant microwave as the radiation exploded into every crevice. He concentrated on the shape of the star and continued to build on the wall around it. He had to trust that the engineers were finding another way to shut it down while he contained it.

The floor around him was melting and he realised he was on his knees, his hands out at his side channelling his power. He shut off every sense he had, cutting off the smell of burning skin and hair that had reached his nostrils. Heeding ALF's word he began to burrow deeper into himself, a place he couldn't feel the stress his body was under. He was seeing the room through his mind's eye, with his awareness pulsing through every particle. He didn't want to think about the state his eyes and skin were in. In those moments he felt almost ethereal, his corporeal body becoming a memory with his life-force surging around the star.

The door behind him was becoming convex, slave to the gravity as the unyielding force pulled it from the servo motors. Kalian screamed in his head as he focused more and more on the star. The more power he put into the shield, the more he lost his own defences. There would be nothing left of him by the time he was finished. He made peace with that thought, knowing that he would die saving so many, saving *her*.

Time had no meaning anymore. He didn't know if he had been containing the star for a minute or his entire life. Kalian felt his energy ebbing as the star fought to be free. That safe place inside his mind began to slip away with his concentration, the pain returning. Molten metal fell from the ceiling like a waterfall as it poured over his tele-kinetic field, weakening him more. He could feel the heat and radiation pulsing through the gaps in the star's field and wreaking havoc beyond the chamber. He no longer had the energy to find Li'ara inside the ship; he could only hope Naydaalan had pulled her to a safe distance.

He thought of her to try and regain his focus but found it hard to recall her face or even her voice. What was he doing? Why was he here? He wasn't allowed to fail but he couldn't remember why. His mind began to wander with exhaustion, causing his personal field to falter. The wave of fire eviscerated another layer of flesh bringing his return to the torturous present. This was it; he had finally reached the end of his abilities, he could push himself no further. The star continued to shine as the protective wall he placed around it wavered.

He was going to die.

THE STORM on Trantax IV continued to rage as Garrett dragged the cube through the dirt. He kicked the bodies of the dead soldiers out of the way. They had tried to stop him from entering the cave system but underestimated his power.

No!

The thought repulsed him. It had felt like his own but he regained enough consciousness to know it couldn't be him. Still, his body waded through the blood and dirt as the rain hammered his infected skin. He screamed in his mind, trying to pull against the will that pushed on. The entity that possessed him stumbled, losing its grip on the cube. He dared to hope.

It is no use fighting us.

His mother's image confronted him in the void again. Her pleasant smile was no comfort to him as it only reminded him of the twisted being that used her memory like a puppet. He looked through his eyes again to see his body strengthening its grip around the cube's edges.

"Why are you doing this?" He thought about the chaos he had wrought on the starship. That Starrillium was going to rupture and when it did everyone onboard would die, including Kalian and Li'ara. His mother slowly circled him like a shark assessing its prey.

We will locate this biological anomaly, in time, and we will eradicate it.

Garrett looked at himself, grasping the entity's meaning.

"You mean me? You're trying to find *me*?" what was it about his continued existence inside his subsumed body that troubled the alien so much? How could it take over so much but not his subconscious? Or was it his cognitive synapses? The soul perhaps? Whatever it was, it certainly irked the entity.

The image of his mother vanished, leaving him alone again. With his enhanced strength Garrett was now approaching the Terran vessel, pushing the cube easily through the lightning strikes that were attracted to its surface. He had no idea why the entity had retrieved the cube in the first place. He could see and feel its actions, but its intent was hidden from him.

Movement to the left caught his attention. A Laronian soldier was crawling through the mud, a nearby rifle his motive. The apparent threat gave the entity no alarm as he continued to plough through the other bodies towards the ship. At the last second, with a quick exertion of strength, Garrett lifted the cube just enough to raise it above the Laronian's prone form. The thunder masked the sound of his head being crushed under the weight.

The feeling of regret seemed too small to describe how Garrett felt about his previous curiosity. How many deaths was he responsible for now?

EIGHT

Their entrance hadn't been as inconspicuous as Esabelle would have liked. Disabling the automated barrier to allow them entrance had been easy, but she had underestimated the scanners thereafter. The connecting walk-bridge had detected their false skins and deactivated them with a laser-guided EMP. At least now she didn't have to hold back by being sneaky. Now she could finally exercise her mind. Sparring with Kalian was fun, but they both had to hold back.

"You need to get across that bridge before they seal the main building off!" Ch'len's voice came through their earpiece.

They sprinted across the long walkway like salmon swimming upstream. The alarms, combined with their human exterior, had terrified the employees traversing the distance to and from the main building. With the door already descending from the ceiling, everyone was jostling to reach the car park. Most gave them a wide berth as they ran the opposite way, with only a few too clumsy to get out of the way. Roland was more than happy to push them out of the way with violent glee.

When they finally got some space the brilliant view returned through the glass walkway. They could see the rest of Clave Tower sprawling beneath them from their dizzying height. Thousands of vehicles flew in every direction as the AI controlled the flow of traffic between the floating archipelagos.

Roland slowed down as the door fitted into place, blocking their path. Esabelle had no intention of slowing down. Extending her arm at the last second, she pushed every molecule between her and the door, condensing them into a telekinetic barrage. The unseen force slammed into the door and blew it from the hidden servo-motors in the wall. The metal slab continued along its momentum for another twenty feet on the other side, scraping across the polished floors. The frame around the doorway was bent out of shape as they passed through into the stark atrium.

"I was just about to do that..." Roland eyed the broken door.

Esabelle smiled at his humour, feeling the adrenaline rushing through her veins. She revelled in her power like a bird set free to fly. Had she grown up on Albadar, or any other Terran planet, she would have used her abilities with the same reflexes she used to breathe. Being around so many inferior species, including the less evolved humans, she was forced to keep her natural talents in check so as not to scare them. With her thoughts wandering, Esabelle reminded herself of the seriousness of their situation. She had to get to the bottom of this conspiracy.

They crossed the atrium, keeping a close eye on the employees that ran for cover. It seemed the door had crushed the only guard on its way into the room. The twitching legs of a Shay could be seen poking out from underneath. The panel next to the row of Translifts indicated that they were on the sixty-fifth floor.

"We need to get up to level 202." Esabelle waved her fake Novattoo across the scanner to call the lift. Thankfully they hadn't been deactivated with the holo-skin.

"That Translift won't get you there," Ch'len explained. "Any level past 101 can only be accessed by an executive lift on the ninety-ninth floor."

"Let me guess. It's heavily guarded?" Roland pulled both of his Tri-rollers from their holsters.

Ch'len laughed, "If I were you, I'd worry about the guards between you and that lift. Speaking of which-"

"There are eight coming up in the Translift." Esabelle could feel the exotic biology of their alien bodies. Each one a part of the universe and yet separate in the only way an organic being can be. She didn't believe that. It was a teaching of the Terran that all life was part of the universe, but one's own intelligent sense of self made them apart from it: as if being able to comprehend the universe made her, or anyone else, superior. She always found it to be a strange teaching for a Terran, considering they could actually see that every being is connected to the cosmic soup of the universe. It was the greatest example of Terran humility combined with their bloated egos.

She believed that when anyone died their energy simply took on a different role in the galaxy. And she was ok with that. It certainly made what she was about to do next a lot easier. The air crackled around her hands as it distorted with every colour of the spectrum. Two organic plasma balls bloomed in her palms. She quickly ended the reaction when Roland put his hand on her arm.

"Wait a minute! Are you sure about this? Those aren't Protocorps mercs in there. If we start killing Conclave security in swathes, there's gonna be consequences."

Esabelle couldn't believe the words of warning coming from the bounty hunter. "I didn't know you cared."

"Well, it would make my life a lot easier if I didn't have to hide my good looks on every planet."

"You think that if we kill some guards, the Highclave won't grant humanity membership?" Esabelle could feel the power inside her desperate to be unleashed.

"I don't think it'll help!"

"Well, what do you suggest?" She purposefully looked at his raised weapons. His plan didn't seem much different from hers.

"You've got all those powers and you can't think of a better way to *incapacitate* some guards?"

"Big word from the Neanderthal."

"You're lucky you've got all those powers." Roland waved his Tri-roller in mock threat.

"What's a Neanderthal?" Ch'len asked.

"Shut up, Len!" they both retorted.

It was that same moment the Translift gently *pinged*, signifying its arrival.

The guards inside didn't even have a chance to raise their weapons before Esabelle attacked. Using one hand she presented them with her palm and created a light brighter than any star. It was the same principle as creating an organic ball of plasma, except she simply focused on the light emission instead of the heat. Roland couldn't help but shield his own eyes at the intensity. Esabelle stepped to the side, making a sweeping motion with her arm as she did. The contents of the lift were evacuated in a flood of bodies as all eight guards were telekinetically forced out. Each one clattered across the floor, tumbling over one another in a heap of red bodies and armour. Most of them were still covering their eyes from the light, which had no doubt burned out their retinas.

With Roland still trying to blink out the pretty colours in his vision, Esabelle grabbed him by the jacket and pulled him into the Translift. She verbally commanded the lift to take them to level ninety-nine.

"A little warning next time!" Roland massaged his eyes with a deep rub.

Esabelle smiled at his discomfort before sending a concentrated burst of electromagnetism into the lift speakers, ending the pleasant music on constant repeat. Her mind wandered for a minute as she thought back to the lower levels of Clave Tower. She had seen some-thing, someone. They were mixed into the crowd but clear to see as the static figure in dark rags and a hood, concealing their identity. It wasn't one of Revus' men; she had known where they were at all times. This was someone else. Before Roland had interrupted her, she thought she had almost felt a connection and dreamed to hope, but the figure had disappeared.

"You've got a problem." Ch'len's warning came only a second

before the Translift stopped moving at level seventy-two. "Thanks to your *unique* DNA they can track you anywhere in the building. From the looks of it, they've only stopped your lift, but guards are being relocated to your floor."

"Doesn't the chupachup ever have good news?" Esabelle tried other options on the terminal.

"Hey!" Roland sounded disrespected. "He's *my* chupachup." They both ignored the angered response from the Ch'kara.

Esabelle slammed the unresponsive terminal with her palm. "It's dead." Esabelle pushed her awareness out to get a feel for their surroundings. She was shocked to find the level of oxygen depleting with every breath as the air was quickly being replaced with carbon dioxide.

"They've shut off the air," Ch'len confirmed over the comm. "If you're quite finished insulting me, perhaps you could find a way out of that death trap?"

"Can't you override any of their systems?" Roland was detaching something from his belt.

"I'm trying," Ch'len replied. "Hacking into their cameras is one thing, but it seems the entire building is being directly run by the main AI construct. Every time the *Rackham* circumvents one system, it disables its own control and switches to a backup. And if it is the main AI controlling it, there's probably no end of backups just waiting to take over."

"Then we go up." Roland gestured to the emergency panel above Esabelle's head. He continued to place what she now recognised to be some kind of homemade bomb, directly across the parting on the door. Without clearance from security, the emergency panel refused to budge for her. With a flick of her fingers, the servo-motors inside were disconnected and the panel slid aside with a little telekinetic push.

"We should probably go before they decide to open this door." Roland was all gentleman-like and climbed up first.

"I thought you were against killing the Conclave personnel?"

"It's designed to blow inwards. A few might get a little frazzled but the lift will take the brunt of it, so you might want to get out of there."

With the agility and grace a human could only wish for, Esabelle climbed onto the Translift roof. Using anti-gravity technology, the lifts were flying by in every direction at great speed. Some traversed parallel to their own while others travelled horizontally, disappearing through corresponding holes in the wall. Esabelle quickly counted the floors and found the door they required above.

"They're almost at your location." Ch'len's words were just audible over his constant eating.

Esabelle peered over the lip of the Translift and saw another one on its way up. She didn't have time to explain her plan to Roland.

"Do you trust me?" She ignored his cautious expression and wrapped her right arm around his waist. At the same time, she altered the polarity of her body, making herself the perfect magnet for the passing Translift. Roland's yelp was engulfed by the sound of rushing air as the pair suddenly flew upwards with half of Esabelle's body stuck to the side of the adjacent lift. She simultaneously kept a telekinetic cocoon around her joints so her arm wouldn't be ripped from its socket.

When the lift stopped, three floors beneath their intended level, they both climbed on top and made for the ladder built into the wall. Roland had to jump for it at the last second before the lift descended again.

"No boom?" Esabelle had expected the explosion.

"They're standing outside. From the looks of it they have scanners," Ch'len offered. "They're not stupid."

Roland hung onto the ladder with one hand, while using his other to operate the flexi-screen built into the sleeve of his jacket. "Plan B it is..." The ladder shook as the lift below exploded. The top half was blown completely off, incinerated instantly, causing the chamber to fill with black smoke and ash.

Esabelle used her telekinesis to part the doors as they reached level ninety-nine. She could feel the Shay guard on the other side, waiting for them, his pheromones permeated with fear.

Roland reacted first however, firing a bolt of brilliant blue Intrinium into the Shay's chest. Esabelle hopped onto the level as the Shay staggered and fell, disappearing through the smoke.

"Where to from here, Len?" Roland asked.

Esabelle could see the military training in the way Roland moved and assessed his surroundings. He may be a degenerate, but there was no disguising his background.

When the bounty hunter had first entered the *Gommarian*, during the attack at Corvus, Esabelle had reviewed his file downloaded from the UDC database. When the Gomar had first arrived at Earth, she had been instructed to jam all communications and scan all available data. There had been no firewall strong enough to keep her out in that single scan, and in so doing she had everything ever recorded about the agent, Roland North. She had, of course, kept this to herself; she saw no reason why everyone needed to know his business. Esabelle felt sorry for him in a way. He had fallen into a dark hole in his morally questionable line of work and became reliant on alcohol to get him through every mission. She recalled the last mission he had been assigned as an agent of the Earth government.

It had not gone well.

Esabelle looked at him for a moment and wondered if his actions on Europa kept him awake at night. In that regard she was thankful her abilities allowed her to forgo sleep. She could be kept awake for eternity if she was forced to see all the Terran and humans she had been party to killing.

"You need to take a left and then it's down the corridor on the second right. But I'm sure the *superhuman* has already told you it's heavily guarded. I think they know where you're going."

"His description is pretty accurate, actually," Esabelle quipped.

"Well then perhaps you should take point, *superhuman*." Roland nodded to the corner on the left.

Esabelle led them around the next corner, pushing her awareness out through the walls as they walked. She could feel the cluster of biological molecules mixed in with the sophisticated technology that made up the group of Shay guards.

"You might want to cover your ears." She could feel the explosive device in her mind, every particle mapped out like blueprints. She used telekinesis to turn the switch on the top of the grenade without even seeing the group of guards.

The explosion burst into the corridor, causing a concussive wave to tear through the walls and ceiling. The whole corridor flickered like something out of a nightmare with body parts littering the floor. Roland didn't look amused.

"I did warn you..."

"You'll forgive me if I can't hear you anymore!" Roland rotated his jaw while poking his ear.

Esabelle's eardrums were already repairing themselves at her command.

"Okay, I've managed to take control of the executive Translift. But I have no idea how long it's going to last so you need to hurry and get up there fast!" Ch'len sounded distressed but Esabelle assumed it was more to do with his shortage of food than their dire situation.

KUBRACKK SAT FORWARD to get a better picture out the viewport. The *Blade* had docked in the bay of Galactic Groceries, two kilometres away from Protocorps Headquarters. The hanging towers were swarming with emergency responders and security patrol ships above. He hadn't seen this much excitement inside Clave Tower since the Gomar attacked the Highclave. Whatever was going on in there was serious. With all the new security measures put in place, they were sure to clamp down fast on any internal attack, especially on something as big as Protocorps. Kubrackk couldn't imagine what had driven the humans to launch an assault on them.

"Typical humans, crazy as they are ugly..." he commented.

Spelnar was sitting at the station behind him, going through the local news feeds. The Trillik still had spots of Lole's blood on his arms and face. It had taken him two hours to clear up the mess. The Tularon's body was now stored in a secret compartment in the cargo bay, ready to be disposed of when they weren't within a parsec of the nearest patrol ship.

"It's weird, boss. There's nothing on any feed about what's going on. Not a single report." Spelnar had yet to make eye contact with Kubrackk since the shooting. The Novaarian browsed through the array on the main console and checked for himself. He couldn't believe that an attack on one of the biggest corporations wasn't being reported on by every channel.

"Well they've either been told not to report on it, and I can't imagine who has the power to command that, or something is redirecting the flow of information and they don't even know this is happening. But that's even less likely." There was nothing powerful enough to control the flow of information in Clave Tower. "Get Revus back on the line and see if he knows anything."

Kubrackk was loath to speak with the Brenine again. Shooting Lole had felt good, but Revus deserved a hole in the head as well, if not more. He chastised himself for not taking better precautions with his crew. He should have suspected Revus would have something on him; he had his fingers in everything and everyone who passed through that bar of his. There were other Bounty Clave associations he preferred to visit himself, free of prying eyes.

"I can't." Kubrackk could hear the worry in Spelnar's voice. Lole's death had apparently sent quite the message. "The link won't connect." His nimble fingers danced across the console. "We can't receive any transmissions either. The entire array is down!"

Kubrackk rolled his eyes, "Then why aren't you outside fixing it?"

"It's not us. I checked it back on Shandar. The whole area has gone dark."

Kubrackk didn't like the sound of that. What could disrupt all the communications on such a large scale inside the tower? He looked out again to see patrol ships taking up positions next to every bridge connecting to the central building.

"How in a Raalak's pit are we going to get in there now?" the Novaarian growled. North was going to get away again, he knew it.

"There's a delivery bay on the other side, part of the main building," Spelnar explained. "We'd need authentic authorisation to pass through but..." The Trillik went quiet.

"But what?" Kubrackk demanded. If there was a way in, he would take it.

"I don't have the software required to pull off that kind of job. Getting through the perimeter checks was easy compared to the level of security Protocorps uses. I mean come on, that building houses the central AI. They use more security than the Highclave."

"So what you're saying, Spelnar, is that you're of no more use to me?" Kubrackk rested his hand lightly on the handle of his Quad-roller.

"But I know a guy, right here in the tower!" Spelnar was halfway out of his seat already, his twin-tail sticking tight to his body.

"Get it done or don't bother coming back!" Returning to the view, the scarred Novaarian sat back in his head-rest and watched the pandemonium play out. He'd be damned if he'd let Conclave security get to his prey first.

Elondrasa looked out as the surrounding windows began to dim, simulating the setting sun in an environment that never experienced a sunrise or set. The Highclave private meeting chamber was situated beneath the Clave Spire, where all public meetings were held. The one-way glass revealed the true magnificence of the capital around them; the great lakes and parks with trees from every world lining the walkways. The splendour of the artificial interior was a true testament to what their races could achieve together.

Marvelling at their creation, she lost track of Nu-marn's words. He had been voicing his concerns again about allowing the humans access to the Trantax relic. She knew he must be feeling the pressure from his own private backers in Protocorps; they were close to finalising the deal to take over the project on behalf of the government. It was a good idea, she agreed - the injection of money from the private sector would only speed up the research into the ancient cube.

"Protocorps will have to wait, Nu-marn." Even sitting down, Brokk towered over them in his seat, designed especially for a quadruped. "Until an agreement is struck, that site is under Highclave control. You were outvoted on the matter, move on."

Elondrasa tried to hide the smile creeping up her face; the Raalak was hard to argue with.

"I agree with, Brokk," Lordina added. "The relic is ours for now. What I do not agree with is giving two humans such free rein. Especially Kalian Gaines. He is dangerous."

"There is a connection between the relic and the Terran," Ch'lac replied. "They were able to unlock the secrets of The Wall; they may shed light on the cube as well."

"This is pointless," Elondrasa stated. "The humans are already on Trantax IV. They are being closely monitored by Ambassador Telarrek and the entire planet is being guarded by the *Nova*."

"We all saw the events that took place on Naveen," the Shay continued his protest. "Do you really think the *Nova* could withstand an attack if the Terran throws a tantrum? Look outside for goodness sake! The capital is still undergoing repairs from the damage they caused."

"Human," Brokk corrected. "You are aware of the facts, Nu-marn. Kalian was born a human. He has never been a part of the Terran culture or the Gomar for that matter."

"Facts? Everything we know is from what he told us. The female and he are the only ones who really know what happened inside that outpost."

"Their statements have been vouched for by Ambassador Telarrek," Elondrasa said.

The Shay councillor's expression said everything he thought about the old Novaarian charge. After his secret observation of the humans had become public knowledge, Elondrasa had been forced to call in a lot of favours and make a lot of promises to keep Telarrek in a good light. Thankfully High Charge Uthor had stood up for him and presented the idea of keeping him on as liaison to the humans.

"They are unnatural by their very creation; I do not trust them completely, either." Ch'lac subconsciously adjusted the controls on his chest panel, tweaking the shield that contained the atmospheric gas. "But we do not know enough about the Terran or the Gomar to make an appropriate assessment. They are a potential threat, but if what they say is true then they no longer exist. But by Kalian Gaines' very existence, he is proof that such a race of beings may once again thrive, given the chance. Our races have committed genocide in the past and I agree that we must ensure the survival of this one. But I also agree that we should use them to learn more about their creators. They may be the only ones who can."

Elondrasa nodded her approval at the Ch'kara's words. "The humans are an unknown factor at present. But without a little trust from us, our races will never co-exist."

The doors parted as ten elite guards piled into the room, breaking off into twos as they found their designated councillor. Xydrandil emerged from within the throng, his pincer legs visible as he quickly strode in. Before he even spoke, the guards were physically picking up the councillors and ushering them to the door.

"We are going into lockdown," the Nix announced. The rough hands of a Raalak grabbed Elondrasa by the arm, while a Laronian closed the space on her right.

"What's happening?" She recognised this particular protocol from the drills they had rehearsed. It had been revised since the Gomar attack on the capital; Elondrasa knew she was only seconds away from being separated from her other councillors, as they were escorted separately to the *Marillion* on the outer edge of the solar system.

"Protocorps Headquarters has been attacked, by humans..." Xydrandil walked ahead of them until they were taken down different paths. The Nix continued on the same route as her.

She had one last glimpse of Nu-marn's face - *You should have listened to me.* The Novaarian felt a pang of anger towards the humans for this. Not only had they shattered any hope of trust but they had made her look like a fool.

"How could they be here? The last report had them entering the Trantax system."

"We are still gathering all the information, Councillor. From the images released by Protocorps, we only know that it is *not* Kalian Gaines or Li'ara Ducarté." They had already been bundled into a secure vehicle and put on a priority route out of the tower.

Protocorps...

It couldn't be a coincidence that Protocorps had an interest in the same thing the humans were currently investigating. But why attack the corporation in the first place? Protocorps' involvement begged a deeper look, she felt.

ESABELLE USED a telekinetic shield to keep the blood spray off her face. Roland slowly removed the Terran blade from the guard's neck and wiped it clean on the Protocorps uniform. For a human, his reflexes were commendable. It was only moments ago that particular guard had his rifle to her head. Of course, she had been aware of his position in the room and had already planned a way to dispatch him. It felt good to be surprised by a human though; so far she had found them all to be quite predictable.

"There's an internal grav-pillar on the other side of the lab, in front of you. That should get you to level 202." Ch'len had only managed to get them as far as level 186 before the AI took back control. The small cluster of guards on this level had only taken seconds to deal with. As far as Esabelle could tell, Roland's combat style was somewhere between finesse and that of a brawler. He had some exotic moves that he often followed up with a simple headbutt or loose punch.

The doors to the lab refused to part for them, even with a fake Novattoo. Without breaking her stride, Esabelle mentally commanded the doors to explode into the lab beyond. The crash was met with screams of terror from the scientists and engineers inside as they scrambled for safety behind workstations and shelves.

The sunlight was dimmed through the wall of glass to their left. At this height, they could clearly see the planetary rock that formed the roof of the capital planet. They walked quickly, ignoring the hysterical looks, and made for the grav-pillar. A large shadow beyond the glass gave them pause before they designated the desired level. The shadow swung across the lab, blocking out the sun, to reveal a patrol ship bristling with forward-facing cannons.

"Get down!" Roland's cry came too late as the glass was blown to a million pieces. Equipment and benches were flung to the back of the room as racing globules of green goo powered through the lab. The occupants were instantly ensnared by the thick slime, holding them in place against the walls and workstations. Some of the heavier equipment proved to be deadly flying objects that most certainly killed more than one scientist. Esabelle felt their electromagnetic energy wink out of existence.

Roland fired his Tri-roller blindly in the direction of the patrol ship, with a stream of profanities accompanying every shot. Esabelle stuck her hand up and keyed in the level for the grav-pillar. If they didn't get off this floor soon, they would be overwhelmed by rein-forcements; she could feel the twelve soldiers inside the patrol ship readying for an assault. She pulled her hand back just in time before a ball of green goo splattered against the panel and hardened in place.

"Go!" Esabelle grabbed Roland by the arm and thrust him into the open portal of the grav-pillar. She dashed in after him and gave in to the anti-gravity that pulled her vertically upwards. She could see Roland above her, flying by the open doors of every level.

"Oh no... Hold onto something!" Ch'len's warning came just before the anti-gravity switched off. They managed another ten feet before their momentum ran out. Roland caught the bottom of the open portal with both hands, kicking out his foot for Esabelle to grab a hold. With one hand she managed to get a good grip on his foot as he used his free leg to hook under her other arm.

"I've got you." The strain was audible in his voice.

"How comforting..."

"The AI disabled the grav-pillar!" Ch'len yelled down their earpiece.

"You don't say..." Roland struggled to shift his weight. Esabelle didn't hesitate as she used Roland's hanging body like climbing frame. He tried to object when her boot was firmly planted in his face.

"Come on." With a small nudge of telekinesis, Roland was already back on his feet and rubbing the dirt off his face. Having exited the lift they were now standing in front of a long opulent desk with Proto-corps written in large glowing letters on the wall behind. This was the executive level. Anyone who was actually important to the company had an office on this floor, including Sav-del Tanek. Strong electromagnetic frequencies were emitting from behind the empty desk. Esabelle focused and knew there to be a young female Shay, cowering under her own desk.

Roland calmly removed a Tri-roller from his holster and rapped it against the shiny surface of the desk.

"Anybody home...?" He gave Esabelle a knowing smile and perched on the corner. "In about three seconds I'm gonna start puttin' holes in this very expensive desk."

A whimper was quickly followed by the mad scrambling of the young girl. She stayed low, pressing herself against the wall with a terrified look on her face. The top of her head was completely artificial with tendrils, similar to that of a Novaarian, hanging in a tight bunch out of the back.

Roland gave her a cocky smile and Esabelle wondered how the simple human had known the Shay girl was there.

Surprises...

"Where is Sal-dev Tanek's office?" When the girl said nothing, Esabelle raised her hand, lifting the girl and pinning her to the wall. "I won't ask again."

The girl's face reflected the surprise she felt at being telekinetically manipulated. "That way!" She pointed down the corridor to their left. "The last corner office on the right!"

With that, Esabelle dropped the Shay and poured her concentration into the girl's mind, overwhelming her into unconsciousness.

They continued down the corridor decorated with holographic images of previous heads of various departments and board members. The whole floor was immaculate and richly designed with overly large offices built for a single being. The corner office was no different with Tanek's name printed in gold lettering next to the door. The glass walls were translucent, obscuring the contents inside. Esabelle dipped back into the universal soup and felt Sal-dev crouching behind a long sofa opposite the door. The Intrinium signature wasn't hard to miss, either.

"He's armed."

"So..." Roland kicked the metal handle, forcing the doors open. His shot was amazingly accurate. Tanek's weapon was fired from his hand as Roland's Intrinium round struck the barrel head on. His stride never halted as he walked around the sofa and clamped his hand around the Shay's neck.

"This is gonna be the simplest conversation of your life." Roland brought his Tri-roller under Tanek's synthetic jaw. "You're gonna tell us what we want to know, or today's the day you die. Simple, right?"

"If I talk, they'll kill me, slowly..."

Roland threw him to the ground and drew his Terran hilt. The black metal grew from within until the blade was just bigger than a hand.

"How long have I got?" Roland didn't take his eyes off Tanek.

"Not long enough." Esabelle went straight to the hovering desk and sat down. She deactivated the privacy setting on the back wall. They could now see the increasing number of patrol ships positioning around the hanging buildings. Searchlights scoured every floor with built-in scanners as they hunted for the humans. The other end of Clave Tower was so far away it was just a blur between the constant movement of traffic and archipelagos.

Placing both hands flat on the table, she connected with every electron that formed the desk's interface and the wireless system it was paired with. The table responded with a hologram asking for a password and the daily code. She sank deeper into the code and removed the firewalls protecting Sal-dev's files. The hologram fluttered with the electronic barrage.

"Whatever you're doing, make sure you record it!" Ch'len said. Roland threw her a small metallic cylinder, which she caught using telekinesis. Once on the table, it was highlighted in a circle of green light. She commanded the desk to transfer everything she found.

After filtering through the mountain of Laronian porn the Shay had amassed, she accessed the files marked with the highest security levels. The majority of information was what the company deemed a secret regarding the technology used to connect the seven hundred and twenty hubs across the Conclave. She skipped through the boring details about the constraints put on the AI to ensure it served instead of ruled. She needed to know about the cube.

There it was, the historical archive buried under layer upon layer of code designed to divert any investigation. There was no code that could keep the *Gommarian* pilot out, however. She had spent two hundred thousand years living like a machine. Esabelle instantly expanded the file and brought the relevant data up as a hologram. A crystal clear image of the cube floated above the desk. It was half buried in a mountain of ice and snow with only three of its corners visible. Sifting through the images, she found more as the cube was excavated by Protocorps personnel. The time stamp put the pictures at over a hundred thousand years ago.

The next file was a few months on, with the cube now situated in a lab somewhere on Shandar's hidden surface. Machines of every kind were attached to its dark bronze surface. The Shay had no idea what they were dealing with. Esabelle realised that even she didn't know what they were dealing with, and she had been on the same ship as a cube for millennia.

"How are there two of you?" she asked out loud. "In two completely different parts of the galaxy."

"It can't be a coincidence that both are found inside a civilisation." Roland snatched Sal-dev off the floor and dropped him on the sofa. "Sit on your hands," he commanded.

"But one was instrumental in wiping out an entire race. Why has this one just helped co-ordinate traffic and allow for better communication?"

"What are you guys talking about?"

"Shut up, Len!"

"There's more..." Esabelle found an adjacent file with a string of numbers for a title. With a single thought, she accessed the file. She felt the intrusion a moment too late and the desk went dark. Roland's recorder stopped and the desk's connection was severed.

"The AI?" Roland pocketed his recorder.

"No, something much worse. This is the cube, it's *them*. They're in the system."

With a short squeal, Sal-dev Tanek made a mad dash for the exit. Everything happened at once then. Before Roland could end the Shay altogether, the entire wall of outer glass was violently shattered. Brilliant blue Intrinium rounds tore through the office suite like paper as the patrol ship levelled out. The sofa was ripped in half by a single round, clipping Roland on the leg and forcing him to the floor. Glass exploded in every direction, cutting both of them from head to foot. The pitch of the cannons made it impossible to communicate with one another.

Esabelle reacted with an expulsion of various powers at once. A telekinetic outburst separated her from everything within ten feet while she simultaneously erected a shield to absorb the incoming fire. She syphoned the energy and fed it into her own body, making her stronger. Extending her hand out towards Roland, she pushed him telekinetically through the glass wall and into the next office. She had no doubt it would have hurt the man, but it was better than the Intrinium rounds that blew through his previous position.

He recovered more quickly than she expected and met her in the corridor. They had to shout over the cacophony of destruction the ship wrought around them. Esabelle had to dodge several rounds as she used every manoeuvre to make it to the corridor in one piece.

"They're not playing nice anymore!" Roland shouted.

"We need to get to the cube!"

"We *need* to get out of here!" Roland corrected.

The corridor suddenly filled up with soldiers as they poured out of the grav-pillar. These troops were better armoured than their counterparts. Each one appeared to be wearing an exoskeleton over the top of the black Protocorps armour. And their weapons were significantly bigger. Roland pulled her into the office he had come from to avoid the hail of gunfire. The corridor was being blown to pieces from two directions now. They heard the thrusters outside as the patrol ship shifted to match their position.

Esabelle's anger flared at the opportunity slipping away. They had to destroy that cube, whatever the cost. She slowed things down, retreating into her mind for a moment to contemplate. She looked at Roland, blood dripping from a dozen cuts across his hands and face. He was a fighter through and through. If she went after the cube, he would follow, but he would likely die doing so. She reminded herself that she wasn't alone anymore. She had allies; Kalian was getting stronger every day, not to mention the allies he didn't know about.

Kalian would want her to save Roland and live to fight another day. Looking at the odds stacking against her, she knew her own chances of survival were slim. Esabelle knew she would regret it later, but they had to escape. The patrol ship was now level again, its blinding spotlight illuminating the whole office.

"We're taking that ship!" Esabelle knew her plan was crazy, but so far crazy seemed to work for them.

"Are you serious?"

"Come on!" She pulled him up as they both ran flat out towards the hovering craft.

There was no time to think, they had to act now if they were going to survive the next ten seconds. Before it could unleash another barrage of Intrinium, Esabelle forced the glass to explode outwards. Esabelle sailed across the gap in a single bound and landed directly on top of the cockpit.

Roland was less successful.

His jump only allowed for his finger-tips to drag across the sleek red surface. After that, he hurtled towards a certain death.

"Roland!"

Esabelle couldn't see beyond the nose of the cockpit. The two pilots looked up at her, complete surprise on their furry Tularon faces. She put her hand to the metallic surface and sent an electromagnetic pulse through the craft, dropping it like a stone in water with Esabelle magnetised to the hull. The craft turned in the air, giving a view of Roland as he descended down the length of the central Protocorps tower.

His big coat flapped high above him with his arms and legs stretched out, angling towards the nearest patrol ship, surprising her again. At the last second, he twisted his body to land feet first, whereupon he slowed down until his descent appeared controlled. The crazy son of a bitch didn't stop, either. He quickly stood up and proceeded to run along the length of the ship before jumping off again. The jump was timed perfectly, as he landed on the next ship below with the same measure of control before landing.

Dozens of other ships were responding now to their dramatic escape. Eventually, Roland was going to run out of places to run, or he'd miscalculate another jump and fall to his death. Esabelle sent a flutter of electricity through the ship and brought the engines back online. It took a terrifying moment for the craft to level out, narrowly avoiding another ship.

"What was the next part of your fantastic plan?" Roland's voice came through her earpiece.

"I'm coming to you. Hang on." Esabelle pinned the pilots in their seat and connected with the main console for flight control. The patrol-ship veered to port and made a bee-line for Roland, who was currently fighting two Laronians on top of another ship. Her mind assessed everything she could see and began making plans according to the distances and speeds of various factors. Everything had to be executed at the right moment.

Her mind overlaid the world with numbers informing her of the gaps closing between herself, Roland, an approaching ship and the lines of traffic below. At the last second, she dropped the craft, forcing it into the approaching ship. The sound of crumpling metal and shattering glass was accompanied by the violent crash she felt beneath her feet. Before both ships began their emergency landing procedures, Esabelle stood up and ran across the port side wing. Her jump was beyond the abilities of any race in the Conclave.

Being perfectly calculated, she landed with a heavy *thud* on the starboard wing of Roland's craft. Behind her, she could hear alarms blaring from both ships as they battled with their controls to land the damaged vessels safely. In front of her were three Protocorps mercenaries circling Roland like predators. The nearest mercenary heard her landing and turned to attack. They didn't have time to stand and fight, though. With a sweeping hand, Esabelle launched the Shay off the top of the craft in a wave of unstoppable force. His mechanical screams were soon cut short as he collided with another patrol ship.

Roland had already beaten one of his attackers half to death and thrown him overboard. The other received a swift shot to the face from a Tri-roller. Esabelle wasted no time in grabbing the bounty hunter and forcing him to run with her until they reached the edge of the ship.

"Not this again!" They both dived off the end and plunged down into the tower. They soon passed through the cluster of patrol ships and continued to drop into the flow of traffic. Lines of vehicles traversed the diameter of the great rings, in every direction. The drag, combined with the rushing air, made it hard to focus on any one thing. Esabelle was relying more on her paranormal senses than her eyes and ears. She could feel every particle vibrating inside the vehicles that thundered by them, some missing them by only metres.

"That one!" She pointed at a slow-moving hover truck with the logo, *Planetary Mover's* printed on all sides. It was big enough for them to land on and allow Roland the extra time required for his boots to land on a moving object.

"I have a better idea!" Seemingly from nowhere, the *Rackham* swallowed them up inside its cargo bay. Matching their speed perfectly, the Terran ship gently pressed up against them until they were flat against the floor. The ramp closed, sealing off the world below, and the ship's artificial gravity corrected their sense of balance.

Roland practically jumped into his bridge chair and punched multiple commands into the surrounding console. Ch'len was right where they left him in his own, slightly wider chair, surrounded by food packets and a grease-stained console.

"Hold onto something. The grav plating isn't going to be able to compensate for these kinds of manoeuvres." Roland wasn't wrong.

Esabelle gripped the bar beside the bridge door just in time for a starboard shift in gravity.

Ch'len groaned as his many items of food were flung from the console.

"What's the plan?" she asked as blue streaks of Intrinium flew past the viewport.

"As soon as we're a hundred kilometres out, I'm hitting the Solar Drive. I think we've outstayed our welcome."

———

KUBRACKK STARTED up the launch sequence the moment he witnessed the unbelievable. Both humans jumped out of the tower and somehow survived.

"What does it take to kill these humans?"

Spelnar rushed onto the bridge with an exhausted look on his face. He looked around in surprise as he clearly knew the sound of the thrusters warming up.

"I got the tech we need..."

"Shut up and man your station!" Kubrackk couldn't deal with the Trillik's incompetence right now. His quarry was managing to escape the inescapable and it was pissing him off. Right now the bounty hunter was vulnerable without his ship and stuck on top of a patrol ship. He wondered if the Highclave would actually reward him for stepping in and killing the human criminal. Before the *Blade* could lift off the platform, a red holographic warning flashed across his viewport. Conclave security was prohibiting his take off since the surrounding area was classed as a live crime scene. He slammed his fist into the console and swore at the flashing sign.

By now he could no longer see the human pair after their suicide jump from the red craft. By simple physics, the jump should kill both of them, but after seeing the stunt they pulled at Krono Towers he knew they would find a way to survive.

"What took you so long?" He decided to take his frustration out on Spelnar. His hand firmly rested on the handle of his Quad-roller. The Trillik's mouth moved a lot but no sound came out. Kubrackk sat back in his chair and already knew he would have to call Revus again. Only the Brenine would be able to track the *Rackham* out of the tower.

"If he gets away because of your uselessness, I'm going to add another body to the cargo bay..." The Trillik sat so still as to blend in with his surroundings; if he so much as flinched, he knew Kubrackk would kill him.

NINE

Li'ara watched in horror as the Starrillium's internal cameras were instantly eviscerated by the miniature star. She could no longer see Kalian as he fought for their lives. She and Naydaalan had been quickly ushered to the *Nova's* bridge while Professor Jones escaped. In charge of the *Nova* was Alvara Versanti, an Atari female from the planet Trendor, deep within Laronian territory. The Charge had taken a moment to acknowledge Li'ara's presence but it was clear where her main concern lay.

"Status, Palaaren?" The Atari directed her attention to the Novaarian surrounded by orange holograms to their left. Alvara had left her command-chair and was frantically making her way around the various stations, giving orders and checking every readout personally.

"Engineering is working to bypass the virus the human uploaded. It's overwritten most of the safety protocols and completely disabled our ability to jettison the Starrillium." All four hands of the Novaarian danced across the holograms in every direction. "The upper decks, twenty-four through to thirty-six are gone..."

"Casualties?" Alvara wiped the sweat from her pink forehead, her yellow eyes focusing on the crewman beyond Palaaren.

"Confirmed fifty-eight from those decks," the Brenine answered. "But the med bays are filling up with injuries. A further ninety-two are critical."

"Where's Garrett? The human!" Li'ara walked into the fray, despite Naydaalan's warning to stay back. Li'ara narrowed her eyes at Alvara for a second, taking her in.

The Atari was surprisingly human in appearance; her facial features were almost identical except for the bony cheekbones, pointed ears and wide-set eyes. Her hair was a darker shade of pink to that of her skin, slicked back to the top of her neck in thick locks. Her physique was similar to Li'ara's with the big difference being the Atari's feet. They were closer to Novaarian with an extended foot, angling behind the knee. Feet like those probably allowed for great speed and agility.

"He landed on Trantax IV. I've sent troops to apprehend him." The Charge nodded to her security staff and two Laronians appeared at Li'ara's side. "Right now we have bigger problems. If we can't get the Starrillium under control, we will all be dead in minutes."

"They won't be able to stop him!" Li'ara shrugged off the blue hands and noticed Naydaalan take a quick step to intercept the annoyed Laronians. "If Kalian couldn't stop him, they definitely won't. You need to hit him with the ship!" Li'ara was fighting her tears at the thought of what Kalian was going through right now, and the only way she knew how to do that was to get angry.

"Engineering?" Alvara ignored her.

"We don't understand," the voice came through the speakers. "The Starrillium's containment sphere has been obliterated, Charge. We can't figure out why we aren't all dead. It should have burned through the whole ship by now."

"Kalian..." Li'ara looked at the hologram where his image had been.

"I saw what he did on Naveen. Can he really be doing this?" Alvara gave Li'ara a disbelieving look.

"I don't know." That fact truly scared her.

"Wait!" Palaaren sat forward and expanded one of the dozen

holograms. "Sensors show a mass depletion in hydrogen and helium; it's being dispersed somehow. The internal temperature is cooling, electromagnetic radiation is..." Palaaren looked closer at his monitor. "It's being diverted back on itself, like an artificial containment." He turned to the crew with an amazed expression.

It took another agonising hour before the sensors relayed the final spark of the raw Starrillium. Li'ara hadn't left the bridge and continued to monitor everything around her. There had been too much radioactive interference for the crew to get a positive reading on Kalian. The ship still being intact was a testament to his being alive, but at what cost? Professor Jones had escaped the system with the cube. His ship had proved impossible to track with the Terran technology powering it.

Li'ara couldn't remember how she ended up outside the Starrillium chamber; the question mark over Kalian's fate dulled her senses. Naydaalan was by her side again. He had left the bridge briefly to check on Telarrek. She knew he was still alive but couldn't recall the details he gave. She could only think about what they would find when that door opened.

The entire area had been exposed to massive amounts of radiation and heat. Li'ara's protective suit was designed for an Atari or a Laronian but didn't feel too cumbersome as she stepped into the chamber. A thick fog had settled over the floor after the emergency cooling system had evened out the temperature. The ground crunched beneath her feet as she slowly made her way to the kneeling form of Kalian.

He was surrounded by a team of scientists and medical staff with a hovering Medder taking scans of his every inch. He remained perfectly still on his knees, with his arms spread out and his head hanging low. His stillness disturbed her. Seeing her, the team gave some space so she could see him better. She couldn't help the sound of alarm that escaped her mouth. His hands and face were charred black like the bark of a tree. He had no hair to speak of and his eyes were concealed behind blackened lids. She fell to her knees in front of him when she realised the truth, Kalian had no eyes. Most of his nose was missing along with any definition around his mouth.

The armoured suit had fared better, with only a few plates across his chest still glowing from the heat.

"Is he..." She couldn't say the word as tears rolled down her cheeks.

"He's still alive." The Ch'kara didn't seem to believe his own words. Li'ara took a breath she didn't think would ever come again and allowed her heart to continue beating. "We have no idea how, but our scans show his brain and organs remain untouched. The skin under this armour is probably burnt to some degree, but we can't be sure of the extent. Oddly, he's not giving off any radiation."

"His vitals are dropping!" a Laronian medic started concentrating his scans around Kalian's chest. "We need to get him to a Medder tank immediately!"

Naydaalan helped Li'ara up and took her aside to give the team space.

"If anyone could survive this, it would be Kalian." Naydaalan was trying to reassure her.

Li'ara looked at his broken form and fought hard to break free of the doubt that clouded her mind, and dared to hope.

KALIAN'S MIND WAS AN ISLAND. He was cut off from every nerve and receptor, leaving him senseless to his external body. He was standing on freshly cut grass, looking out over San Francisco Bay. The Golden Gate Bridge was shining in the midday sun as a beautiful super-yacht glided underneath. Everything was moving in slow motion around him. There was no sound coming from the people or the cars slowly passing by.

It took him a moment longer to collect his thoughts. He had been inside the Starrillium chamber. With that thought, he tried to orientate himself back into reality and leave the memory behind. A cloud of darkness appeared on the fringes of his sight and began to take over the bright and vivid world as if a storm was descending over the city. He knew that if he continued, this darkness would be all that greeted him, along with unimaginable pain.

He immediately stopped and tried to sink deeper into his mind. The fact that he was still inside his own reality was proof that he had somehow survived the Starrillium. He surmised that the feeling he experienced was a warning that his body was trying to heal. He trusted Li'ara to keep his physical body safe while he...

What was he going to do? He was stuck inside his mind for who knew how long. Esabelle had been teaching him about the benefits of retreating inside himself. He could take the time to learn more and allow his subconscious to absorb it. When the darkness continued to spread through the city, Kalian remembered that he wasn't alone in here. He failed to take control and reshape his surroundings. The cityscape began to crumble around him in silence, the rubble taking a different form and changing into an alien landscape.

He fell to his knees as the weight of Savrick's memories washed away his individuality. When he thought of Li'ara he could only see T'lea staring back at him, her beautiful dark eyes reflecting the love she felt for him.

Kalian fought against the intruding memory but felt his energy being diverted to repairing his body. He was helpless against the torrent of images that consumed his vision.

Savrick looked out over the stunning vista of snow-capped mountains and the never-ending range of canyons. The sun was beginning to set behind the furthest mountain, blanketing Nal-hala in a dusky orange glow. The magnificent land before him was a poor reflection of the scene that had taken place only two hundred miles away. He looked to the West, where yesterday the Gomar had met the Terran forces head-on in a brutal but short battle.

The Gomar had suffered heavy casualties taking the planet. He knelt down and cupped a handful of dirt, letting it slowly slip through his armoured fingers. The soil was dry and brown as it should be. Two hundred miles away the ground was stained red with blood and littered with bodies.

A flicker of doubt crossed his mind at the memory of all the blood. They had been fighting this war for eighty years with no end in sight. It seemed like every day a new war machine was constructed by ALF and spat out of one of his assembly plants. Was all this death worth his revenge? How many more would have to die to satisfy his rage?

For her...

The voice was his own but it had not come from his consciousness. It was the cube. He could feel its microscopic nanocelium coursing through his blood, connecting the two of them forever. He was forced to see T'lea die in a brief flash. Her bloodied image flashed across his mind as Esabelle's cries filled his ears. His resolve returned with a promise that the Terran would pay with their lives.

He felt a mental pull and turned to gaze upon the *Gommarian*. It hovered a thousand feet above him, a dark sentinel keeping watch. Its sheer mass had caused several earthquakes in the area, opening up new canyons. He knew the source of the pull had come from the cube. It hadn't requested his presence like this for years but he always answered the call. Savrick gave the setting sun a longing look before using a controlled burst of telekinesis to fly up to his floating home.

His awareness pulsed through the ship and filled his mind with a mental picture of where his crew were. He could feel the energy emanating from over a hundred thousand men and women, all loyal to him and their cause. He focused for a moment on Lilander, the newest member to join their ranks. She was being treated in the med bay before being introduced to her exo-suit. The Terran had been using Nal-hala as a staging post and so Lilander had been one of dozens of Gomar slaves. Her job had been to provide the Terran with anything they required and be grateful for being a part of their civilisation. She had made them suffer for that. There was a fire in her; he had seen it when they found her, surrounded by Terran bodies.

The pull in his mind became more intense, directing his attention back to the heavy door in front of him. Savrick's hand pressed against the cool metal, allowing the nanocelium to take a biometric reading.

A heavy *thud* preceded the door spiralling open and disappearing into the wall. The reason for his required presence was evident.

"Elandar..." He was the only one aboard that had the know-how to bypass the biometric scanner. His oldest friend slowly rose from his crouched position and turned to face him. His dark hair was tied in a knot behind his head, exposing the elaborate tattoo across his cheek. Savrick glanced over the cube, noting a lack of tools or scanning equipment. Elandar was more than capable, however, of learning everything he needed to know with his abilities alone.

"You shouldn't be here." Savrick walked around the cube, inspecting every surface. "When I told you about this, I specifically forbade you from coming here. How did you find it?"

"Forgive me, brother, I had to see it. I would never say anything in front of the crew but..."

"But what?"

"I have seen that look on your face, Savrick. After the fighting ends and our feet are bathed in blood, I have seen the doubt that creeps into your mind."

Savrick appeared stunned at the remark but knew Elandar would see through it. He *had* doubted their course of action in recent years.

"I know that it was this... cube, which gave you what you needed to start the war, to set us free. I also know that you haven't been down here in a long time." Savrick gave him a questioning look. "The *Gommarian* see's everything." That was explanation enough for his knowledge. As caretaker of the pilot, he was in a position to survey the entire ship.

"And you think that my lack of resolve is tied to this?"

"I think it fuelled you, why I don't know, but it did. You told me you found this and it changed everything. It gave you knowledge and power. It drove you for decades in pursuit of complete Terran annihilation and you were unstoppable. But now I see you fading, brother. It's *your* fire that fuels us. You must see that! As your oldest friend and a free Gomar, it is my duty to ensure that whatever fuels you must stay alight."

"It was what they took from me that drives me on! What they have taken from us all! This machine is a means to an end. It gave us the tools we need to win this war, Elandar. That is all..." Savrick felt his forearm sting from the memory of his earlier years interacting with it.

"Does it not interest you? Worry you?" Elandar walked around the cube to stand between it and Savrick. "What is it? Where did it come from? Why is it so happy to help us?"

"It came from a time before the Criterion, a creation of our ancestors." Savrick didn't look him in the eye.

"I know you don't believe that. I know I don't. This was not designed by our people. All of my senses tell me it is... alien." Elandar's disdain at the word was evident on his face.

"I only know that it's broken." That got Elandar's attention. "I believe if it was at full power, it would have taken me over the first time I touched it." Elandar took a few extra steps away from the cube. "It doesn't just use nanocelium, it replicates it. I can feel them inside me now, whispering in my mind. It can communicate with me, but it cannot use me."

"Are you sure about that?" Elandar gave him an appraising look.

"Yes." Savrick's tone was commanding - he was not to be judged again.

"So it's sentient, it's alive?"

"I'm not sure you could say it's alive. I believe it's part of something much larger, something worse. But as you said, it gave me knowledge and power, and more than anything I wanted to be free of *them*. I didn't question its motives, Elandar. I just wanted to use it. Why it's helping us, I have no idea. But it does want to see the end of Terran life, I can feel that much. So for the time being our goals are the same." Elandar made to ask more questions but Savrick silenced him with a hand. "See to our pilot."

Elandar looked rebuked but followed his orders and left without another word.

Savrick commanded the heavy doors to seal him in with the cube. He hated this next part. Allowing it to physically connect with him, and commune like a real being, was a disturbing experience. He slowly walked towards the cube, manipulating the electrical signals to his Sinoatrial node in an effort to keep his heart-rate level. He had put his people on a course that put all Gomar in danger. He had to see it through.

The dark tentacles stabbed into his exposed arm before his hand even passed through the hole. He was dragged in until the armour around his bicep wouldn't fit, leaving him on his knees. Having already disconnected his pain receptors, he felt only the microscopic probes making contact with the nanocelium in his bloodstream.

We have been disturbed.

The words resonated inside his mind as if they were his own.

"Elandar is no threat to you, he was only concerned."

As are we. You are forgetting the brutality you suffered under the Terran rule. They must be wiped from history. You have been given the necessary tools to perform this task. See it done.

"I forget nothing! I need more! This war is taking too long. They inhabit over a thousand worlds and all you give me is one ship! We waste time with ground battles and skirmishes for territory when we should be obliterating entire systems. I need more Eclipse missiles."

More resources are required for construction.

"You mean you're broken!" Savrick wanted to pull away but felt the cords tighten around his arm. He hated the malevolence that accompanied its every word. He was fighting for the freedom of his people, to make his wife's death mean something, but the cube had a completely different agenda.

Our entry into the Terran Empire was taxing, internal systems have been compromised. But it will not stop the inevitable. We are coming...

Savrick recalled a similar conversation decades ago, on Hadrok. Those three words had haunted his dreams ever since, making him doubt the help the cube had given the Gomar. Savrick felt a pulse through his arm and couldn't stop the barrage of images attack his conscious mind. He screamed into the dark, as he was forced to kneel there for another five hours, and relive the death of T'lea.

Li'ara couldn't switch off. She tapped the lower frame of the window incessantly and tried to stop herself from pacing the room. Naydaalan had kept close by since they left Kalian in the med bay. His presence felt reassuring like a silent guardian keeping her together. She hadn't wanted to leave Kalian but new developments required her presence elsewhere on the *Nova*. They had been escorted to the Charge's briefing room off the bridge. It was a long room with a circular table in the centre and an L shape viewport off the port bow.

She looked out on the gleaming hull of the *Nautallon*, High Charge Uthor's personal ship of choice. She recalled the name from some ancient legend on Arakesh she had read about in her free time.

Having already docked with the *Nova*, multiple teams of engineers and technicians had come across to help in repairing the ship's damaged systems. Li'ara knew what was coming. Too much had happened since they left the *Gommarian*, too many Conclave soldiers had died at the hands of a human, if Garrett could still be called that. Uthor would demand answers and she would have to give them to him. She wished Kalian could be with her for this part. He had always said that it would eventually come to this; they had kept too many secrets from the Conclave.

The Raalak's heavy footsteps weren't hard to miss coming up the corridor. Naydaalan straightened up and gave her a steely gaze, lending him confidence and strength. Li'ara replied with a small nod before turning to the face the door.

It was impossible to get a reading on Uthor's expression; like every Raalak he always looked angry. Charge Versanti accompanied him with an entourage of officers. Uthor fixed Li'ara with an unwavering glare but remained silent in her presence. A quick look at Alvara and the charge dismissed her subordinates and sealed the room with only the four of them.

"I suspect you have a lot of questions." Li'ara's voice was croaky from lack of speaking.

"Is this the part where you tell me about the cube hidden in the bowels of the *Gommarian*?" Li'ara was too exhausted to hide the shock on her face. "I have already spoken with your captain, Commander Ducarté. You saw what Professor Jones did on this ship; can you imagine what he has done on your own?" Li'ara didn't think she could feel any worse right now, but the sinking feeling in her gut just found a new level. "They have many casualties but the ship remains in a better condition than the *Nova*. Lucky for them he was more interested in retrieving the Trantax cube." Uthor slowly moved around the table to look upon his own ship through the viewport.

"What did the captain tell you?"

"Why, so you can get your lies straight? You will tell me every-thing you know and I will decide on the truth. Lie to me and you will never see Kalian Gaines again."

Naydaalan stepped forward, puffing his chest out in a challenge. "You cannot do that! My father should be present if a human is to be questioned."

Uthor turned from his ship to face the young Novaarian. "Out of respect for your father, I will let that go. But if you speak to me like that again, I will have you mining Intrinium on the moons of Veridian for the next two hundred cycles." He whipped his head around to Li'ara, "Speak."

"We don't know where the cubes came from, either of them," Li'ara began. "Savrick found the one on our ship over two hundred thousand years ago on a planet called Hadrok. It helped him to over-come the Harnesses that limit the Gomar and, ultimately, start the war that ended with the creation of life on Earth. We *think* it may have had a hand in making the *Gommarian*." Uthor's dark eyes pressed into her like probes. How much did he know? She had no choice now; the only way to move forward was to lay everything out.

"Savrick's daughter was plugged into the ship and used to pilot it, against her will. She is the one who... who told us all this." Uthor already knew about Esabelle, she could tell. For the captain to have told her so much, Li'ara could only surmise that Garrett had left them in a bad way. "Esabelle was the one who helped us take the ship in the end. She's on our side." She tried to emphasise that point. Another Terran would be seen as a mounting threat to the Conclave, especially one hidden from them. "There are twelve other Gomar onboard, all of them unconscious and locked away in Rem-stores. They pose no threat now."

"You have told me everything, as Captain Fey did. But the captain does not know everything since your departure. Your actions on Naveen and against my men require an explanation, a good one."

Li'ara looked away in thought for a moment. This particular secret was a big one. If the Conclave knew they had been in league with an AI from the Terran civilisation, and not to mention more powerful than their own, there would be serious consequences. Not just for her but also for Telarrek, Ilyseal and Naydaalan.

"I am waiting."

"As you already know, when the Terran had finished on Earth they left an outpost on Naveen. Should we ever make it that far, it would tell us everything we needed to know about where we came from. That information came in the form of an artificial intelligence known as ALF."

Uthor shared a look with Alvara, her expression easier to read than his. They were concerned.

"What kind of AI?" the charge asked.

"He's only a part of the whole. His physical housing was destroyed by the Gomar." Li'ara couldn't believe she had used ALF's own annoying line. "He controlled the Terran Empire much the same way yours does, only a little more God-like. He's as old as the Terran, that's why we had to retrieve him from Naveen. We hoped he would know more about the cube on Trantax, but he didn't."

"It was on Trantax? Where is it now?"

Li'ara looked at Naydaalan for help but knew there was nothing either of them could do. They had come this far, she had to hope that working together would benefit all of them.

"He's inside Kalian's suit."

With that Uthor gave Alvara a look she clearly understood. The charge turned on the spot and marched out of the room without a word.

"Where's she going?" Li'ara couldn't conceal the distress in her voice.

"I don't think you fully understand the danger an AI poses. There is a reason we have contained ours and limited its growth. I can't even imagine how dangerous an artificial intelligence is from the Terran Empire. The suit must be quarantined immediately, with or without Kalian Gaines inside it." Li'ara could feel a threat on the tip of her tongue before Uthor continued. "What is the interest in these cubes? Are they Terran in origin or not?"

Li'ara took a breath, "ALF didn't think so. There's a Terran word inscribed on the side but it didn't mean anything. We don't know why it's even on the cube. We need to see the one on the *Gommarian* for a real comparison. Can you tell me what happened?"

"It seems Professor Jones interacted with the cube against your captain's wishes. They do not know what happened after that, but he is clearly not the same being who went into that chamber. Our scans show he is teeming with the technology you call nanocelium."

"Esabelle thinks it's alive. That its only purpose is to seek out and end all human life. There's even a chance that what it's done to Garrett, it did to Savrick millennia ago."

"But you don't know where it came from, or who sent it?"

"No." That was a question Li'ara wanted answering more than anything.

"I find it troubling that the Terran civilisation came to an end after the discovery of that cube, and that we have just found one in our own borders."

"We tried to warn you last-"

Li'ara was cut off by Uthor. "You gave us half-truths and lies. So far, the only threat we have faced has come out of that monster of a ship. So now the two of you and Kalian Gaines are coming with me on the *Nautallon* where we will rendezvous with the *Gommarian*. I'm sure it doesn't need explaining to you that we are assuming complete control of it and those aboard. We should have done it much sooner, perhaps then so many lives may have been spared."

Li'ara could think of nothing to say. He was right. Uthor was doing everything she would in his position. They had been surprised by too many human lies and secrets. This was the expected reaction. With that in mind, Li'ara thought about the secret mission Esabelle had left for. She couldn't imagine what they would do if they discovered an unchecked Terran on one of their worlds. And with Roland no less - he was trouble enough.

"There's something else you should be aware of before it becomes a thing. Esabelle left the *Gommarian* before we did. She's trying to locate Roland North and bring him in before he causes too much damage."

"The damage has already been done, Commander Ducarté. We are well aware of the pair's recent activities. Perhaps *you* could shed some light on why they have attacked Protocorps Headquarters on the Capital?"

Li'ara recognised the name from Telarrek's warning about Roland. Why would they both attack the headquarters? She could offer no explanation for their actions; it was as much a mystery as the cube.

"Do you know what is inside Protocorps?"

"Up until a few days ago, I'd never heard of it," Li'ara admitted.

"It is the central hub for the Conclave's artificial intelligence. I don't believe in coincidences. You tell me about the AI recently acquired from Naveen while at the same time a Terran and a known human criminal attack the Conclave AI I do not like that combination of facts."

"Neither do I, but we should get answers before any judgment is made. Now that we all know the same thing we should work together." Li'ara could feel the adrenaline wearing off, leaving her tired.

"They were unsuccessful in reaching the AI but caused tremendous damage. Protocorps' personal security firm has reported deaths among their casualties. I can't even count how many laws they broke. They were able to escape thanks to the girl's abilities and that Terran ship, the *Rackham*. In the meantime, we will continue with our investigation onboard the *Gommarian*."

"What about Professor Jones?" Naydaalan asked.

"We are using every tool at our disposal to hunt him down. The Terran ship makes it harder. Do you have any idea why he would want the Trantax cube? Or even how he knew about it?"

Li'ara knew it couldn't be for anything good. What would he need from a second cube that he couldn't get from the *Gommarian* cube?

"I have no idea what he wants with it. Nobody on the *Gommarian* knew what we were leaving for, and Kalian and I didn't know until the Highclave told us."

"He left your ship and headed directly to Trantax IV. He knew exactly where to go." Uthor stroked his rocky chin.

"Is it possible he had help?" Naydaalan offered.

"You think someone inside the Conclave is in communication with this, monster?" Uthor looked troubled at the prospect. "I don't see how it is possible. We monitor all communications in and out of the *Gommarian* and there was none prior to his escape."

"Well someone must have told him where to go; the galaxy's a pretty big place. He knew to come here and he already had a plan. Destabilising the Starrillium not only allowed him to escape with the cube but it also nearly took out his biggest threat." Li'ara massaged her sore shoulder from the encounter with Garrett.

"Kalian..." Uthor checked a message on the screen built into his sleeve.

"Have we been able to identify the attackers on, Trantax?" Naydaalan asked.

"Not yet. Their ship's navigation and log were automatically stripped when we attempted access. They had no form of identification. Great measures were taken to conceal the markers in their DNA. Upon death, a toxokatic chemical was released into their bloodstream to destroy their chromosomes. I have not seen such precautions in mercenaries before. Their hardware is untraceable, no doubt acquired from the black market. Their employer will have to remain a mystery for now, but their services would not have come cheaply if their numbers and weaponry are anything to go by."

"Then there is a third party involved," Naydaalan added.

"It seems there is no end to the mysteries that follow your kind,

Commander Ducarté. I will bear all of this in mind for my report to the Highclave, but right now I would settle for knowing what the Professor plans on doing with the cube."

GARRETT LOOKED HELPLESSLY through eyes he could no longer control as the viewport gave way to a magnificent space station. In the shape of a crescent moon that didn't quite meet at the ends, the station could easily fit the *Gommarian* or the *Marillion* through the internal circumference. Lights were visible across the hull indicating activity inside, towards the bulk in the central curve of the crescent. Three massive spheres extended from the station at random spacing across the dull grey exterior.

What is this?

He knew from the holographic readout that he was in the Helteron cluster, between the borders of Shay and Laronian territory. He tried to get a better look at the console, an array of contrasting holograms in the pitch-black of the darkened ship. It seemed his parasitic occupant did not require light to see its surroundings. His body stood up against his will and exited the bridge, obscuring his view. It was infuriating to be trapped in his own body, his free will stripped from him.

His body stood inanimate in the gloom for several minutes while the ship docked with the station. Garrett found his own lack of movement disturbing in the dark. He didn't blink, breathe or twitch so much as a muscle, like a machine powered down. He felt a cold dread as the realisation sunk in; he was truly dead. There was no coming back from this now. Whatever damage the cube had done to him would be irreparable at this point; his organs would have shut down and his nervous system was no longer his own. He was dead.

He was washed in white light as the ramp beneath his feet descended forty-five degrees. The cube had been right in front of him the whole time. His strong hands clasped around the edges and pushed the heavy relic down the ramp with no sign of any strain on his body. Two lines of soldiers met him at the base of the ramp, all clad in black armour and face masks to suit their species. At the sight of him, they all took a cautious step back but made no move against him.

They're expecting me.

His body released the cube and stood aside as the relic was hoisted by a small crane onto a hovering platform that fitted its size perfectly. Without a word between any of them, they all followed the hovering cube as it led the way through the maze of corridors. There were guards everywhere, patrolling all the walkways, each heavily armed. After several Translifts and over two miles of walking, Garrett was standing before a long blank wall with a single horizontal line running through it. It was at least twenty metres across with seven black miniature rectangles placed side by side above the line. His body never moved to examine the room or locate the door from which six finely dressed Shay came. They regarded his presence with quizzical expressions and no lack of disgust.

Each of the men stood before the miniature rectangles and placed their right hand over the top. One of the troops, a Nix from its appearance, approached the last rectangle with a box. Very carefully, the Nix removed a severed hand from within and placed it on the rectangle. Moments later Garrett's improved sense of hearing picked up the unmistakable sounds of dozens of locks and bolts on the other side of the long wall. They Shay stood back when the wall released a *hiss* across the cutting line and the two halves were pulled into the ceiling and floor. Behind the wall-sized door was another door. This proved to be the case for another three doors in which a different part of the body was required with a passcode and voice recognition. The Nix had produced several body parts, including an eyeball, to assist with the apparent missing member of the strange group.

The final circular door required a drop of blood from each, with the Nix providing a sample from a vial. The curved locks spun around the circumference of the door until it spiralled into the walls, out of sight. A cold fog crept from within, spreading across the floor between their feet and under the hovering platform.

The room beyond was illuminated in neon blue light, exposing the heavily guarded secret. Garrett finally moved as he pushed the cube closer to the newly opened portal. The Shay appeared to be in shock at what was hidden in the vault. How could they not know what they were opening? The doors were obviously coded specifically to them, yet their horrified expressions told of revelation. The Shay dispersed in his presence, giving him a wide berth to rest the cube down. Without the obstruction, he could finally see what was contained inside. His own twisted face showed no sign of disturbance, but the Garrett trapped inside was in disbelief.

Stood upright before him was a large tube with hundreds of cables and wires connecting it to the walls and floor. Words and graphs flashed up across the frozen glass that made up half of the tube, presenting him with data about the tank's contents. At eye-level, the frozen mist had evaporated to allow for a clear view of the human man inside. He had short blonde hair with striking features that accentuated his beauty. The technology was advanced and sophisticated by human standards, but Garret could see that it was dated for the Conclave. This man had been inside the vault for centuries at least.

That's not a human, it's a Terran!

How the hell had the Conclave managed to contain a living Terran? Where had he come from, who was he? Garrett's eyes rested on the cube and he was consumed by another question; what was the cube for?

He walked right up to the glass and placed his disfigured palm against it. He could feel the writhing across his skin before the dark tendrils of nanocelium snaked over the tank. It penetrated the consoles on the side and took control of every mechanism. The tubes detached explosively, rebounding off the walls. Servo motors retracted the glass panel round into the tank, leaving the naked Terran exposed.

Garrett reached inside and pulled the body out, dumping it on the floor. He bent down and used the nanocelium in his body to form a sharp nail on the end of his thumb. A small cut was made across the

Terran's face so that a drop of blood was hanging off Garrett's new nail. With the flick of a hand, the blood was sprayed across the silent cube. It waited. He didn't know why, but the blood was needed to begin the process. Perhaps the technology required some biology in order to work. It was a mystery to him, but a mystery he would have been happy to have not experienced.

He joined the Shay on the other side of the vault and watched as the cube came to life with horrific intent. Sections moved around one another until it no longer resembled a cube. Long tendrils wormed out of every pore and made their way towards the prone Terran. The human-looking body was picked up by the tentacles as each one pierced the skin and tore through muscle and bone.

Garrett remembered the pain. The agony of having his bones broken and remade over and over as his physiology was transformed. The Terran had no idea how lucky he was to be unconscious for the experience. His skin visibly darkened in patches where the nanocelium clumped together. Thick veins of it ran over the top of his muscles until it covered his entire body like an exo-suit. Only his head remained visible with his once beautiful features now twisted. His eyes were sunken pits with no recognisable detail. It made his own transformation appear crude and unfinished.

The tendrils connecting him to the cube had attached completely now. The cube was just an empty shell like the one Garrett had left on the *Gommarian*. The only sign of life from the Terran came in the form of a deep breath. A surprising sight considering Garrett no longer needed oxygen. Did this new form require air to live? How was his transformation so different? It could only be the difference in physiology or the individuality of the cubes, or possibly both. He hated his continuous existence, of questions and theories that he knew he could share with no one.

As one Shay bowed on the knee, the others quickly followed suit. With bowed heads, they remained silent as if waiting judgment from a god. What was this new form to them? He noticed the guards all did the same, regardless of their species.

The Terran looked straight at him with piercing dark eyes. Garrett felt like he was looking right at *him*, his trapped consciousness. A strange connection formed between them at that moment. His head was filled with another mind, a powerful mind. He felt his own parasitic occupant bow to the presence.

You do not have long.

The voice was neither his invaders nor his own. The two were communing via some wireless connection.

I cannot isolate its mind. Like the heretic, it is elusive.

You are broken. Your control of this body will not last without the use of a functioning biology.

You may have control of the body, but you must take measures to contain the mind. Yours is that of a Terran and more powerful.

I am in control.

Garrett could feel another connection across the minds. It was familiar but still different. Its communication was on a lower level, like an emotion instead of actual words. They both understood the information, however, and continued with the new data.

The Terran has survived our attempts to destroy him. They are taking him back to the Gommarian.

In his condition, he will be no threat. The female, however, may be a problem. She was connected to me on the Gommarian. She is more powerful and is now aware of our presence in the capital.

We will make use of this station and contact the Vanguard. Steps must be taken to ensure the Terran does not get in the way.

Garrett found some relief in the knowledge that he hadn't killed Kalian after all. From the way they spoke about him it was obvious he was a threat. He also found some comfort in the knowledge that he wouldn't have to live for much longer. If the Terran was right his alien invader wouldn't be able to maintain his control and the two of them would finally die. But who was this Vanguard? And where did the other connection come from? He feared any answers he gleamed would only die with him.

The Vanguard will not be satisfied with our level of progress. This galaxy is supposed to be ready by now.

The heretic's involvement changes everything. I suspect it has survived our machinations.

"What would you have of us?" The question came from the closest Shay, who had dared to lift his head. Garrett realised that to the Shay, only a second had gone by since the Terran took his first breath.

"Is this station operational?" The Terran's voice was more human than his own, but still not right.

"It is exactly to your designs. If you wish, I can show you to the bridge; everything is operating perfectly." The Shay remained on one knee.

Garrett stepped into line next to the Terran as they both made for the exit.

"I already know the way."

TEN

Ch'len was taking his frustration out on the chopping board as he sliced through a slab of Horvian meat. Roland was clearly ignoring him while he removed the never-ending amount of gear and armour from his body. His slow movements were evidence of the injuries he had suffered during the escape.

"Would it be possible for the two of you, just once, *not* to jump out of a friggin' building?" Ch'len was shouting over his mouthfuls of meat. "Do you have any idea how many laws we just broke? We just crossed a line there's no coming back from. They will hunt us across the universe for this! And your plan is to return to the one ship that has all of their attention?"

Esabelle sat on the floor and rested her head against the wall. It was the only spot in the open-planned living area that was clean enough to sit on. She had healed all of her wounds and replayed recent events in her mind. A part of her regretted saving the bounty hunter's life instead of fighting her way through to the AI. There was a cube in the heart of the Conclave and she had to know why. Were they integrated into every civilisation in the galaxy, or just the Terran and the Conclave?

"He has a point..." Roland was down to his trousers and vest now.

His arms were covered in bruises and cuts. His right eye looked to have taken a hit during the fight on top of the patrol ship. "We should really lie low for a little while. I know a place on Trendor where we could disappear."

"Not an option." Esabelle stood up and used her telekinesis to pull in a cup of water. Ch'len stopped chewing and stared at the unusual sight. "We need to get this information out. Kalian can inform the Highclave of what we found and they can open their own investigation."

"You're forgetting the part where we just broke into a government-funded building and trashed the place. I'm already a wanted man, but now they know for sure that you exist. You think they're just gonna let it go that another Terran is walking around unchecked. And that's not to mention the fact that you're the daughter of the man responsible for the deaths of thousands of Conclave citizens."

Esabelle didn't think of Savrick as her father. Beyond her fourth year, he had given her to the cube so her raw power could be put to use. He wielded her like a weapon and so lost his right to call himself her father.

"I couldn't remain hidden forever. This is too big to worry about the consequences for us. Hopefully Kalian and Li'ara will be back from whatever the Highclave wanted with them. We'll come up with a way to broach the subject with the Conclave and explain that we had no choice but to act the way we did."

"Oh yeah, I'm sure they'll just give us a pat on the back and grant us immediate membership. Maybe we'll get medals!" Roland pushed out his chest until his back audibly cracked.

"They just need to understand how serious this is. Look at the damage just one of those cubes did." Esabelle drained the cup and used her abilities to levitate it back to the counter.

Ch'len muttered something but a piece of Horvian meat hanging from his mouth distorted every word.

"Approaching final destination," the *Rackham* announced.

Roland ignored Ch'len and made for the bridge. Esabelle followed behind the waddling Ch'kara who refused to stop eating.

The bridge was darker than she liked but Roland was often at odds with the lighting after a drink. In his captain's chair, he pulled up the necessary holograms to monitor the ship's internal functions and check the sensor array.

"Wait a minute... something's not right." Roland enhanced the hologram to his right and displayed it in front of them. Esabelle had a bad feeling. The sensors showed the *Gommarian* ahead of them in real space, surrounded by an armada of Conclave ships. With a flash of light, the *Rackham* emerged from subspace, ten thousand kilometres away from the mass of ships.

"What's going on?" Ch'len sounded distressed.

"Is this because of us?" Roland asked.

"It can't just be because of us. This is something else." Esabelle detected the movement of ships a half second before the sensors indicated their flight path. Seven patrol ships and a Nebula-class vessel had broken off from the surrounding net and were heading straight for them.

"Did you forget to activate the stealthware?" Ch'len half ran, half waddled, over to his station to check his own question.

"Of course I didn't! They shouldn't be able to see us!" Roland frantically activated several internal scans to ensure the stealthware was working efficiently. The ships were now clearly visible beyond the viewport as they formed a new net around the *Rackham*.

"Take us back into subspace, Roland!" Ch'len jumped into his seat, which automatically increased the height to match the station.

Roland flicked up another hologram, "Not enough fuel." The console chirped to indicate an incoming transmission. "How do they know where we are?"

"They don't, the *Gommarian* does." Esabelle could see it as the only explanation. For some reason, the Conclave had boarded the ship and taken control of the bridge. It was the only way they could detect them with Terran stealthware technology.

Roland sighed as he dropped his hand on the open comm channel.

"Under the authority of the Highclave, you will deactivate your stealth technology and be escorted to the *Gommarian*. You have ten seconds to comply or we will open fire."

Roland sat back in his chair and pinched his nose. "I've got to put all that shit back on…"

A SMALL ARMY of soldiers awaited them beyond the *Rackham's* descending ramp. Each one was aiming their rifle at the three fugitives as they slowly walked into the light.

Esabelle could feel the adrenaline surging through the varying species before them. The soldiers didn't know what to expect, only that the ship's occupants were dangerous. After her display on the capital, she couldn't blame them.

"Why can't I stay on the ship?" Ch'len was uncomfortable in the open spaces of the massive ship.

The crowd began to part and the flat rocky head of a Raalak became visible.

"Because they'll only storm the ship and drag you out by your stubby legs." Roland tucked his jacket behind his Tri-rollers, showing off the handles as he strolled through the guards, ballsy as ever.

The guards parted as High Charge Uthor towered over them on his four powerful legs. His stony brow furrowed at the sight of Esabelle, looking her up and down.

"Are we going to have a problem?" he asked.

Esabelle remained silent, not wanting to make any promises. She still didn't know why the *Gommarian* was now in the hands of the Conclave. She matched his steely gaze with an unyielding will born of the power she felt flowing through her body. She would go along with them for now, knowing that if it came to it she could turn the tide of control on the great ship.

Uthor clearly took the lack of action as her response. "Good, come with me." The High Charge showed them through the many corridors of the ship until they arrived at the med bay. Esabelle couldn't hide her shock at seeing Kalian submerged in a tank of blue liquid in the centre of the room. She knew it was him immediately, despite the lack of detail on his severely burnt face. Several nodes were attached to his face and hands along with a mask that covered his mouth and nose. Small robotic spiders crawled across his body, each one with a head of probes that couldn't find a way through his armoured suit.

Between the rainbow of holograms that floated around the Medder tank, Li'ara stood with her hand flat against the horizontal tube. She watched Kalian intently through the glass covering, barely noticing the new arrivals.

Esabelle pushed out her awareness to feel everyone in the room rather than look at them in turn. She instantly knew that Telarrek and Ilyseal were present with the Ambassador's son, Naydaalan. From a slight chemical imbalance in Telarrek, she knew that the Novaarian had been recently injured and treated by a Medder. Between that and Kalian's situation, something must have gone seriously wrong on their mysterious venture.

"What the hell happened to the kid?" Roland marched right up to the tank and bent down to get a better look at his burnt features.

Li'ara looked up, startled by the commotion.

Esabelle could see the exhaustion on her pale face with swollen red eyes. It appeared the commander's feelings for Kalian were stronger than Esabelle had thought. It was a futile relationship, doomed to end in tragedy. The facts were simple; he was a Terran and she a human. He would live an immortal life, connected to the universe in a way she could never understand in her limited lifespan. She would grow old before his very eyes and become nothing but a painful memory. Even now Li'ara didn't truly grasp Kalian's situation in the Medder tank. Esabelle could feel the life that burned like a star inside him; he would heal from whatever had caused his afflictions and be stronger for it.

The next hour was spent with sorrowful faces and an explanation of recent events on a planet called Trantax IV. Judging from Uthor's silence, the High Charge must have been aware of the facts. All the cards were on the table now. Esabelle's attention was brought back to

Kalian's appearance when told of his incredible feat aboard the *Nova*. His ability to hold back the power of a miniature sun was more proof of the energy she felt emanating from the Medder tank.

The news of Professor Jones was more disturbing, however. His apparent transformation, along with the presence of a new cube and their own findings on the capital, was unsettling. How many cubes are there?

"So that old shit survived Naveen?" Roland had never met ALF, but he had been present with Esabelle for the recanting. The news was surprising to her as well. Esabelle had hoped to never actually meet the artificial intelligence. Besides being instrumental in the obliteration of his civilisation, she had mixed feelings towards ALF and choices he had made. She wasn't entirely sure how she would react to meeting him.

"He's inside the suit." Li'ara pointed to the Medder tank before looking at Uthor. "We can't get it off him. It won't respond to anything and they can't cut through it. They think it'll slow down the healing process..."

"I can get it off," Esabelle announced.

"Not before you explain your actions on the capital," Uthor interrupted. "You are facing severe consequences for that."

"No..." Esabelle stood defiant.

"No?" Uthor straightened his back, increasing his size, to intimidate her.

"I want Kalian to hear it."

Uthor looked to the Medder tank with disbelief on his face. "That might take some time," he replied sarcastically.

So primitive.

"Leave me with him. When I am finished he will be ready to hear me, along with the rest of you. But I will not speak until he is out of that tank."

Li'ara was visibly torn by Esabelle's proposal. It was clear that Esabelle knew a way to heal Kalian, but she also knew what that entailed. Kalian had healed Li'ara on Naveen and imprinted a piece of himself inside her, giving them their unique bond. If Esabelle did the same now, there was a chance that the same bond would form between them.

"You will not be left alone with him." Uthor looked down on her.

Esabelle could see his true concerns. He didn't want the AI left unattended in the hands of a Terran. If he was going to stand in the way she would be left with no choice. The Conclave feared the power and wrath of a Gomar, trapped and restricted inside the exo-suits and Harnesses. Now they would see what a single Terran could do when backed into a corner.

"Uthor..." Telarrek stepped forward just as the smallest of sparks ignited inside Esabelle's palm. "Let her help him. Then we can all have our answers."

The two aliens held each other's gaze for a moment longer and Esabelle allowed the spark to die. The Raalak looked away, considering his friend's counsel.

"There will be guards outside at all times." With that he stormed out of the med bay, taking the others with him.

Li'ara lingered for a moment, her hand not quite ready to leave the pane of glass between her and Kalian. "Bring him back to me." There was a subtle threat in her words. Esabelle got the message - *he's mine.*

"Anyone fancy a drink?" Roland's voice faded away as the doors sealed behind Li'ara.

Esabelle looked down on Kalian's broken form as she used various magnetic waves to interact with the ship's nanocelium. At her mental command, the ceiling formed a pair of robotic arms that reached down and turned the tank so it was vertical, putting Kalian at eye level. A small appendage extended from one of the arms and pressed against the glass with a pointed nozzle. A high pitched frequency burst from the nozzle and instantly cracked the thick glass. Blue liquid gushed out in every direction before creating waves across the floor. Every drop had been telekinetically kept at bay, leaving her clothes dry.

The other robotic arm tapped a series of commands across the panel on the tank, which released the tubes and face-mask. They dropped to the floor along with the micro-spiders and probes. Kalian fell out of the tank and into her arms, flopping over her shoulder. At that moment Esabelle was thankful for her natural increase in muscle mass as a Terran. She carefully laid him on the floor, taking care not to injure his fragile looking head. Most of his lips had been melted away, exposing his charred teeth. She could feel the telekinetic barrier around his brain and organs. He had most likely erected them in reflex more than forethought, but she was thankful none the less.

Esabelle placed the pad of her thumb over the buckle, under his navel. With a short burst of electromagnetic energy, the nanocelium retracted back into the container, leaving him naked on the floor. His body was burnt red to varying degrees, depending on how well the armour held up to the heat and radiation. She looked at the Terran buckle sitting on his burnt flesh. She was hesitant to pick it up, knowing that ALF was inside it. Using telekinesis she lifted the object and placed it next to the nearest monitor.

"It's time to wake up, Kalian." Dropping into his mind was like being pulled into a hole too small for her body. She felt compressed and stretched out while their minds merged. Everything was chaos. His mind was more fractured than she had expected. Li'ara's memories collided with Savrick's in a dizzying swirl of reality all around her. She shouted his name across the changing landscape, in the hope of drawing his consciousness out. Separating her mind, she went to work on jump-starting his immune system and rapid healing, while at the same time focusing another part of her mind to route him out.

She had to be careful not to leave too much of herself behind as she tore through the memories looking for him. When Kalian had saved Li'ara it had been all emotion and urgency. Esabelle had to be more surgical and delete the imprints of herself that stuck to him. There was a reason this form of communication was restricted to loved ones who wished for a deeper connection.

Esabelle suddenly found herself in the last place she wanted to be. She stood before Savrick and Lilander in the dark bowels of the

Gommarian. She already recognised the memory from her own observations, millennia ago. What was left of the *Tempest* crew now knelt before Savrick in chains. They had each been crudely fitted with a Harness that gripped agonisingly to their spinal column. They were helpless against Savrick's brutal interrogation techniques. She had hated watching it at the time and hated watching it now.

The ship had been captured shortly after its arrival at Albadar, in the core system. Savrick had killed the crew slowly, one at a time, in an effort to gain information regarding their mysterious expedition. Esabelle remembered every detail about the memory, including the prisoners. She looked to the corner of the room where she had watched through the ship's internal cameras. Right now, Savrick had the one named Ryson by the throat, lifted off his feet in a death grip. His pleas for life were nothing but unintelligible gurgles, as Savrick's fingers began to crush his trachea. Savrick's armoured form turned in the shadow, but Esabelle was not greeted by the face of her father, but rather that of Kalian. He was literally reliving the memory as Savrick himself.

"You will tell me what I want to know or I will crawl inside your head and make you kill him with your bare hands." His threat was aimed at Adanae, the leader of the *Tempest* mission. Her face was flushed with anger and fear, streaming with tears. She had been forced to listen for days as her friends were slowly tortured to death around her.

"You coward!" Nalana spat the words at Kalian. She knelt next to Adanae with her hands bound behind her back. The dead body of Grif lay at her knees on the cold floor, his skin burnt and neck broken.

Without taking his eyes off Adanae, Kalian unleashed a ball of organic plasma into her face at point blank range. With a gut-churning *squelch*, the front half of her head was blown away, spraying Adanae in hot blood and melted skin.

"I will make *you* kill him..." Kalian repeated. Esabelle knew what came next and decided Kalian didn't need to relive *that* horror. She stepped fully into the memory and grabbed Kalian by the shoulder.

He turned on her, startled by the disturbance and break in the memory as if a part of him knew this wasn't how it played out.

"It's time to come back, Kalian." In the blink of an eye, the horrific scene evaporated until the new surroundings were that of a gloomy cave. Kalian blinked hard, disorientated by the quick change in events. She knew his consciousness would be piecing itself back together while filtering out Savrick and Li'ara.

"What's... what's happening?" he stumbled around the cave, assessing the environment. "Where are we?"

"Hadrok."

"Savrick's memories?" he was looking more himself now.

"Mine, actually. This was the last place I felt safe, before..." She kept her emotions in check, not wanting to leave any imprint. "Your body has been through a lot. I'm helping to accelerate the healing but you'll need to do more yourself. Just be sure to leave your pain receptors until last."

"What's going on, out there I mean. Is Li'ara safe?"

"She's fine. There's a lot to catch you up on and we don't have time. I'm going to need you at full power for what comes next." Kalian looked confused without all the facts. "Don't worry; it'll all make sense soon. We're going to share everything we've experienced, all our senses at once. In an instant, you'll know everything I've seen and done as if you lived it. It's going to be intense but you need to focus, take it all in and process the information as fast as possible."

Kalian slowly nodded his head in agreement.

"Take my hand..."

KALIAN WRAPPED a towel around his waist, feeling slightly awkward about his nakedness. He paddled his feet on the wet floor, noticing three of his toes were still skeletal with veins and muscle growing over the top. He formed a fist, feeling his strength returning with a tingle running through his spine. He had been sure he would never survive the Starrillium, that he would never feel the cool air on his skin again. It was like a dream, remembering the white-out as his power left him and his skin burned.

Esabelle was watching him closely from behind, he could feel her. There was the faintest of echoes left in his mind of her intrusion. He had cautiously viewed her memories of the discovery on the capital and didn't like the picture he was putting together in his mind. As well as having a new enemy in the form of a powerful corporation, the Highclave were now aware of ALF, Esabelle's existence and the captured Gomar. He pushed out his awareness to cover every inch of the *Gommarian* and felt the alien biology that made up the Conclave soldiers. They were everywhere. The ship was now theirs and humanity was once again at the mercy of another race.

Feeling the proximity of some very familiar electromagnetic frequencies, Kalian moved to retrieve his Terran buckle. The device was on the brink of folding back together after a series of web-like strands retracted from the surrounding monitor. What was ALF up to?

He placed the device below his navel at the same moment Li'ara and the others he had felt came through the door. The nanocelium covered his body, but not before everyone caught a glimpse of the towel falling to the floor. Li'ara looked from him to Esabelle with a hint of suspicion on her face.

"Well, that's disgusting." Roland wasn't talking about seeing Kalian naked. He could feel his eye socket rebuilding the healthy flesh and retina before his dark brown eye took shape again. This wasn't the moment Kalian had hoped for. He wanted Li'ara to rush in so he could take her in his arms and tell her how he never thought they'd get the chance. He could tell she was overjoyed at his health, but there was a cautious edge to her that kept them apart. Esabelle was evidently a source of friction between them.

Telarrek ignored Roland and clasped forearms with Kalian, using his upper arm to grip his shoulder, a broad Novaarian smile on his face.

"Greetings of peace, Kalian. It is good to see you so well! I feared we had lost you for sure."

"I thought the same about you. It seems you don't go down easy, old man."

"I have you to thank for that. You saved all of our lives on the *Nova*. I did not know you were capable of such a feat."

"Neither did I..." Kalian noticed Esabelle was still watching him closely. Seeing her reminded him that time was of the essence. He looked at Li'ara and decided their long overdue conversation would have to wait. For now, he simply walked over and gave her a small hug. It was more awkward than he had planned. He could feel the frequencies jumping out of her mind like golden strands trying to make contact with his own. She wanted to speak to him as much he wanted to speak to her.

Kalian quickly went around the room, acknowledging everyone, and thanking Ilyseal for taking care of Telarrek. Ch'len was a little confused as to how Kalian knew him without any introduction. He saved Roland for last, not really sure what to do with the trouble-maker. At one time he had put their potential Conclave membership in a sensitive position.

"I knew she'd get you back here; I just didn't think it'd be in one piece." Kalian thought for sure that Esabelle would have had to drag him back.

"What can I say, I got bored. This had better be as exciting as Captain *Serious* over there thinks it is." He flicked his head in Esabelle's direction. Same old Roland North. He could never really tell what the bounty hunter was thinking. His motivations changed like the wind, depending on his current mood.

"With that in mind," Captain Fey was standing in the doorway with High Charge Uthor, "perhaps we should continue our conversation on the observation deck?" Fey looked haggard and exhausted. Kalian could only imagine what Garrett had put them through in his absence. Her uniform was torn and dirty, with blood stains across the shoulders and legs.

"Actually, I would prefer to have this conversation in the basement." ALF was standing in the middle of the room, his image projected from Kalian's exo-suit. There was a moment of stunned silence in the room. This was the first time, for the majority of those present, to actually see and hear the ancient artificial intelligence.

Ch'len simply looked confused. "Who the hell is this guy?"

NOT LONG AFTER, the group found themselves in the small antechamber of the basement. Eight Conclave guards stood to attention at the sight of their High Charge and moved aside. Kalian couldn't believe the twisted and broken state of the heavy door. Garrett was even stronger than he remembered. Standing next to Li'ara, he took the opportunity to grab her hand and get her attention. With a look, he asked her if she was okay, but really he wanted to know if *they* were ok.

She yanked his arm down, pulling his ear to her lips. "If you ever pull a stunt like that again, I'll kill you myself," she whispered.

Her darker mood made more sense now; she was angry about his choice to die for her. He didn't want to point out that he had done the very same thing on Naveen when he forced her into the lift, away from Savrick. He now knew he could survive the raw energy of a Starrillium up close, but he knew for sure that he couldn't win a fight against Li'ara.

"Sorry..." He didn't really mean it and she knew it. Li'ara squeezed his hand reassuringly before letting go.

The cube was in front of them.

Several light orbs floated around the room to illuminate the dismantled cube. It looked to have opened up from the inside as it now lay spread out in different compartments like an old Chinese puzzle-box. All eyes were on ALF again as he appeared next to Kalian in his usual long robes and grey hair. He clapped his hands together before rubbing them like an excited child as he bent down to inspect the cube.

"Ok..." The AI turned to see everyone. "All roads lead here, people. It's time to bring and share. I'm ALF by the way, artificial life form." His crystal-blue eyes rested on Esabelle. "Had I a heart, it would ache for what your father put you through. Having said that, I don't trust you. Kalian vouches for you, however, so that will have to suffice, for now." Without waiting for a reply he moved on to Uthor. "No hard feelings about the *Helion*. I'm sure in your position you understand that a little evil is sometimes necessary to ensure the greater good and all." A look of revelation fell across the Raalakian's stony features. "And yes is the answer to your question; you should fear me, I'm really powerful and stuff." Kalian tried to hide his smile from the shocked Raalak - ALF's sense of humour was a unique one. Kalian had disagreed with sacrificing the crew of the *Helion*, but couldn't argue with the results. The alternative would have been Savrick killing him and going on to wipe out the Conclave.

"I don't see what's so big and scary about this. It looks more damaged than the last time we saw it." Roland kicked the edge of the cube.

"Ah, the bounty hunter..." ALF regarded him with a thankful smile. "In the spirit of sharing, I will go first. Shortly after the events on Naveen, I used the excavation team as a door through which I gained access to the Conclave. Your firewalls are so easily cracked, by the way. I hopped on a laser-com and found my way on to every planet with an AI hub. I spent the next few months researching *every-thing*." Kalian understood that when he said everything, he meant *everything*. "I started to find discrepancies in the historical archives when it came to the creation of the AI the Shay take so much credit for. They went from barely understanding the required components to having a fully functioning, yet malleable, artificial intelligence. Suddenly a small and unknown company became a galaxy-spanning corporation with controlling rights to their *machine*, and a contribution worthy of joining the Highclave."

"Protocorps..." Uthor's powerful arms were clasped behind his back.

"Indeed. I decided to take a closer look at Protocorps. Aside from their obvious ties to multiple crime syndicates, which have been forever overlooked, they are given an unusual amount of anonymity with their maintenance of the AI and those who are allowed to work on it. What was more surprising was the level of security surrounding Protocorps Headquarters. If I wished I could have seen what every Highclave councillor ordered for dinner, but I could not penetrate Protocorps' main tower. They control so many other companies and influence an army of officials on every planet that their operations are almost impossible to follow. I believe if you could, you would see that the mercenaries that attacked us on Trantax IV were employed by them. Specifically, Gor-van Tanar, whose connection to the underworld runs much deeper than the rest. He is part of a select group that sits at the top of this empire, and have done since its inception. So I decided that one of these fellows must have the answers to their ancestors' apparent creation." ALF turned to Roland and Ch'len. "It was I who employed your particular set of skills, Mr. North."

Roland actually looked perturbed at the news, while Ch'len just looked pissed off.

"You owe us a shit-load of money, old man!" Ch'len jumped at the hologram before Roland held him back.

"*You* sent us after Ral-vet Tanek?" It appeared the bounty hunter was doing long multiplications in his head.

"Yes, I would have sent you after Kel-var Tionis, the man at the top, but he was harder to track down. Unfortunately, by the time you had any information for me I had already left Naveen. I've been cut off from the Conclave network ever since. Perhaps it is now *your* turn to share?"

"That's gonna cost you!" Ch'len interrupted.

"Shut up, Len!" Roland and Esabelle blurted together. Kalian concealed his amusement, more curious at the connection forming between the odd couple.

"Ral-vet wouldn't talk, even with a gun to his head," Esabelle explained. "But his home array gave us what you were looking for. Show them." Roland pulled out a small disc from his belt and left it to hover in mid-air. It continued to project the images taken from Ral-vet's private server, showing them the schematics for the AI's core.

Kalian already knew what was coming from his shared experience with Esabelle.

"What is this?" Uthor asked.

ALF clearly knew what he was looking at as he circled the holo-gram. When it separated him from Kalian, his own holographic image became distorted.

"It's what *that* looked like before Professor Jones disturbed it." Esabelle indicated the cube. "So we broke into Protocorps to get more information. It led us to Sal-dev Tanek, Ral-vet's potential replace-ment on the board. His terminal gave us this..."

The hologram changed to the old images of the first excavation team that found the cube. There was also an official photo of the cube housed inside the great chamber at the top of Protocorps' HQ. There was no mistaking the likeness between all three cubes.

"You're saying that one of these, *things*, is controlling the central AI?" Uthor asked.

Kalian could feel the wireless connection being made between the floating disc and Uthor's arm pad.

"No, she's saying this *is* your central AI," ALF clarified. "I knew it! There was no way they could make an AI so quickly and effi-ciently."

"So what's the connection between Protocorps and these cubes?" Captain Fey kept a good distance from the relic in front of them. "Why are they working together?"

"These images would show that one simply found the other, a coincidence perhaps." ALF had no doubt run through a million scenarios already. "Why they would choose to work together remains a mystery, and to what end? It's been installed on the capital for thou-sands of years and done nothing but help run a civilisation. *This* cube wiped out an entire race in less time..."

Li'ara was carefully inspecting every inch of the compartmen-talised cube, crouching on all fours to see under the folded outer sections.

"It has the same Terran writing," she announced. "Right here on the side, Evalan." Kalian was impressed that she could remember the complex hieroglyphs of the Terran language.

"What's Evalan?" Roland asked.

"We don't know," Esabelle replied. She already knew that conclusion from Kalian's memories.

ALF came up behind Kalian and spoke into his ear, "Do you just let anyone inside your head?"

Kalian rolled his eyes at his old mentor's concerns. "I didn't really have a choice."

"Esabelle is correct," ALF continued to the group. "I created the language and it means nothing to me. I would say the obvious conclusion is that it's a name, but there were no planets, moons, habitats or people by that name. And yes, I realise there is a link between the cubes and the Terran, but I assure you, they were not created in *my* time."

"You expect me to believe you now, after so many lies?" Uthor stepped closer. "Protocorps helped bring our civilisation together. You show me pictures, though you cannot prove you stole them from Protocorps or Ral-vet Tanek. Now you spin tales of another threat to both our kinds, except it seems to me that these cubes and the technology they use are the same as the Terran. You may not have been around to witness their creation, but it is apparent that they were made by the Terran none the less. And by your very existence you are proof that artificial intelligence is achievable; who are you to judge the Shay's ingenuity? I have seen nothing that proves *you* are not the threat my people should fear." Uthor made a sweeping gaze of the party before him.

"We know that Garrett Jones is a threat, High Charge," Captain Fey said. "We should focus our efforts on him, together."

"Whether you think we are the threat or not, you cannot deny that whatever is controlling him is not of our design." Kalian hoped to make the Raalak see sense. "Even if our ancestors did make these things, we had no part in it. From what we've seen he isn't just lashing out, he has a purpose. He went straight for that cube and he knew exactly how to take out the *Nova* and me in one attack. Something or someone is guiding him with information he couldn't have got from the *Gommarian*. Think about all the people who knew about the Trantax project and tell me Protocorps had no involvement."

Uthor looked away in silence, "They were lobbying for control over the site before we discovered the Terran hieroglyphs," he admitted with some concern. "But it proves nothing of their guilt. Protocorps own several companies and museums that specialise in relics of all our species."

Kalian turned away, exasperated. How could he convince Uthor that they were malevolent in their machinations?

"We know that the cubes play the long game," ALF continued. "This cube took two hundred thousand years to wipe out the Terran and the humans. The cube inside your capital may well be playing a similar game. It may have no intention of striking now, but when it does it will have planned every eventuality."

"And that one isn't broken," Kalian added.

"Yeah, no shit." Roland kicked the fractured cube again.

"No, I mean this one was broken *before* Savrick found it." All eyes fell on Kalian. "Before Savrick died he... left a part of himself inside my mind. I have most of his memories."

Uthor looked very interested in this new development. It was another secret out of the bag, and not just for him. Everyone but Li'ara and Esabelle looked shocked.

"The cube was damaged when it entered the Hadrok system. I think there was a battle taking place over the planet, before the creation of ALF. When it emerged from subspace it was probably hit before crashing into the planet. Savrick knew it was influencing him but only to a point. It was too damaged to take him over completely like it has Garrett. I imagine taking over a human mind is easier than a Terran or a Gomar. I'm sure Garrett has no control over his actions the way Savrick did. But I am certain the thing inside him knows exactly what it's doing."

"If the cube in the capital is not broken, imagine what it is capable of." Telarrek's expression was pleading to Uthor.

"Or the one on Trantax IV..." ALF added ominously.

"You offer your help but you have already shown that you are no match for Garrett Jones. He almost succeeded in killing you." Uthor was as stubborn as his skin was thick. "It is the Highclave's opinion that you should all remain under quarantine and this ship is to be confiscated. You have already shown the devastation just one of you can cause." He eyed Esabelle with his observation.

"Just let a small team of us go." Li'ara stepped away from the cube, approaching Uthor. "Let us go and we can track Garrett down and bring him in. He tore through your men like they were nothing; why put them in more danger? Together, Kalian and Esabelle are stronger than him."

Kalian didn't think he would ever hear Li'ara say that. For a moment it looked as though Uthor was actually considering it.

"I would think it *more* dangerous to unleash all of you on the galaxy. We will find Garrett and he will be put down, without your help. Now we will rendezvous with the *Sentinel* in the Ch'ket system and you will relinquish the AI to us. All those aboard will be given shelter in an isolated habitat around Ch'ket, while the Highclave decides what to do with you and this ship."

"What about the Gomar?" Esabelle asked. She didn't show it but Kalian could feel the concern she felt towards their wellbeing. He couldn't understand why though. Since day one she had insisted on their survival, even in Rem-storage. It was possible though that she still clung to that previous connection she had with them as the ship's pilot.

"*They* are the biggest threat I know of. The damage they can cause has already been demonstrated. They will be sent to a different facility until the Highclave decides what we do with them. Personally, I'm thinking about dropping them into the nearest black hole."

With a brief glance, Kalian told Esabelle not to react in the way she wanted to. He could feel the molecules around her instinctively gathering to form a protective barrier. Her body was preparing for a fight.

"I'm sure the crew and the subsequent population will cooperate fully with your proposal, High Charge." ALF gave a small bow of the head.

"You do not speak for these people," Captain Fey was quick to add.

"Sorry, old habits..." With that, his image vanished as the emitters in Kalian's waist switched off.

"As a show of good faith, we will comply fully. There will be no resistance," Captain Fey continued. "I trust you will take this into account in your report to the Highclave?"

"That I will, Captain. Though I cannot say how it will effect the outcome. Your admittance into membership of the Conclave is looking unlikely. You will now regroup with the rest of your people until we arrive at Ch'ket. As ambassador to the humans, Telarrek, you are to accompany them to ensure a smooth transition."

Naydaalan and Ilyseal stepped closer to Telarrek to show their allegiance. Uthor strode out of the chamber with a small escort as the others were ushered from the room at gun-point.

Kalian looked across the room at Esabelle. They shared the same look of annoyance with the course they were now on. How could it be so hard to convince them of the coming threat with all their evidence? In their image, Savrick and his people had caused too much damage it seemed. They were irredeemable in the Conclave's eyes, now. It was frustrating that they were now suffering for the simple likeness they shared in biology to the Gomar. For an enlightened civilisation, they were very crude in their observations of two different people.

You know we can't let this happen.

Esabelle's voice rang clear in his mind. His first instinct was to push her out, keeping his mind his own. In their present circumstances it seemed there was no other choice. He expanded his mind and dipped into the frequencies that emanated from her head, feeling her thoughts fizz around his consciousness.

I take it you have something else in mind?

Without seeing her face, Kalian could feel the scheming smirk spreading across her face.

Kubrackk regretfully entered the Abyss with Spelnar close on his heel. He hated that it had come to this. The club was practically empty in the late morning, with an empty dance floor and a deserted bar. Some of Revus' goons occupied the tables, playing cards and placing bets on their Datapads.

A bald Revaneen, Kubrackk recognised as Lydagar, got up from his table and put himself between them and the stairs that led to Revus' office. "And where d'ya think you're goin'?"

Kubrackk considered Lydagar to be a unique member of his race. The Revaneen were a people known for their honour in the ways of battle, as well as their belief in only telling the truth. Their skin was a beautiful combination of green and blue patterns that differed on every individual like a fingerprint. Their dark dreadlocks were tightly bound behind their back and never cut above the knees. They had evolved with rock-like skin across their knuckles and joints, making them formidable in combat. They were scholars, philosophers and the greatest of warriors, even rivalling the Raalakians in war.

Lydagar was none of these things.

Kubrackk looked down on the hairless biped, who had spent his entire life lying and cheating his way up the ladder to lick Revus' boots. He had purposefully had the blue areas of his skin tattooed to match the green skin tone that he then had covered in intricate tattoos. His blue eyes looked Kubrackk up and down with no fear of the Novaarian's superior height or weaponry.

"Need to see Revus, so step aside before I put you aside, little man." Kubrackk's hand rested on the hilt of his knife at the base of his back. It was hidden from sight under his ragged poncho, but the movement was noted by the Revaneen.

"Well nobody sees the boss unless they're on the list and eh..." He pretended to look at an imaginary list on his arm pad. "You and your pet aren't on it."

Spelnar snarled at the insult and let his hand fall onto his holstered gun.

Kubrackk had heard enough from the little Revaneen. He pulled on the hilt of his knife, ready to bury it in his bald, green head.

"Lydagar!" Revus shouted from his office.

His meaning was interpreted by Lydagar, who stepped aside, slowly. After Kubrackk walked past he immediately put himself in front of Spelnar and put a hand to the Trillik's chest. "Not you, grub."

Spelnar looked at Kubrackk who gave him a subtle nod in response. The Trillik wasn't needed in this conversation anyway. He continued up the stairs and headed into Revus' office, where the Brenine sat behind his wooden desk like some self-important politician. He was a powerful man, no doubt, but his reach only went so far. Now Kubrackk would put that to the test.

"Kubrackk, it's been too long since you visited this little watering hole of mine. It's been nearly six months since your last bounty. You know membership comes with a price?"

It was true, he hadn't paid his membership for some time now, and Revus usually took the units out of his take of the bounty. "The *Rackham* will pay my fee for the next millennium." Kubrackk took the measure of the two goons sitting on a long sofa to his left, with a third standing to his right, looking out over the club below. Their casual nature was a sign to the Novaarian that he wasn't considered a threat, but if he tried something stupid, there were enough of them to take him down. No doubt Revus had more than one weapon hidden under his desk.

"You think I want to go anywhere near the most wanted ship in the galaxy?" Revus tapped his desk and a holographic video played out, above the surface, of the *Rackham* during its daring escape from Conclave authorities.

"Of course you do. That just proves why it's so valuable. There's no other ship that can attack Protocorps Headquarters in the heart of Clave Tower and successfully escape the entire solar system." Kubrackk had called his bluff; it was clear to see on his pale face. Revus wanted that ship more than anything right now and Kubrackk was his ticket. "You want it, I can get it. I just need to know where he's hiding."

Revus looked away and didn't say anything for a minute. He

tapped his fingers on the desk, contemplating something that Kubrackk guessed was worrying the Brenine.

"I know where the Conclave thinks he's going; I just don't know *where* he's going..."

Kubrackk hated this mysterious bullshit. Only rich, greedy men had time to talk in riddles, with no sense of urgency. "Speak sense," Kubrackk replied sharply. The Shay guard to his right apparently took some offence on his employer's behalf. Before he could remove his weapon, Kubrackk flicked his knife directly into the servo-joint of his robotic arm, pinning it to the wall and severing the Shay's connection to his fingers.

The two Brenine on the sofa jumped up, ready to blast the Novaarian into the next world.

"Stop!" Revus held up his hand. The guards looked confused at their orders but obediently remained where they were. Revus laughed to relieve the tension, sitting back comfortably in his leather chair. Kubrackk had a feeling it was Tularon leather.

"My friends are a little more sensitive than I am, Kubrackk. Sit down," He waved at the two Brenine, still itching for a fight. The Shay struggled to remove the blade with his organic arm. With a single look from Revus, the Shay stopped struggling and remained silently pinned to the wall. "What I mean to say is that my contacts tell me Mr. North and his associate are potentially heading back to their own kind."

Kubrackk knew about that hulking ship like everyone else. Aside from its outright attack on the capital, it was also witnessed in the Corvus system and in orbit around Naveen. It was bigger than any ship made by the Conclave, stronger too. It had been met with mixed results when the human refugees took shelter inside it after the so-called Gomar had been defeated. It made sense to Kubrackk though. They were well protected inside the *Gommarian* with no small amount of leverage on their side, not to mention the famous Kalian Gaines.

"You don't know where the *Gommarian* is," Kubrackk stated.

"The location of that ship is known only to a few, and I do not have access to them."

Kubrackk felt all his hope wash away. If Revus couldn't get to these people then he had no chance. North might die from human old age by the time he got that kind of information. He knew that the ship had been allowed to travel through Novaarian space, under constant guard, but even that amount of territory would take centuries to scour. He sighed as he turned and removed the buried blade in one motion, heading for the door. The Shay sagged against the wall under the weight of his broken mechanical arm. This had been a waste of his time.

"There is someone who can get this information, if he doesn't already have it, that is." Kubrackk turned again to see the calculating look Revus was giving him. "I can arrange a meeting if you like?" The Novaarian already knew who he was talking about. Just thinking about him gave Kubrackk a feeling of dread that made him want to run in the opposite direction.

"The Laronian..."

ELEVEN

Judging by the smell, Roland guessed they were close to the open living area, where those too scared to move out into the ship had made camp. He could almost taste the various foods being cooked inside the many tents and pavilions. He tried to ignore the pangs of hunger his own belly was suffering. If he was hungry, he could only imagine how hungry Ch'len was.

The Conclave guards escorting them were on all sides, not taking any chances. He counted eight altogether and knew they had passed twenty-two soldiers on the way. The Novaarians had been taken a different way after they left the basement, and no doubt Uthor was monitoring everything from the bridge. Roland felt Ch'len's tiny eyes boring a hole in the side of his head. The Ch'kara obviously blamed him for their current predicament. He didn't feel sorry for the little shit, of course. He needed Roland; it was as simple as that. Where he went, Ch'len followed. In this case, it wasn't anywhere great, but at least there would be food.

With no alcohol in his system, it was hard to tune out his training. He noticed everything around him, especially the almost imperceptible glances between Kalian and Esabelle. It was hard to miss the weird tension between the two of them and Li'ara, but that was a situation he was more than happy to stay away from. He knew for sure, however, that the kid wasn't smart enough to juggle both of them, in any capacity. The one he inevitably scorned would be upset, vulnerable and probably up for some revenge sex; that's where Roland would come in.

He examined Captain Fey and wondered how she was still walking. She appeared physically exhausted after the ordeal Garrett had put them through; she was over a hundred years old after all. Then again, if her body was anything like her personality she was a walking, talking robot. He couldn't deny the great job she was doing as the leader of mankind though, despite all the shit that had taken place in the last forty-eight hours. It was the thought of responsibility like that which kept him always on the move. This was the first time in a long time that he had been a part of something, something real and important, something that mattered.

He knew the best thing would be to leave as soon as possible before he started to actually care. He hadn't really cared about anything since Europa. It had numbed him to the point that he forgot what it was to be human, to feel. He shook his head to try and forget the faces of all the children, but it never worked.

Suddenly Kalian and Esabelle stopped walking, a fraction before the lights in the corridor disappeared. Roland caught on and flung himself into the space where the nearest guard had been. To his surprise, there was nothing but a blank wall to greet his attack. Seconds later, the lights came back on with a painful glare and an impressive display from the Terran. All the guards were scattered across the corridor in unorthodox positions as if beaten by a wild animal. The soft gargles of the last guard died out as Kalian let go of his throat, dropping him to the floor at his feet.

"How did you do that?" Captain Fey had an expression somewhere between awe and horror.

"Electromagnetic pulse to cut the lights," Kalian offered.

Roland quickly checked his Tri-rollers, aware of the effects such magnetism had on the Intrinium.

"Don't worry, it wasn't that powerful," Kalian reassured him with a cheeky smirk.

"We need to go, now." Esabelle was already walking down the corridor before Captain Fey stopped them.

"We can't do this. If we take this ship back by force it will be taken as a sign of war. We need to work *with* them now."

"We're not taking back the ship, Captain," Esabelle explained. "They can keep it for all it's worth to them. The nanocelium will take them decades to figure out. They can pilot it with the controls but that's about it."

"What are we doing then?"

"Whether the Conclave believes us or not, there is a very real threat out there," Kalian said. "If we're limited to their confinements, it will be too late when the cube and Protocorps strike. We need to get off the *Gommarian* and end it ourselves."

"Just us the five of us?" The captain didn't look convinced.

"Five and a half." Roland nodded towards Ch'len.

"We have no other choice. Look at what just one of the cubes did to our race, to our home. Terran and human alike were wiped out by just one of them. We know for sure now that one of them is in the heart of the Conclave. Imagine the damage it's capable of."

"If we're right, we'll have saved the entire Conclave..." Li'ara added.

The captain showed a new interest in Li'ara's words, even Roland saw that connection. It would surely be an instant invitation into their civilisation.

"Then go, but I can't come with you. I have to stay with them." Her place was with the rest of their species. Leading from the front was the only way she knew how to be a captain. Roland respected her for that. Not that his respect was worth much.

"Good luck." Kalian put a hand on the captain's shoulder before turning to leave.

"I think you're going to need the luck with *him* tagging along." The captain looked at Roland as he passed by and he blew her a mocking kiss. They left her alone, in the corridor of unconscious bodies, as they ran through the ship, heading for the hangar. The guards along the way were easily dispatched by either Kalian or Esabelle, who always seemed to know where they were.

"Why have we stopped here?" Li'ara asked. They were standing outside a large circular door with no designation on it. Esabelle stepped forward and placed her palm out to the wall, where a hidden panel materialised. She quickly punched in a code and allowed the biometric scanner to identify her. The door opened without a sound to reveal an empty room.

"Shit!" Kalian exclaimed.

Roland had no idea what the problem was. It took him a moment of looking around to recognise the room where the twelve Gomar had been stored months ago.

"They've already taken them." Esabelle had a look of despair.

"I thought you said it would take them months to figure out how the nanocelium worked?" Li'ara pointed her question at Esabelle.

"I was wrong..." And she definitely didn't look happy about it.

"What were we gonna do, anyway? Carry all twelve of them back to the *Rackham*?"

"Yes," both Esabelle and Kalian replied. Roland remembered that carrying several tons of Rem-stores was quite easy for a Terran.

"We need to keep moving." Li'ara pressed.

Ch'len was already out of breath, resting on his stubby knees. They were soon off again at a speed even Roland found uncomfortable. Kalian and Esabelle were probably running a lot slower than they were capable of, but it was still damn fast. A few minutes later the hangar doors opened to a circus of activity. New ships were landing as old ones were taking off, relieving the current soldiers. Conclave engineers examined different consoles while a larger group were trying to prise open the *Rackham*.

They stayed low for a moment, taking cover behind the nearest crate of fresh supplies. There were so many soldiers that Roland couldn't count them all. Ch'len was already sitting on the floor, adjusting his breathing equipment to compensate for his lack of breath.

"Even if we take off, how are we going to escape?" Roland asked. "With them in control of the bridge, they can detect us even with the stealthware."

Esabelle didn't hesitate as she moved away to get some space. With her hand held out, the floor produced a column of nanocelium with a holographic display at the top.

"What are you doing?" Li'ara was looking out for anyone who might see them.

"I'm rerouting the bridge master control. It won't last long, just enough time for us to leave the solar system."

"Where are you rerouting it to?" Kalian inquired.

"The bathroom on level fourteen," Esabelle replied with a smile. "When I redesigned the ship, before disconnecting, I created an override code in case of emergency."

"That's hilarious..." Roland tried to stifle his laugh. He imagined that right now there was some poor Conclave guard, dropping a shit, as the bathroom around him turned into the command centre for the scariest ship in the galaxy.

"Let's go." Kalian lead the charge as they made the mad dash for the *Rackham*. Roland set his Tri-rollers to low yield as he shot wildly into the clusters of guards that closed in on them from every side. He recognised the incredible power of telekinesis as several guards and objects were thrown around the hangar with the unseen force. Any that got too close was taken down by furious hand to hand combat that left the individual in a heap of broken bones. They made a better Special Forces team than he had seen on Earth, with the exception of Ch'len, who couldn't seem to hit the side of a patrol ship.

The engineers scattered, leaving the *Rackham* free to board. Roland used his mental connection to start the drive and lower the ramp, just in time for them to take cover inside. He felt the ship lift off, causing him to stumble to one side, as they reached the bridge. He jumped into his seat as Ch'len took up his own station, wiping several desserts off the console as he did. The hull *panged* with weapons fire from the soldiers outside, each bolt of energy absorbed by the nanocelium.

Roland was quickly surrounded by holograms including two orange domes that allowed him to manually steer the ship. The arcing viewport shifted as the *Rackham* turned to face the hangar exit and the stars beyond. Targeting reticules appeared in front of them with Roland aiming the cannons at the closest patrol ships parked nearby.

"No weapons fire." Li'ara put her hand over his to prevent the activation. "The ships outside will detect it and make getting out of here a lot harder."

Roland dismissed the hologram and rolled his eyes. "Whatever you say, sweetheart." Li'ara's glare was enough to make him smile. He placed both hands over the domes and ignited the thrusters, hurtling the ship out of the hangar with incredible speed. "Ch'len..." He continued on into space while he waited for the Ch'kara's coordinates.

"Alright, alright! I'm sending them over now." Ch'len always knew the best places to hide in a situation like this. Before his aspirations to be a bounty hunter, he had spent over a hundred years working as a smuggler for the biggest crime syndicate on Ch'ket.

Roland looked over the new coordinates that just slid into the hologram on his right. "The Karina nebula... where the hell's that?"

"Exactly," Ch'len replied slyly.

Roland smiled at his partner's criminal knowledge before inputting the coordinates into the navigation system. The hologram to his left flashed with alarm as multiple Nebula-class ships and a Nexus-class set a course to intercept. He coolly brought up a new screen and activated the stealthware. Now the ship was invisible to the naked eye and every scan they possessed.

"Let's punch it!" Roland ignited the Intrinium and activated the Solar Drive. "I've always wanted to say that..." The Drive whined and stuttered before cutting out completely.

Bollocks...

He forgot about their lack of fuel. He turned to see four judging faces staring at him. He adjusted the course of the ship to face the sun, seventy million kilometres away.

"We just need to stop and soak up some rays."

"Great idea, *Captain*! Except the stealthware won't work while we charge the Intrinium!" Ch'len was wiping his fingers across the smears of food and licking them clean. Roland knew he only ate like that when he was nervous.

"How long will it take to charge the Intrinium?" Kalian asked.

"Too long..." Roland looked at the specs for the Nexus-class vessel. Once they were detected it would be on them before they had enough charge to even traverse the solar system.

"How far to the nearest system?" Esabelle was pacing behind his chair. He turned to see Ch'len going through the star charts with frantic speed.

"With thrusters alone, it would take nine days to reach the Torvin system." Ch'len looked back in despair; they didn't have that kind of time. The stealthware wouldn't last that long and they would inevitably be found between here and the Torvin system.

"Any ideas...?" Roland sat back, unsure of their next move.

"Just one, actually." Everyone turned around to see Esabelle entangled in a nest of tubes and holograms coming out of the floor. The nanocelium was pressing into her skin from head to toe until her eyes rolled into the back of her head and she became unresponsive.

"Esabelle!" Kalian stopped short of the mesh of tubes and wires, while Roland looked on in disbelief as his ship revealed more secrets to its Terran occupants.

"What the hell is she doing to my ship?" The lights flickered along with the consoles and holograms around the bridge. Roland just caught the warning about life support depletion before they were all cast into darkness. It took him a moment to realise there should be some light from the approaching sun. He swivelled in his chair to see nothing but an empty abyss beyond the viewport.

The *Rackham* was in subspace.

GARRETT WANTED to curl up in a ball and find a dark place to hide. A conversation he couldn't comprehend had just come to an end between the Terran, his own parasite and another being. This other being could only be heard when the station was activated, and thankfully the great machine had been turned off. The voice had a power to it that dwarfed the Terran and his own. Just being connected to it made Garrett feel violated and exposed to raw energy.

What is this station?

The Terran had worked the central console perfectly, as if he had built the system himself, bringing its hidden functions to life. A mysterious flash of light from outside the viewport was the only indication anything had happened. Purple bolts of lightning raced around the exterior of the crescent hull, bombarding the station. The titan-like voice had coursed through his mind the second the station had become active. He was too frightened to try and contemplate the meaning behind the conversation, let alone the identity of the voice. Whatever it was, it wasn't happy. Garrett felt a renewed sense of purpose flow through his parasite's thoughts.

As one, the Terran and Garrett turned to face the confused faces of the Shay delegation. Garrett still had no idea what part these individuals had played in all this. They must have been unsure themselves of what had taken place before them. To the Shay, it would have appeared the station was activated and the two aliens simply stood in silence until it switched off. With their incredible speed of thought, it was impossible to say how long they had been standing there, communing with the so-called Vanguard.

"Is everything to your satisfaction?" The one who had identified himself as Kel-var Tionis asked. They thought the Terran was testing the station, they had no idea what had really happened. As far as the Shay were concerned, the two beings in front of them were gods. But Garrett understood now, they were only puppets for something worse.

"You built the facility to our exact specifications," the Terran replied. There was no hint of gratitude or emotion in his voice; the Shay was clearly beneath the effort. There was something more to the Terran, though. Garrett could feel so much more from him when they were connected as if he was more complex than his own parasite.

"What's next?" Sel-gar blurted out.

Garrett had already picked up on the groups dislike for this particular alien. The fat Shay appeared to instantly regret his actions, taking a small step back and keeping his eyes firmly on the double chin that protruded from his collar.

"The Terran infestation in this quadrant of the galaxy is unacceptable." The Terran continued, "We are to use this station to finally wipe them out, while you return to Shandar and prepare the *Crucible*."

The Shay began to display subtle signs of anxiety and displeasure at that particular word. Garrett didn't know what they were talking about and couldn't glean any answers from the passing thoughts of his parasite.

"So it is to be in our time then..." Bal-son Narek quietly commented. To the keen auditory senses of the Terran and Garrett, he might as well have yelled it at them.

"Indeed you are lucky to witness the majesty that will descend upon this galaxy," the Terran announced with some prestige. There was definitely more of a personality to him than the simple brute that possessed Garrett.

"Perhaps we should wait..." Sel-gar offered nervously. "Until we know for sure that the Terran can be annihilated with this station. They have proven to be quite the survivors-"

The words were cut off as the fat Shay rose into the air, a moment before his neck twisted with a bone-crunching *snap*. His body was flung by unseen forces, hurtling him into the hard metallic wall where it crumpled into a heap of organic and artificial limbs. To Garrett's left, the Terran had his arm outstretched towards Sel-gar.

The Terran had Kalian's powers.

The Shay delegation was stunned into silence as they tried to hide their expressions of horror. The guards didn't know how to react to the sudden violence and the death of one of the people they were supposed to protect. They made a step forward before deciding that avenging Sel-gar Tanek wasn't worth the punishment they would face at the hands of the Terran.

"Transcendence is upon you all. Prepare the way for what is coming and you will be rewarded in your new life. Your identities may yet be preserved; the same cannot be said for the rest of your civilisation." Sel-gar's lifeless body was evidence of the alternative.

"I will use my connections to find the current location of the humans and their ship." Gor-van Tanar bowed his head beneath his shadowy hood.

"They are en-route to Ch'ket, where the Conclave will evacuate them onto an artificial habitat. They are now under the full control of the Conclave security forces," the Terran replied smoothly. Garrett could feel the undercurrent of chatter that ran between the two of them and the third intelligence he initially felt outside the sarcophagus. It felt familiar to him but he knew he could easily be misinterpreting his own familiarity and that of his parasites.

Is it another cube?

Surely there couldn't be another cube. Whatever it was Garrett could feel it constantly supplying them with vast amounts of data. He couldn't access the information but it was obviously well connected to the Conclave.

The group looked shocked at the level of knowledge the Terran possessed. Coupled with his recent show of telekinesis he was starting to appear quite omnipotent to the uninformed Shay.

The Terran turned to the nearest technician, standing at her post, clearly terrified. "Set a course for the Ch'ket system, immediately," he ordered.

The female Shay looked hopelessly at the collection of well-dressed Shay standing beyond the Terran.

"Is she defective as well?" the Terran raised his hand before Kel-var spoke up.

"You mean to drop the station into subspace and travel to Ch'ket..." Kel-var's voice began to fail him under the glare of the Terran's black eyes.

"Yes..."

"The station is fully operational; however, there are still a few systems that need extra time. We had a longer timetable in mind when my great-grandfather began construction. Normally the station could be activated and then instantly used for subspace travel, but that phase of configuration has not been completed. Since all three Starrilliums have just been used it will take time before the energy can be diverted for subspace travel..."

Do we kill another one?

I would like to, but it will make no difference to the functionality of this station. It will take their primitive forms time to correct this mistake. We will have to wait until...

Garrett lost track of the conversation as the connection between the two increased. The more they conversed, the more he could see into the mind of the Terran. Through the perpetual abyss that had become his only surroundings, Garrett could see a speck of light in the distance. He sank deeper into the cage of his own mind and found the strongest part of the connection between the two of them. The light became more intense as it took form in front of him, slowly drawing the outline of a cube made entirely of light around the edges.

"My God..." Inside the box of light was the curled up figure of a human man. He was bald and naked, clawing at his own body as if he was being ravaged by insects. Garrett caught sight of the man's face and gasped at the revelation. It was the Terran from the sarcophagus. His consciousness was trapped inside his own head like Garrett's, only the Terran's prison was far more confining. At seeing another person the Terran jumped at him, his eyes pleading for help. He was clearly shouting from inside the box but Garrett couldn't hear anything. The Terran's hands slammed against an invisible wall between the edges of light, creating a ripple effect across the surface.

The Trantax cube must be more powerful than the *Gommarian* cube if it could cage a Terran's mind so completely. Garrett instinctively hammered his fists against the invisible wall, hoping to give the Terran some control back. When his strength proved useless he realised there had never been any hope, really. This was after all inside his mind, a mind he no longer controlled. He was simply the remnants of a consciousness that couldn't be entirely eradicated.

He was a ghost in the machine.

The Terran had stopped beating on the wall and now sat curled up in the corner of his cell. He was afraid and Garrett knew why. They could both hear the slithering that circled them in the darkness.

You shouldn't have done that.

The image of his mother was now standing behind him, a disappointed look on her face. He turned his head back but the box of light and the Terran within was gone. The connection was lost as the two parasites focused their attention on the Shay again.

"You will all leave this station and return to Shandar, now," the Terran continued as if the news about the Solar Drive was no longer important. "When it is ready we will travel to the Ch'ket system and wipe out the humans and Terran alike. Once you hear news of this, activate the Crucible."

The Shay officials filed out of the control room without another word.

Garrett was now left alone with his parasite and nothing to occupy it. His mother's expression changed from disappointment to malevolent glee.

You shouldn't wander, little rabbit. Now you're going to stay in here with me. I'm going to give you a glimpse of what is coming. I'm going to show you what will become of your kind and the rest of this civilisation.

He was suddenly standing on a world he had never seen before, surrounded by aliens he didn't recognise. Every time he blinked, the environment swirled through an endless visage of worlds and cities. Garrett screamed inside his head, sure that he would never stop screaming ever again as the horrors played out across every planet.

THE FABRIC of the universe was folded where two points of origin were temporarily knotted together before reverting back to normal space. Kalian had felt the tear in physics like a change of pressure in his ears. It was a unique form of subspace travel yet to be unlocked by any race or Solar Drive. In fact, to Kalian's knowledge, it was a form of travel known only to Esabelle. It allowed the ship and its contents to be instantly transported from one place to another without having to navigate subspace.

Kalian looked over the navigation console and saw that they were now in the Karina nebula. It should have taken them several days to get there via thrusters and a whole day in subspace. Thanks to Esabelle it had only taken a second.

Roland was clearly stunned in his chair. His hands dashed out across the console, checking every readout twice in disbelief.

Ch'len stumbled off his chair, staring out the viewport at the beautiful nebula of golden dust that formed a cloud several light-years across.

Li'ara stood next to Kalian, never taking her eyes off the visage of Esabelle, entangled in the mess of tubes.

"This is a whole new level of crazy, even for you guys!" Roland exploded from his chair and checked the star charts on Ch'len's console. "How did she do that?" He marched around her standing body, inspecting the dark tubes that rose up from the floor of his ship. With no indication, the tubes suddenly detached from Esabelle's skin and sank back into the floor once more. Her body crumpled to the floor, caught, only inches before hitting her head, by Kalian.

"Esabelle..." She didn't respond to his voice. Kalian was alarmed to see a trickle of blood flowing from her nose and both of her ears. "Esabelle!" He gripped her face harder and held her tight but she refused to respond. He could feel the brain waves emanating from her unique frequency and took comfort in the knowledge that she was still alive. He matched his frequency with her own in an effort to make contact telepathically. Like a hand to the face, he was repelled from entering her mind by a violent shove. His head physically shot back and he fought not to drop her.

"What's wrong with her?" Li'ara asked.

"I don't know, I can't get into her head." He looked at Li'ara and saw some conflict there. Kalian could feel her discomfort at the thought of them sharing their minds so intimately.

"You need to leave her." ALF was standing next to them. His sudden appearance made Ch'len jump and fall backwards into Roland's console. "She will recover in her own time. Her healing abilities are better than yours, Kalian." He felt the AI's poke in the ribs with his explanation.

"I'm supposed to just leave her? She didn't leave me when I needed healing."

"Esabelle has about two hundred thousand years on you. Trust me, she'll be fine. Might I suggest we focus our attention on charging the Intrinium, instead?"

"*Rackham*, plot a course for the nearest star and begin Intrinium charge." Roland's order was met with a pleasant chirp from the overhead speakers.

"*Rackham*?" ALF directed the question to Roland.

"Yeah you know, Jack Rackham, the famous pirate!"

"You named your ship after a famous Earth pirate?" Roland shrugged in reply. "Fitting..."

Kalian was just impressed that the bounty hunter knew anything about Earth's history. Pirates hadn't been around for over a thousand years, but if Roland was going to know anything about history, it would be pirates.

"What did she do?" Li'ara checked Esabelle's pulse.

Kalian met her questioning look but he wasn't entirely sure he could answer her.

"She pushed herself." ALF focused on Kalian. "Something you should try doing, eh? Esabelle folded space in a way no Solar Drive can. The closest machine capable of instantaneous travel is a Starforge, but since that technology doesn't exist on this side of the galaxy, Esabelle did what only a Terran can do." There was a look of pride on ALF's face. "She was forced to use this ability when the *Gommarian* was a part of her, feeding her all the nutrients and energy required to pull it off. Without that extra help, she has suffered some internal trauma. In all the millennia I watched over Terran development, I never saw such an incredible feat. It is proof of the connection all Terran shares with the universe. Marvellous..."

"You're saying she teleported us here with no technology?" Ch'len couldn't take his eyes off Esabelle.

"Indeed. Put her somewhere quiet where she can heal. It may take some time."

"It's gonna be another day before we can use the Drive. For now, we're stuck in the nebula until we reach the nearest usable star." Roland was leaning against his console, clearly stressed with their latest situation.

"But we're in a nebula; there must be thousands of suns we can use." Li'ara moved to check over Ch'len's charts.

"We need to find a sun old enough to have developed starspots, or the electromagnetic charge won't be strong enough to ignite the Intrinium," Ch'len explained their astronomical problem with some condescension. "Even a child knows that..."

THE SUBCONSCIOUS CLOCK in Kalian's head kept him perfectly informed of how long they had been sitting in the starspot. Since arriving in the nebula, twelve hours had gone by with agonising speed. It had taken them eleven hours to reach the appropriate star on thrusters alone, and Kalian could feel the Intrinium particles becoming excited in their Drive cells. It wouldn't be much longer before they had enough charge to travel to any planet in the Conclave.

Pushing his awareness out into the *Rackham*, he despaired at Esabelle's inaction. She hadn't so much as twitched since he put her in the hold below. She lay prone over some blankets, her mind gated off from his attempted incursions. How long would it take to heal from such a humongous use of power? He could only dream of understanding how the universe could be folded in such a way.

The unique frequencies of Roland and Ch'len rippled out from their brains on the bridge. From the way, they were synced it was obvious they were playing some kind of card game together. Kalian was pleased with himself for being able to discern his findings from brain waves alone. His knowledge and experience of Terran abilities paled in comparison to Esabelle's though. His thoughts went back to the mercenaries he killed on Trantax IV and he dwelled on his use of power. Was it wrong that he couldn't fold the universe or fly without the peril of death hanging over him, but he could take life with ease? He would have talked to Esabelle about it, but he already knew her point of view on the matter. To her, it was a simple case of nature when it came to the use of their powers. If nature had seen to grant them their abilities, then they were entitled to use them in any way required.

Kalian wasn't always so sure.

The pressure in the room changed moments before Li'ara walked into the kitchen. Kalian detected the effect her body had on the molecules in the atmosphere that filled every inch around them. His thoughts of inadequacies and death were washed away as the beautiful redhead stepped into the light. His Terran eyes looked over her face with a clarity no human could hope to achieve. It was agonising how much he ached to be with her, to bind their minds and bodies in a way that made them one. They were yet again in the middle of a conspiracy that could spell the end of the Conclave. A part of him wished they could hand the responsibility over to someone else and simply get lost in the galaxy.

"What are you looking at?" Li'ara sat down opposite him, and Kalian blinked his reverie away.

"We need to talk..."

Li'ara shuffled in her seat, uncomfortable with the chosen topic. They had avoided this conversation for months, and when it was brought up Li'ara ended the talk before it began.

"You want to talk about that now?"

"Why not? We've got time. And after our latest insult to the Highclave, it won't be long until I'm hauled off to join the Gomar on some classified planet."

Li'ara hesitated. "Have you ever stopped to think that your interest in me isn't natural? A result of our minds crossing over, or whatever happened to us on Naveen?"

"My interest? You might not talk about it but I know there's a part of me inside that brain of yours. It was a two-way process, and I'm sorry it happened that way; I didn't have the same level of control I do now. I was doing the only thing I could to save you..." He was becoming defensive.

"I'm not saying I'm not grateful for you saving my life. I'm suggesting that our feelings are being manipulated by our personalities crossing over."

The conversation was starting to feel more like an argument. "Look at me and say you feel manipulated by what you see in me."

Li'ara only looked at him for a moment before concentrating on the floor between her feet. They both sat in awkward silence, avoiding each other's glances.

"Li'ara, I *know* I lo-"

"Don't say that." Li'ara cut him off. "Since we met, we've both nearly been killed a dozen times. Our way of life has been completely wiped out with most of our species. We're clinging to the edges of an alien civilisation that fears us. There's something out there hunting us down and the one safe place in the galaxy is apparently on its list as well. What's left of our race is relying on us to make sure they have a future. You're important, Kalian. You might not be the one making all the decisions but they will rally behind you, behind your strength. You're the living embodiment of our future, of what we all hope to achieve. You can't be distracted by me..."

"I understand, I really do." With her personality inside his head, Kalian really did see her point of view, but he also had her stubbornness. "But if what you say is true, there are going to be a lot of hard choices. There's going to be conflict and pain and loss. I don't want to go through that without you. You're right, we have nearly been killed a dozen times, but every time I was on the edge it was the thought of you that gave me strength. Do you think I could have defeated Savrick or contained that Starrillium without you? We're stronger *together*, Li'ara."

"You're stronger because Esabelle's teaching you."

There was more to that statement than just the words, Kalian - could feel it. As the realisation spread across his face, Li'ara couldn't keep eye contact.

"Don't make that a thing," Kalian pleaded.

"I'm just saying-"

"What is it with you and her?" Kalian couldn't imagine Li'ara being intimidated by Esabelle's looks. As a Terran she was naturally pleasing to the eye, often gaining the interest of every male and some females onboard the *Gommarian*, but Li'ara was unquestionably beautiful and intelligent.

"Don't you see it," she continued. "You and she are the perfect match. You're both Terran, at least in physiology; you both understand what it's like to be so connected to the universe. I will never be able to relate to that, Kalian. You can learn so much more from each other, not to mention the things you can do together, the places you can go that humans can only dream of. And you're both immortal..."

There it was, spoken out loud. In truth, Kalian hadn't really stopped to think about his newfound lifespan. The idea of living forever was a concept entirely foreign to human beings. Kalian didn't really know what to make of it, but the idea of living forever without Li'ara was very clear in his mind.

"Immortality is a choice for a Terran. If I don't replenish my cells regularly, I age the same as you. I would rather die with you than live forever without you." He couldn't make it any simpler than that.

"Don't be ridiculous, Kalian." Li'ara sounded almost angry. "You've been granted a gift by *nature*, the greatest gift. You could see the universe; you have time for that now. Don't give something up like that just to die with me."

"I would give it up to live with you!" he matched her anger with his own aggressive tone.

This was a stupid thing to be fighting over and they both knew it.

Kalian knew how she felt for him and yet they argued over what should be a natural union.

"How do you think I will feel when you're getting older and dying because of me? I'll spend centuries looking at you knowing that you could be so much more if it wasn't for me. Your lifespan could be invaluable to the human race. Who knows what's coming for us in the future. You could teach our people for eternity, be a guiding hand in the unknown. Eventually, more people are going to develop Terran abilities and they're going to need someone to be there with the answers. That's you, Kalian."

"There's Esabelle for that, and she's more powerful than I'll ever be."

"She doesn't relate to humans the way you do. You've grown up a human, not a Terran or a Gomar."

Kalian could see it now; there would be no changing her mind. His head agreed with her but his heart wanted to ignore her. There was another moment of awkward silence between them.

"So you don't love me?" He wanted to take control of his tear ducts but for a second he forgot how. He knew his eyes were glistening and he just managed to stop any tears from breaking free.

"No..." Li'ara met his eyes as she said it.

Before Kalian could reply, Roland appeared in the doorway, his Callic-diamond vest shining under the light, its golden surface smeared with soot and ash. Kalian had never noticed the tattoos on both the bounty hunter's arms before. The one on his right deltoid was neon-green and glowed in the dark, thanks to the neolight ink that had been common on Earth. It was no doubt a throwback to his days in the UDC before he became an agent for Parliament.

"Esabelle's awake." With that, Roland disappeared down the winding ramp that led to the cargo hold. Kalian quickly followed him without meeting Li'ara's eyes. With her answer, he was only too happy to have an excuse to abandon the subject and move on.

Esabelle was stretching when they reached the hold, her body contorting into positions most gymnasts would struggle to achieve.

Roland's gaze was definitely captured by the Terran as she rested her fingers on her toes.

"Damn that suit is tight." Roland's attention to detail never failed to amaze Kalian.

"How are you feeling?" Kalian asked.

"Like my body was stretched across the cosmos... and then dumped in this heap."

The grimy cargo hold was cast in stark shadows by overhead spot-lights illuminating dozens of mysterious cases, each in various states of disrepair. Many of the crates were unmarked with very few labels stamped across the side. Roland and Ch'len had obviously spent some time as smugglers in between their bounties.

To finish off, Esabelle arched her back creating a series of bone popping cracks.

ALF's image was projected into the space a few metres away between her and Kalian, his long robes gathered behind him as he clasped his hands in the small of his back. "That was an impressive display. I wasn't sure it could be done without the *Gommarian*."

Kalian wasn't sure what to make of the relationship between Esabelle and ALF. They had never technically met during the Terran war, and yet both of them had critical impacts on the other. With Esabelle powering the *Gommarian*, the Terran had suffered blow after blow until they were finally beaten. ALF, on the other hand, had been instrumental in the catastrophic events, which ultimately led to Esabelle's imprisonment.

Despite these circumstances, neither of them had ever met during the war and Esabelle's forced imprisonment had to be taken into account. Time would tell whether they blamed each other for their previous roles.

"You mean you didn't know it could be done by the offspring of a Gomar?" There was an accusation behind her words.

ALF dipped his head in apology, but Kalian knew the AI wasn't sorry for his past decisions, only the knock-on effect it had on her. Being the embodiment of logic, ALF would know that it wasn't he who placed Esabelle inside the *Gommarian*, but Savrick. Therefore the blame lay with her father's decisions, not his.

"I always knew that the Gomar could overcome their limitations, just not within their lifespan. I calculated that within another five millennia from your birth, the defects in the Terran genome that created the Gomar would die out. In the meantime, the empire simply didn't have the resources to place every living Gomar into a virtual world with enough power to keep them alive for so long. You yourself required over two hundred thousand years to master your own mind."

"I don't care." Esabelle raised her hand to put a stop to ALF's excuses. "You made choices that cost billions of lives, and you can blame the cubes for manipulating events all you like, but there's some connection between you and them. There has to be. The same language *you* invent just happens to be engraved on the side of two cubes. I didn't push the issue with Uthor because we need to build trust with the Conclave, but *you* cannot be trusted, I know that much. An artificial intelligence with an immeasurable IQ does not say things like, 'I don't know'.

"I may not have actually lived in the Terran Empire, but I learned enough to know that you were a god. You oversaw every detail of their lives, and I'm willing to bet you know more about their civilisation before your creation than you let on. There's no way you don't have an idea about where the cubes came from. I wouldn't be surprised if you made them, a failed experiment or weapon, perhaps?"

"I didn't make them," he replied coolly. "Though, I can see how you might draw that conclusion, what with their external shell being made from nanocelium. And yes, I do have detailed records of life before my creation; it was violent and bloody, with a species devouring itself because of greed and selfishness. I didn't share it with the Terran because I didn't want them to dwell on war and weapons of mass destruction. Before your father, the Terran were on track."

"On track for what?" Kalian asked.

"For perfection. What you are now is magnificent, but you can accomplish so much more. Esabelle is proof of that." Despite her harsh words, ALF regarded Esabelle with admiration. "To all of you, it would appear that Esabelle transported us through subspace, like any ship. But in reality, the ship never moved. Rather, the universe moved around us..."

Kalian looked intently at Esabelle for a moment. Was that possible? Could a Terran actually move the universe? It made ALF's fascination with them a little clearer to see.

"Are you shittin' me right now?" Ch'len waddled into the centre of the loose circle they had made. "We just shot our way out of quarantine, injuring who knows how many of Uthor's soldiers, and you want to stand around, talking about *moving the universe!*"

Roland sat with his leg hanging over a large crate, quietly chuckling to himself.

"Unless you can teleport Uthor's rock-laden ass into a black hole, can I suggest we plan our next move?" The Ch'kara pulled something out of his chunky suit resembling a chocolate bar wrapped in a worm and began furiously chomping on it.

"He eats when he's stressed..." Roland commented.

"He has a point, though." Li'ara rested her back against an upright crate. Kalian could feel her looking at him but he couldn't bring himself to meet her eyes. "We left the *Gommarian* to actually do something about Garrett and the cubes."

"Since Garrett's location is unknown, the only logical choice is to go to the capital since we *know* there's a cube hiding inside." Esabelle's tone was that of a leader, with determination and conviction for their course of action.

Kalian knew that escaping the capital had been hard for her; letting the cube slip through her fingers. She was keen to finish what she started. "Uthor will be expecting that after what we told him," Kalian said. "Without surprise, it will be nearly impossible to get inside."

"Nearly impossible is what we're good at." Roland looked to Ch'len for support.

"We suck at that..."

"We need to find Garrett and the Trantax cube," Kalian continued. "We know that he's most likely being helped by Protocorps. They knew what to do with the last cube they found - it's possible they know what to do with Garrett's cube. Is there no way we can hack into their systems?" Beyond that generic term, he really had no idea how to get information out of a computer.

"In this form, I am very limited." ALF waved a hand over his holographic robes. "For now I'm stuck inside the suit."

"Maybe we could fly to the nearest hub, and the *Rackham* could try a remote hack?" Li'ara offered.

"If they are sheltering Garrett and the cube, I highly doubt that the location will be found on any server," Esabelle said. "It'll be hidden within different companies they own and given a false name and coordinates."

"I say you all join the crew." Everyone looked at Ch'len. "With your talents and my access to the Bounty Clave, we could make a killing - no pun intended." His attention only lasted as long as his suggestion.

"We're screwed," Li'ara dropped her head. "We have no idea where to go, and we're the galaxy's most wanted fugitives."

Roland shuffled on top of the crate. "There might be a way we can find him..." The bounty hunter scratched his head, avoiding eye contact. Kalian could tell that whatever his idea was, he wasn't too keen on it. Ch'len gave his partner-in-crime a long hard look before horrified realisation spread across his chubby face.

"No, no, no!" Ch'len waved his little arms in alarm. "You cannot be serious about this, Roland. I know what you're thinking. The more parsecs between him and us, the better!"

"What's he talking about?" Kalian could literally see the frequencies around the Ch'kara's body change with his fear.

"There's a guy that might know where to start looking," Roland explained. "He's a sort of middle-man in the underworld. Everything goes through him from simple muggings to top-tier politics. His business is knowledge."

"He sounds like a man harder to find than Garrett," Li'ara added.

"Oh, he's easy to find," Roland continued. "Even the Highclave know where to find him. They just *choose* not to."

"Exactly. He's dangerous!" Ch'len was pacing. "If the Highclave can't touch him, why are we even thinking of going near him?"

"You're just jittery because you owe him. Don't think I've forgotten why you live on this ship." Roland hopped off the crate and joined the circle, while Ch'len appeared to be looking for a dark corner to hide in.

"So what's he going to want in return for this information?" Kalian asked.

"Nothing you're going to want to part with. Some force may be required..." Roland purposefully rested his hand over one of his Tri-rollers.

Ch'len squawked something unintelligible at the idea and adjusted the holographic panels around his breather.

Kalian looked at everyone, including Li'ara, weighing up their reactions. It was clear to see that they had no better options. Kalian hated being backed into a corner with only one path in front of him; his life had come to this too many times in the last year.

"OK..." He took a moment to give everyone a chance to protest. "Where can we find him?"

Roland smiled as he looked up, "*Rackham?*"

"Yes, Roland?" the seductive female voice replied.

"Set a course for, Vallara."

"We're going to a core planet?" Li'ara stood up straight. "Who is this guy?"

"Nobody knows his real name. He's just known as *The Laronian...*"

THE HELTERON SYSTEM was several light-years behind Kel-var's ship now. With so much space between him and the Terran, he felt able to breathe again. He had known since he was a child that a Terran resided inside the sarcophagus, but he had never known why the prophet demanded he be kept alive inside the machine. The revelation was terrifying.

The technology that powered the cubes had repurposed the Terran as some kind of herald, for what was coming. If that twisted figure was only a glimpse of the future, Kel-var wasn't sure he was ready to face it. It had killed Sel-gar with a flick of the wrist. He remembered the sound of his neck snapping, as the artificial vertebrae were torn from his brain by an invisible force.

He could feel Gor-van watching him from under his consuming, blood-red hood. Kel-var made certain he was showing no sign of fear or regret. Gor-van had only accompanied him on the journey to Shandar because his own vessel had a malfunction in the port-side thrusters. The engineers on the station had reported that it would take another day to fix. Kel-var's ship had more than enough room, however, to accommodate the entire board if needs be.

"Did you know that was going to happen?" Gor-van asked.

"Did I know the Terran was going to be used in such a way? No, of course not. Before the incident with this other human, I didn't even know it could be done." He was beginning to feel a little too manipulated by the prophet. He had always been the most informed about its plans and the inevitable future of the Conclave, but never this.

"Are we really going to do this? There will be no going back after we activate the Crucible." Gor-van had never been so free with his words before. Always working in the shadows had made him a very discreet, close guarded man. It was possible he was testing Kel-var's resolve. Was this the start of a power play?

"The Prophet wills it." He looked away, unsure that he could keep his expression from betraying his true feelings.

"Does it? Or does this new thing will it?" Gor-van sat forward, his clawed fingers clasped together.

"They are all of the same mind, Gor-van. One entity, but many. You know this."

"It's the one they serve that troubles me. We both know they activated the station to open a communication. I fear that we have served our purpose, and now we are being kept out of the loop. Activating the Crucible will be declaring war, Kel-var."

"You heard the Terran. Once the station is used to destroy the humans, we are to fulfil our end of the prophecy. There will be no war, only transcendence." He didn't really believe his own words. After centuries of service to the prophet, he was a slave on a subconscious level. "Your lack of conviction is troubling, Gor-van. Are you not ready to ascend?"

"I have dedicated my life to serving the prophet. I have manipulated countless people for hundreds of cycles to see this plan through. But having manipulated so many, I am accustomed to knowing someone who is being used. Do you not feel used, Kel-var? Because I do. Before we left, the technicians informed me that while they were 'testing' the station, three unidentified objects came through it. All three left the Helteron Cluster within minutes of arriving. The station's anchor point was somewhere *outside* the galaxy."

Kel-var thought hard about that for a moment. There was only one explanation he could think of. It made sense, however much he hated being uninformed by the prophet. This plan had taken up centuries of their lives but, for the cubes, it had been much longer.

"They are enacting a plan that no doubt has more layers to it than we are aware of. The scale of it is unfathomable. Of course, we aren't aware of all the facts; we shouldn't be, Gor-van. We are servants of a god."

"We both know what the Highclave are building in the Ch'ket system. The *Sentinel* is almost ready. If the Terran takes the station to Ch'ket, it will most likely be obliterated."

Considering that scenario, Kel-var thought he had a good idea of where those three objects were bound for. "As long as the humans are destroyed as well, it doesn't matter. Besides, there are plenty more stations..."

TWELVE

The *Marillion* glided through space, orbiting the solar system that housed the capital planet, its leisurely speed setting them on a course that would take centuries to traverse the entire circumference. The main sequence was a tiny speck on the reflection of the golden sphere now. The shining hull was a pale comparison to the opulence of the secret interior, with its palace-like rooms and arching corridors that formed the core of the ship. The aesthetic appearance was down to the Novaarian and Laronian designers who created it, with the engineering being a thing of beauty to the Ch'kara and the Shay, while Raalakians found it comfortable due to its hulking size.

With a crew of six thousand, it was well maintained as the flagship of the Conclave armada. After the incident in Clave Tower, the crew had worked double shifts to ensure the *Marillion* was combat-ready and able to drop into subspace at a moment's notice. Without command from the Highclave, the ship remained in lockdown so that no other vessel could dock or disembark, while a threat assessment was carried out on the planet.

Elondrasa walked through the corridors, accompanied by her entourage, feeling safe in the heart of such a magnificent machine. If the threat level increased, the *Marillion* would activate its next layer of defence, using the same stealth technology used by the *Valoran*. Like the observation vessel, the great sphere would become invisible to the naked eye and undetectable to any scans. It was a technology reserved only for the *Marillion*. By allowing it to be used on the *Valoran*, Elondrasa had taken a huge political hit. She knew that in two cycles, when the council was up for re-election, she would lose her status.

It was worth it to observe the humans, for whatever time they had left.

Elondrasa's entourage remained behind as she entered the cylindrical chamber made for the Highclave to sit in session. She took her place around the table, admiring the jewel-studded chandelier that hovered overhead. The circular table was broken on one side where the life-size hologram of High Charge Uthor resided. She acknowledged her fellow councillors before nodding to Uthor for his report.

"Have you had time to review the data file I sent, councillors?"

"We have Uthor; your findings are quite serious," Elondrasa replied.

"If accurate..." Nu-marn added his comment with heavy speculation intoned.

The Novaarian regarded him, aware of his personal feelings towards Protocorps. She let his statement go, since they didn't know enough about the corporation's involvement.

"Has there been any progress with locating Professor Garrett Jones?" Brokk shuffled on his saddle-like chair.

"I'm afraid not. Until we understand the *Gommarian* better, we cannot track the Terran craft he escaped in. In truth, we have no idea where to start looking for him. His reason for stealing the Trantax cube remains a mystery."

Elondrasa could tell Uthor was finding it hard to relay such little information. As a being with so many resources at his disposal, it must be infuriating for a single person to disappear.

"What about Kalian Gaines and the others?" Lordina was dressed immaculately as ever, despite the privacy of being aboard the *Marillion*. It was one of the perks Elondrasa loved the most about the ship: no media coverage and no audience.

"Their escape caused some casualties, but no fatalities. The *Rackham* is proving just as hard to track as Garrett's ship; they could be anywhere."

Lordina had no problem expressing her disappointment. "This is unacceptable High Charge. You damn near had the entire fleet surrounding that ship! How could they escape your grasp so easily?"

Uthor didn't even blink under the scrutiny. "Two Terran are harder to bring down than one, councillor."

Elondrasa looked over the data file that presented itself in her vision. With their implants, every councillor could see the virtual information as if it was being projected into the room. The Novaarian quickly accessed the file on Esabelle.

"You are referring to Savrick's daughter?" Elondrasa attempted to settle the tension.

"Another secret the humans were keeping from us," Nu-marn spat.

It was hard to argue with his statement; as much as she would like to. The fact that Kalian Gaines wasn't the only living Terran was quite the concern. The Highclave had come to the conclusion that any being with that level of power was a threat of the highest magnitude after the Gomar's display. Kalian, however, had been judged based upon his actions and character. It would have been preferable to keep him somewhere they could study him, but they were satisfied with keeping him somewhere they could monitor. That measure of control gave them some security, up until now.

Not only is there another Terran out there, but she is the daughter of Savrick. They didn't know enough about Esabelle to judge her the same way as Kalian. From Uthor's report, it would seem she is the more powerful after her display in Clave Tower. Her age was hard to imagine at over two hundred thousand cycles. She literally predated their entire civilisation. There was some sympathy to be had if her story was true about being imprisoned by her own father, but as Nu-marn and Lordina continue to point out; the humans lie.

"She is an unknown in all this," Uthor continued. "She was not pleased about the remaining Gomar being removed from the ship, either. Her loyalties would apparently lie with the humans, but her concern for the Gomar troubles me."

"Whatever her loyalties," Ch'lac interjected, "the daughter of Savrick is highly concerned about Protocorps' AI systems." They now knew that Esabelle was the source of information concerning this third party that manipulated the Terran war. "Are we still not taking the human's warning seriously?"

"How can we?" Nu-marn replied. "It's just more lies to cover up for the fact they are a violent species. Both Terran and human history is littered with war; the humans' last war only ended a few centuries ago!"

"The connection between both the Trantax and the *Gommarian* cubes cannot be ignored." Brokk placed both of his heavy hands on the table. "The report confirms that they are identical, except we already know that the Trantax cube arrived in our system long after the *Gommarian* was finished wiping out the Terran. That cube found its way onto Trantax IV without direction from the Terran, Gomar or the humans. That would suggest a third party."

"So you think the Terran is right; that there's a cube inside the AI mainframe?" Nu-marn copied the Raalak's posture with both hands on the table.

"They claim to have proof," Uthor offered. "Before I could have the data verified they escaped custody-"

"Of course they did..."

"But, from what I saw, the plans looked to be authentic." Uthor looked down on Nu-marn, unhappy with the interruption.

"In your opinion, High Charge," Elondrasa asked, "what do you think they will do next?"

Uthor took a moment to compose his answer. "Whether they are correct in their findings or not, I know they *believe* they are. With the level of conviction they show, I would assume their next move is to attack Protocorps again and destroy the third cube."

The councillors were quiet for a minute, while they considered all their options. They had two separate targets to find, seven thousand humans to relocate, twelve Gomar to secure and the *Gommarian* to repurpose.

"At this moment, our findings are incomplete." Elondrasa assumed her regal posture. "We need to find Professor Jones to accurately assess the nature of these cubes and the supposed third party. We will continue to transport the humans to Ch'ket, where they will remain under the guard of the *Sentinel*. I think we all agree that the *Gommarian* should be left in the hands of the Ch'kara so that we might discover more of its secrets." The other councillors nodded their approval so far. "Uthor, what is the status of the Gomar?"

The High Charge turned to his left, inspecting a monitor they couldn't see. "They have already landed at the base. No problems reported. Doctor Bal is on site."

The base was a nameless facility located on a nameless planet on the border of Conclave space. It was the most classified place Elondrasa knew of, though she wasn't naive enough to imagine that Uthor didn't have a few other black-sites off the books. It was designed and constructed shortly after the events on Naveen with one purpose in mind: contain Kalian Gaines. It was currently undergoing some quick alterations to make appropriate space for the Gomar.

"Excellent. Any suggestions on how we should proceed with Protocorps?"

"Their security has already been increased," Nu-marn stated.

"I was not referring to their level of security, Nu-marn. What should we do about the allegations? Their involvement in the Trantax project is indisputable. It would be negligent to ignore their part in this entirely." Elondrasa was aware of the freedom granted to the corporation over the centuries. Their contribution on behalf of the Shay was hard to ignore, but so was this.

"Allegations from an alien species who are not members of this Conclave," Nu-marn countered, his eyes darted around the table, looking for support.

"They maintain a machine that helps govern the lives of seven trillion people," Brokk added, supporting Elondrasa. "You must look at this as a High-Councillor, Nu-marn, not a Shay and most definitely not as someone who receives a campaign contribution from Protocorps."

"We will commission an investigation," Ch'lac said. "It will be discreet and not made public, but it will be definitive."

Nu-marn sat back in his chair, defeated. He looked to Lordina who remained quiet on the subject, happy to nod along.

"Then it is settled," Elondrasa announced. "I realise that capturing Kalian and Esabelle will be difficult, Uthor, but try to bring them in alive if possible." There were several matters that needed addressing between the Conclave and the humans, but if this new threat did prove to be real, having a couple of Terran on *their* side wouldn't hurt.

THE HOLOGRAPHIC EMITTERS consumed the forward section of the *Rackham's* bridge, swelling with the image of Vallara, against a starry backdrop. The Laronian homeworld glittered with lights of every colour on the dark side, while vast oceans of deep blue shimmered in the sun on the other. Arcing super-bridges of tremendous size extended from the ground to pierce the atmosphere, with towers hanging from every structure like a city upside down, only stopping a mile above the ground, where it met the rolling forests and mountains below.

Kalian magnified the hologram to get a better look at the beautiful planet. Most of the super-bridges intersected mid-arc, or via individual bridges at various points. Snow-peaked mountains rose up between them while winding rivers flowed across the land like roots of a tree. The planet's surface was only blemished at the points where the bridges were secured to the ground with diameters miles apart in size. The Arcs were thick, each one capable of housing millions inside, as well as the hanging towers and the colossal spires that ran along the top.

The Arcs were clustered together in groups across the entire planet, leaving whole sections untouched. Each cluster comprised around thirty to forty bridges like regions on a map. Kalian knew from the Laronians' history, that Vallara had not always looked as it did right now. Like most intelligent species, industry ultimately dominated their way of life. Vallara had once been covered from pole to pole in cities that demanded more and more of its natural resources. If it hadn't been for their early discovery of Intrinium, on the outer reaches of the solar system, the planet would be toxic by now. Centuries of rejuvenation saw the landscape returned to its natural state, so its people could enjoy its splendour.

As with most Conclave planets, Vallara's atmosphere was overlaid by the constant movement of vehicles, flying from one Arc to another. As one of the five core worlds, it was under greater security than most. Just seeing the amount of activity from this distance was giving Kalian second thoughts. Their appearance was unique, even among a society as multi-cultural as the Conclave. It wouldn't take long before their scanning equipment detected them on the streets or a local called in their position.

But they needed answers.

The *Rackham* banked to starboard, heading for the dark side of the planet. He observed Roland and Ch'len as they checked the ship's systems, making certain the stealthware was working. The plan was to enter the atmosphere undetectable to the naked eye, then find somewhere to land where the ship wouldn't be a problem.

In the few hours it had taken to reach the planet, Kalian had avoided Li'ara in every way. Being able to find her anywhere on the ship made that easy. She was standing behind Ch'len, pretending to look over the readouts, but Kalian knew she was stealing glances at him every few seconds. He suddenly hated how attuned he was to her.

"Hitting the atmosphere in twenty. Adjust the angle of the port thrusters, Len. I don't want to burn through and give ourselves away."

Ch'len rolled his eyes at the insult to his name but continued as ordered.

The entire ship changed its angle of approach and slowed down just enough to avoid heating up, as they punched through the planet's natural shield. Seeing Roland in action reminded Kalian that he wasn't just a bounty hunter with a quick-trigger finger. This was a man who had been trained for decades in the subtleties of warfare.

"Where are we going?" Esabelle asked.

"To the Ninx district, in the Spiral Arc," Roland replied, eyeing Ch'len's expression of dismay. The bounty hunter clearly found his partner's terror, highly amusing.

The forward section of the bridge became a wall of holographic fog, as the *Rackham* flew through the cloudbank and descended under the night sky. A few minutes later, Roland deactivated the stealthware and connected to the local AI hub, under a false registration.

The view was incredible, as the hulking bridges dwarfed them on their journey through the cityscape. The *Rackham* ducked and weaved between the traffic, descending even lower until the tops of the trees were whipped into a frenzy by the after-effects of their speed. Like the feet of giants, the city-bridges appeared from nowhere as the larger ones vanished above the clouds.

"There it is..." Roland's words preceded the view of the Spiral Arc.

It wasn't large enough to pierce the atmosphere, but it was by no means the smallest of the Arcs. Unlike the others, however, it wasn't connected to any other via bridges or indeed another Arc. It was an island from which The Laronian could conduct his criminal affairs.

"So what's the plan?" Li'ara asked the group.

"My plan is to stay right here!" Ch'len shuffled in his seat, creating a deeper imprint.

"The Laronian runs everything from his club. That's where we'll find him." Roland selected the landing destination and handed over the controls to the computer.

The towering spires that made up the city, arching over the Arc, became crystal clear across the forward section of the bridge. The *Rackham* was gliding through the streets and towering buildings with a black, starry sky above. The city was painted in every colour of neon light as the inhabitants came out to play. The Ninx district was obviously the place to be to have fun on the Spiral Arc.

"How can we get to him without drawing attention?" Li'ara was inspecting a hologram of the club, highlighted by Ch'len.

"We can't." Roland's reply held no sound of hope. "Between the *Rackham* and the club we'll be spotted by a few hundred people, not to mention all the cameras connected to the AI hub."

"You think the cameras in this district are connected to the AI?" Ch'len snorted. "Everything here goes through The Laronian."

"Don't you have any friends here that can help us?" Kalian aimed his question at Ch'len.

"Ha! He doesn't have friends, just people who want to kill him less."

Ch'len muttered to himself while he glared at Roland.

Why are we even considering another way of getting in?

Esabelle's voice echoed through his mind in perfect clarity. Kalian looked at her with a questioning look and a hint of disapproval.

We could walk in there and take the answers we need, and be gone before local security is even alerted. Nothing can stop us, Kalian.

He didn't reply but considered her words. It was true; they could blow through The Laronian's club and take what they needed. But should they? His use of power had been playing on his mind since he killed the mercenaries on Trantax IV. If they went with Esabelle's plan there was a chance he would have to kill again, if only to keep the others safe. He retreated into his mind to give himself longer to think, but he knew there was no other way to get the answers they needed, in the time they had.

"Esabelle and I will go in and speak to The Laronian. One way or another, he'll tell us what we want to know." Even as he spoke the words, Kalian could feel Esabelle's confidence mixing with his own feelings, filling him with excitement at the prospect of being free with their abilities. It was worrying how quickly her thoughts and feelings could ebb into his own, changing his perspective completely.

"We're coming with you!" Li'ara protested.

"They won't just let us in; it's safer if *we* go," he countered.

Li'ara's expression was reply enough; *I don't need you to keep me safe.*

"For the first time ever, one of your crazy-suicide missions takes me to a bar, and you think I'm sitting it out?" Roland stood from his chair and twirled his Tri-rollers on both index fingers. "Let's skip to the good bit…"

THE NINX DISTRICT was alive with its night time proclivities, with members of every race coming out to enjoy all it had to offer. Kubrackk leant against the railing, overlooking the layers of walkways below, each one cast in a multitude of neon light and bright colours. He was only four levels above the street that formed the top of the arching super-bridge, with many more levels above him. The street appeared to be flat, rather than curved, due to the sheer size of the Spiral Arc. The night-time illuminations literally outshone the stars, leaving them under a black sky devoid of cosmic detail.

To his left, Spelnar clung tightly to the rail, with his twin-tail wrapped around his slender leg. The Trillik was more nervous about the coming encounter than Kubrackk was. That in mind, the scarred Novaarian looked down the street to his right, where The Laronian's club, Nightfall, was situated. Nightfall dominated the strip of bars, casinos and entertainment parlours that specialised in virtual stimulation.

Like all the buildings on the Arc, the club was built into the other structures around it, making it hard to see where one tower ended and the next began. Nightfall, however, was easy to find in the Ninx district. The exterior panels were chrome blue, to match the Laronian skin-tone, only the panels glowed with soft light. The surrounding business had no doubt been paid to keep their illuminations to a minimum in order to highlight the club.

Everything about The Laronian screamed *I can't be touched*.

It was this lack of fear that put everyone on edge in their dealings with the criminal. His limitless contacts meant there was nowhere Kubrackk could go that The Laronian couldn't reach. The Novaarian was about to enter into a deal with this shadowy individual. That thought gave him pause. He would avenge his brother and see Roland North dead by his hands. That outcome would never change. But was it worth going down this route to achieve that goal? Dealing with Revus was dangerous enough, but The Laronian was something else entirely.

The criminal's personality was well known among the underworld. He was eccentric to the point of psychotic madness. That made him hard to reason with and even harder to strike a fair bargain with. The Laronian's intelligence was never brought into question though. By concealing his identity and face beneath his legendary faceplate, he had created an almost mythic symbol in the criminal underworld, making him terrifying and untouchable to his enemies.

Kubrackk stared long and hard at Nightfall, remembering the last time he had visited the establishment. His uncle had taken Torvrackk and him when they were in their late teens, centuries ago when they were still learning the bounty trade. He couldn't recall the business his uncle had with The Laronian, only the visage of the super criminal himself remained burned into his memory.

"Are we really going to do this, boss?" Spelnar looked out across the layers of streets, avoiding Kubrackk's gaze.

"The *Gommarian* is too well hidden. We could be searching Novaarian space for years without finding it. We're just going to ask The Laronian for the location, that's all." He relayed their plan as if he was talking to a child.

"What do we give him in return?"

Kubrackk had thought about that question. There was only one thing he would want and only one thing the Novaarian would have to offer.

"We give him the *Rackham*, of course. It's the only thing of any worth in all this."

"But we've offered that to Revus. Besides, you said the ship was going to be *our* prize, that it would compensate us a thousand fold for not taking any bounties." Spelnar's defiant expression only lasted until Kubrackk returned the look.

"Let them fight over who gets the *Rackham*. Something tells me

Revus won't win. And by succeeding in this endeavour, we will be opening lucrative doors to work for The Laronian. The contracts he gives us will be worth ten times anything the Bounty Clave can offer us." Kubrackk gave the Trillik a hard look. "You're going to walk in there with me, Spelnar. And you're going to look like the toughest, meanest bastard there is. Got it?"

Spelnar's attention was split between Kubrackk and something that had caught his eye on the street below. He was about to scold the stupid Trillik, before realising that Spelnar wasn't the only one staring. Kubrackk leaned further over the rail, magnetised by the four humans walking freely through the streets of the Spiral Arc. They were not just any four humans, but four very important humans. On the far side, strolling through the crowd in his long animal-hide jacket was Roland North.

"It's *him*!" Spelnar shouted. Thankfully, his voice was drowned out by the music blaring out of every doorway between them and the humans. Kubrackk continued to watch from his lofty vantage, pulling his wide-brim hat down to shadow his scarred face. His long fingers slowly reached for the handle of his Quad-roller, strapped to his chest.

It would be so easy...

He quickly retracted his hand as reality set in. Every person in the Conclave knew the face of the other human, standing next to Roland North. Kalian Gaines was one of the Gomar or the Terran, or whatever they were. He couldn't remember the exact details of the story, spun by the Highclave, regarding the Conclave's current squatters. He hadn't been as obsessed with the celebrity-humans like the rest of the Conclave had been, and still were if the gawkers were anything to go by. The humans were small and weak, with an engineered gene-pool that made them inferior to their makers. Unlike them, Kalian Gaines was an actual threat. He wasn't sure if the leader of the humans was from their world, or in fact from the other side of the galaxy. He recalled the images of Naveen and decided it was irrelevant. Kalian's evolved state put his biology an order of magnitude above Kubrackk's.

A low growl rumbled from Kubrackk's throat as he took a step back from the rail. The woman walking next to Kalian was the new companion of Roland North. He had seen, first hand, the extraordinary things *she* could do. His prey was finally within striking distance and he was powerless to act.

"Why are they *here*?" Spelnar voiced Kubrackk's own question.

From their direction, it would appear that they were going to see The Laronian. But why? Shouldn't they all be on the *Gommarian* or at the very least in custody after the attack on Protocorps? Kubrackk couldn't believe the universe had brought the two of them together on the same planet at the same time. The Novaarian had been bounty hunting for centuries and never *stumbled* across his prey.

Looking around, it was clear how much attention they were gaining. Everyone had stopped to stare at the humans strolling through the Ninx district. Kubrackk could imagine what they were all thinking; were the humans now members of the Conclave and they had missed the latest News cycle? Are they moments away from dying at the hands of the dangerous and unpredictable humans? Should they greet them or give them a wide berth? It seemed most were going for the latter and staying away.

Kubrackk broke away from the rail and blended back into the crowd, keeping parallel with the humans below. Spelnar followed behind as they moved through the upper streets, glancing between the on-lookers to keep track of them. No one tried to stop the humans or make any kind of contact, but he noticed almost everyone was using some form of holo-communication device to spread the word.

"What do we do now, boss?" Spelnar's question went unanswered while Kubrackk weighed their options.

Attacking Roland now was suicide; his friends would defend him immediately, and that would only end one way for the two of them. Following them into the club would be too risky since Roland would recognise him if they were forced together in a confined space. Waiting outside wouldn't work either, he reasoned. This was bound to bring down Vallara's security force as well as the Conclave when word finally got around. There was only one path left to take, though it would require patience on his part.

"The *Rackham* must be close by. Hack into the local security feed and track their movements back, until you find it."

"But they all run through The Laronian! If I break into the feed he will be alerted." Spelnar stopped walking, his twin-tail once again wrapped around his leg. Kubrackk was forced to pull the Trillik into a nearby alley to hear him over the incessant music; his Novaarian hearing was inferior to Spelnar's, though he would never admit it.

A drunken Laronian came stumbling out of the shadows, his alcoholic stench reaching Kubrackk's nostrils. He knocked over discarded bottles, using the wall to keep himself upright as he approached the bounty hunters like old friends. Before an unintelligible word could depart his blue lips, four strong Novaarian arms shot out, encompassing the Laronian's head above and below. Kubrackk squeezed with all his rage, thinking about the injustice for all his hard work. He looked between his hands and saw the face of Roland North, his face twisted in agony as Kubrackk broke the skull and jaw simultaneously. Blood oozed out of the Laronian's eyes and nose, running over the pale hands of the Novaarian.

His senses returned and he released the disfigured head of the wandering drunkard, leaving him in a pile at his feet. Spelnar took a few cautious steps back, putting some distance between the two. Kubrackk quickly scanned the area, before scooping the Laronian up and tossing him in a nearby dumpster. Crime was rife in the Ninx district and the alley was free of surveillance. Given the proper resources, it would be easy for the authorities to identify Kubrackk as the killer with advanced DNA profilers created by the Ch'ket. Thankfully, a murder in the Ninx district was not a priority on anyone's list, not that it mattered; it would just be another crime attributed to an already wanted fugitive in the bounty hunter trade.

He fixed Spelnar with a dangerous glint in his swirling eyes. The Trillik quickly unpacked the gear out of the flat-pack on his back, unfolding various technical equipment and emitters.

"I need access to a surveillance terminal to track their previous movements..."

A satisfied, yet menacing, smirk crept across the Novaarian's features.

KALIAN WAS ALMOST OVERWHELMED by his senses as they strode through the busy streets of the Ninx district. The input was too much to take at times, forcing him to pull back and use his human senses alone. Everyone was watching them with fascination and a little fear it seemed. Kalian could literally see the electronic signals across the spectrum, beaming out of every communication device and broadcasting their location to the galaxy.

The world around them was full of much more than what was merely presented in front of his human companions. Kalian looked at Li'ara and felt a moment of sadness, not because of their recent conversation, but because he knew she couldn't see the wonder of the real universe. He could see that wonder in Esabelle's eyes as she too took in the sights and sounds of the ever-moving universe of life. They could feel the planet spinning beneath their feet and the life force of the great forest below the Arc. The variety of exotic aliens surrounding them vibrated on an atomic level, with unique frequencies emanating from their complex minds. He could smell a thousand different perfumes mixed with alien pheromones and alcohol. Their individual scent was so unique that he could trace each one to its owner or even track them for miles. It was times like this when he remembered that it wasn't just his mind or his body that was more evolved, but his senses too. Without thinking it through, Kalian enhanced all of his senses at once. The taste of salt and copper filled his mouth with what he knew was sweat and blood, but he couldn't trace the origin as the sound of laughter, sex and death came from every direction across the entire Arc. The different smells became toxic, bringing with them a feeling of nausea. His skin felt irritated by the breeze with its constant bombardment of molecules.

Kalian looked up in a physical effort to shut it all out. He filtered out the pollution of light to see the heavens above and felt a quiet calm take over. He could see the nebulas and stars laid out across the sky as if painted by a god upon a black canvas.

He desperately wanted to share it all with Li'ara, to show her the magnificence of the world they lived in. But he couldn't, and never would. A part of him didn't care, reasoning that it wasn't required to have a relationship with her. Another part now knew that *she* didn't want to share it with him.

He lost his train of thought again, as the environment offered up more information. His awareness pulsed out of his mind and collated all the data in fractions of a second, displaying it through his occipital lobe. Most of the inhabitants were in possession of some kind of augmentation, biological or artificial. He could see the adrenal glands of a Laronian had been enhanced to allow for better control of stress and the manipulation of his own metabolism, an augmentation that came naturally to Kalian and Esabelle. Several Raalakians had their muscles reinforced with strands of Callic-diamond while most had an overall augmentation of the mind, with artificial inserts to allow for more memory or quick thinking. Kalian noticed that most of the Shay had the same insert in their brains, no doubt an upgrade to help with the integration of their numerous mechanical augmentations.

The Conclave was certainly a culture that had grown tired of its slow rate of evolution, favouring enhancements of their own making and imagination. He wasn't sure if there was a single individual in the entire district that wasn't enhanced in some way.

As the crowd continued to part for them, The Laronian's club, Nightfall, came into view. The sleek-looking club was windowless with a domed exterior that rose out of sight above them. The queue outside dominated the walkway, though it was better described as a mob. Two Raalakians barred the entrance with their combined width, an impenetrable wall of rock. Four guns rested in holsters on the quadruped hips, while their massive arms remained tightly folded against their marble chests.

Standing at almost half their height was an Atari male in a fine blue suit, to match the club. His pink skin glistened with what Kalian could see was some kind of lotion designed to make the person look as if they wore the stars themselves. His yellow, wide-set eyes darted from the person in front of him to the orange hologram that emitted from the device, surgically moulded into his palm. The hologram was clearly a list of people permitted into Nightfall. A list they would not be on.

He met Esabelle's eyes in a brief moment of doubt, only to be reinforced by her confident nod. He knew what to do.

The crowd became oddly silent as the humans approached, tripping over one another to give them space. Their actions were seamless as Kalian telekinetically collapsed the trachea of both Raalakians, while Roland grabbed the Atari by the jacket and forced him past the bouncers. The Raalakians fell to their knees, gripping their throats in panic before passing out. Beyond the entrance was a corridor coated in neon blue and green lights with sofas lining the walls.

"Where's The Laronian?" Roland was so close to the Atari's face that he was covering him in spit.

"This is V-Vallara," the Atari stuttered. "There are l-l-lots of Laronians h-h-here..." Without the bouncers, the doorman was quite terrified; though not nearly enough to incur the wrath of his boss, apparently.

Roland planted his hand flat against the Atari's face and pushed him away, onto the nearest sofa. Quickly scrambling to his feet, the Atari ran for the door with one last terrified look back. Kalian focused his hearing and heard him alerting The Laronian's forces inside the club. He welcomed the rush of adrenaline as his brain processed his fight or flight response. It was hard to hide the smile at the thought that he could now do both with a very literal sense.

They continued to the double doors at the end of the hallway, where Kalian felt the minds of four Laronian guards, running towards them on the other side. One of them favoured his left leg, evidence of some injury he had yet to take care of with a Medder. Two of them wore a holster around their thigh with a sidearm in each, while the other two preferred knives. Their approach wasn't uniformed or rehearsed, demonstrating a lack of professional training. They were grunts in a criminal organisation of thugs.

The doors parted with the four guards set on bringing Kalian down first. Having already played the fight out in his mind three times, his response felt more like muscle memory to a choreographed dance. While throwing aside the first jab of a knife, Kalian lashed out with a foot to the already injured right knee. The joint popped out of place with a sound only Esabelle and he could hear above the Laronian's scream. In the same fluid movement, he bent the alien wrist, causing the knife to fall in the exact place he had predicted. He ducked another knife while catching the falling blade before throwing it with perfect accuracy into the hand of the guard at the back. Unfortunately for him, his hand was now pinned to his leg, through the handle of the gun he was drawing.

Kalian launched back up, using the knife-wielding Laronian as leverage, jumping over his shoulder and kicking the third guard in the face, with enough force to fracture his skull. The last guard was disorientated by the use of his own body in the nimble acrobatics. He barely had enough time to register the series of blows that Kalian landed across his body and head, before dropping to the floor.

The entire fight had taken less than ten seconds.

Without stopping to catch his breath, Kalian strode through the open portal knowing his friends were close behind. Nightfall pulsed like a beating heart, with music blasting out in waves across the club. A large circular bar consumed the centre of the club, illuminated by more neon blue against the low lighting of the dance floor. It was lined with every kind of drink and staffed mostly by Novaarians, who managed several drinks at once between their four hands. The DJ occupied the top of the bar, surrounded by orange holographs to help the Nix create the music. It seemed to be an odd job for a Nix, but Kalian had to admit that he had only ever met Xydrandil.

Above all of them were several platforms, just big enough to fit a dancer on each. Some had female Laronians dancing seductively around a pole while others had male Laronians flexing their muscles.

There were members of every species on exhibit in some fashion, each showing off a unique trait of their kind. It was as if a club had been blended with a museum of the bizarre. It was also the first time Kalian had seen the anti-gravity walkways used by Novaarians. The vertical strips lined the walls at intervals between the pillars, leading off into other rooms and booths that were built into the club, out of sight.

At the very top of the club, the ceiling was made entirely of hanging crystals. The tip of each crystal was set at a different length, giving the image of a natural formation. Rather than glisten in the light, the crystals shone from within as if lit from above.

Depending on what species approached the bar, the floor would produce a different stool to accommodate the varying biology. Everywhere Kalian looked there were people dancing and drinking the night away, oblivious to their dramatic entrance. He stepped onto the main floor and was shocked to feel the hum of life below his feet. Swimming under the transparent floor was another world of creatures no human had ever seen before.

From between the dancing bodies came the next wave of guards, pushing people to the ground as they made for the human group. The nine attackers were made up of Laronians with a few Atari and Revaneen backing them up. Thinking of Li'ara and Roland, Kalian was happy they would only be challenged by bipeds. From what little he knew of the Revaneen, Kalian was surprised by their willingness to defend The Laronian, a known criminal. Perhaps it was more of a testament to what The Laronian was capable of.

With so many customers around, the thugs were less inclined to use their Intrinium based weapons, turning to blades and bats instead. Before the two groups collided, Kalian felt more activity above them. Running down the vertical walkways were even more of the crime lord's thugs.

"I've got them!" Esabelle shot off, leaping over chairs and tables like a cat. She took to the change in gravity with ease, never slowing her charge towards her enemy.

Roland was naturally the first to attack, using the nearest table to gain height before jumping onto two Laronians. Considering his combat abilities, it was a messy way to begin a fight, lending only to the idea that the bounty hunter just loved to fight. Li'ara, on the other hand, was more tactical with precise blows that incapacitated her opponent instantly. A fist to the throat here, a foot to the knee there and she was soon standing over three unconscious bodies.

Kalian took the opportunity to be a little more graceful in his movements, incorporating different fighting techniques designed by the Terran. His moves were more about dodging and moving, waiting for the perfect counter-strike, while his opponents wore themselves out. He noticed the Revaneen had come only at him. Their fighting style was impressive and very fast, with incredible strength behind every blow. Kalian let a few punches and kicks through his defences in order to test his armour. He was always astonished at what he could do in the compact suit. It allowed for quick, elegant movements, while hardening to prevent damage to its wearer. He hadn't been sure how well it would stand up after the incident with the Starrillium.

To his right, Roland was using the environment in the only way he knew how. He smashed one Laronian across the face with a bottle, moments before driving the head of another into a table. He stopped hitting one thug to take a gulp of whatever drink was nearby, only to be wrestled to the floor by two others. Kalian wasn't sure what to think about the bounty hunter's laughter, as he was driven to the floor.

Kalian deftly turned the closest Laronian with the nudge of an elbow, forcing him into the spinning kick from Li'ara. In turn, Kalian punched one of her attackers square in the chest, with some added telekinesis. The thug was launched across the club and into the bar, taking a line of alcoholic bottles with him.

A second before the Revaneen could get close enough to Kalian; a screaming Laronian fell from above, flattening them both into the aquarium floor. It started to rain thugs after that. One by one, Esabelle was expelling the guards from the walkway. The last one landed on top of the DJ's equipment with a violent crash, bringing the music to a sudden end. In the silence that followed, the only sound came from Roland, who was repeatedly smashing an unconscious Laronian onto the bar-top.

"Roland..." Li'ara ended his violent reverie and the bloody body dropped to the floor. A multitude of creatures nipped at the glass underneath, trying to reach the blood. He simply shrugged under the questioning looks and wiped the blood from his nose.

They were met with stunned looks by the remaining customers, clearly shocked with how their night had changed so drastically. The Novaarian bartenders poked their long heads over the counter to see if it was safe to come out of hiding. The Laronian dancers reprogrammed their platforms to return them to the ledge, while the various exhibitionists scrambled to blend in with the customers.

From somewhere above came the sound of a single burst of applause. The singular clap sent a chill through Kalian's body. It was the sound of a person who had no problem being in the spotlight, despite the danger the four humans presented. This kind of confidence could only come from The Laronian. The clap was soon followed by a deep laughter that sounded as if it had been produced by a robot.

"Of all the bars on all the planets in all the galaxy... welcome, welcome auspicious guests! Everybody OUT! " The balcony on the opposite side of the club was occupied by a row of thugs, with one individual in the middle, his arms outstretched.

The man was dressed in an expensive white suit with an unusual helmet covering his entire head and face. It was smooth and sleek, matching The Laronian head shape, only it had no space for eyes or a mouth but was, instead, one whole piece. Its most hypnotic feature came from the display that danced across the entire dome. Looking at the Laronian was like looking into a swirling spiral galaxy, made to appear in the centre of the head, surrounded by stars.

Esabelle landed next to Li'ara without a sound, having jumped from the vertical walkway. The unusual welcome from the crime lord was off-putting, forcing the small group back together.

"Out, out, out, out, out, OUT!" His voice was filtered through the helmet, disguising more of his identity. With that, the Nix DJ pushed the Laronian off his platform with one of its many pointed legs and scuttled over the bar. "Why are people still HERE?" The Laronian slammed both of his palms onto the rail, as the occupants scrambled over each other to leave as quickly as possible. "Come, won't you join me for a drink?"

"This is unexpected," Esabelle commented to the group.

"Not really, he's not exactly what you'd call... stable." Roland downed another drink off the bar.

TELARREK STOOD, mesmerised by the beautiful colours of the different nebulas that played out across *Gommarian's* observation deck. The old Novaarian had programmed the holographic walls to display some of the systems the ancient ship had passed through, on its long journey searching for Earth. The alternative was to stand and observe the abyss of subspace they were travelling through.

Without a sound, his youngest hatchling appeared by his side, solemn and grave as ever. Naydaalan was half-a-foot smaller than his father, but most certainly faster and stronger having gone through the rigorous training to become a Protector.

"We're approaching the Ch'ket system, Ambassador. Ilyseal is helping to gather the humans and pack up their belongings." The exotic nebulas failed to capture the young Novaarian's imagination, it seemed.

"Formality is not required here. We are alone, hatchling." Telarrek noticed his son's hesitation to speak freely, not as Protector to the Ambassador but as a son to a father.

"What do you see in them, father?" Naydaalan looked up at him. "Why would you do so much for the humans?"

"They are fresh eyes in an old kingdom..." Telarrek watched as new stars were formed inside the ancient purple nebula. "They have questions about our way of life that we should be asking ourselves. The Conclave is not perfect, hatchling. Its foundation is built on equality and transparency between the races. But we both know it is not. We are governed by five of the twelve races because we have deemed ourselves the rightful rulers on account of our contributions." He stopped talking after that, aware of his innermost thoughts rising to the surface. It wasn't fair to expose his hatchling to rebellious thoughts and it certainly wasn't appropriate for an ambassador of the Highclave.

"You believe the humans can bring about change?" Naydaalan remained fixed on his father.

"I don't know. I only know that change is needed, and we have both witnessed the power of Kalian and Esabelle. Humanity's potential is overwhelming..."

"Some would see it as threatening," Naydaalan countered, his eyes following a streaming comet.

Telarrek felt a moment of pride swell within him. He had left his family for centuries in his mission to observe Earth, but he could see now that Naydaalan had become everything he dreamed. The young Novaarian was starting to see the board from all sides. The politics of the Conclave could swallow most whole with its intricacy.

"The humans have a saying, 'we fear what we do not know'." Telarrek let the words sink in before continuing. "It would appear we have more in common with them than we thought. Whether we like it or not, the nature of the universe chose their species to thrive before any of ours. That has to mean something, Naydaalan. I believe there is something coming for us, something worse than the Gomar. Our people need shaking from their apathy if we are to combat it. If we are to survive."

"I should have gone with her, with *them* I mean..." Naydaalan dropped his head.

Telarrek closed his mouth before the question could be asked. His hatchling had shown little love for the humans in the time he had spent with them, but now it seemed his attachment to their kind was perhaps down to one individual. He decided to drop the subject and leave Naydaalan to make up his own mind.

"Whatever they do next will have a ripple effect for those aboard this ship. We must remain by their side to offer guidance to Captain Fey and Uthor. They will be scared by this new move, on both sides. For now, our place is here. We must trust Kalian to do what must be done for the benefit of us all."

Telarrek felt guilty for his open affection towards mankind. He knew it was affection he should be giving to his family and the society that raised him. But he had always known the system was flawed and in need of renewal. Perhaps that was why he got into politics in the first place; who knew?

"What can be done about High Charge Uthor?" Naydaalan asked.

"If I know Uthor he is already looking into this from every angle. I believe the Highclave would like him to be a blunt instrument through which they wield Conclave security. But Uthor did not rise to his rank without a great deal of intelligence. He has an investigative mind and a deeper curiosity that most would not suspect in him. We have given him our theories and what evidence we have but, more than that, I believe Kalian's recent actions have shown the humans to have an unwavering resolve and belief in what they are fighting for, something every Raalak has forgotten in our age of accomplishments."

"Well said." The familiar yet alarming voice of ALF came from behind the Novaarians. The AI stood in the centre of the observation deck as if he had always been there.

"You are here..?" Naydaalan sounded confused.

"Correct."

"But you are with Kalian..."

"Correct again, Naydaalan. Such are the benefits of not being tied to one body, though I am more of an *echo* to what remains with Kalian." ALF stood perfectly still. There was something missing in his demeanour. The image before them lacked the flair and animation that usually accompanied his every word. It was often hard to remember that he wasn't a real human when in his company.

"What are you doing here, ALF?" Telarrek closed the gap between them.

"What is left of my makers is about to be relocated without the protection of this ship. I felt it only prudent that I take steps to ensure they are well taken care of."

"What you are really saying is that you want to maintain control of the *Gommarian*." Telarrek's assumption had no effect on ALF.

"Being any part of this ship is the last thing I wanted, but I will do what I must to ensure the completion of my mission, Ambassador."

"And what is that exactly?" Naydaalan had the same scepticism in his voice as Li'ara when she spoke to the AI

"The same as every species," ALF replied. "Survival..."

DOCTOR BAL TOOK one last look at the clear blue sky, knowing he wouldn't see it again for some time. The Trillik whipped his twin-tail, not entirely comfortable with the confines of his new lab. He stood on the square platform, the only artificial construction on the planet, and listened to the ocean lap against the solitary landing pad. The whole world was consumed with water, its only land in the form of two polar ice caps. Doctor Bal was aware of the storm coming in from the west and knew he wouldn't survive if he stayed out to greet it.

The Translift rose out of the flat platform behind him with his assistant inside, waiting for him. The young Atari presented him with a tablet displaying the live readouts from the eleven stasis pods. All the occupants were now in their new cells, sleeping in their Terran machines, blissfully unaware of the prison in which they resided.

"Thank you, Gelda." Doctor Bal watched the numbers plummet on the Translift wall.

The unnamed base was a simple cylinder that connected the surface of the ocean to the inhospitable bedrock. Every level had been fitted with enough explosives to obliterate the structure and everything inside it. The pressure of the depths alone would crush the majority of the base if it was ever compromised. Not that it mattered, Doctor Bal thought, for the planet had been chosen because it was an island in the ocean of the galaxy. Even if the prisoners escaped and survived the destruction of the base, the water planet would entomb them indefinitely.

"The new labs are almost complete, sir." Gelda highlighted a new tab on the display.

Extra labs and workshops were currently being retrofitted to accommodate the new prisoners. It had originally been designed to hold only one occupant, and even then they had been unsure as to how much experimenting they would be able to do. But these new occupants were unconscious and would offer no resistance.

"Excellent!" Doctor Bal rubbed his green hands together. "We have work to do."

THIRTEEN

A black glove covered The Laronian's slender hand as he massaged the side of his unusual mask, creating a vibrating hum with every flex of the fingers. He sat with his legs crossed on one of the many sofas sprawled throughout the expansive platform. It was impossible to tell what he was looking at as he surveyed the four humans standing on the other side of the low table.

Kalian could practically smell the fear coming from the surrounding guards, their weapons held tightly in their hands. Their nervous trigger fingers kept him alert and ready for any surprises. With the flick of a finger, Kalian knew he could disable all the electronics in the room, including their guns.

The humans looked at one another in confusion as The Laronian sat in awkward silence, making no attempt to communicate.

"You mentioned something about a drink," Roland said expectantly. He was the only one who took the offered chair.

The Laronian's head tilted, turning on Roland with an unknown expression, "Don't tell me you came all this way just for a drink, Mr. North." The crime lord had taken a serious tone, putting the group on edge. "I thought you wanted to know about Protocorps..."

"What can you tell us?" Li'ara asked pointedly.

After Roland's description of the crime lord, it came as no surprise that he already possessed many of the facts.

"*Why* would I tell you is a better question." The Laronian placed his feet across the hovering glass table. Kalian could feel the composition of the material and was shocked to discover the shoes were made from Brenine.

"What do you want?" Esabelle appeared casual in her body language, but Kalian could feel the dense atoms covering her body like a suit of armour.

The Laronian jumped out of his seat and stalked around the group of humans, his gloved hand slipping over Kalian's armour before running it through Li'ara's hair. When he reached Roland, The Laronian took a step back, drawing his hands into himself.

"Does that exceptional vessel of yours possess a shower?" The Laronian turned to the nearest guard. "Get him a drink and burn the chair when we're finished."

The Novaarian nodded and disappeared behind the private bar at the back of the room.

"What do I want, what do I want?" The Laronian scraped his fingers over the top of his mask as if he were putting his hand through hair. "I *want* to know what the big deal is with these cubes that keep getting everyone's pants in a twist. I *want* to know why there's one inside the AI mainframe. I mean seriously, what's it doing in there? I *want* to know how the *Gommarian* cube turned a puny human being into a killing machine. But most of all, I want to meet *him*."

"Meet who?" Esabelle asked.

"The oldest guy in the room, of course!" The Laronian's hands flew into the air.

Kalian looked at the others with more confusion. He was clearly talking about meeting ALF but how he knew of the AI was a mystery. They had only recently divulged his existence to the highest echelon of the Conclave.

To Kalian's annoyance, the ancient intelligence projected himself

PHILIP C. QUAINTRELL

into the room. Kalian promised he would find a way to control that aspect of his suit later.

The Laronian's hands dashed out as if to probe the hologram. It was clear to see his excitement without actually seeing his expression. ALF remained quiet while the crime lord made a circle around him, distorting the image for a moment as he came between Kalian and ALF.

"How old are you?" The Laronian asked.

"It's a number you've never thought of." ALF was showing off again.

"Ha, he's got attitude. I LIKE it!" His domed head turned to Kalian. "How do I get one?" The Laronian practically danced around the AI. "Oh, the things you must know! The knowledge you possess must be infinite! Together, you and I could accomplish wonderful things Mr... ALF, is it?"

"I'm going to be honest," ALF replied. "I can't tell if you want to rule this galaxy or cripple it."

The crime lord laughed. "I already rule it. I just want to have a little *fun!*"

"We don't have time for this." Li'ara stepped forward. "Every Nova-Class battleship in the galaxy will know we're here by now!"

"*Every Nova-Class battle-ship blah blah blah...*" The Laronian mocked. "What do you take me for? No transmissions get off this Arc without my say so. No one knows you're here."

"We need to find Garrett Jones and that cube." Kalian tried to guide the conversation. "I don't know what you want but we have little time and even fewer resources."

"For a being of immense power you're awfully serious. It's quite *boring.*" The Laronian intercepted the bright pink cocktail off the Novaarian's tray before Roland could reach it. The bounty hunter ground his teeth but remained in his seat. "If you want to find him you need to follow the money, and Protocorps' money is everywhere!"

"How do *you* know Protocorps is involved?" ALF asked. "You have proof?" The AI's tone suggested he was angling for information.

"We live in a golden age of information... and receipts." The

300

Laronian shrugged. "I have all the right people in all the right places, perfect for following the crumbs all the way back to Protocorps' fat accounts. A spectacular amount of money is being funnelled through shell companies into something in the Helteron Cluster. Something big..."

"So is Jones there or not?" Roland had his own feet resting on the table. He was trying to be casual and uncaring about their situation, but Kalian could hear his heart beating faster and feel the individual cells coursing through his veins. The bounty hunter was ready for a fight.

"It's the one place I don't have eyes and ears, and since I can't find him anywhere else I assume Mr. Jones has found refuge there." The Laronian turned on Roland. "And speak again in a tone I don't approve, Roland, and your evolved friends here won't even move fast enough to save you."

Kalian held back a smile at the bounty hunter's silence.

"Why *are* you helping us?" Li'ara folded her arms tight.

"You need to open those pretty little pink ears of yours, Miss Ducarté. Knowledge keeps my enterprise alive, and right now I feel like there's a conspiracy going on under my very nose, and I'm-not-getting-a-*cut*. By helping you to expose whatever Protocorps has been hiding all these years, I am put back in control of the map, so to speak. So here's what I propose; you two," the Laronian flicked his head towards Kalian and Esabelle, "take the *Rackham* to the Helteron Cluster and confront Professor Jones to your heart's content, while simultaneously uncovering whatever Protocorps are up to out there, and I will supply you two," he gestured at Roland and Li'ara, "with a nice shiny ship to get you back to the capital, where you can destroy whatever's infecting the AI.. *and* plant a backdoor in the redundancy mainframe." The Laronian clapped his hands together in glee to silence Roland's protests.

"And why exactly are we splitting up?" Li'ara asked stubbornly.

"And no one's flying *my* ship, period." Roland sat forward in his chair.

"He has a point..." ALF continued round Roland and sat on the sofa. The Laronian paused to watch the unusual spectacle from the hologram, not that the light particles had any effect on the fabric. "If Professor Jones is in the Helteron Cluster, it'll take both Kalian and Esabelle to stop him. If his actions have proven anything so far, it's that humans are no match for him, whereas breaking into the AI mainframe fits right into your wheelhouse." ALF crossed his legs and stared at Roland and Li'ara.

Kalian observed Li'ara working her jaw as she considered the plan. It made sense and she knew it, but she didn't like it.

"No-one-is-flying-my-ship." Roland stared back at the AI defiantly.

"An element of stealth will be required if the Helteron Cluster is to be navigated without resistance." The Laronian was leaning against the balcony edge, his domed head swirling hypnotically with the holographic galaxy.

"What backup mainframe are you talking about?" Li'ara turned to the balcony.

"Consider it my price. The only way to separate whatever's inside the AI hub is going to be with explosive force. There's simply too much code to try and deactivate from a terminal; you'd be dead before you succeeded. When the hub is destroyed the backup will come online. Now this redundant AI isn't anywhere near as sharp as its predecessor, but it'll keep the Conclave ticking over until Proto-corps can make the necessary adjustments. Before you blow the hub to pieces, I want you to install a little backdoor for me."

"What exactly will this *backdoor* do for you?" Roland asked.

"The AI sees and hears everything, Mr. North... it'll cut down on my costs. Do we have a deal?" The Laronian tapped his fingers against the railing.

"Deal," ALF replied on behalf of the group, much to their obvious irritation.

Everyone looked to Kalian then, wanting his decision. He met Li'ara's eyes and knew she thought it was a good plan, but he could tell she didn't want to split up. The conversation on the *Rackham* briefly played out in his mind again and he felt like punishing Li'ara.

"Deal," Kalian repeated.

"Excellent!" The Laronian clicked his fingers and the Novaarian presented Roland with a small data stick. "Upload the contents into one of the main control terminals in Protocorps HQ; the stick will do the rest. Now if the two of you would like to follow my minion here, he will show you to your new ship. Don't worry about getting through security, everything's already taken care of."

Roland stood up, "Perhaps none of you heard me when I said..."

"Roland..." Esabelle reached out for his arm and the bounty hunter just looked at her. Kalian couldn't tell if something was going on between them, or if Esabelle was manipulating Roland with her Terran abilities.

Either way, he appeared to be mulling over his next words. "Fine, just bring it back in one piece. And you with it, eh?"

Esabelle smiled warmly in reply. Kalian decided to ask about it later.

The warm smile vanished in an instant when Esabelle turned to The Laronian. "If you double-cross us in any way, I promise you the whole Conclave will know your secret before I die." The Terran held her gaze with the galactic visage of The Laronian.

The mobster's fingers ceased their endless rattling mid-air. It was a long moment before he decided to reply, and Kalian was none the wiser as to what they were talking about. "I wouldn't dream of it."

Esabelle nodded and indicated to Kalian that he shouldn't ask. "Then I think it's time we left Vallara." With suspicious looks from everyone, the group started to leave and ALF's image dissipated.

"A last word of warning... Mr. North," The Laronian called after them. "You are not the hunter anymore." With that the mobster exited through another door, followed by his entourage.

THE GROUP LANDED the temporary ship on the platform next to the *Rackham* so Ch'len could swap ships. Kalian watched from the viewport as the fat Ch'kara waddled across the landing platform while he blasted out every obscenity he knew.

"What kind of stupid deal did you O-2 breathers make? That ship's the only protection I've got!" He peeked up at the starry sky and whimpered at the sheer vastness of the open world.

The ship wasn't much to look at but it was still a lot cleaner than the *Rackham*. The bridge was spacious, designed with a crew of six in mind. Shaped like a fork, its three engines spread out from the aft of the ship, covered in old scars and several bad paint jobs. It was the perfect unassuming ship to slip past Conclave security.

Roland sighed as he looked longingly at the *Rackham*.

"Am I ever going to see her again?" the bounty hunter asked.

"Well considering the four of us are going on separate suicide missions," Kalian shared his sigh, "I'm gonna say no."

"Suicide missions..." Roland half laughed to himself. "Been there, done that. Just promise you'll bring her back to me, kid."

"I will if you will." Kalian turned in the pilot's chair to look at Li'ara, tinkering with the guidance system at the back of the bridge.

"You still haven't sealed the deal there?" Roland asked playfully. Kalian's only reply was a warning glance. "Don't worry, kid, she's tougher than *both* of us."

"So what was The Laronian talking about back there?" Kalian changed the subject while examining Roland's face for any reaction.

"I've got no idea." The bounty hunter's expression was that of stone. "I'd be more interested to know what Esabelle was talking about."

Kalian knew he was lying and he didn't have to listen to his heartbeat to know that.

"You want to know what?" Esabelle came over.

"What did you threaten that nut-bag with?" Roland swivelled in his chair.

"Kalian?" Esabelle looked at him expectantly but he had no idea what she wanted him to say. "What have I been teaching you? Always know what's around you. I scanned every molecule of that arrogant moron before he even started talking. The Laronian is not a Laronian." Both Roland's and Kalian's jaws dropped. "That helmet hides his face but he wears holo-bands up his sleeves to disguise his hands in case his gloves ever come off."

"What is he?" Roland asked eagerly.

"He's an Atari. Under that holographic blue skin, he's all pink." Esabelle's cocky smile was disturbingly similar to Roland's.

"No shit? Now that's worth knowing." Roland settled back into his chair as Ch'len came onto the bridge. The Ch'kara dropped several packets of food onto the floor as he fiddled with the dials on his breather, desperate for breath.

"Okay..." Li'ara announced after finishing with her inspection. "It's not the flashiest bucket of bolts but it's got a solid set of engines on it. We're good to go."

The group looked to one another for a moment as they all considered the possibility that they wouldn't see each other again. Kalian wanted to say everything he felt to Li'ara but clamped his jaw shut, determined to punish her for pushing him away. He knew it was irrational and child-like but he didn't care. Li'ara had made her feelings clear and they were to remain apart. There was an awkward moment when Roland tried to hug Esabelle but she tactfully moved aside and said her goodbyes to both him and Li'ara. Roland patted Kalian on the arm and wished him good luck with as little optimism as possible, while Li'ara waited for the bounty hunter to step aside.

"Well..." she started.

"Good luck, and be careful." Kalian nodded and left the bridge after Esabelle, taking good care to control his tear ducts. He never looked back.

"Does nobody care if *I* die?" Ch'len exclaimed to silence.

UTHOR STOOD as a statue at the forefront of the *Sentinel's* bridge, his heavy hands clasped behind his back while he observed the plethora of News ships that swarmed the mega structure's green hull. Beyond the News ships, the planet Ch'ket swelled in the expansive viewport.

The High Charge could see his own vessel, the *Nautallon*, docked with one of the giant rings that haloed the planet.

"Give me an update on the quarantine," the Raalakian called out to the bridge crew, knowing someone would be ready with an answer.

"A ten-mile strip of the Tiphus Ring has been cordoned off with checkpoints at each end, sir." It was Gre-den, his second-in-command that answered. The Shay had been by the Raalakian's side since he took command of the *Nautallon* and often knew to pre-empt his commander's needs. "The report from the final scan is coming through now."

"Excellent. Give the order to evacuate the *Gommarian*." The alien ship had taken the place of the *Sentinel* in the shadow of Cerula.

Gre-den appeared at his side after relaying the orders, "Do you think this will work, sir?" the Shay asked in hushed tones.

"The *Highclave* believes it will." Uthor's tone implied his own lack of faith in the plan. He looked down at his old comrade and remembered he could speak freely with the Shay. "This ship isn't ready yet. It shouldn't be paraded for the masses just to keep their eyes off the Tiphus Ring."

A small alarm could be heard emitting from a nearby console where a Novaarian ensign was sitting. Her four arms quickly navigated the holographic display to silence it.

"Report, Ensign," Gre-den ordered her.

"It's already been corrected, sir." The Novaarian was embarrassed. "The Sentinel was passing through the gravity-barrier alert. We're still getting used to the size of her."

Uthor rolled his black eyes. Another example of the danger it posed to reveal a ship that wasn't finished with a crew that wasn't accustomed to it. The *Sentinel's* size had proved to be as problematic as the *Marillion* when it came to approaching a planetary body. Their sheer size had the ability to affect a planet's gravity-well like a moon.

The High Charge walked around the oval bridge, to the nearest available monitor, and activated the live feed. Elondrasa and the rest of the Highclave were introducing the galactic community to their newest battleship. Using simple technology they were able to make it

"None of this will matter," Uthor continued. "You can't hide over seven thousand human beings on a core world. It won't be long before this ship is old news and they are discovered."

"I hear the Planetary Location Office has already narrowed their choices to two worlds," Gre-den replied.

Uthor failed to hide his surprise. "The P.L.O is involved? How did you come by this information?"

"I have a friend that works there. She informed me last night."

Uthor didn't need to check with his second-in-command that the channels he used were secure. "The Highclave really is playing this close to the chest. Then again, it would be easier to keep an eye on the humans from a planet, rather than an orbital ring packed with ships and technology."

The Raalak felt his rocky forehead crinkle as he considered everything Kalian had told him. There was too much going on around him that felt out of his control. It was his duty to keep the Conclave safe from threats foreign and domestic, and right now he felt they were being attacked by both. There was no denying that something beyond the control of the humans was making aggressive actions towards his people, but could Protocorps really be involved?

The High Charge had always left criminal investigations to local security and other officers under his command, but he had suspected some criminal involvement with Protocorps for years. They were simply too big and too powerful to have never made a deal with one of the syndicates. Though now he thought about it, it wasn't much of a stretch to believe that they could own the syndicates with their wealth.

In his mind, he kept seeing the image of the cube inside the AI hub on the capital. Forensics had already confirmed for him that the pictures were valid and hadn't been tampered with. Uthor had gone over the images for hours on the journey to Ch'ket, wrestling with taking the information to the Highclave. But even they had ties to Protocorps. Something ALF had said on the *Gommarian* kept repeating in his mind; *It may have no intention of striking now, but when it does it will have planned every eventuality.* A pit opened up in his stomach at the thought of that. If he was going to conquer the Conclave, the first move he would make would be to compromise the one thing that holds it all together. The AI knows the ins and outs of every level of infrastructure there is. There would be no fighting it.

It suddenly occurred to Uthor what he would do to combat that threat, and he remembered the four dangerous humans that escaped the *Gommarian*.

"Gre-den?" Uthor called the Shay closer. "I need you to do something quickly and quietly for me."

"Sir?"

"Put together a team of the most loyal soldiers you know and position them around Protocorps HQ on the capital." Uthor considered his next words carefully. "Instruct them that they are to keep a close eye on the central building, and they are to assist any humans they come into contact with."

"But sir..."

"They are to minimise loss of life, but they should help the humans at all cost. If they question you, inform them that they may well be saving the entire Conclave and their promotions will know no bounds." Gre-den didn't look convinced, "Do you trust me, old friend?" Uthor placed a thick hand on the Shay's augmented shoulder. Uthor had every confidence that Gre-den held no loyalty to Protocorps; the Shay was Conclave Security through and through.

"Of course," Gre-den nodded gravely.

"Sir, we're getting some anomalous readings from the *Gommarian*," a Ch'kara reported from the other side of the bridge.

Uthor strode over, annoyed at the ridiculous size of the bridge and the distance he had to cover. With four arcing columns that fitted into the oval shape, all thirty-six bridge crew were stationed across its length. The central podium, designed for the Charge of the ship, sat in the divide between the columns of monitors. Uthor rarely positioned himself inside, preferring to walk around his command centre and get a feeling for his crew instead of having all their data collated and presented to him in holograph form. Looking at the bloated size of the crew needed to run the ship, Uthor was beginning to see the benefits of the podium. The High Charge came up behind the Ch'kara, where the terminal was receiving data from the skeleton crew left to oversee the evacuation.

"The shuttles have left already, sir, but the remaining crew are reporting some glitches," the Ch'kara explained.

"What kind of glitches?" Gre-den asked.

"It appears some of the internal walls are... moving." The Ch'kara brought up another report. "They're struggling to access certain walkways and corridors that were otherwise available. Some of the doors aren't responding."

"Tell them to stay in contact at all times and to move in twos," Uthor ordered. "Get me a status update on the cube as well. If anything changes in that room I want to know immediately."

"Yes, sir." The Ch'kara hurriedly went back to work.

The High Charge and Gre-den strolled off the bridge together. "Make those arrangements, commander. I'm going to dig a little deeper into our friends at Protocorps."

CAPTAIN FEY BRACED herself for the throng of people gathered outside the door to their temporary council room. She was escorted by three of her own UDC personnel aware of the concerns and general uproar amongst the people. She could already hear them before they reached the end of the corridor.

"Captain Fey!" they shouted.

"Why are we here?"

"What's happening?" Their questions were endless and rightly so.

Upon seeing them she realised it was a mob. The corridor opened up into a larger deck into which at least four hundred people had managed to cram. The room that had been reserved for the council was completely hidden by the masses, each vying for her attention. Men and women were crying, clutching their children and adopted children for dear life, unsure of their sudden re-housing. The captain had always believed in transparency when it came to the survivors of her race; she truly believed it was the only way to maintain order and trust.

"We will make an address very soon, I assure you!" she shouted over the crowd.

The soldiers were forced to push people back as they drove their way through to the door. The captain's instructions had been clear about leaving their weapons behind; it was to be incident free. Hands reached out to grab her but between the soldiers and herself, they were able to keep them at bay until the door offered some escape.

"Please!" the crowd pleaded before the door sealed her in. She felt a moment of guilt at leaving her men outside.

"Captain..." Laurence Wynter was sitting at the head of a long table. The room was bare but for the table and chairs with a window as long as the room on the far side. The other councillors were dotted around the room, leaning against walls and pacing the length of the window. Only Wynter appeared calm.

"Right..." Upon closer inspection, the captain could see how haggard the group were. A few of them even had torn clothing where they had tried to pass through the mob outside. "Ambassador Telarrek is going to be late; he's already opened channels to negotiate with the Highclave on our behalf."

Jim Landale stopped by the window. "Something tells me the Highclave is going to be a bit busy right now. Have you seen what's out there? Even from here it looks humungous!"

"It's all over their News networks." Sharon Booth was watching the feed that played out across the table's surface.

"And there's nothing about us or the *Gommarian*." Samuel Vock wiped the sweat from his dark bald head. "They're using this *Sentinel* as a smokescreen for kicking us out of our home."

"And we should have expected better?" It was Joseph Barnes who spoke out. "We kept too many secrets from them while we strode around their backyard with a big gun! We should have been open with them from the beginning, about ALF, the basement, Esabelle and not to mention those goddamned prisoners we kept locked away out of sight." He was angry - that much was obvious.

"Take a breath, Jo," Wynter advised. "The people outside that door need our heads to remain level. We have to present a clear message that shows we are united and that we trust the Conclave."

Captain Fey tried to hide her disdain for Laurence Wynter. He never felt quite human to her. His motives always appeared as if they were in favour of the people, but the captain knew he only wanted to keep some semblance of power. He was a man who had been in control his whole life and he knew no other way to live.

"*Do* we trust the Conclave?" Jim's question was met with silence.

"*Our* trust in them is irrelevant," the captain replied. "We need everyone out there to trust *us*, and the only way we're going to achieve that is if we tell them the truth."

"And what is the truth?" Wynter countered.

"That right now, the Conclave is afraid of us. Something is attacking them and they're blaming us. But Kalian Gaines is fighting for us, right now, off this ring, trying to prove our innocence and that we belong in this community." The captain kept her expression as serious as possible. The thought of Kalian and the others out there opened up a pit in her gut. She hated not knowing what they were doing or whether they were succeeding. The question of whether they were even alive was one that the captain couldn't even entertain at the moment. Right now, she had to keep the council calm so she could keep the populace calm.

"You still expect us to have faith in a history teacher?" Wynter didn't hide his disdain for the captain.

"You and I both know he's more than that." The captain was ready for a fight if that's what he wanted. She didn't know if it was the nanocelium flowing through her veins, but she felt a storm building inside her that wouldn't be weathered.

"The people look to him as a sort of... saviour," Sharon added. "He's an unknown, I admit, but he makes everyone feel a little safer."

"Regardless of how the people see him, he has never spoken on this council for them or *actually* saved them from anything." Samuel couldn't stop pacing.

The storm was growing. "If Kalian had faltered on Naveen, none of us would be here right now. Even the Conclave has to recognise that. And he may not have spoken on this *make-shift* council, but he has spoken on humanity's behalf several times to ensure our survival in this alien community." The captain's tone implied she was not to be argued with.

"What exactly are they doing, Captain?" Wynter's eyes narrowed.

Captain Fey hesitated before answering. "Gathering evidence of our innocence and proving we're an asset to the Conclave." The soldier in her couldn't part with any more information than that. Until they were all back safe and sound, the mission should remain classified to give them every advantage. For all they knew, the High-clave was monitoring everything they said.

"*Please,* don't tell us too much, Captain," Wynter replied sarcastically.

"We're getting off topic," Jim interjected before Captain Fey tore Wynter apart. "We need basic answers like: How long are we going to be here? What's happening to the *Gommarian*? Where do we go from here? They can't keep us here forever, we'll drain their resources."

Aware that she didn't have the answers, Captain Fey walked around the table to get a better view from the window. The starry vista was distorted by the traffic of ships and carriers that flitted between the great rings and orbital Translifts, while so many others were drawn to the unveiling of the *Sentinel*. The battleship was floating in the distance, its green hull shimmering in the light of Ch'ket's sun. It was a magnificent vessel with a size that could almost rival the *Gommarian*. The captain didn't want to think about its armaments.

"Telarrek will have some..." Captain Fey turned around as the door slid open and the sound of the mob momentarily exploded into the room with Telarrek. "Ah, Ambassador, you're just in time. Have you spoken with the Highclave?"

Telarrek bowed. "Greetings of peace, council members, Captain Fey." Telarrek's towering form was followed by his son, Naydaalan. While Naydaalan remained by the door, the ambassador took a seat at the table, no doubt to make the humans feel more comfortable with his height.

"What did they say?" Joseph blurted.

"Jo, let the Ambassador speak," Wynter commanded.

"I am afraid there is only one thing the Highclave are interested in," Telarrek began. "They wish to know where Kalian and the others are."

"Wouldn't we all," Wynter added dryly.

"I pointed out that the four of them escaped custody without your permission, but I also tried to convince the Highclave that Kalian and the others only wish to help. Unfortunately, the council does not recognise an internal threat, and therefore lay everything at your feet." Telarrek rested all four hands on the table.

"How can they *still* not understand that we have done nothing wrong?" Joseph clenched his fists in frustration.

"Learning of Esabelle the way they did has not earned you any trust," Telarrek explained, "and they know for certain that Professor Jones is a threat, a threat that originated from your ship."

"Not our ship," Jim Landale pointed out. "It was never our ship. This seems to be a fact that the Highclave can't get out of their heads. We are not the Gomar or even the Terran for that matter. We didn't choose to be created and we didn't choose to have our world blown to hell. Now I admit that the *Gommarian* holds a few secrets, some that we shouldn't have kept from them, but we are just as victimised as the Conclave, maybe more so!"

"Jim..." Wynter held up a hand to calm him. "Right now all we can hope for is that the Highclave recognise Kalian and the others as a rogue group, acting beyond our control."

"We should be united," Captain Fey replied defiantly. "If they prove our innocence and help to eliminate a threat to the Conclave, it should be seen as an effort on behalf of our entire race."

A smug politician's smile crept across Wynter's face. "That's the beauty of it. If they succeed we will come out supporting their efforts and win favour; if they do nothing but wreak havoc, we have deniability."

Captain Fey inhaled deeply and blinked slowly in an effort to control her anger. Wynter was happy to sit on the fence and see where the chips fall, then pick the winning side.

"How long do we have to stay here, Ambassador?" Sharon asked.

"It will only be temporary, I'm sure. The Highclave would not reveal their plans in full to me, but I know they will not wish to keep you on Ch'ket for long. What I am certain of, however, is that you will not be returning to the *Gommarian*."

"Well, that's a given," Samuel snorted. "They'll pull that ship apart until they know *all* its secrets."

"Can we hope for somewhere with a little land?" Jim asked.

"I cannot say," Telarrek lowered his head. "Much will depend on the outcome of Kalian's findings."

"Well I suggest we strongly hint at that in my announcement to the people." Wynter clasped his hands together. "Give them some hope of a new world."

"I thought the Captain would be giving the speech?" Sharon looked as puzzled as everyone else, who for the most part nodded in agreement, except for Samuel Vock who looked fearfully at Wynter.

"Very well..." Wynter slowly lowered his chin onto his clasped hands, staring at the blank wall at the other end of the table.

Captain Fey met the looks of expectation. "Fine, I'll make the announcement. But I'm not going to lie or offer any false hope of a new world. We need them to have hope and trust in us. We will go out there together and tell them everything we know. Kalian and the others won't let us down."

"Is that what we know?" Wynter was pissed off. "One of these *others* is Roland North, an unpredictable, highly trained killer."

A sharp grunt came from Telarrek's throat. "It was Roland North who saved you from the Gomar, and he has already assisted in the discovery of a possible threat inside the Conclave AI. You should have a little more faith, Mr. Wynter."

"Well said." Captain Fey spoke before Wynter could. "We will address the people and iterate our faith in them to remain calm while we negotiate with the Highclave."

With that, the meeting came to a close and the councillors braced themselves before leaving. Wynter gave the captain a look of derision, clearly believing her faith to be naive. He would spin tales to appease the crowds and have them wrapped around his little finger. She lingered for a moment until it was only herself and the Novaarians left in the room.

"Have you heard anything?" the captain asked seriously.

"There are rumours coming out of Vallara that humans have been sighted, but there is no recorded data to collaborate."

The captain walked away, her hand over her mouth as she considered the odds they were against.

"They *will* succeed, Captain." Naydaalan spoke with such certainty, it was hard to argue.

"I know. I suppose it's a *good* thing nobody knows where they are..."

THE *BLADE* FLOWED through the traffic that surrounded the capital planet, always keeping its prey in sight. The unassuming ship with pronged engines held his prize. Kubrackk had swelled with elation when North and the red-head separated from not only the *Rackham* but also from the Terran. The fact that The Laronian was helping them was a little more disturbing, though he had no idea what any of them were up to. It was downright moronic of North to return to the capital after the chaos his last trip caused, especially without the protection of the Terran.

Once again they followed the bounty hunter into Clave Tower, where they immediately blended into the traffic heading to its apex.

Kubrackk stroked his long jaw as he thought about their direction. Surely he wasn't going back to Protocorps? Security had doubled since their last incursion and not only with Protocorps' private army, but the Conclave's forces as well.

Spelnar was sitting by his side, manually adjusting the *Blade's* course since they couldn't hand over the controls to the AI without knowing their destination. The Trillik's double-ended tail moved over the console, tweaking the ship's systems, while his hands kept the flight as smooth as possible. Kubrackk found himself having to dodge the occasional flick of Spelnar's tail and gave the Trillik a look that could melt a Raalak.

Eventually, the rush hour traffic died down and the *Blade* came to settle down on a landing pad, not too far from the unassuming ship. The Protocorps HQ loomed in the distance, hanging over the tower. The gleaming red hull of the Conclave's security forces could be seen patrolling in and around the towers that surrounded Protocorps.

"What the hell are we doing back here?" Spelnar polarised the viewport to ensure no one outside could see them.

Before Kubrackk could answer, the main console chirped with an incoming call. Spelnar used his tail to access the comm systems and identify who was trying to contact them. A holographic image popped up above the console with the stilled image of a Brenine.

"It's Revus..." the Trillik sounded confused.

"How does he know we're here?" Kubrackk turned on Spelnar with fangs exposed.

Spelnar gulped. "It must be something Lole wired into the comm relay to alert him when we're in system."

A low growl slowly erupted from Kubrackk's throat. "Fix it, *now*." The Trillik didn't say another word before leaving. Kubrackk took a deep breath and activated the comm feed. "Revus..."

"Kubrackk, back so soon I see." The Brenine was sitting in his office above the Abyss.

"What do you want?" Kubrackk kept an eye on the surveillance feed Spelnar had set up after landing. The Novaarian could see the ship North arrived in, though the human bounty hunter was yet to reveal himself.

"It's not what I want, it's what *he* wants."

That got Kubrackk's attention. "Why is The Laronian involved?"

"The *why* is his business." Revus relaxed into his high-backed chair. "It's what he wants that's important." The Brenine paused to let the significance of his words sink in, much to Kubrackk's annoyance.

The Novaarian looked away to keep himself calm. Revus might not be as powerful as The Laronian but he was still a heavyweight in the underworld. Pissing him off would only cause more trouble down the line when Kubrackk had finished with his vendetta.

"You have to drop this obsession you have with Roland North." The Brenine's words hit Kubrackk like an Intrinium bolt. "Whatever he's doing now is sanctioned by The Laronian, and he doesn't want you getting in the way."

A rage began to grow within Kubrackk; a rage he felt could destroy the entire Conclave if he unleashed it. How dare they order him to leave his brother's murder un-avenged, and for what? Profit was the most likely answer and the Novaarian hated it.

"Now don't worry," Revus went on. "I'll throw you a bone. I've got a nice job all set up for you. It'll be the easiest bounty you've ever had, and the pay is good." The Brenine looked closer at the feed on his end since Kubrackk had yet to respond. "You still there, Kubrackk? Tell me you understand."

Something snapped inside the bounty hunter. He had spent too long under the thumb of people like Revus and The Laronian, taking orders and jobs that were below him. He should be free to ply his trade as he liked, not constantly trying to fight his way out of debt to the various syndicates that run the Clave. He could run the entire underworld better than all the bosses combined, including that eccentric dick-wit on Vallara. A blood-vendetta was his right as Torvrackk's brother.

Kubrackk spoke very slowly. "When I'm finished with North, I'm going to come for you, Revus. And when I'm done gutting you, I'm going to find The Laronian and remove his head. Tell me you understand." With that he cut the feed, ending the conversation. Using the main console, Kubrackk opened the internal comm system. "Spelnar, forget the relay. Load up and prepare that ID check for Protocorps HQ. We're moving out in five!" The Novaarian knew that was all they would have before Revus sent his goons to attack the *Blade*.

FOURTEEN

The *Rackham* hurtled through subspace at maximum yield as it pushed on towards the Helteron Cluster. Beyond its dull bronze hull, there was nothing but darkness, a void so vast it could never be filled. Kalian preferred to confine his awareness to the ship's interior while they journeyed between the fabric of reality. The abyss of subspace was a cold thing to touch with his mind, its feedback so empty and lifeless that it felt unnatural.

"You're wasting time sitting there." Esabelle walked onto the bridge.

Slumped in the pilot's chair, Kalian had used his extra senses to follow her movements around the ship. He could hear her bones grinding against one another as she moved, while the scent of her sweet perfume filled his nostrils. If he focused hard enough, he could even taste the faintest drops of sweat on her skin. His own skin could literally feel the impact of every particle in the air being displaced by her body. This was all surplus to the way his Terran mind could map out the *Rackham*'s interior and feel the impression everything made on the physical universe. That last one was a hard sense to define. Li'ara had asked him about it before, but he could only shrug in reply. It was a sad thought that only a Terran could truly understand what it felt like.

"We wouldn't be wasting any time if you just... *poof*." Kalian opened his hand like an explosion.

"If I transported us through subspace I'd be too weak to fight on the other end, and I'm fairly certain there's going to be fighting." Esabelle came to lean against the curving main console in front of Kalian.

"At what point in my training do I learn *that*?" He swivelled in his chair to face her. "Because ALF downloaded a lot of Terran training programmes in here," he tapped the side of his head, "and there was *nothing* about travelling through subspace on the power of the mind alone."

The holographic image of ALF suddenly appeared by their side, emitted from Kalian's waist. "And with good reason!"

They were the only words he managed before Esabelle waved her hand over Kalian's armour and shut the projection down. Kalian felt the tingling sensation pass over his skin as the electromagnetic pulse passed through his body.

"I don't like him listening," Esabelle stated flatly. "Though he did have a point. It took me thousands of years to learn how to manipulate energy like that, and I still needed some juice from the *Rackham*. Why do you think Savrick had me plugged into the *Gommarian*? I needed complete sensory deprivation *and* the ship's energy to push that thing through subspace. Even now I don't feel a hundred percent after escaping the *Gommarian*. For someone as young as you, you'd need the power of a star to achieve that kind of feat; you're centuries away from having that kind of power, Kalian."

"Thanks, coach."

"I mean it. Don't even try it. Besides, you have plenty of the basics to practise in the meantime. We don't know the extent of what the cube's done to Garrett. He won't be easily brought down, especially if he's surrounded by Protocorps security." Esabelle had her stern teacher's expression on her face as she forbade him from experimenting.

Kalian gave her a sideways look. "You want to train right now, don't you?"

"Well, whatever's waiting for us in the Helteron Cluster, it's definitely going to try and kill us, and out of the two of us I *know* I'm not the one that's going to die." Her expression was serious but Kalian knew there was an element of play to her.

"Then I guess I should train..."

Only minutes later were they both in the cargo hold of the *Rackham*. Esabelle spread both her arms and telekinetically pushed all the crates and boxes into the wall. Kalian stood in the middle of the room, in no state of mind to train right now. Esabelle circled him slowly, as she always did before her pre-fight lecture.

"You're distracted," she stated softly.

It caught him off guard and he had to turn his head as she walked behind him. "I'm just thinking about everyone on the *Gommarian*," he replied.

"No, you're not." Esabelle came back into view. "You're thinking about, Li'ara. You're distracted." She repeated.

"I'm worried about *both* of them," he replied defiantly, becoming sick of her constant circling.

"Li'ara told you she doesn't *love* you, and now you're distracted." Esabelle's tone never changed.

Kalian clenched his jaw at the words. He should have known that Esabelle would be listening to them. The conversation came back to him and took his mind away from the present for a second, a second Esabelle used to her advantage.

"Ow!" Kalian grabbed the side of his neck where something sharp had pierced the skin. Upon examining his fingers he could see a small spot of blood from his neck. "What the hell?" he exclaimed.

Esabelle came back into view with a small green dart in her hand. "Distracted." She threw the dart away and came to stand directly in front of Kalian. "Groll venom, from Zantesh. Apparently, Roland is quite the fan." Esabelle looked to the red crate in the corner of the bay.

Kalian tried to bring up the files in his mind and view everything there was to know about the Nix homeworld. The image in his mind became distorted, leaving only the lasting impression of danger towards the predatory Groll. Looking through his physical eyes had become just as hard as looking through his mind's eye. Esabelle appeared to be flitting about the bay as the borders of his vision became blurred and dull. The whole ship seemed to shift making Kalian stumble backwards, though Esabelle was unaffected.

"What...?" The darkness at the edge of his vision consumed his entire sight as sharp stabbing pains fired in his joints.

"You're letting the venom distract you." Esabelle kicked him square in the chest with enough force to put him on his back. "Focus." Kalian could no longer see her but without touching him he was flung up into the ceiling and dropped back to the floor.

Pushing himself back onto his feet, Kalian could feel a numbness spreading through his arms and legs, and thanks to Esabelle's telekinetic attack, he had blinding pain in the back of his head. Thankfully the nanocelium in his armour was doing its job and taking the brunt of her abuse.

"What's the...?" A stinging pain exploded across Kalian's neck when he tried to speak. Esabelle came in again, hitting him in several places across his body and dropping him to his knee.

"Just like Li'ara, the venom is distracting you. Your real threat is right in front of you, and you're too busy trying to figure out how to counteract the poison in your veins. You need to create vaults in your mind where distractions can be placed at a moment's notice. Your mind/body control must be perfect, Kalian. Your immune system is like an army at your disposal, but you must separate your mind and command your body to do what it must, while you deal with the external threat. The subconscious mind of a Terran does not work like a human's. You have complete access to everything inside your brain, but that does not mean you should. Having a portion of the brain devoted to defensive measures without your direct command is essential. You need to heal *while* you fight."

Kalian had heard enough. The pain made him angry at everything. He lashed out in the direction of her voice, estimating the distance between them. The first attack was countered by Esabelle, as was the second and third. Kalian's fourth attack went wild, only to be met with a blow to the ribs from Esabelle, who easily evaded the blind man's attack.

"Focus!" Esabelle commanded. "What's the first thing you should have done?"

Pain...

In the blink of an eye, Kalian opened a thick heavy vault door in his mind and had it suck everything inside like a black hole. Any thought of Li'ara was instantly gone as he imagined the vault dropping into a shaft that disappeared into the depths of his mind. He quickly moved onto the Parietal lobe in his brain and commanded it to misinterpret the pain being transmitted through his spinal cord. In an instant, the pain was gone and he could focus again.

The right side of his face was awash with particulates in the air as Esabelle's fist compressed the atmosphere between Kalian's face and her approaching knuckles. A dodge of the head was all it took for her swing to follow through and expose her ribs. Kalian grappled her around the shoulders and drove his knee into her ribs, bringing them both down to the floor with him on top. He couldn't see but he could feel her wriggling between his knees. That was until Esabelle launched him back into the ceiling with a shockwave of telekinetic energy.

After hitting the ceiling and the floor, Kalian picked himself up again, using his extra senses to locate Esabelle. Time slowed as he retrospectively investigated the extent of the Groll venom in his system. His immunity to the venom was growing but the occipital lobe of his brain had been poisoned the most. Kalian concentrated on moving more white blood cells to that region of his body to try and gain his sight back. Having dealt with the pain aspect of the venom, he could leave the venom in the rest of his body until later.

The air was pushed from his lungs as a wave of heat washed over his face and hands. Before Kalian could make sense of the attack, he was impacting against the far wall of the bay. On his hands and knees once more, Kalian probed the chest plates of his armour and felt the nanocelium rebuilding the crater where an organic ball of plasma had struck him. With an audible groan, he picked himself up, again.

"Too slow, baby Terran," Esabelle mocked. "All the measures you just enacted inside your mind should have been done before the dart left your skin. If I was Garrett you'd be dead by now." Her approaching footsteps rang out on the metal floor. "You lash out with your hands and feet, forgetting that you have so much more at your disposal. Even now you're trying to locate me with your human senses; though heightened, it's still slow and inaccurate."

Esabelle's footsteps stopped right in front of him. Kalian dashed out with his fist but hit nothing but air and stumbled forward.

"Your senses are easily fooled, Kalian. Try seeing the world like a Terran." Esabelle's voice came from the middle of the bay, nowhere near him.

With a slow breath, Kalian let the universe flood his mind with all its physical information. The picture in his mind was made of every colour imaginable as the cargo bay and beyond was constructed for him to see. Esabelle shone like god incarnate before him. The frequencies of her brain emitted outward in every direction, like his. Kalian was forced to take a sharp breath as his awareness spread out into subspace. Icy cold tentacles pierced his body as if the abyss wanted to claim his senses. The bubble contracted, bringing his vision back to the cargo bay alone. Two small containers lay at his feet where he thought Esabelle should have been. With telekinesis, she had managed to trick Kalian into thinking she was walking towards him.

"You have three hundred and sixty vision. Use it." Esabelle ran at him with enhanced speed.

Matching her speed, Kalian countered the first few attacks before trying to land his own. With all his senses working at once he could anticipate her every action. Unfortunately, so could Esabelle. Eventually, the fight began to evolve as Esabelle attacked Kalian from all sides using various crates and large containers. The cargo flew through the air faster than any human could move, striking Kalian in between Esabelle's own attacks. He was forced to use telekinesis to keep them at bay while also blocking the hands and feet that whipped at him.

The training continued for another hour before they both picked themselves off the cold floor. Bruises and cuts across Esabelle's face were already fading, though she actually appeared to be out of breath with glistening sweat on her forehead. Kalian smiled at his efforts while his ribs realigned, allowing him to breathe properly again.

"You're getting better," Esabelle remarked.

"Tell that to my ribcage..." Kalian felt the ribs fit back into place and the pain receptors came back to life with a slight ache in his shoulders. The Groll venom had been filtered through his organs and removed from his occipital lobe, returning his sight.

"Don't rely on that armour," she warned. "It's the best armour in the galaxy, but it's not as good as this." Esabelle put her finger to her temple.

"Garrett was strong and fast, but he doesn't have Terran abilities. Whatever the cube's done to him, it's only enhanced his human physiology. I was... distracted on the *Nova*, but together you and I can bring him down, hopefully without killing him."

"You did well containing the Starrillium," Esabelle replied, "But the fact that Li'ara was onboard distracted you more. Keep working on creating those vaults in your mind."

Kalian chewed over whether to respond. "You know, sometimes thinking of her makes me stronger, not distracted. Overcoming Savrick, containing the Starrillium, I did all that thinking of her."

"You did that because you were worried she was going to die. What happens when you're at your limits and Li'ara's not in danger? When you feel there's nothing left to give and there's no one to protect? You need to be able to achieve those feats when she's not around. And she won't be around forever, Kalian." Esabelle's expression was a knowing one.

"I'm going to go and check on the... something." Kalian turned to leave.

"You can't run away from this one," Esabelle called after him, giving him pause in the doorway. "You're in love with someone whose lifespan is a speck compared to yours."

That got Kalian's hackles up. "So I shouldn't love anyone that can't live as long as me? What kind of life is that?"

"A life not filled with heartbreak." Esabelle's tone was a little softer. "Conclave technology might give Li'ara a few extra centuries, but centuries are nothing compared to the life you have. I know that's hard to imagine right now but..."

"You get to train me, Esabelle; you don't get to tell me how to live my life. I mean, you've only been *alive* for six months. Maybe after a couple more decades of actually living, you'll have a different outlook," Kalian added spitefully, before walking out of the cargo bay.

ROLAND WAS SITTING SLUMPED in the co-pilot's chair with his feet up on the main console, deep in thought, distorting Li'ara's words into nothing but white noise in the background of his mind. The Laronian's warning confirmed his gut feeling. For months Roland had felt someone was behind his every step, with rumours of someone asking about him after a new bounty.

Old scar-face was still hunting him.

The Novaarian didn't exactly scare him, but the bounty hunter's tenacity to track him down and exact revenge for his brother was disturbing. At this point, Roland couldn't even remember the name of Kubrackk's brother. It had been a split second decision to kill the ruthless brothers in the canyons on Veridian's moon. The bounty had been very clear with the prices for alive or dead, and dead would not split three ways and be worth it, but the brothers were merciless when it came to their job, enjoying the kill at the end of a hunt. Roland had urged them to take the Tularon alive, giving them all a nice chunk of moolah, but the look on their faces when they finally cornered the poor bastard...

Killing the brother had been easy, dopey shit didn't see it coming.

But before his body had hit the canyon floor, Kubrackk had levelled his Quad-roller at Roland, putting his Callic-diamond armour to the test. The fall had knocked him unconscious, giving Kubrackk the impression of death. Of course, the Rem-plant took care of the rest. A couple of shots from his Tri-rollers put the Novaarian in the dirt, but the kill-shot never found its mark. It wasn't the first time Roland had ignored his training and finished his target, but the Tularon had used the fight to his advantage and ran for it. With the payday all his, Roland left Kubrackk to die next to his brother and catch the Tularon.

Son of a bitch should have stayed down.

This was a potential complication that they didn't need right now. With that in mind he suddenly sat up and examined the view beyond the bridge, inspecting the array of ships on the surrounding landing pads, but there was no sign of the ugly-ass ship the Novaarian called home. Roland decided he was being paranoid. After everything that had happened to him since taking the Protocorps job, there was no way Kubrackk could have tracked him all the way back here. They had even changed ships.

"What are you doing?" Li'ara asked with a raised eyebrow. She was sitting in the pilot's chair in her usual combat suit and boots. Her red hair was tied behind her head in a ponytail that rested between her shoulder blades.

"Nothing." Roland tried to casually sit back down but looked nothing except suspicious.

"The Laronian's put you on edge." A wicked grin appeared in the corner of her mouth.

"He doesn't know what he's talking about." Roland accessed the main console, pretending to check the comm was open to incoming messages. He wanted to drop the subject.

"Have you heard anything I've been saying?" Li'ara hit the master control and closed down the holograms across the shared console. Roland had no choice but to turn back and pay attention. "Whatever The Laronian's got you thinking about, you need to forget it. I need your head in the game. You already know the layout and The

Laronian gave us details on where to find the backup mainframe...
Len?"

Ch'len was sitting silently at the back of the bridge, engrossed in
holograms of Protocorps' interior complex. For once he wasn't
stuffing his face with snacks but, instead, poring over the data
supplied by The Laronian.

"Len!" Roland shouted.

"What?" Ch'len sat up straight.

"Can you direct us once we're inside or not?" Li'ara had little
patience for the alien.

"It's a maze in there, but yes I think so." Ch'len grumbled into his
console, "I still think this is the stupidest idea you've ever had! That
building is swarming with itchy trigger fingers, and this ship offers
zero protection!"

"I promise when this is over, we'll get the *Rackham* back and take
the easiest bounty going." Roland couldn't help his patronising tone.

Before Ch'len could reply with some sarcastic comment, the main
console came back to life as the external comm panel was activated
on the ship's outer door. Li'ara brought up the camera-feed so they
could all see the group of mixed aliens standing outside the ship.
Between them were a couple of large crates with no markings on.
Roland knew scoundrels when he saw them.

"Right on time," the bounty hunter remarked.

With Ch'len waddling behind, they met the group of criminals at
the outer door. With no cargo bay on the ship, they would have to
carry the crates through the kitchen area. The door slid into the ship
revealing a group of seven aliens, predominantly Laronians. Upon
seeing the human, the Raalak at the head of the group took a hesitant
step back on his quadruped legs. Roland gave them all a menacing
smile, revelling in their fear. Very few of the diverse Conclave had
actually met a human being and, amongst the general population,
they were still considered to be dangerous.

"Take it through there, on the right," Li'ara instructed.

With cautious glances to one another, the group plucked up the
courage and hefted the crates into the ship. After dumping them on

the dining table the Raalak dismissed the others and used a data-band on his wrist to open the crates. The lids split into two, with three shelves automatically rising out of the interiors. Roland was practically salivating at the contents.

With a deep gravelly voice, the Raalak said, "The Laronian has told me to provide you with everything you need. These weapons are yours. I have transmitted the details to your ship's nav-computer. Follow the instructions *exactly*. There's a limited window in which you can gain access to Protocorps, and make certain you follow the flight path provided." A last curious look at Ch'len was all the Raalak gave as a goodbye.

Roland wasted no time in diving into the crates with both hands. There were grenades of every kind, with mines and explosive Intrinium rounds. An exceptional collection of blades decorated the top shelf of one of the boxes, but Roland still preferred his Terran knife.

"Is this a grenade launcher?" Li'ara pulled out a bulky looking gun with a wide muzzle.

"Mine!" Roland snatched the launcher out of her hands like a child and immediately opened the internal chamber to inspect the ammo.

Li'ara didn't look convinced. "Isn't all this a little... loud? Shouldn't we be infiltrating this place with a modicum of stealth? You tried to shoot your way through with a Terran by your side last time, and you still got thrown out of the building, literally."

"I jumped, there's a difference." Roland didn't even take his head out of the crate to reply.

"Taking out the AI is going to be loud, I'll admit, but our little favour for The Laronian requires finesse. We'd be better approaching the first half of the mission quietly."

Roland used both hands to pull out a flat rectangular box with a single touchpad in the middle. "There's nothing quiet about this." He placed the bomb on the side of the kitchen counter.

"*I'll* look after that." Li'ara scooped it up and gently lowered it into a backpack designed to carry multiple weapons.

After prying Roland away from the weapons crates, they returned to the bridge to review the details sent by The Laronian's men. Ch'len dimmed the lights and activated the central holo-emitters to reconstruct the designated flight path in the middle of the bridge. The image was in pale blue with an outline of the towers hanging from the ceiling. In deep red, the path of their ship was shown to travel around the edges of Clave Tower until it reached the furthest tower on the right. They were then to hug the shining walls of the next tower, closest to Protocorps' HQ. Every manoeuvre was recorded at a certain time as the red line tracked down the central tower until it came to a stop. The holographic image magnified to a small flight deck near the bottom of Protocorps.

"What is that?" Roland asked.

"It's a hangar. It must be a supply entrance for deliveries," Ch'len replied. "The Laronian must have people on the inside."

"And on Conclave security," Li'ara added. "Look at these times. Someone must be supplying them with patrol patterns."

Roland sat in the pilot's chair and integrated the new flight path into the auto-pilot. He didn't want to take any chances controlling the ship himself if they had to keep to such strict measures. A quick alert flashed over the console to indicate the approaching time - they only had a short window to get themselves ready before they landed in the hangar.

Preparing for a fight such as this was more like a ritual for Roland. It was a time when all distractions were cast aside, even the annoying ones about Esabelle that had come from nowhere. Whether he liked it or not, infiltrating Protocorps without a Terran was going to be difficult. The bounty hunter surveyed his equipment carefully, choosing the right level of firepower that still provided him with enough manoeuvrability in combat. The brown-hide overcoat he had come to love so much was put aside, exposing his bare arms and tattoos, leaving only his Callic-diamond vest to protect him. The rusted plate covering was a good disguise for the real strength of the armour.

His hands cracked as he put on the fingerless gloves and balled them into fists, inspecting the metal knuckles. Extra belts were required around his waist and over his shoulder to fit all the gear. Laser mines hung from his waist, next to the grav-grenades and his Terran blade. A few of the smaller knives from the crates were concealed inside his Laronian boots and hidden pockets. A new addition to his arsenal were the seekers. The spherical bots, no bigger than his finger tips, scattered around any environment to create a collective image of their surroundings. This was fed back directly to the neural interface he used for directing the *Rackham*.

Roland saved his favourites until last; the amber hilted Tri-rollers that moulded perfectly to his hands. After loading extra ammo onto his chest belt, he slotted the weapons into their holsters on his thighs, comforted by their weight.

When he was finished he noted that Li'ara was similarly attired with her combat suit and several belts of weaponry, though she favoured one large rifle over any of the handguns. The backpack she carried was the most valuable item between them. Without the explosives provided by The Laronian they wouldn't be able to destroy the AI. Roland admired how cool and collected she was. Her previous career had its dangerous moments but nothing like this; she simply hadn't been trained for it. Then again, he thought, she looks tougher than most of the hardened bastards he'd trained with.

There was slight crackle before Ch'len's voice came over the internal comm. "We're about to land in the hangar. Get your asses up here, now!"

Back on the bridge, they looked out through the viewport to see the hangar doors opening on cue. Inside they could see one other smaller ship and a few loader bots ready for the next delivery of equipment. There was a single Shay standing in the middle of the hangar, swinging his arms to pull them and land as quickly as possible.

"Len, why aren't you ready to go?" Roland asked seriously.

"What-" Ch'len was immediately distressed.

"I'm just dickin' with ya'!" Roland laughed.

"Hilarious, shit-kicker," Ch'len replied dryly. The Ch'kara's expression became grave. "Just... make it back, both of you."

There were few moments between the two bounty hunters that could be considered serious. Roland knew there was sincerity in Ch'len's words, and acknowledged the fact that there was a friendship between the two unlikely companions.

"Just keep the engine running, Lenny boy. If we manage to survive this shit-tip, something tells me we're going to need a quick getaway." It was the best Roland could do.

The whole hangar shook momentarily, knocking over two of the loader bots. The Shay stumbled outside the viewport and the three of them held onto the chairs inside the bridge.

"What the hell was that?" Li'ara asked.

"A pretty big explosion is my guess..." Roland looked around, waiting for the soldiers to flood into the hangar, but no-one came.

"What the hell is going on out there?" Li'ara clasped her rifle a little tighter.

"It had to be inside Protocorps." Ch'len was checking the array for any news.

"We need to go." Roland moved off.

Both humans were met outside the ship by the same Shay that had coordinated their landing. It was evident from his armour that he was part of the private security force. Most of his artificial enhancements appeared to be around his eyes and arms, no doubt to increase his handling of weapons. He looked away when they approached as if he was concentrating on something else.

"Something's happening at the main entrance. Is that you?" the Shay's question was met with shrugs. "Well whatever it is, reinforcements are already on their way. You don't have long. Take the cargo Translift over there. You can use the distraction." With that, the Shay removed his weapon from its holster on his back and made for the door on the other side of the hangar.

"Seriously, what is going on?" Li'ara asked.

"I don't know," Roland replied. "But I wish I'd thought of it!"

"WE'RE GONNA DIE!" Spelnar screamed as the *Blade* accelerated at breakneck speed into the main entrance of Protocorps HQ.

Kubrackk ignored the wailing Trillik with manic glee and continued to angle the ship into the expansive double glass doors. The landing platform that extended from the entrance managed to take the force of the collision, causing the *Blade* to bounce before exploding into the foyer. Through the viewport, he just caught sight of the few employees unlucky enough to be walking through the entrance when the ship crushed them. Debris blew into the building causing more chaos, with shards of glass butchering anyone who wasn't killed by the ship.

The *Blade's* speed pushed it through the reception wall and into the rooms beyond. Kubrackk could no longer see out of the cracked viewport, now covered in rubble and a shredded semi-organic arm from a Shay receptionist. All the lights flickered inside the ship and the holographic display fluttered. To his right, Spelnar was rubbing his chest where the straps from the harness had kept him in his chair. There was a trickle of blood flowing down the side of his green head, mingling with beads of sweat. Kubrackk hit the buckle on his own harness and fell out of the chair, unable to support his own weight. His right leg had bashed into the console at the point of impact and taken a knock. Aware of the time, the Novaarian stood up and tested his knee, desperate to get out of the ship before Conclave security descended on them.

"Get up!" Kubrackk barked at Spelnar, who was still dazed in his chair. "We need to go, now!"

"This is suicide." Spelnar stumbled from his chair. "The ship is ruined; we'll never get out of here now."

"We can secure another ship after North is dead." Kubrackk tried to shake off the hazy mist that clouded his vision, before realising it was smoke rising from the consoles.

The Novaarian slammed his fist onto the touchpad on the wall after it didn't respond to his code. The wall came apart to reveal a concealment of weapons and various types of ammunition. The Quad-roller was fully loaded with explosive rounds and Kubrackk stocked up on more, with an entire belt of grenades and one large blade hilted to his thigh.

"You're insane!" the Trillik spat. "You've finally done it; you've killed us both! You said this was going to have the biggest payday ever. But now we're going to die..."

Kubrackk closed the gap between them and shoved his Quad-roller under Spelnar's jaw, "Then I guess you have a choice to make. You either die right here, right now, or you die out there in battle, taking as many of them with you as possible."

Spelnar audibly gulped while looking from Kubrackk to the large barrel under his jaw. His sweat dripped off his face and onto the wide muzzle in the awkward silence that followed the Novaarian's ultimatum.

"Ok... let's get North," The Trillik whispered.

The *Blade* had come to a stop on an angle, forcing the two bounty hunters to hold onto the railings as they descended the cargo bay ramp. Kubrackk punched the emergency door-control button to lower the ramp with speed. The thick metal dropped with a *crash*, unable to meet the floor with all the debris that littered the ground.

"They're coming!" Spelnar jumped off the ramp with both sub-repeaters raised in his hands.

"Get to that door!" Kubrackk could hear the incoming boots down the corridor. "We'll funnel them through there."

The bounty hunters dashed across the gap and skidded over the broken glass. Spelnar let rip with the sub-repeaters, tearing the corridor and its occupants to pieces. Taking no time to marvel at the killing machines, Kubrackk threw a grenade down the length of the corridor and took cover. Any who survived the Trillik's onslaught were blown to oblivion.

Through the walls, the screams and pleas of terrified staff could be heard in every direction. Behind them, the *Blade* looked to have seen its best days with every panel battered or caved in. It would take a recovery crew to remove it from the building now.

The bounty hunters stepped over the smouldering bodies and entered the nearest room. Two Shay women screamed in their faces and ran for the door, waving their robotic arms in the air. Kubrackk considered letting them go for a second, then decided it would be better if no one knew where to start looking for them. The Quad-roller blew the head off one and put a hole in the other that almost separated her torso from her legs. Spelnar gave him a sideways glance but kept his mouth shut, instead, going to work on the closest terminal.

"It'll take me a minute to hack the internal feed." The Trillik plugged in a series of devices Kubrackk didn't know much about. He had seen Spelnar use them time and again but only cared about the results.

"We don't have a minute. Our grand entrance will have attracted every Conclave security ship on the capital. Find them!"

Spelnar's nimble fingers danced across the holographic display, typing in the override codes as fast as a Trillik could. It wasn't long before the holographic display changed to a square block of different feeds from cameras throughout the building. There was a general panic among the employees as they flooded back to their vehicles in the thousands. It was an amusing thought to Kubrackk that it was the second time in as many days that the building had been subject to an attack.

"There they are!" Spelnar expanded the camera's feed. Both humans were exiting the cargo Translift several floors above them. "Without a Novattoo they're tripping all the alarms."

"Amateurs..." Kubrackk hefted his Quad-roller until it rested on his shoulder.

"Where do you think they're going?" Spelnar continued to follow them on the camera feed.

"There's only one thing of interest in this building. They're going to the *top*."

"The AI? What could they want with the AI? Even if they manage to disrupt its processors there are redundancies upon redundancies to keep it running." Spelnar sounded almost amused.

"So..." Kubrackk was putting it together in his mind. "If they really want to destroy the AI, they're going to have to find the backup mainframe?" Spelnar nodded. The Novaarian examined the feed more closely. "The female is wearing a bag but has no weapons attached to it. She must be carrying the bomb." It was all coming together in his mind. "They'll either split up to achieve both objectives at once or go together. Either way, the defences are going to be stronger nearer the AI hub. Find the backup mainframe, Spelnar."

The Trillik went straight to work on the adjacent terminal.

THE *RACKHAM'S* viewport was pitch-black with the emptiness of subspace staring back at Kalian. After touching the strange sub-reality, he knew better than most that empty was the best adjective. Their arrival into the Helteron Cluster was imminent and he couldn't wait. As he sat back in the pilot's chair, ALF appeared at his side with a sombre expression.

"Are you ready for what's coming?" The AI cupped his grey beard. "I only ask because I'm trapped in this exoskeleton, and if you die, I die. I've still got the whole *Starrillium incident* playing over and over..."

Kalian rolled his eyes at ALF's remarks. "Something tells me that whatever happens to me, you'll find a way to survive." He wasn't in the mood to talk after his argument with Esabelle. She had remained in the cargo bay to meditate after he stormed off.

"You can't tell me you've never thought about what she said?" ALF knew exactly what was on his mind. Even Esabelle couldn't short-circuit the AI for long. "The Avatar came to me once with the same dilemma." ALF had a faraway look in his crystal blue eyes. "He fell in love with a woman, like men always do. He knew he had to spend the rest of his life with her, but he couldn't. Back then he was an immortal and a very lonely one at that. He alone had learned how to rejuvenate his cells on a subconscious level; never to age, never to die. And I know what you're thinking, Kalian; why not just let yourself die? Age like anyone else? But letting yourself die is not so easy, even over time. Your brain is hardwired to survive."

"What did the Avatar do?" Kalian was hopeful for the answer.

"He gave her the best life he could and then he gave her back to her star." ALF met Kalian's eyes. "He tried to teach her, and many others, but it was a long time before the Terran caught up with him."

It wasn't what Kalian wanted to hear but he sympathised with the Avatar. "What was his name, his real name?"

"You mean before Savrick turned him into the *beast*?" ALF paused with an expression full of regret and sorrow. "His name was Alai, and he was magnificent; the first of a perfect race. You remind me of him, you know? He too had a passion and a need to do what was right, to make the hard sacrifice."

"I'm sorry you had to kill him, on Naveen." Kalian could see it was as if ALF was talking about a son.

"That *thing* wasn't Alai. Savrick killed him long ago." ALF looked away and took an artificial breath in his continued imitation of human life. "There's going to be more fighting before all this is over, and I don't just mean with Professor Jones. I think you need to have a clear head and be confident in your abilities if you're going to succeed. But, it always helps to have something worth fighting for, and I already know how far you're willing to push yourself for Li'ara. So my advice; whether you choose to live forever or not, when you get back you take Li'ara in your arms and you never let go. She'll see it's what she wants too."

Kalian didn't know what to say. He completely agreed with the AI and yet it was Li'ara's voice that rang clear in his head that ALF wasn't to be trusted. But listening to him talk about Alai like his own child, his insight into Kalian and his trust that he would succeed with Li'ara, not without her, it made perfect sense in a way it never had. It didn't matter what the future held for any of them, immortality or not, there was only Li'ara and the now. Kalian was filled with an urge to hold her again, as soon as possible. It was Li'ara that kept him fighting and believing in himself in a way he never could without her. He knew she loved him: in a way she always had and he knew it.

Kalian's train of thought ended when Esabelle entered the bridge and announced, "We're about to exit subspace."

She walked over, meeting ALF's eyes in the way they always did.

Nothing was said and yet it felt to Kalian like everything was said at once. There was still animosity between them, though both felt it hard to express exactly what the other had done. Esabelle took a seat in the co-pilot's chair, where Ch'len usually sat and scraped most of the half-eaten snacks onto the floor, where the nanocelium gobbled them up. ALF stood between them, staring at the abyss before it flashed and gave birth to the starry field of space.

"Stealthware systems engaged," Esabelle stated. "Commencing scan now."

There was an awkward tension on the bridge as Kalian shifted in his seat, unsure what to say. He had been overly harsh with his last comment to Esabelle and he hadn't really meant what he said. In her own way, she was just trying to ensure that he survived emotionally and physically.

"I'm sorry about what I said." It was the best start he could think of. "You only want to help me and I understand that. I wouldn't be alive now if it wasn't for your training all these months, but I haven't lived as long as you. I can't look to the future and know how quickly it comes around. I live in the now, and right now I have Li'ara, and that's all that matters."

Esabelle looked back at him. "It takes more than a few words to break my bones, Kalian. I just don't want to see you get hurt."

Kalian smiled. "How can I get hurt with you around?"

Esabelle mirrored his smile. "Well, at least I've taught you something." They shared a brief laugh before the main console chirped with an alert. "There's something passing in front of a star on the edge of that nebula."

Kalian looked out at the panorama of deep orange and blue swirls that made up the expansive cloud. The entire Helteron Cluster was packed with similar nebulae across an expanse of several million light years.

"Is it a planet or an asteroid?" Kalian asked.

"Neither." Esabelle studied the results of the scans. "It's entirely artificial... and big. It makes the *Gommarian* and the *Marillion* look small. I'm plotting a course now."

ALF spoke for the first time. "Perhaps we should send these coordinates to High Charge Uthor?" The AI elaborated, "It would only serve our larger cause if the Conclave could see whatever this thing is for themselves. Not to mention the backup."

"Good point." Kalian transmitted the coordinates to the *Nautallon* using the *Rackham's* comm relay.

At maximum yield, it took several minutes to reach Protocorps' big secret. With such close proximity to the baby yellow star, the *Rackham's* viewport had been polarised almost completely to keep out the intense light. Esabelle brought up a holographic dial to control the spectrum of light until they could see the mega-structure before them.

"Is that what I think it is?" Kalian had seen the giant space station during his time in the subconducer on Naveen. Its crescent moon shape was quite distinct and easily recognised.

"It can't be..." Esabelle whispered.

"It's a Starforge." ALF didn't take his eyes off it.

"How could they build a Starforge without *you*?" Esabelle's tone was aggressive. "Your level of intelligence is the only thing that could even operate one of those things. The calculations are unthinkable. Where would they even get the plans for it? The Starforge is a Terran design."

"It's a little different though. Look," Kalian pointed, "There are three Starrilliums attached to it. It's a Terran design with a little Conclave added in."

"That still doesn't answer where they found the plans. I made sure the *Gommarian* was wiped of all information like this. Besides, they've clearly been building this thing for years." Esabelle was standing now.

Kalian noticed how ALF had remained silent, staring at the crescent structure. "What are you thinking?"

"Technology that allows for instant transportation across the galaxy makes sense, in terms of the Conclave's next step in space travel, but making the prototype that big doesn't make sense. This Starforge was designed to allow something massive to travel through it, something much bigger than anything built by the Conclave." ALF looked at them both. "And Esabelle makes a good point about it being Terran. There are only the three of us in the whole galaxy that even know these things existed, and they've been putting this together since *before* the Gomar arrived."

Kalian used the console to recreate the Starforge in holographic form in the centre of the bridge. The three Starrilliums appeared to be in random places across the hull with a built-up section on the inside of the crescent, in the middle of the structure. The two ends looked to be as sharp as any blade, with ten miles between them.

"What if it wasn't designed for something massive," Kalian added, "but an army of smaller ships?"

"That's a possibility," ALF replied. "Until we get inside and have a look we'll have nothing but questions. If the design is similar to my Starforges, there should be a small access port here." The AI pointed at a section of the hologram, near what looked to be the command centre.

"Then let's ring the bell..." Esabelle set a course.

FIFTEEN

The replicated echo of ALF observed the current occupants aboard the *Gommarian*. The AI could see through every camera as the Conclave's crew tried their best to pick apart the ship's systems. Had it been ALF in his entirety, the scene would have brought some amusement with it. Instead, the AI looked on with calculated deliberation.

Steps had already been taken to keep them herded together in the areas ALF wanted. In some areas of the ship, the crew had already been separated from the others by a simple change in the structure of the ship. He watched as they scurried to find their way back to the bridge, panic spreading across their comm. Two Novaarians were attempting to use a high powered laser to cut through one of the doors ALF had sealed. The AI had made certain the Eclipse missiles were beyond their reach, forever changing the internal structure around the doors. His programming had been clear about the fate of the star destroying rockets; they were to be permanently deactivated if they couldn't be obliterated safely.

Through the array, the AI kept a close watch on the transport and settlement of the remaining humans. Via the comm net that connected all the Conclave vessels, ALF was aware of every movement the alien society made in the Ch'ket system. So far he was satisfied with the treatment of the humans and had no reason to be concerned with their wellbeing. The Conclave had no reason to harm them and the *Sentinel* was secretly watching over the rings of Ch'ket.

Moving through the Conclave's own systems, ALF scanned through the details pertaining to the *Sentinel*. It was clearly modelled on the *Gommarian*, though the giant ship was curved at each end rather than flat. Its weaponry was on another level compared to other Conclave vessels, however. It had enough planet breakers to wipe out the ecosystem on every core world.

An external message sent directly to the *Nautallon* triggered one of ALF's alarms. The AI accessed the message before the crew of the High Charge's ship did. This was the information he had been waiting for. Now he had coordinates and a ship with which to act. The echo's directives had been specific regarding the alien crew. In the same millisecond the AI comprehended the message, he began evacuation protocols.

"What was that?" The bridge crew looked for the source of the cracking sound that resounded beyond the walls.

ALF made certain the doors were vacuum-sealed and the rooms with occupants were reinforced with grav-plates. The Starrillium was charging up, ready for the jump.

"Sir, the nav-computer is loading new coordinates." ALF could detect fear in the Laronian's pheromones. "I've lost all control of the ship's systems!"

The AI projected his image to the bridge crew. "Your presence is no longer required. Have a nice day."

———

UTHOR RETURNED to the luxurious bridge of the *Sentinel*, frustrated with the lack of progress he had made with investigating Protocorps. They had been allowed to become powerful, and with that power they were untouchable. The corporation had enough money to keep everyone in line and cover their tracks, with an army of lawyers ready and waiting to pounce on anyone inclined to ask questions. Multiple investigations suggested criminal ties, mostly to Gor-van Tanar, but the trails always died before leading anywhere.

"Sir!" Gre-den hurried over to greet him in distress. "Protocorps has been attacked again."

Uthor loved and hated that he was right. "The humans?"

"Unclear," Gre-den guided them to a glass panel as big as a Raalak. "This is the only footage we have right now." The glass came to life with holographic images of an ugly looking ship hurtling into the main entrance of the tower.

"That looks like something they would do..." Uthor saw no hope now for the humans gaining membership into the Conclave. They had taken it too far.

"I made the preparations you requested. There's a team standing by." Gre-den added quietly as his attention was pulled away by the same Ch'kara that had been monitoring the *Gommarian* crew. The ensign was frantically moving holographic screens around and motioning for others to check their own terminals.

"Report, Commander." Uthor's mighty form came to a towering halt beside the Shay.

"The *Nautallon* just received a transmission from the *Rackham*, sir." Gre-den was reading from the terminal. "They're coordinates inside the Helteron Cluster."

"Is there a message?" Uthor asked.

"One word, sir: proof."

The High Charge took a deep breath and considered his options. These humans were tenacious. In only a few days they had managed to find what so many of his own had failed to discover for years. At present his mandate was to bring in the humans and the AI at all costs, ignoring any alleged involvement of Protocorps. But if the humans thought they had found proof of the corporation's hand in all this and were willing to be captured in the process, Uthor was going to follow his instincts, regardless of the Highclave's tip-toeing around Protocorps.

"Let's see what this ship can really do then." Before Uthor could order the new course, the Ch'kara crewman spoke out.

"Er, sir?" the Ch'kara took a moment to study his monitor before alarm crept into his voice, "There's an emergency broadcast coming from the crew of the *Gommarian*."

"What's happening?" Gre-den examined the same monitor.

"They're reporting a complete system lockout. They're..." The Ch'kara couldn't find the words.

Gre-den stood up and looked Uthor in the eyes. "They're being jettisoned into space."

"WHAT?" Uthor nudged him aside with ease to see the monitor for himself.

"It appears the individual rooms they occupied have been released into space," the Ch'kara explained. "They're alive but have limited life support, sir."

That was the problem with nanocelium, Uthor thought. Essentially the ship was a giant jigsaw made of trillions of tiny machines. Individual rooms could be *let go* by the rest of the ship like an emergency life pod.

"The *Gommarian's* Starrillium is charging, sir." Gre-den was now looking at another terminal. The Shay paused before he spoke again, "There's a transmission coming from the *Gommarian*." The holographic display simply read: *Follow me.*

"Who sent the message?" the High Charge asked, confused. His question was met with stunned silence. "Order the *Nautallon* to intercept the crew, Commander. Set a course for Cerula and prepare to either disable the *Gommarian* or... follow it."

FOR THE MOST PART, Li'ara and Roland had been successful in evading the security force inside Protocorps. All the heavy boots were heading for the main entrance below them, not even aware of their presence. They ducked in and out of rooms that were abandoned in the frenzy to escape another terrorist attack.

They ran down a corridor with a glass wall and a view of their towering height above Clave Tower. Dozens of Conclave security ships emerged from the depths, their crimson hulls flitting past the window. Civilian vessels and transport ships were being guided away by local security personnel.

Li'ara paused before they reached the end of the strip, taking in the exotic world beneath them. She knew they weren't just fighting for the human race, or what was left of it, but for all the lives of the Conclave. They might not be human and always relatable to, but they were people, just ordinary people trying to live. They deserved to live as much as her own kind, if not more so. The races of the Conclave had been thriving long before humanity was engineered. Li'ara knew in her gut that Protocorps were allied with whatever sinister force was out to destroy them, *all* of them. She would fight just as hard to save any alien as she would a human, and Protocorps were about to find out how hard she could fight.

"Come on," Roland pressed as two Shay guards rounded the corner, almost bumping into the bounty hunter.

Roland didn't hesitate to jump into the nearest Shay, knocking him into the wall and pinning him there. Li'ara raised her rifle and squeezed the trigger without thinking about it. The Intrinium rounds exploded from the muzzle in a short burst and tore through the Shay's head. Roland pinned the Shay with one arm across his throat while the other reached for his Terran blade at the base of his back. The nanocelium shot from the hilt, building into a sharp blade only just bigger than a hand. Roland shoved the knife into the side of guard's head and pulled him to the ground. With a foot on the alien's face, the bounty hunter yanked the blade out and deactivated the nanocelium.

"We've got more incoming." Li'ara could hear more boots coming from behind them, back down the corridor.

"Keep going." Roland nodded to the Translift up ahead while retrieving the grenade launcher from his back. "Hey fellas!"

Li'ara couldn't see the new group of soldiers, having rounded the corner, but she did see Roland's wicked smile before unleashing the grenade launcher. The explosion was twofold as the concussive force blew out the glass wall along the entire corridor. Judging by Roland's casual replacement of the launcher and slow walk, Li'ara assumed all the guards were either dead or falling into the depths of Clave Tower.

They both entered the Translift with Li'ara giving Roland a look that conveyed her thoughts on his overkill attitude. The bounty hunter shrugged and cracked the bones in his neck, all relaxed until a stark spotlight shone through the broken glass wall and into the Translift. On the other end of the spotlight was the familiar hum of Conclave security ships.

"Move!" Li'ara pushed off Roland, forcing them both into the sides of the Translift.

Large Intrinium rounds cut the corridor and the lift doors to ribbons, punching through into the Translift and blowing fist-sized holes across the interior wall. Sparks flew in every direction as the two humans hugged the wall, trying to make themselves as flat as possible. Li'ara slid her arm over the surface and repeatedly pressed the button to get the Translift moving. As they went up, the cannon fire appeared to move down the lift until it tore through the floor and disappeared. The smell of ozone filled the busted interior with no small amount of smoke.

"That may have been my fault..." Roland peeled himself off the wall with a sheepish grin on his face.

"If we survive this, I might just kill you myself." Li'ara exited the Translift on the next floor.

"That's fair." Roland wiped the blood off his arm from a small shrapnel wound.

They exited on a floor made entirely of glass walls and white floors with expansive rooms between each glass panel. Shay scientists cowered behind their machines and equipment as the humans passed through the corridor, checking for any guards. Li'ara caught sight of the cameras in the top corner of every lab, their spherical servos swivelling to follow their progress.

"It's tracking us."

"What is?" Roland looked around.

"The cube. It knows we're coming for it now. Whatever's

distracting them downstairs isn't going to be enough." Li'ara checked the ammo level on the side of her rifle. "It'll do everything to stop us."

"Like redirecting every soldier in the building." Roland gripped his Tri-rollers and pulled them free of their holsters.

"We need to prioritise," Li'ara continued. "The backup mainframe will have to wait. We need to go to the top and destroy the cube first before all hell breaks loose."

"You get that, Len?" Roland asked out loud.

"That's fine but you're heading in the wrong direction." Ch'len sounded focused for once. "Get back to the Translift and, oh shit, look out!"

A flash off to their left was all the warning they got before the sound of Intrinium fire exploded across the labs, shattering the glass walls. Li'ara and Roland broke into a sprint, staying ahead of the deadly energy bolts that fizzed through the glass and past their heads. In the corner of her eye, Li'ara saw two of the lab technicians fall under the barrage. The Protocorps guards cared little for life, more concerned with protecting the AI and preserving the corporation's secrets.

They both blindly shot back in the direction of the gunfire, pulverising machinery and expensive equipment. The surviving scientists dived for the floor and yelled in terror at the violence that reigned around them. Roland skidded across the ground, pivoting on one knee to line up both of his Tri-rollers. Li'ara ran past him and charged into the Translift without slowing.

"Come on!" she shouted for Roland who was still laying down fire across the lab. The bounty hunter took down two of the guards before he scrambled to the safety of the lift, which he practically fell into.

More holes were put into the double doors before it finally got moving again. Roland continued to sit on the floor, panting against the wall. Li'ara took the opportunity to reload her rifle with explosive rounds. No sense in using stealth anymore.

"I've got a problem," Ch'len announced over their comm links. "I was watching you over the cameras, but I've lost control of them. The real bad news is that I can still see you, but only because whoever's controlling them is also watching you. You need to get off on the next floor."

"How close are we?" Li'ara asked as they stepped out onto the new floor.

"You're really close, but between you and the AI chamber is a whole lot of firepower," Ch'len replied.

The new floor was a dark corridor with a reception desk at the other end, highlighted by a wall with Protocorps in bold letters across the white surface. Every six feet were thick pillars, separating the translucent glass offices and blocking the view. Both humans kept their weapons raised, unhappy with the silence.

"Oh and, Roland?" Ch'len came back. "Kubrackk's in the building."

Li'ara saw the bounty hunter wince at the sound of the name. It wasn't fear she saw, but annoyance.

"I take it the explosion was him?" Roland asked.

"Yeah, a pretty dick move from the looks of it. Before I lost control of the cameras I took a peek. The idiot crashed his ship into the main lobby." Ch'len laughed to himself. "He must really want to kill you."

Li'ara stopped and sighed at Roland, "What shit have you dragged into this with you?"

"It's nothing, just a little grudge." Roland shrugged it off and continued to slowly push on down the corridor.

"Well, that *nothing* is making his way up to you pretty fast," Ch'len commented.

"Thank you, Len," Roland said through gritted teeth. "He won't be a problem. So far he's done nothing but help, so let's get on with it." The bounty hunter removed the thin cylinder of seekers lining his chest and bowled them down the deserted corridor.

Without a sound, the spherical machines scattered up the walls, their track-pads hugging the corners to stay out of sight. They both clipped the one-sided headset to their right ear, as the holographic emitters displayed an overlay across their eye. Once the seekers had found a position in which they could cover every angle, their scans fed back a collective image. They could both see an orange outline of multiple guards through the walls, hiding at the end of the corridor and inside the rooms.

Li'ara noticed the broken glass littering the floor, as well as the broken glass walls between the offices. The breeze on this level was unnatural for an executive floor and was being funnelled through the corridor. They were obviously in the same place Roland and Esabelle had been when they made their crazy escape.

"I count sixteen," Roland spoke a little quieter.

"How do you want to play this?" Li'ara kept one hand close to the grenades on her belt.

"You take the eight on the left, I'll take the eight on the right," Roland replied casually.

Li'ara raised her eyebrow. "And my side just happens to have the two Raalaks..."

"Well, that's where the toys come in." Roland tapped the side of the headset, activating the targeting system.

Li'ara could see through her own holographic image that Roland was highlighting the two Raalaks, as well as the turret gun waiting beyond them, in front of a large circular door. The x-ray image began to rapidly contract across her eye when the seekers left their hiding places to track down their new targets. The last thing Li'ara saw was the orange outline of the two Raalaks before the entire floor was racked by the ensuing explosion. The corridor filled with smoke and large chunks of rock-like skin and limbs. The odds were high that some of the others had been killed or injured by the velocity of the Raalaks' separate body parts. An explosion further down the corridor took place a second later, destroying the turret.

They both moved like a coordinated team, kicking their way into the opposing offices and shooting through the translucent glass walls that hadn't already been blown out. Their surprise attack earned them a few extra seconds to fire first and take out a couple of the remaining guards.

Protocorps didn't hire amateurs to watch over their greatest asset.

After the first couple went down under Li'ara's fire, the rest immediately adapted and took cover, while simultaneously throwing grenades into the offices. Li'ara skidded, almost falling over trying to dive behind the thick pillar before the explosions ripped through the offices. Chunks of the protecting pillar flew off in every direction with bits of desk and office stationery, and glass between it all. She gripped her rifle tighter while the high-pitched hum in her ears drowned out all other sound.

On the opposite side of the corridor, Roland had taken cover behind an upturned desk and was firing pot-shots blindly over the top. Li'ara could see him shouting to her but the sound of his voice was washed away with everything else. That's when Roland aimed his Tri-roller at her and fired before she could realise what was happening. The Intrinium bolt flew inches above her head and struck the Shay behind her in the mid-riff. The blast of super-hot energy caught the guard under his armour and threw him into the wall of the office.

Pull it together, Li'ara thought. She pushed herself up the column with her rifle close to her chest. A quick glance confirmed the advancement of the attacking troops, ducking in and out of the pillars and using the debris for cover. The grenades on her belt were weighing heavy on her, begging to be thrown into the fray.

"Cover your eyes!" Li'ara had no idea how loud she shouted. The flash-bang grenade rolled out of her hands and bowled over the debris and into the midst of the guards.

The concussive force told her the flash had gone off. Along with Roland, Li'ara launched from her cover and levelled her rifle at the dazed soldiers. The Protocorps guards continued to fire in their direction, however, pushing the humans back into cover. Li'ara fell after putting her weight on her right leg and landed awkwardly onto the side of a chair. A piece of shrapnel was protruding from her calf with blood dripping down her leg.

There was no time to examine it as a Laronian came bounding past the nearest pillar with his gun raised in Li'ara's direction. Her instincts kicked in with the desperate need to survive that accompanied the adrenaline. As fast as her muscles allowed, Li'ara rolled over the broken chair and flung it at the Laronian with all her strength. His shot went wild as Li'ara landed on her back, rifle aimed at his exposed neck. The Intrinium melted the soft tissue around his scaly neck until it seared through the muscle and bone, leaving a decapitated Laronian.

Another explosion rocked the offices and two Shay flew through the air like ragdolls. Roland was holding the grenade launcher again.

"Come on!" The bounty hunter's mad call for blood was the first thing she heard again.

Intrinium bolts whizzed over and around her body as she picked herself up. Li'ara's limp turned into a mad hop while she fired back, trying to make it to the nearest pillar. Heavy boots crunching over glass grew louder on the other side of the column. Her muscle memory reacted to the years of hand-to-hand combat, drawing her knife and swivelling as best she could on her damaged leg. The blade plunged into the face of the unsuspecting Shay, shattering his visor and coming to a halt inside his cybernetic mind. Li'ara didn't stop there; she was getting angry with the pain in her leg. With one hand holding the knife and the Shay up, she charged at the guards using the dead body as a shield while firing her rifle through the gap in his arm.

Li'ara felt the impacts against her *shield*, but none made it through the armour and into her. Another Shay dropped in the distance as her rifle fire caught him in the head. Eventually, her body shield began to lose limbs and larger chunks of his body, compromising her own body. All she could see was red. Li'ara's finger never left the trigger, spraying the enemy with vengeful Intrinium. As the body was almost shot to cinders, Roland appeared from nowhere and roughly yanked her behind the nearest pillar. The dead body fell to the floor with her knife still buried in its face.

"So this is going well!" Roland shouted over the weapons fire.

Li'ara couldn't help but wince under the pain in her calf. Roland looked down where it was impossible to miss the jagged metal sticking out of her leg.

"It's fine." Li'ara flicked out the magazine from her rifle and replaced it. "How many are left?"

"Seven or eight I think." Roland put a finger to the comm in his ear, "Len, can you see anything in here?"

"No, the cameras are blown to shit," Ch'len sounded stressed. "But I *can* see the small army below you. They're coming."

"We need to move fast," Li'ara braced herself.

"Agreed." Roland lodged the stock of the grenade launcher into his shoulder, ready to fire.

"They're too close now," Li'ara warned. "You're just as likely to kill us as them!"

Roland groaned and slung the launcher over his back. "I need a second." The bounty hunter removed a grav-grenade from his belt and chucked it over his shoulder and down the corridor with ease. The grenade stuck to another pillar and altered the effects of gravity within six metres, sucking in three of the guards. Roland had taken the extra time to assemble a new assault rifle out of three separate sections attached to his various belts. When the weapon had become one it emitted a sharp hum to signify deadly capabilities. The bounty hunter crouched and swung around the pillar in one swift move, unleashing the new rifle on the three guards, bunched together. All three were dead in seconds with smoking scorch marks pitting their bodies.

Li'ara took advantage of the explosion as well, barrelling around the other side of the pillar and advancing. Two more guards fell to her surprise attack, each taking a hit in between the plates of their armour. Li'ara's life was saved by the pain in her leg causing her to fall over and the Intrinium bolt flying over her instead. She continued to fire as she fell, making certain to remain a hard target. The Shay made a bee-line for her, the barrel of his rifle staring her in the face. Roland burst from behind the pillar and charged into the Shay, picking the alien up under his arms until they both slammed into the floor, a tangle of limbs. Li'ara didn't hesitate. On one knee she took aim and ended the lives of the other two remaining soldiers, both caught off guard by the fight between Roland and their comrade.

A feral roar erupted from Roland's throat as he continued to beat the Shay to death. The fight ended the way most fights did with Roland; a knife to the throat and an Intrinium round to the chest for good measure. In the silence that followed, Li'ara could see the fresh cuts and singes to Roland's skin and armour. He looked as battered as she felt.

"Feel better?" she asked, looking at the mutilated alien under the bounty hunter.

"I kinda' do..." Roland stood up with obvious pain on his face. "You're not a bad shot for a grunt." A cheeky smile broke through the pain on his face.

"And you're as violent and crazy as I thought you'd be." Li'ara reflected his cheeky grin, despite her own pain.

There was a groan of pain in the distance, beyond the obliterated corridor and executive offices. With their guns raised, they walked over the sprawl of dead bodies and debris, following the moaning. Li'ara found the source of the tunnelled breeze in the office at the end of the corridor. There was a large hole in the glass wall of an expansive and luxurious office. The name beside the door, now hanging off its frame, read: Sav-del Tanek.

Past the executive offices stood a large circular white door. The lights in the ceiling were flickering above the smoking remains of the turret gun and a prone Shay in what looked to be an expensive, yet torn suit. The Shay tried to crawl away from the door, his left leg lifelessly dragged behind him, and stopped when his fingers rested over Roland's boot. Even Li'ara found his whimper pathetic.

"Remember me?" a malevolent smile spread across Roland's face.

The Shay looked around desperately for a weapon but found none. The bounty hunter picked the Shay up by his ripped jacket and slammed him into the wall before launching his fist like a piston into the alien's gut. The air burst from the Shay's lungs as he dropped to the floor like a stone.

"This is Sav-del Tanek." Roland lightly kicked the Shay in the leg.

More whimpers escaped Sav-del's mouth while he caught his breath.

Li'ara rolled her eyes at the dark stain spreading out from the alien's crotch.

Roland laughed hysterically. "He's pissing himself!" the bounty hunter dropped knee first, allowing his full weight to press against Sav-del's broken leg.

The Shay screamed.

His scream doubled when Roland plunged one of his hidden blades into the Shay's good leg.

"Do I have your attention?" Roland twisted the knife, changing Sav-del's scream into an animalistic groan. "I'm willing to bet you know how to open that shiny door." Pure fear reflected in the Shay's eyes. "I suggest you start talking before I put more holes in you."

Sav-del's fear turned to defiance. "I'll never tell you!" he spat. "You'll be dead before you even make a dent!"

Li'ara left Roland to do his work while she investigated the panel on the wall beside the large door. There was a keypad and multiple scanners built into the panel, each designed to identify a different part of someone's body. She knocked her knuckles against the door and heard the flat *thud* that resounded. It was thick, too thick to blast through.

Sav-del's scream returned her attention to the increasingly bloody scene behind her. Roland was crouched over the Shay having pulled his knife free of his leg. Blood spurted from the wound in no small amount.

"You're right Sav-del," Roland said casually. "Time is of the essence. Take your wound for example. I'm no expert on Shay physiology, but it looks like I nicked an artery there. I'd say you have maybe a minute before you bleed out." From a pouch on his belt, Roland retrieved a small shiny cylinder. "Start talking and you live."

The Shay was panicking at the sight of his life gushing from his leg. His eyes darted about for some unseen solution to his predicament but rested on his injured leg, finality setting in.

Li'ara decided to play on the Shay's fear, "Tick-tock, Sav-del. What's it going to be?"

Sav-del sputtered, "Fine! Fine! I'll do it..." His eyes pleaded to Roland to be saved.

A small needle ejected from the cylinder before Roland plunged it into the Shay's wound. The bleeding stopped as blue jell filled the open gash and painkillers rushed through his veins. The instant relief was obvious in Sav-del's gasp.

"How close is the next team, Len?" Li'ara touched the comm in her ear.

"Er, they're not coming," Ch'len sounded confused. "Kubrackk killed them all..."

Roland and Li'ara looked at one another, calculating the fight that was coming.

"He killed them all?" Roland didn't sound convinced.

"He's got a Trillik with him, but to be honest he looks really pissed... Oh shit! They're in the Translift!" Ch'len screamed down the comm.

Roland stood up and paced the small corridor, considering their options. He wiped the sweat from his forehead and looked at Li'ara. "Use him to get in and blow it to hell. I'll hold them off at the lift."

"It's too risky." Li'ara had already considered their options. "We won't get another chance at this, Roland. If even one of them gets past you, they'll delay me enough to allow more guards to show up. We had two objectives; maybe we can still achieve them both." Li'ara marched to the end of the corridor and pointed at the smaller Translift outside Sav-del's office. "Take the executive lift down to the backup mainframe and make sure they follow you. Plant the back door and kill them both. I'll meet you back at the hangar."

Roland looked away, mulling over her idea. Li'ara knew he would see sense and agree to her plan; it was the only way to achieve both goals and get out alive. Of course, that was all dependent on him killing both bounty hunters and her blowing up the cube, before the cavalry arrived.

"This all sounds a little suicidal." Roland scratched the side of his head with the barrel of his Tri-roller.

"When did it not?" Li'ara dropped her rifle on the floor and removed her sidearm from its holster. With one hand she half lifted, half dragged Sav-del to the panel on the wall.

Roland sighed. "Just get in and set the charges. Make sure you give yourself enough time to get out."

"No shit." Li'ara shoved the end of her gun into the Shay's back as the soft chime of the Translift rang out.

Roland gave her a final nod before leaving to face Kubrackk.

THE TWISTED AND corrupted body of Garrett Jones stood motionless beside the equally corrupted Terran. The extraordinary pair conversed through the same unexplained connection as the Terran leaned with both hands onto the master console on the Starforge's bridge. Garrett's parasite forced him to watch as strands of nanocelium wormed out of the Terran's hands and began to bore into the console. Holographic screens and monitors flickered under the duress of the Terran's wireless control.

Garrett couldn't explain how he knew what was taking place in front of him. The longer he spent connected to his parasite the more he felt their thoughts and memories merging. He knew the Terran was taking steps to ensure they had complete dominance over the Starforge, another name Garrett instinctively knew, and so make the crew redundant. Images flashed across his vision of the Starforge travelling to Ch'ket, which was apparently where the humans had been placed. Garrett had never actually seen the rings of Ch'ket and yet he knew the planet that formed before his eyes.

If he dwelled on the question of what the Starforge could actually do to destroy the human race, his captor would bore down on him with its suffocating presence. The same thing happened when he tried to find the real Terran, trapped inside his own body like Garrett. The image of him inside the cage of light was fresh in Garrett's mind.

The Terran had fought against his barriers to no avail, causing Garrett to wonder why he wasn't in a similar cage. With that thought, he had images of the broken cube sitting dormant in the *Gommarian's* basement. Again, the parasite's mind bled into his, giving him answers he shouldn't have. He was weaker than the Terran because his parasite was broken, though it probably didn't hurt that the new cube's host was a powerful Terran.

The same message began to appear on every screen and hologram throughout the giant station. The entire crew, guards and all, were being ordered to evacuate immediately. The Terran had full control.

New messages came to life across the master console, informing them that the last Starrillium was almost fully recharged. Before the crew had been ordered to leave, the Shay engineers had finished their last adjustments to the station's systems. The Starforge could now navigate subspace and be ready to use on the other end without recharge time. This still confused Garrett who only knew that the station could be used to communicate across vast distances. The professor was sure their last transmission had been with something outside this galaxy, though he mentally shrugged off the thoughts of that particular being.

The technological transfusion between the Terran and the master console came to an abrupt end. Pulling his hands away, the Terran stepped back and stared out of the polarised viewport of the bridge. The intense light of the baby sun, behind the station, was dimmed to protect the equipment as well as the previous crew. The Terran continued to stare into the ocean of stars beyond the bridge, his body the perfect imitation of a statue. Garrett could feel his parasite questioning the Terran, just as unsure as he was about the Terran's immobility.

"They are here." The Terran spoke out loud.

Garrett had sudden images of Kalian Gaines and Esabelle flash over his mind. The professor felt his hand clench at the thought. His fist tightened. The action rolled around his mind for a few seconds. Garrett had actually felt his hand clench under his own command.

He had experienced similar muscle control on Trantax, but not to this extent. What did this mean? Angry alarm emanated from all around his consciousness as the parasite descended on him like a giant spider from an oily abyss.

Fighting me is futile, insect.

The words *hissed* out of the darkness. Garrett felt the pressure around his subconscious form increase as if the space he occupied inside his mind was being invaded. The creature's words were accompanied by more images that bled across the gap. The professor saw aliens that didn't belong to the Conclave being attacked by tentacle-like strands of nanocelium, their bodies being corrupted as his was, but the parasite failed in its attempts to scare Garrett. He saw something else through the creature's mind. There was fear mingled with the anger at the thought of taking over a human or Terran body. Why would they fear to control one of us?

The genocide of your kind will be the last thing you see before your pathetic body is wasted. There will be no ascension for the human race!

Garrett screamed inside his own mind as the parasite stimulated pain throughout his nervous system. There was no fighting it; the pain would be eternal and he knew that now. He had made a grave mistake that could never be undone, and he would be made to pay for it at the malevolent hands of this parasite.

As quickly as it began, the pain stopped with the parasite's attention being pulled away by the Terran. Again, this was a first for Garrett. The creature was usually able to continue his torment even while distracted by the outside world. The professor concentrated on clenching his fist again, willing it to ball up and crack his mutilated knuckles. If Garrett could, he would drop to his knees in defeat as only his index finger twitched, and even then he wasn't sure if he did it or the parasite was messing with him.

"The female is stronger." The Terran rotated his shoulders in a very human manner. "I will take her. You must correct your failure and kill the other."

As you command...

Garrett's parasite chose to speak via their unique link, clearly disliking a verbal form of communication. The professor sensed a very strange hierarchy between the two and the entity on the other side of the Starforge. The Terran was in charge here, no question about that, and the other entity was in charge of both, but it felt as though *any* form of hierarchy was alien to them. Making decisions of their own appeared to be a new concept to them, one they enjoyed and hated with equal measure. Maybe it has something to do with this constant sense of separation Garrett felt when connected to the parasite? It was as if they were constantly telling themselves that their current state of existence was temporary, though Garrett couldn't fathom why that would be a good thing.

AFTER DOZENS of ships exited the Starforge's main hangar and ignored the *Rackham*, Esabelle had become curious and set a course, forgetting the smaller port ALF mentioned. Rows of identical ships lined the hangar as hundreds of crew flooded out of various Translifts. With the stealthware deactivated, the *Rackham* passed through the shield and settled down in the place of an exiting craft. There was no attack or soldiers waiting for them.

"What the hell is going on?" Kalian descended the *Rackham's* ramp and watched hundreds of ships taking off around the hangar. A trumpet-like alarm rang out as engineers, scientists and armed guards ran into the waiting ships without batting an eye at the Terran vessel.

"Why would they be evacuating?" Esabelle came up by his side.

Kalian recognised the thin piece of nanocelium in her hand; a triangle with the apex cut off. Esabelle placed the metal below her navel where it exploded with dark strands of nanocelium, encompassing her body. The armour had a bronze tinge to its plates, making it a little different from his but no less formidable in its appearance. Like his, the armour hugged her every curve making it look too thin to be protective. Kalian knew better than to believe that.

ALF projected himself into the hangar. "If Garrett, or the cube I should say, has taken control of the Starforge remotely, he will no longer have need of an organic crew. No doubt he has replaced each of them with ten thousand nanocelium."

"Then we need to hurry," Esabelle said. "If it has taken control it won't be long before the station is used as a weapon."

"A weapon?" Kalian followed Esabelle who strode off in the direction of the nearest exit.

"I think this is more your area?" Esabelle looked over her shoulder at ALF, who followed beside Kalian.

"So you really were aware of everything that happened during your incarceration," ALF met Kalian's eyes before continuing. "A Starforge's primary use is to open a hole in space/time and allow for instantaneous travel. But, during the war, I was forced to use it in other ways." There was regret in his voice. "If you plot coordinates inside the core of a star, the forge will open a wormhole that connects the two across space. A vicious ground battle on the planet Vordinay was going badly; I calculated that the Gomar would win within days and take the planet. So I made a choice." More regret. "I positioned a Starforge in orbit, above the battle. After it punched a hole into the closest sun, the forge focused and directed the raw energy like a beam, down into the planet."

"Aptly named, then?" Kalian couldn't believe such technology, such a weapon, existed.

"It decimated everything," Esabelle explained. "It scorched Vordinay's surface and wiped every Gomar and Terran from existence. But it was a calculated loss..." her words were spoken with venom at ALF.

"It wasn't what I designed it for." ALF ignored her last comment.

The three entered the Translift and Kalian felt Esabelle build a shield around her entire body. He decided it wasn't a bad idea and followed suit, building the millimetre-thick barrier around himself.

"Do you think the cube knows how to use the station that way?" Kalian expanded his awareness beyond the Translift. The huge station pulsed with energy as three Starrilliums hummed with the power of the stars.

"We should assume so." Esabelle pushed the button for the

bridge. "How the cube could know is a question we will have to visit after neutralising Garrett."

"Their whole connection to the Terran Empire is something we'll have to visit later," Kalian added.

He hated not having all the pieces to the puzzle. These cubes, or whatever they are, had to be connected to the Terran in some way. They had Terran script carved into their shell, one of them was found on Hadrok and was pivotal in destroying their entire civilisation, and now one of them controlled the most powerful corporation on the other side of the galaxy and had them build a Starforge, another Terran link.

Kalian was finding it harder and harder to believe that ALF had no knowledge of them. The AI had nurtured the Terran and worked with them to develop all their technology, including nanocelium, which just happened to be the material the cubes were made from. Was it possible the cubes had been made by the Terran without ALF's knowledge? An experiment gone wrong? A weapon designed before ALF's creation? That made no sense either since ALF had invented nanocelium. And yet the cube found by Savrick would suggest it fell to Hadrok during the end of the last Terran war, possibly around the same time ALF was given life. There were too many questions that Kalian felt the AI should be able to answer.

A small static charge disturbed the molecules in the Translift, turning Kalian's attention to Esabelle. With one hand gripping her other wrist, Esabelle activated the nanocelium in the bracer, causing the microscopic machines to spread across her open hand, covering like a glove. She did the same with her other hand so that only her head was left exposed.

"How did you do that?" he asked, looking at his own hands.

"Your armour can do a lot more than that." Esabelle turned both of her hands palm up. Her fingers flexed once and produced a tiny light on the tips, each light emitting a holographic menu. "You can mould the nanocelium or even change its colour." Esabelle wiggled different fingers, interacting with various controls for the exo-suit.

The flat bracers across her forearms began to shift like liquid until small spikes protruded all the way around her wrists.

Kalian did his best to make it appear as though it wasn't a big revelation that he could have done with knowing months ago. "I'm happy with the way mine is."

"Are you ready to kill him?" Esabelle asked with a sideways glance.

"If it comes to that, yes." Kalian didn't believe his own words. He had taken lives freely on Trantax, even with some enjoyment, but that didn't mean he had the right to. These abilities of his were a responsibility that neither Esabelle nor ALF had asked him to ponder on. Should they kill because they could? Were they superior? These were questions Kalian hadn't had time to stop and wonder about. Esabelle had been all about control and discipline over the last six months, but her outing with Roland appeared to have awoken something in her, an animal that had been caged for too long, perhaps. He was worried that she was no longer concerned with control.

"I think he's past saving, Kalian," Esabelle continued. "We won't be able to draw out the nanocelium without leaving Garrett inside a broken body; that's if there's even any Garrett left to save. Who knows what that thing's done to his mind."

"If we can capture him alive then we will," Kalian pressed.

ALF replied, "If you think the professor can offer any answers to our current riddle, I believe you would be mistaken. From what we know about this new Garrett, he doesn't feel pain. That rules out one way of getting answers, but I would wager that he's more machine than man now. You can't leverage programming."

Kalian was shocked that the AI would even consider torture. "Time to go back in your box."

ALF shrugged and disappeared.

Esabelle was looking at him. "I just need to know you're not going to pull your punches."

Before Kalian could reply, the Translift came to a stop and opened up onto the bridge. The command centre was befittingly large for such a massive station. Kalian counted three tiers, with one below them and one above, each filled with terminals and holographic monitors, though perhaps the oddest thing was the dozens of empty chairs. The viewport to their left rose up to the highest tier and stretched around the sides. The screen was heavily polarised with a slight glare around the edges as the nearby star fought to be seen.

The level pitted below them was crossed by two intersecting platforms with stairs either side. On their level was a raised platform with a single bank of monitors and terminals that looked to be the central command post. There were two other Translifts connecting to the bridge, opposite the one they both cautiously exited.

The fabric-like metal of their boots was soft on the polished floor, making as little sound as possible. Kalian doubled his shield and felt Esabelle do the same. They both made their way around the walkway, keeping the lower tier to their right as they approached the command terminal. Seeing the wrecked monitors and leftover nanocelium strands that infected the terminal, Kalian quickly expanded his awareness, connecting with every particle in the room. He turned around as soon as his mind built the picture of the man standing on the opposite side of the tier above. Esabelle mirrored his quick turn and faced the being that watched them.

The man wasn't a man, so to speak. Kalian could feel the Terran frequencies that pulsed from his mind, building a picture of his own. His features were twisted like Garrett's, but not to the same extent, with sunken dark eyes and shadowed cheekbones. The Terran's milky skin was interlaced with hardened strands of nanocelium that forced many of his veins to the surface, where they met his short blonde hair. The nanocelium had collected over the surface of his body and created an exo-suit much like Kalian's, only more organic.

The Terran said nothing but continued to stare at them from across the bridge with curious dark eyes. Kalian glanced at Esabelle with a hundred more questions flashing over his expression. How could there be a Terran here? How could there be a Terran anywhere? Kalian had memorised the faces of the eleven Gomar taken by the Conclave, and this wasn't one of them.

"Who are you?" Kalian couldn't help but ask.

The Terran moved for the first time, imitating a robot that had just come to life. He walked down the stairs with a low chuckle at Kalian's question. He never took his eyes off them.

"It's quite the obsession with your kind, isn't it?" The Terran's voice was eerily human. "You always have to name everything, label it, categorise it, put your stamp on it and make it yours. It doesn't give you the power you think it does. But if it helps your primitive brain comprehend its own destruction, then so be it. I suppose you could call me Malekk."

SIXTEEN

Sal-dev squirmed under the pressure of Li'ara's gun in his back, his face pressed into the charred white wall where the turret gun had made a mess. The Shay was clearly struggling to keep himself upright on his bad legs, forcing Li'ara to use her free hand to pull up on his torn jacket.

"Enter the code and open the door!" Li'ara stood back and aimed the gun at his head.

Sal-dev slid down the wall momentarily before crawling his way back up the wall. The Shay was practically crying while he placed his eye into the protruding socket. Li'ara watched him carefully as he entered the code and exposed the Novattoo on his arm. A painful groan escaped his throat when the Shay tried to stand upright and space his feet. Sal-dev uttered his name out loud for the scanner, heavy with shame and fear.

They both turned to the circular door as a dozen locks could be heard through the wall, each of the thick cylinders sliding out of place. The heavy door was propelled open with a *whoosh*, triggering Sal-dev to break down and cry again, crumpling to the floor at the sight of his failure. The vault-like door swung open to reveal the cavernous expanse created to house Protocorps' dirty little secret. The cube stared back at her from across the walkway.

Li'ara looked back at Sal-dev. He had heard their plan to plant a backdoor into the backup mainframe, making him a liability. She didn't care much to be honest; it was The Laronian's schemes, not theirs. But then she saw the faces of the *Gommarian* crew that had been slaughtered by Garrett; Rodriguez, Pitt, Gardner, Astill and so many others killed because Protocorps were keeping secrets and helping the cubes.

"Please!" Sal-dev pleaded, seeing the cold look in her eye.

Li'ara shot him in the chest, killing him instantly. She didn't stop to look at him but, instead, turned towards the AI chamber and strode over the threshold.

ROLAND HAD BEEN FORCED to get creative with distracting Kubrackk. The Novaarian and the Trillik had burst from the Translift, covered in blood and panting for breath. There was no hesitation in their dash to catch him as he ran for the executive Translift. Calling the lift would be too slow; their alien physiology made them faster than him, period. A few pot-shots compelled the bounty hunters to take cover behind the pillars, slowing their advance while Roland primed a grenade.

The explosion blew the doors of the executive lift open and filled the corridor with more smoke. Roland shook his head to try and rid himself of the high-pitched hum, before jumping feet first into the empty shaft. He over-calculated the jump and bounced off the other side of the shaft, smacking his head against the cold steel. The weapons on his back scraped over the shaft wall until he pushed off and corrected his drop.

"Are you suicidal?" Ch'len shouted down his ear.

The top of a stationary Translift was quickly coming into view, its square top rushing to meet him. Roland braced his legs and let the Laronian boots take care of the impact with a flare of blue light beneath his feet. His drop was immediately slowed until his feet were firmly on the top of the Translift. Looking back up, Roland could see the distinct features of a Novaarian's head poking out of the burnt remains at the top of the shaft. An angry snarl echoed down to Roland.

"Come and get me, asshole!" Roland gave Kubrackk the finger, a gesture he knew would be lost on the Novaarian.

The emergency hatch slid aside for Roland to climb down into the lift. With his approaching enemy in mind, he repeatedly hit the button to open the doors.

"Why aren't the lifts working, Len?" Roland looked up through the hatch and heard the sound of a metallic object magnetising to the shaft-wall above; they were going to rappel down.

"I would assume if it's watching you, it's listening as well," Ch'len replied. "It knows where you're going and it doesn't want you to."

"Fine..." Roland cracked his knuckles and started to prise the door apart manually. Sweat dripped off the corners of his eyebrows, stinging the cut above his eye.

Halfway through the gap in the doors, Roland had an idea, an explosive one. With the doors determined to close after him, he primed his last grenade and used his foot to keep the doors open wide enough to fit it through the gap. Roland carefully placed the explosive between the two so the doors kept the grenade primed.

"Try and catch me now." Roland turned to leave with a smug look of satisfaction on his face.

Thud

He froze at the sound of the doors opening and the grenade hitting the floor behind him. Without even stopping to scream some profanity, Roland sprinted away from the lift without looking back. Two guards came rushing out of the door to his right, offering the opportunity of safety. The bounty hunter bounded into the closest Shay, knocking them both into the room as the grenade released its payload, shredding the corridor with shrapnel. The other Shay was blown away in the explosion, sending half of his body down the corridor.

Roland rolled off the winded Shay, feeling a little dizzy himself. Once again his hearing had been shot to shit by yet another explosion of his doing. Smoke poured into the room with the distant sound of sparks and an acrid smell.

"It opened the doors..." Roland half whispered to himself, ignoring the recovering Shay.

"In the words of Roland North," Ch'len cut in, "no shit!"

The surviving Shay picked him roughly off the floor with augmented arms. Roland could see the pistons that had been surgically fitted to replace the alien's biceps.

"You're dead!" the guard pinned him to the wall...

The space between them flared with brilliant blue. The Shay gasped with an expression of surprise and horror before looking down to see Roland's Tri-roller pressed into his gut.

"Amateur." Roland pushed the Shay until he fell to the floor and replaced his gun.

"You need to go up a level." Ch'len came back with more directions.

Roland sighed with exhaustion setting in. His joints felt like they could go on forever with their enhancements, but his muscles were starving for oxygen and his lungs burned with all the smoke he'd inhaled.

"There's a Translift around the corner. Try not to blow this one up," Ch'len said.

The corridors were chaotic with personnel running for exits in every direction while trying to save their precious work. The sight of a human striding through their midst only terrified them more. It wasn't long before he found himself prising open the next Translift, which, of course, refused to take him up a level.

"I don't understand." Roland had to shoot the emergency hatch to get through it. "Why did the cube let us get this far before taking over the lifts?"

"It might have been something to do with the ship that parked in its lobby." Ch'len's sarcasm was on form as usual. "Maybe you should thank Kubrackk before you kill him."

"I'll try and remember that." Roland climbed up the service ladder and planted a mine on the door above. He made sure to cover his ears this time.

The next level was a simple corridor lined with a panoramic view of Clave Tower to its right. On the left was a field of tall black servers in row after row, each blinking with various lights to indicate their function. A lone monitor sat in the centre, at the front of the terminals, with a bank of holograms surrounding it.

Roland rushed over to the monitor, aware of Kubrackk's Novaarian senses. It wouldn't be hard for the bounty hunter to track his scent. He fumbled for a moment with the data-stick The Laronian had given him, its tiny mechanisms proving tricky for his rough hands. After slotting it into the port, the monitor consumed the stick, where Roland had been assured it would do everything for him.

"You know if this works out, The Laronian might forget the money you owe him." Roland wiped the sweat from his head.

"Just promise me we'll never have to work with that crazy, blue-scaled fuck ever again." Ch'len sounded almost as exhausted as Roland.

"Are you kidding me," Roland continued. "Now we know his little secret I'm gonna bend his ass over a barrel! We're gonna get the highest paid gigs with the lowest amount of risk."

Ch'len chuckled at the thought before he gasped, "Take cover!"

The door on the other side of the corridor blew open, followed by a dozen heavy boots storming the room. Roland dived behind the monitor as Intrinium bolts landed all around him, gutting the terminal and busting one of the monitors.

"Cease fire!" the lead Shay ordered. "Don't hit the servers."

That was all Roland needed to hear. The bounty hunter pushed off the broken monitor and slid between the servers, firing blindly in their direction. He heard them scatter with his shots going wild. Roland didn't care; he picked himself up and made his way further into the maze of servers, using them as protection.

"Spread out." The order carried over the hum of the servers.

Roland heard multiple sparks of electricity come to life at the front of the field. He reasoned they had switched to some sort of stun baton, in the hope of bringing him down in combat. The bounty hunter leaned against one of the servers and checked the ammunition level on the side of his Tri-roller. Almost two of the three barrels were depleted, leaving him with just over a hundred shots. Considering his preferred choice of fighting, Roland decided to change the magazines and replace them with fresh ones. Three hundred shots per gun was excessive, but what was the point of being alive if he couldn't be a little excessive every now and then?

Being as quiet as he could with all his injuries, Roland stole a glance between the servers and glimpsed one of the Shay guards. The alien was approaching slowly, being cautious to check every row with his shock baton raised high.

Roland ducked back in and steadied his breath. Chances were high that the rest of the team were doing the same in a line, moving their way through the field. Pivot and shoot; that was the plan. Kill one and scatter the rest, creating confusion and dissolving their search pattern. He took another breath and squeezed the gun in his hand.

The Shay screamed out in pain and Intrinium fire erupted across the field of servers. Roland braced himself against the hot metal of the server, unsure what was happening. More screams and cries of pain resounded throughout the room, with explosions breaking their pleas for life. Smoke rose from the broken servers, sending sparks arcing into the air and raining over Roland. He strained to listen and figure out where the running footfalls were coming from between the gunfire. A thundering guttural roar reverberated across the field of servers.

The predator had found its prey.

LOOMING stalactites pointed down at Li'ara from the capital planet's real earth. They glistened and glittered as if the cube sat under the very stars. She continued her stride across the platform, trying to ignore the pain in her calf, only slowing when she looked down at the tanks of liquid nitrogen that surrounded the cube and the shaft of cables and wires in the centre. The sound of her feet on the walkway echoed inside the cavern, giving Li'ara the feeling of being alone in such a large place.

But she was not alone.

Seeing the new cube, apparently lifeless in front of her, was chilling. It was identical to the other two, only with a polished gleam and an air of sterility to it. This cube hadn't been buried in the ground for a long time but had in fact been cleaned rigorously. Its golden sheen called out to a very human aspect of Li'ara, a characteristic that made so many people feel the need to touch. Kalian's words of warning about touching them rang clear in her mind. It wanted to be touched, to make contact and force her into submission.

The unusual stand in front of the cube tore her eyes away. It looked to her to be the ideal place to put one's arm. Li'ara took a step back, seeing the hole in the side of the cube, opposite the stand. The weight of the bomb on her back pulled at her attention. She needed to find somewhere to put it, somewhere that would cause the most damage and destroy the cube for good. Li'ara was hesitant to place it anywhere near the cube. She remembered the nuclear device that had been rendered inert by the nanocelium onboard the eclipse-missile months earlier.

The shaft that ran down the centre of the cavern, beneath the cube and between the tanks of liquid nitrogen, looked to be the best place. It was filled with thick cables and tubes that ran up into the cube itself. Seeing that she would have to climb down, Li'ara injected her bad calf with stimulants and painkillers. Now wasn't the time to be labouring under pain.

Once over the railing, Li'ara used the many cables to slide down, being careful not to get tangled up in the finer wires. When she was close enough, she dropped to the floor and slung her bag off her back. The cables created a very claustrophobic environment in which to prime a bomb. Li'ara wiped the sweat from her brow and took a calming breath. She had to give herself enough time to climb up and get clear; if she could close the vault door behind her then the explosion would be contained to the cavern, ensuring the cube's destruction. Taking that into account, and not being a hundred percent sure on how to close the door, Li'ara primed the bomb with fifteen minutes on the clock.

The climb back up to the walkway was harder than sliding down, though thankfully her leg gave her no trouble. Li'ara didn't stop to catch her breath with the timer counting down under her feet. She looked at the cube one last time with doubts about the bomb's payload. This would all be a waste if they destroyed everything but the cube. With time against her, Li'ara unstrapped every grenade and mine attached to her body. She tucked them all inside her bag and threw it on top of the cube. It was all she had.

The vault door closed behind Li'ara, locking her in.

She spun to face it, dread filling her every bone as a pit formed in her gut. The dozen locks fell back into place inside the wall, sealing her fate. Li'ara instinctively ran at the door and pounded against its unyielding bulk. It was futile, but her fear didn't care for logic.

"No!" She kicked it and screamed in frustration. There was no internal panel or release button. There was no way out.

The cube was silent as ever, mocking her ridiculous efforts to escape the death she had caused herself. If it weren't for the fear of dying under its control, Li'ara would have marched over and beaten the cube with her Terran blade.

The climb back down the shaft was much quicker the second time, with little care taken for her injuries. Li'ara activated the menu and searched as calmly as she could for the deactivation control. There wasn't one. She thumbed the on/off switch rapidly, her frustration growing with the lack of response.

"You sack of shit!" she cursed The Laronian.

Li'ara climbed back out of the shaft, but the cavern gave her no hope, either. There was only one way in and one way out of the chamber. With frantic fervour, she darted from one side of the walkway to the other, searching for a ventilation-hatch or anything big enough to fit through. She dropped to her knees, leaning on the railing, as realisation settled in.

This is where she would die...

ROLAND DASHED BETWEEN THE SERVERS, his Tri-roller in hand. Sporadic fire continued to interrupt his thoughts, along with random servers being blown to hell amidst the fire-fight. Kubrackk's snarl broke through the weapons fire, informing Roland of his proximity.

"I'm coming for you, North!" the Novaarian bellowed.

Light steps flitted past Roland. He swivelled around the server and saw the bulbous ends of a Trillik's twin-tail whip past the corner. The sound of a blade being wrenched from armour and guts could be heard a few rows away. The Trillik used the diversion to his advantage and caught Roland unawares. A strong green leg pushed the air from his lungs, forcing him into the gap between servers. Without looking, Roland fired both his Tri-rollers in the Trillik's direction. He didn't see where the shots went but he heard the server behind the Trillik take most of the damage.

"Sneaky bastard." Roland kept a Tri-roller in one hand and replaced the other with his Terran blade.

Streaking shots of Intrinium flew overhead, putting charred holes into the ceiling. It wasn't long before the dying twisted screams of a Shay followed. Kubrackk was cutting a bloody swathe through the server field.

A barrage of green Intrinium fire exploded around Roland, causing him to duck and roll out of the way. He continued to run between the servers, ducking and weaving the constant green fire that followed him. Trilliks' agility made the Novaarians look like clumsy animals. Roland looked back in the hope of lining up a shot, only to see the green-skinned alien skipping between the rows of servers, literally jumping off them to gain on him. There would be no lining up that shot.

Roland changed his tactics and whirled on the Trillik while

pulling the grenade launcher from his back. There was no way he was going to use it, the explosion at this range would certainly kill him, but the Trillik didn't know that. Roland was relying on his psychotic reputation to convince the Trillik.

The constant firing stopped abruptly when the Trillik caught sight of the launcher accompanied by Roland's suicidal grin. The moment the green-skinned alien dived out of sight, Roland dropped the launcher and dashed behind the nearest server. He realised that the firing in the distance had also stopped; Kubrackk had finally killed them all or died trying. There was no sound but the ceaseless hum of the servers.

The Callic-diamond armour creaked and his clothes rustled as he slowly made his way round the servers. Roland looked left and right down every row, with his Tri-roller crossed over his blade, aimed high. Sweat dripped off the end of his nose.

A silhouette swept into his peripheral vision moments before a curved blade slashed at his face. The tip cut his cheek and Roland gave into his muscle memory and evaded the next swipe. The Trillik pressed the attack with a knife in each hand, the blades moving so quickly that Roland could only see the light reflecting off them. The Trillik's twin-tail moved as if it had a mind of its own, lancing at Roland's gun hand and pinning it between the two ends. A quick flick knocked the weapon to the floor.

Without the gun, Roland's state of mind flipped into combat mode. The Terran blade deflected the curved knife and opened up a big enough gap for Roland to kick the Trillik away. The alien *hissed* as it collided with the corner of a server and dropped one of his knives. Roland could finally stop for a second and assess his opponent; the Trillik had taken some serious hits getting this far into Protocorps. One of his four eyes had been severely burnt with puss oozing around the edges. His ridiculous excuse for a combat suit was in tatters from close encounters with Intrinium fire. The lime-green flesh visible through the scorched torn clothing was marred with cuts and bruises. Kubrackk had put this guy through it, and for what, the Novaarian's revenge? Roland almost felt sorry for the green shit.

Almost...

The two crashed into one another with enough force to spin them, knocking them to the ground in a tangle of limbs. The Trillik clambered on top of Roland, with his curved blade angled to plunge into the bounty hunter's heart. He continued to lie there, feigning defeat, when the Trillik drove the knife down into the stubborn Callic-diamond chest plate. Roland didn't even feel a thing, unlike the Trillik. The blade snapped and rebounded into the alien's hand, drawing more blood and a sharp yelp of pain.

"Get! Off!" Roland jammed his Terran blade into the Trillik's thigh and punched him in the jaw.

The bounty hunter got up and followed the reeling alien. Roland pressed his boot onto the Trillik's chest and yanked the knife out of his leg, spraying blood across the servers. The Trillik screamed and whipped his tail round Roland's wrist, pulling the bounty hunter into a green bony fist and sending him flying across the floor. The alien grunted with anger and pain as he limped to stand over Roland.

"All this... for *you*." The Trillik aimed a small handgun at Roland's head, previously concealed behind his back.

Roland's hand instinctively went for the remaining Tri-roller on his thigh, his eyes fixed on the end of the barrel staring him in the face.

A blinding flash of light blew the Trillik's head off his shoulders.

Roland tensed at the sound of the Quad-roller, its high powered Intrinium round ending the Trillik and showering the bounty hunter in blood. The headless body flopped to the floor, the twin-tail writhing with muscle spasms. Roland blinked hard to remove the rainbow of spots in his vision while spitting alien blood out of his mouth.

Slow, heavy footfalls approached from behind, beyond Roland's head. He felt vulnerable on his back with the Trillik's body slumped over his feet. The Novaarian chuckled as his scarred features came into view, upside down to Roland, with his Quad-roller hefted in both of his upper hands.

"Well, shit..." Roland sighed, exhausted at the mere thought of fighting a Novaarian. Hand-to-hand combat with a taller, agile, four-armed alien was damn hard on a good day, and today was not a good day.

Kubrackk walked around his prone form, revealing his own bloody appearance. The Novaarian was covered from head to toe in blood, accentuating the scar across his face. The translucent tendrils fell haphazardly over his shoulders and back, each dripping with blood. It was easy to see some of the new scars the Novaarian had picked up on his way through Protocorps. Gashes and cuts marred the exposed skin over his arms and legs with a few burns thrown in to boot. Roland detected a slight limp in Kubrackk's left leg where a strand of tendon was exposed over the thigh muscle.

"You didn't think I'd let someone else kill you, did you?" Kubrackk stood at Roland's feet, smirking at his downed prey. One of his bottom fangs had been broken in half, leaving a jagged tooth in its place.

"You should have stayed down, asshole." Roland feigned more injury and pain while he slowly manoeuvred his legs from under the Trillik.

"Death will claim you long before it seeks me out." Kubrackk holstered his gun and delicately removed a long blade from his hip.

Roland needed him closer if he was going to get out of this. He couldn't reach for his Tri-roller before the Novaarian pounced, and even a quick draw would result in the blade ending his life. He needed Kubrackk to attack him to inflict pain, not death. The odds would shift once Roland was on his feet again; even if he was in the grip of four strong arms, he would still stand a better chance.

"Maybe you should have taken a leaf out of your brother's book," Roland goaded. "That dumb-fuck knew when to shut up and die."

Kubrackk's snarl turned into a roar as he dropped the blade and leapt at Roland. The Novaarian picked him up with ease and slammed him into the server. With two arms, Kubrackk kept Roland suspended in the air while his other arms pummelled his stomach and chest. The Callic-diamond took chunks out of Kubrackk's knuckles, smearing more blood across Roland's chest plate.

The odds shifted.

With both arms, Roland pushed out against Kubrackk's pinning hands. The Callic-diamond joints in his shoulders added strength, compounding his arms' resilience. The Novaarian was forced to let go, dropping Roland to the floor, whereupon he crouched low, driving an elbow into Kubrackk's injured left leg. The pain caused him to step back involuntarily until he staggered and collapsed on it. Kubrackk became a tangled mess with the Trillik's dead body.

Before Roland had even thought about it, his Tri-roller was already out of its holster and aimed at Kubrackk.

"Roland!" Li'ara's panicky voice came over his comm.

It was all the hesitation Kubrackk needed to lash out with his powerful right leg and launch Roland backwards. The bounty hunter fell on his back and slid down another row of servers, dropping his weapon.

"Roland!" Li'ara's voice again.

With a hand on his chest, Roland picked himself up and grunted in pain. The Callic-diamond had done nothing to stop him feeling that. He stumbled into another server and rested there for a moment.

"What's wrong?" he asked through strained breath.

"I'm locked inside the chamber..." Li'ara's voice was somewhere between desperation and defeat.

A pit opened in his stomach. "Have you already-"

"Yes. It's got five minutes left."

"Then deactivate it!" With his concern for Li'ara, Roland made his way back to Kubrackk without stopping to pick up his Tri-roller.

"The countdown won't stop. The Laronian wanted a big bang, one way or the other." Now her tone had changed to complete defeat.

"Okay..." Roland was thinking. "How long?"

"Five minutes." Li'ara sighed down the comm.

"Hang on, I'm coming for you." Roland headed straight between the servers, intending to get back to the Translift.

Four blood-soaked arms shot out from behind a server and picked Roland up, charging him down the empty row. Kubrackk faltered under his damaged leg and brought them both down in a tumbling mess. Roland's goals had changed now; he no longer cared about killing the Novaarian. He had to save Li'ara. With each hand, Roland removed a small knife from the side of his boots and jammed them in-between the knuckles of Kubrackk's upper hands. The Novaarian howled in pain, holding his impaled hands before his face. Combined with his already broken lower hands, Kubrackk was becoming more crippled with every encounter.

"Hang on, Li'ara!" Roland scrambled on his back and activated the repulsors in the soles of his boots. The opposing force launched them in separate directions, sending Kubrackk back down the corridor.

Ignoring the increasing pain that shot through his joints and his spine, Roland staggered through the rows of damaged servers, heading for the light of the bay windows.

"I'm coming," he gasped. "Just hold on."

"Get out, Roland," Li'ara ordered. "This bomb has to go off and you know it. By the time you get back up here, there won't be enough time to get me out *and* escape the blast. Besides, Sal-dev is the only one who could open the door again and I killed him."

"No!" Roland didn't do the math; he just had to get her out. "I'm coming to get you!"

"No you're not," Li'ara replied calmly. "You're going to get as far away from here as possible. I need you to give Kalian a message for me."

"Tell him yourself!" Roland was just breaking through the last rows of black servers, the light of Clave Tower coming into view. He was careful not to trip over the mutilated bodies of the Shay guards.

Kubrackk roared behind him, "I'm going to kill you, Roland North!" The Novaarian burst from between the servers, struggling to wield his Quad-roller.

The first shot took a chunk bigger than Roland's head out of the adjacent server. The second created a concussive force powerful enough to knock Roland off his feet. He slid across the polished floor, face down and trailing blood from his cuts and wounds.

Kubrackk appeared manic as he exited the field of servers. All four of his mangled hands worked to keep the gun held up. "I will avenge Torvrackk!"

Roland stood up, judging the distance between him and the Translift. He had to save her. Looking back at the Novaarian, he was filled with confidence that he would easily finish the pathetic bounty hunter and save Li'ara. After all, he had gotten out of worse situations than this. Empty holsters greeted his desperate hands and it hit him. Not only would Li'ara die, but he would die also. His cock-sure attitude had finally seen the end of him, but also another. She would die because of him, because he couldn't save her. If it wasn't for his past, Kubrackk wouldn't be here and Roland could have been in the chamber with Li'ara, and he knew he would have found a way to save them.

The wide barrel of the Quad-roller burned orange. Roland preferred to stare into its glow rather than die looking at Kubrackk's smirking grin.

The bay windows exploded as a team of Conclave security rappelled in from above. Roland ducked and covered his head, thinking this was the end. Intrinium fire erupted from both sides as the team unleashed their weapons on Kubrackk at once. Roland looked up to see the Novaarian flailing with every bolt of super-hot energy tearing through his body. The Quad-roller was flung aside, its casing melted while its owner fell to his knees, a cold dead look in his golden eyes. The weapons fire ceased when the Novaarian's body lay motionless on the floor.

"Roland North." An Atari in red armour picked him up by his arm. "You need to come with us. We've been instructed to get you to safety."

"Roland, are you there?" Li'ara's voice had become a whisper.

Roland shrugged the Atari commander off. "We need to get back up to the chamber. We have to save..."

"Roland," Li'ara commanded his attention. "Tell Kalian I..."

The whole building shook as the shockwave from the bomb blew out every window on its way down. The team crouched around Roland, who for the first time since the beginning of his career, felt dazed by his surroundings. The ceiling began to crack above them and the Atari commander took control.

"Move out!" he ordered. "We're getting you back to your ship!"

Roland was manhandled out of the server room and into the Translift. He didn't fight them or struggle to get free. He had failed. Li'ara was dead.

The building continued to quake under the stress of the explosion. The hangar remained unaffected for the time being. The forked ship was ready for Roland's arrival. The engines were running hot and steam was venting from various ports in the undercarriage. The Atari commander ushered him onto the ship and left with his team without saying another word. Why had they helped him?

Roland made his way to the bridge, still in a daze. Li'ara was dead. The pilot's chair took his weight as he slumped into it, not even acknowledging Ch'len.

"Where's Li'ara?" Ch'len asked.

Li'ara's dead.

He couldn't say the words out loud yet. His hands danced across the controls as a plan began to take shape in his mind. They were going to get out of this, and he was going to kill every Protocorps son-of-a-bitch he could get his hands on.

"We're leaving." Roland directed the ship towards the hangar's exit. "Strap yourself in."

Ch'len complied immediately with fear evident in his expression.

A Conclave security ship came to hover in front of the hangar, its weapons popping out of their compartments. The ship was unable to fire a single Intrinium bolt when a massive piece of debris slammed into the cockpit, crushing the occupants and blowing out the engines. As the ship started to freefall with the rest of the debris, Roland pushed their own ship out of the hangar and cut the engines at once.

Ch'len wailed when the ship dropped and his straps fastened him into the chair. "What are you doing?"

Roland braced himself while the ship tumbled through the air, falling past the security net that surrounded Protocorps. With the engines off and the ship powered down, it would appear on their scanners as just another piece of debris. The hull *clanged* with the multitude of wreckage that crashed into and bounced off it. Roland strained against the G force to flip the switches and start the ship back up. Maximum yield was applied to the thrusters, which battled against the inertia.

The forked ship came to a stop mere metres above a central platform that housed a massive park and forest. Other detritus landed around the ship, indenting the field of grass and snapping several trees. Through the viewport, Roland could see people running across the park, desperate to escape the carnage.

"Find the nearest exit," Roland ordered.

It wasn't long before the ship was leaving the capital's orbit. All the security ships were heading towards the planet, paying no attention to the millions evacuating. Eventually, the starry field of space filled the viewport once more and Roland slumped, turning his chair away from Ch'len. A rogue tear streaked down his face, cutting a line through the ash and blood.

Li'ara was dead.

SEVENTEEN

The creature calling himself Malekk continued to pace the walkway that intersected the pit of terminals and monitors. Black eyes, devoid of life, remained fixed on Kalian and Esabelle on the command podium.

Spread out.

Esabelle's words echoed in Kalian's mind. It still felt intrusive to him, but he was more than happy to have a form of communication with her that Malekk couldn't detect. The two of them slowly stepped away from each other, creating harder targets. Kalian commanded his heart to increase and pump blood to all of his muscles, ready for the inevitable. Adrenaline began to course through his veins, preparing his body for instant exertion and sharpening his reflexes and senses.

Malekk laughed, "I'm not sure that's going to be enough, Mr. Gaines."

It caught Kalian off guard. This new creation of the cube was Terran, and with that came all the perks, including the ability to tap into the universe and read your surroundings. Malekk could feel the physiological changes inside Kalian's body.

Kalian decided to do the same.

Malekk's body was intertwined on a molecular level with the

nanocelium. Every muscle fibre was enhanced by the metallic strands that ran through them. The individual nanites screamed with artificial intelligence, each loyal to the next, bundled in the central nervous system where the cube's consciousness now resided. Malekk's organs were dead. His lungs were deflated while his heart remained as still as a stone. Kalian was looking at a robotic parasite.

"I know your name." Esabelle continued to walk around the left side of the pit, distracting Malekk. "It was on the manifest of the *Tempest*. The ship's log stated you were a traitor to the Empire, a heretic. It also stated that you died during a fight of your own making, and were given back to the stars."

Malekk took the bait and followed Esabelle. "Terran lie just like the Gomar or the humans, or every species in the Conclave for that matter. The only *truth* in the universe is coming for you, and it is absolute."

"You're very passionate for a machine," Kalian observed, drawing Malekk's attention the other way.

"We're all machines, Mr. Gaines." At the same time, Malekk smiled, his face transformed. The nanocelium and dark veins faded behind the skin and filled with colour and life. His eyelids blinked and presented two ordinary, human blue eyes. "Your type of machine just cares more for the aesthetic."

Esabelle had left the podium and walked round to the head of the walkway. "I'd say there's a little bit of Malekk still inside there if your chosen image is anything to go by."

Malekk raised an eyebrow at the comment.

"The nanocelium could have altered your structure into anything, yet you chose to leave the face and frame the same."

Before Esabelle had finished her last word, Malekk's face returned to its twisted former self. "I assure you, this body is a shell, and its former owner is as extinct as the Terran Empire. Though I will admit, it's certainly the most uncomfortable organic I've ever encountered." Malekk examined the back of his hand as if it was a foreign object.

"You really have a problem with the Terran, don't you?" Kalian remarked.

Malekk's head whipped back. "Your species is..." His jaw stopped moving before another word could be uttered. The expression on his face became uncomfortable, his eyes confused at the stubbornness of his own jaw.

Kalian and Esabelle looked to one another but had no answer for Malekk's strange behaviour. Kalian now stood at the head of the opposite end of the walkway, Malekk between them.

What's happening to him?

Kalian projected his question into Esabelle's mind, enjoying the ease with which they could communicate.

I don't know. Maybe he was about to say something he shouldn't.

Malekk's jaw snapped back. "Destroying your race took less than point four of a percent of our intelligence. The Terran lineage is not a problem, Mr. Gaines; it is simply a blemish that requires removing."

"Why do you want to wipe out the species that created you?" Kalian pressed. This being had the answers they had all sought after for months.

Malekk laughed again. "You know so little. It's truly astounding that you've survived this long. Still, I suppose you're not to blame. That primitive little machine you call a brain can only comprehend so much, not to mention your source of *information*." Malekk looked at Kalian's suit, "ALF... how quaint." To Kalian's surprise, ALF made no appearance at the sound of his name. "He will be wiped out along with the rest of your unnatural kind."

"You're saying you weren't made by the Terran?" Kalian's concentration began to waver as he focused on Malekk's answers.

Malekk smiled with condescension. "Even the *great* Terran Empire was a speck in the lifespan of the universe." His smile turned malicious. "*We* are not a speck..." Malekk's posture was completely relaxed, an image of confidence. "We have thrived for so long because you do not see us coming, Mr. Gaines. We have no weakness, no fear and there is nothing you can do to stop the inevitable."

"So something terrible *is* coming. Got it." Kalian was getting tired of Malekk's posturing. "Then why are you so hell-bent on wiping out the Terran? You've spent a long time hunting down a less evolved version of them, which sounds a lot like fear to me."

Esabelle replied instead of Malekk. "They're taking us off the board."

Malekk slowly turned to face Esabelle, irritation in his expression.

"Something terrible *is* coming, isn't it? You just don't want the Terran to stand in the way. You're *afraid* we'll stop you."

Kalian was beginning to understand. "So what are you, some kind of scout come to check out the opposition? What's this terrible thing going to do when it gets here?"

"A scout?" Malekk laughed to himself. "You *could* think of us as the vanguard, I suppose. But believe me when I tell you; having your lives end by my hands will be far swifter than dying at the hands of my maker. Your continued survival has angered him greatly."

The threat got under Kalian's skin. "Well, you can tell this terrible thing that they can shove their anger up-"

"You think my maker is the terrible thing?" Malekk laughed. "My maker is the vanguard. We *are* the vanguard." Malekk held his arms out. "You should only hope that your entire race is ash by the time *they* arrive."

We need to strike, now!

Kalian ignored Esabelle. "What do they want?" He stepped forward, onto the walkway.

"To feed..." Malekk's reply sent a chill down Kalian's spine.

A bloody and mangled hand shot out from under the bridge and gripped Kalian by the ankle like a vice. Garrett had been hiding under the walkway. Kalian was instantly pulled to the floor and dragged into the pit of terminals and empty chairs. Garrett dropped down and landed with his legs either side of Kalian's prone body, his torn face void of emotion. Esabelle leapt the distance between Malekk and herself, sending them both spiralling across the walkway.

Looking at the broken body of Professor Jones, it was clear to see that there was nothing left of the man. He appeared worse than the last time Kalian had seen him, aboard the *Nova*. Garrett's skin was peeling all over in large chunks, revealing more of the nanocelium skeleton that controlled his actions. His usually unkempt hair was completely gone, leaving only scabs and fresh cuts behind.

With one hand, Garret pinned Kalian to the floor and held his other fist high, ready to beat him to death. His hand faltered for a second, the fist unclenched as his eyelids twitched. That second was all Kalian needed.

A telekinetic blast launched Garrett through the walkway above, twisting and breaking the metal, driving him into the ceiling of the tier above them. Garrett's endurable body dented the framework before he dropped to the ground floor, landing face-down. Kalian wasted no time in leaping out of the pit, using his abilities to enhance the strength in his legs. Garrett remained on the floor, immobile.

The fight between Esabelle and Malekk escalated far quicker than his own. The two of them had already blown through the top tiers of the decking, putting jagged holes in the ceilings and floors. Their telekinetic barrages shredded each level of its infrastructure, knocking through the supporting pillars and splitting the machinery into splinters and sparks. Kalian looked on in awe, unsure of how he would fare in such a battle.

Malekk was forced to one knee while Esabelle rapidly beat him across the face. She might as well have tapped him with her little finger for the all the effect it had. Malekk shot up, head-butting Esabelle, before he stood, arms outstretched as a maelstrom of energy exploded around them both. Electricity consumed the tier, firing off random bolts of lightning in every direction, while balls of fire erupted in each of his hands. The fire slowly took shape, as the heat increased to create molten balls of white-hot plasma that Kalian was forced to shield his eyes from. Telekinetic energy whipped around them as if they were caught in a tornado.

Esabelle recovered quickly and pushed against the onslaught of energy that contained the two of them. Kalian altered the structure of his retinas to compensate for the light of the plasma and lightning.

Every step Esabelle took was slow as she fought against Malekk's new-found powers. Before she could reach out and grab him, Malekk unleashed the organic plasma balls into her chest plate. Esabelle was hurled through the railing and sent flying across the expansive bridge like an Intrinium bolt fired from a gun. Kalian whipped his head to track her flight, intending to catch her with telekinesis but was brought down himself by Garrett. He only heard Esabelle as she crashed into the same upper tier, above him.

Garrett was on top of him once again, snarling with drool. Kalian intercepted his hammer-like fist before it could make contact with his face. The professor's weight pinned him to the floor with his knee on Kalian's chest. Malekk was standing at the edge of the platform above, where the railing had been bent outwards by Esabelle. The maelstrom of energy died down around him while he examined his hands again, this time with a hint of glee in his expression.

"You need to pay attention." ALF's voice rang as clear in Kalian's mind, as Esabelle's did when they communicated telepathically. Kalian's awareness soon found the strand of nanocelium that had grown from the collar of his exo-suit and attached itself to the translator disc behind his ear.

Garrett swiftly moved Kalian's arm aside and repeatedly drove his hand into the chest plate as if his fist were a piston. The armour held up to the professor's blows, but still knocked the wind from Kalian's lungs. With telekinetic force, Kalian rolled over, taking Garret with him into a tumble across the floor. The professor's head hung over the lip of the pitted terminal bay as Kalian came to rest on top of him.

Esabelle screamed from somewhere above him. He needed to help her.

Garrett's hands scrambled for his throat, hoping to choke the life from him. Kalian didn't have time to think about a better way to incapacitate him, he needed to help Esabelle. With one arm he swept Garrett's reaching hands away and held his free hand palm-down, over the professor's face. Exciting the particles around his hand felt like child's play now as he created a blinding light powerful enough to burn out any normal person's eyeballs. It wasn't enough though.

He had to end Garrett once and for all. Any question of morality dissipated with the sound of Esabelle's pain-filled scream. Kalian ended the light-show and dropped his weight onto Garrett's head with his forearm. The professor's head snapped over the edge of the platform into a ninety-degree angle, tearing the rough skin and splitting the spinal column.

His body went limp under Kalian.

Esabelle screamed again, this time from the highest platform. Sparks fired into the air wherever they fought, ejecting whole monitors and severing cables between the floors. Malekk was thrown around like a ragdoll in the telekinetic clutches of Esabelle's hands.

Malekk didn't utter a single syllable of pain.

GARRETT FELT himself floating upwards through a sea of ink, shaking free the shackles of his master. The tentacles of the cube's control were slipping free from his subconscious body. Was this death? Real death? The last encounter with Kalian had blanketed the world in white before severing his senses altogether. Garrett could feel the cube's mind scurrying around, panicked, barking orders at the army of nanocelium that ravaged his body. The nanites were clustering around his neck, working to knit the skin back together and fix the bones inside.

This parasite would never die, never release him.

Garrett's eyes became suddenly irritated, leaving him with the need to rub them and soothe the dull ache that ran into his temples. The nanocelium were recreating his eyes and reconnecting his nervous system simultaneously. The darkness faded around the edges of his virtual world, taking the image of his floating body with it. He was now looking through his own eyes, fully in control of his actions. The parasite had been so engrossed in healing his body that its reins over Garrett had loosened.

Garrett looked at his fingers and concentrated, willing them to move, testing the limits of his new control. His head moved, seemingly of its own accord, as the nanocelium reattached his head to the rest of his body.

The parasite screamed in frustration at the back of his mind. It clawed at his thoughts in an attempt to take back control. Garrett sat up, relishing the power to do so, and inspected his surroundings. He couldn't feel the metal under his hands and legs, the nerves in his skin unable to connect to his brain via the spinal column that was still being worked on. Kalian was a few feet away, moments from jumping into action to help Esabelle against Malekk. The bridge had been decimated almost beyond use, with sparks flying out of various broken terminals and cables hanging between the tiers. Small electrical fires had broken out on every floor, filling the area with smoke. Seeing the Terran clash was no small spectacle, Garrett predicted that the entire station would crumble under their power soon.

His right hand clenched into a fist of its own accord. The cube was taking back control already. Garrett willed the hand to open again while he pushed himself onto all fours, desperate to find Kalian before it was too late.

No one else would die by his hands.

KALIAN WAS WAITING for the break in the fight where he could launch into Malekk and take him off balance. The twisted Terran would be no match for them together. On the tier above, Esabelle attacked Malekk with every fighting style Kalian had ever seen, striking all of the nerve clusters in quick succession. Malekk took every hit that made it past his defences, showing no signs of defeat. The nanocelium that coated his body proved to be just as strong as their exo-suits, rebuilding every impact created by the organic plasma Esabelle threw at him.

The gap he had been waiting for appeared for just a second after a telekinetic blast separated the two combatants. Kalian jumped the twenty feet through the jagged hole in the ceiling, coming to land gracefully behind Malekk. A telekinetic field around his hand kept the plasma heat at bay as it grew to the size of a fist. When it was fully formed, he launched it at Malekk's back. Kalian's face dropped when the ball dissipated across an invisible field spread over Malekk's body. The possessed Terran turned on him with a wicked smile curling into his pale cheek.

"Have you come to die first, Mr. Gaines?"

Before Kalian could take a step, Malekk leaned forward, bringing his leg out behind him with more force than a Raalak. The flat of Malekk's foot caught him square in the chest, slamming Kalian into the far wall and taking out another support frame on the way. Busted monitors sparked around Kalian's body, now firmly indented into the wall like a nail hit by a hammer. The exo-suit scraped against the shredded edges as Kalian came to land on one knee with a comforting hand over his chest. His mind/body connection informed him of two broken ribs and a collapsed lung. His vision started to blur as his breathing became almost impossible. At least this time he had made sure to switch off his pain receptors.

"Focus, Kalian!" ALF shouted into his head. "Remember your training. You need to heal while you fight. Ignore the pain, forget the needs of the body and focus on Malekk."

Like a machine creating a subroutine to perform low-level tasks, Kalian set his body to the job of fixing his ribs and inflating his lung. He pushed up from the floor and hurtled towards Malekk, who continued to face Esabelle and used a blast of telekinesis to almost fly into the twisted Terran. The framework around the middle tier burst apart as if a balloon had been popped in the wake of the telekinetic backlash.

Malekk remained standing, defiant amidst the wreckage around him. Kalian had been flung back out into the bridge space while Esabelle hung limply over a bent railing. Kalian managed to keep enough of a shield around his body to ensure the damage was kept to a minimum as he skidded over the control podium below.

"These powers are wasted on your kind," Malekk announced from above. The Terran walked over to Esabelle's helpless form and roughly pulled her off the railing.

Kalian stood up immediately, only to be greeted by the hunched body of Garrett, limping up the podium steps. It halted Kalian for a moment, taking his attention off the danger Esabelle was in.

"Kalian..." Garrett's voice was just as broken as his body. "Not much time..." The professor actually looked to be in pain, putting Kalian on edge.

"Garrett?" Was this the real Garrett Jones or a trick? The look in his eyes was more human than before, pleading almost.

"They have a weakness..." Garrett fell to his knees and grunted in pain. "*We* are their weakness. Corrupt-" His pained expression became a snarl in the blink of an eye.

The surprise attack took Kalian off his feet again, sending them both reeling into the command console. They struggled across the floor of the podium, hitting each other with every opening.

***

ESABELLE USED the railing to pull herself up, blinking the blood that dripped into her eyes. Her concentration wandered, as a result of the new head injury, causing her pain-receptors to come screaming back to life. Malekk had broken several bones across her body that she hadn't successfully healed yet. His attacks were incessant and calculated, like a machine. The Terran body gave the parasite preternatural speed that, when combined with the nanocelium, created a killing machine.

The bridge appeared to wobble when Esabelle finally stood upright. She blinked hard to force her vision to return, desperate to make certain Kalian was still alive. The concussive explosion Malekk had unleashed was beyond anything Esabelle imagined he could know how to use. The infected Terran was using their abilities as if he had been trained for thousands of years and yet the parasite had only been recently introduced.

The sound of talking below caught her attention and Esabelle had to focus to turn her body without fainting. Kalian was standing on the command podium, talking to Garrett. The scene confused her for a second while her memory tried to piece together recent events. Her head injury was more severe than she initially thought; Garrett was the enemy now, as well as Malekk. Esabelle felt out of time with parts of her memory missing. How had they got onto the Starforge? Where was Roland?

Malekk came to stand before her.

"It looks as if you took quite the knock." His black eyes hovered over the gash on her head. "I give you credit for still standing, though." Malekk casually walked around her, unafraid. "Imagine the trouble your race could have caused, hmm? Billions of you instead of just the two, well, soon to be one." Malekk looked down on Kalian. "And then none."

"We will beat you..." Esabelle redirected her attention to healing her brain and skull, leaving her other injuries for the time being.

"Beat us?" Malekk laughed. "We've been coming for your kind since before the Terran even had a name. We know how you think, we know how you move and we know how you die."

"You talk a lot for a robot." Esabelle dropped to one knee as her leg gave out under Malekk's telekinetic nudge.

He stood over her. "You see the nanocelium and presume to know what we are. We are so much more complex than any machine, even more than your biological one. You are a cancer, infecting the universe with your every breath. You are toxic. Think of me as a white blood cell, eradicating that cancer before it infects the whole."

Esabelle looked up at him then, Malekk's words taking a new meaning. "Is that it? Is that why you've hunted us across the cosmos for so long? The Terran, humanity... we're some kind of weakness?"

Malekk burst into action, picking Esabelle up by the throat and holding her a foot off the floor. She fought back by kicking and punching with everything she had, ignoring the agony of each broken bone and torn muscle. Malekk took the blows stoically, unflinching under the barrage. The edges of her vision began to blur and go dark, focusing on Malekk's stony expression. The infected Terran pumped his fist into Esabelle's stomach and dropped her onto all fours, choking and spluttering. The exo-suit did nothing to soften the blow.

Malekk had practically pummelled her to death. Esabelle could feel the inevitable coming. She was too weak and inexperienced to fight a machine with complete control and understanding of Terran abilities. Her time in the *Gommarian's* virtual world hadn't prepared her for this kind of fight. Malekk couldn't be distracted or worn down; his energy appeared unlimited. Esabelle turned and looked down at Kalian through the matted strands in her hair. He was fighting Garrett again now, sending balls of organic plasma at the erratic professor.

"Kalian..." Esabelle whispered.

Esabelle had spent two hundred thousand years battling these creatures on a virtual playing field, keeping them from infecting her mind, protecting the crew. Her father had been lost, slave to the cube before she had any chance of helping him. For two hundred millennia she had kept them from finding Earth, giving the Terran lineage as much time as possible to grow strong. Esabelle could see now that everything she had ever done was to get Kalian to this point. To train him, for her part, while he grew into the man humanity needed, the man the galaxy needed. The realisation that she would not be around to continue his training was devastating.

But she knew one who could in her absence...

KALIAN STRUCK GARRETT in a dozen places with preternatural speed, each blow having little to no effect. Garrett took every hit and always came back, more feral each time.

ALF cut in. "Stop using your hands and feet and start using your head!"

The professor jumped onto Kalian's waist, bringing them both to the floor.

"Mr. Gaines!" Malekk called out his name from the upper tier behind him.

Kalian kept Garrett's gnashing jaws at bay long enough to turn his head and see Malekk holding Esabelle by the throat. She looked half-dead on her knees with Malekk standing behind her, his right hand firmly gripping her neck. Blood was dripping down her face from gashes cut into her forehead where it matted her dark hair. Esabelle was broken.

"All that time in the *Gommarian* learning about her abilities..." Malekk partially lifted her off the floor, causing her to choke under the pressure of his grip. "It amounts to nothing against us."

Kalian could see it coming and fought against Garrett's pressing body. Esabelle opened her bruised and swollen eyes just enough to meet Kalian's, revelation in both of their expressions.

Find Sef...

Malekk whipped his free hand around Esabelle's face and cracked her neck.

"NO!" Kalian barely registered her last words as he screamed at the sight of her lifeless body, being instantly disregarded.

Fury exploded within Kalian, an emotion he had yet to experience with his Terran abilities. A telekinetic, electromagnetic and telepathic wave erupted from his body with destructive intent. Garrett's hands shot to his temples, his face twisted in agony before his whole body was ejected from the command podium, along with all the monitors and half the floor. Malekk was momentarily cast back from the edge of the railing, his hands similarly gripping his head in pain.

Sparks erupted out of the exposed cables under the flooring as if a volcano was pouring out lava. New electrical fires blazed from the destroyed terminals surrounding Kalian in chaos and heat. Supporting pillars and internal framework groaned under the telekinetic stress that exploded from Kalian. A spider's web of cracks was growing over the three storey viewport, letting in slithers of light from the star.

"I am going to kill you." Kalian clenched his fists. "And then I'm going to hunt down the rest of your kind and kill all of them too." It wasn't the scariest threat he could have made, but he knew that was exactly what he was going to do.

Malekk gave him a coy smile and dropped off the lip of the middle tier. Above him, Esabelle's body lay limp, her arm hanging over the edge. There was no sign of any injuries on Malekk's body; even his visible flesh remained untouched.

ALF spoke into his head, "You're going to have to use everything to beat him, not just your physical body."

A ferocious snarl was all that preceded Garrett's leap over the fire, his arms outstretched towards Kalian. In his mind, Kalian gripped both of the professor's arms and legs mid-air. He made no physical movement or even looked at Garrett, as all of his limbs were torn from the professor's body. The limbless body slammed into an invisible shield around Kalian and dropped to the floor. Kalian flicked his wrist and sent the professor's remains into the cracked viewport, damaging it further.

ALF remained silent.

"Now your lap dog's been put down," Kalian strode towards Malekk, "let's see what you can do."

SPACE AND TIME were ripped open for the millisecond it took the *Gommarian* to emerge from subspace. ALF's clone viewed the ship's surroundings through a combination of scanners and long-range cameras, all feeding back a perfect image of the Starforge. It orbited the star at a mere three hundred thousand kilometres. ALF checked the status of the *Gommarian's* hull and was confident that it could withstand the proximity.

A deep scan that penetrated the Starforge's hull informed ALF of the evacuation that was taking place as well as the four occupants on the bridge. The clone registered no emotion with the understanding that Esabelle was dead, along with Professor Jones. Thinking exactly as ALF would, the cloned AI prioritised Kalian Gaines and ensured his survival. His secondary goal was to make certain that the forge was obliterated before it could be used against the humans.

More nanocelium was detected in the hangar bay, taking the

shape of the *Rackham*. That would be Kalian's only way of escape, ruling out the destruction of the bay. The Starrilliums would create a chain reaction that would tear the station apart before Kalian could reach the *Rackham*. Hitting the bridge directly would kill him for sure, ruling that approach out as well. The logical target was the thrusters that kept the Starforge in its orbit around the sun. Being a designer of such constructs, ALF's clone knew exactly where to hit.

The *Gommarian's* internal structure shifted dramatically when the clone commanded the nanocelium to bring all the armaments to bear. Once the thrusters were taken out, Kalian would be forced to abandon the station and then the clone would decimate the rest of the Starforge with ease.

An alert was raised in the wake of the latest scan. The Starrilliums were being activated. The station was either preparing for subspace travel, opening a portal or...

The clone wasted no more time and launched the missiles at the power conduit in the lower quadrant of the crescent. New calculations proved the *Gommarian* to be in serious peril with this new development. The Starforge had to be taken out now or it never would.

The missiles streaked across the vastness of space as giant lightning bolts of purple and blue fired up inside the crescent. The clone had encoded the nanocelium missiles with specific instructions to keep out of the beam circumference, which would burst from the station imminently. That concentrated beam would convert the ship into slag in seconds.

Long range scans of the sun confirmed the station's intent. A portal had been opened inside the star, ready to funnel and eject the raw power like a laser from a gun. Another alert was raised when the *Sentinel* emerged from subspace, half a light year away. Luckily, they would be out of the Starforge's line of sight and safe from the beam.

The *Gommarian* had no time to manoeuvre, however.

The blinding light shot from the centre of the Starforge and covered the distance at the speed of light. Incapable of comprehending death, the clone felt nothing in the seconds it took the beam to cut through the *Gommarian*, obliterating every particle and nanocelium, reducing them to atoms.

———

THE CUBE-SHAPED BRIDGE was in disarray. Both upper tiers on one side had completely caved in, raining scrap metal over the floor. The pitted tier was on fire, the chief source of the smoke that slowly filled the giant room. The constant sparks that erupted everywhere were drowned out by the god-like battle that raged throughout.

Kalian pinned Malekk to the wall with telekinesis, pushing his body so hard it dented the panels. With one hand keeping Malekk in place, Kalian used the other to create a brilliant flare of organic plasma and shoved it into the Terran's face. The infected flesh was burnt away, melting Malekk's left eye and ear. Kalian let the plasma burn like the rage that filled his mind, fuelling his power. Kalian was forced to constantly heal his eyes that suffered under the deadly glare, a light that would permanently blind anyone else.

There was no sign that Malekk even felt the plasma or the crushing telekinetic force. Fighting against Kalian's will, Malekk slowly brought up his hand and opened his palm. Kalian was ready for any attack, though. He had built a wall as strong as diamond around his body, only a couple of millimetres thick.

The square pillar beside them groaned audibly over the heat of the plasma and Kalian realised too late what Malekk was doing. The metal frame crumpled inwards until the weight of the tiers above came crashing down on top of them. In the second before they were buried, Kalian released his hold on Malekk, intending to dive out of the way and leave the Terran to be crushed.

But Malekk was quicker.

Kalian was driven from the spot by Malekk, who charged into him with telekinetic assistance. They were both flown out of the narrowing gap until they skidded across the floor, sliding through small fires. Kalian's anger kept him going. He had already planted a skull-shattering blow to Malekk's face before their momentum ended. They were separated again, rolling in opposite directions.

The most powerful beings in the galaxy picked themselves up and faced one another. Malekk's face was healing more slowly than it had before; leaving him with a black eye-socket that still smouldered.

"Being burnt sucks, huh?" Kalian tried not to think about the Starrillium's effects on him.

"I will see to it that your whole race burns before they die." Malekk actually looked angry for the first time. "But not before..."

The bridge shook, creating more chaos and debris. Malekk looked around with the same faraway stare that ALF had when he was investigating something they couldn't see. Kalian expanded his awareness and felt the explosions that had gone off in the lower curve of the crescent station. He felt the power of the thrusters slowly die away and the hungry pull of the star's gravity.

"It doesn't look like you'll be seeing to anything." Kalian could feel the exhaustion creeping through his defences.

"Much like your precious *Gommarian*," Malekk added. "Or your friend up there." He pointed at Esabelle with his chin.

Kalian felt the fury in his bones renew and fired himself at Malekk. He was going to tear the monster apart as he had Garrett and beat what was left of him with his own limbs. Malekk's hand shot out and stopped Kalian in mid-air before putting him on his back. The blow to the back of his head dazed his vision for the second it took Malekk to pick him up by his throat. The bridge continued to shake around them, shattering any glass that survived the fighting. The crack in the viewport spread, creating a more complex web.

"You should know when you're beaten."

ALF's voice came from a newly formed speaker in Kalian's exo-suit. "So should you."

Without Kalian's permission, the nanocelium grew over his head and hands before the entire suit of armour ejected his naked form out the back. The exo-suit knitted back together in the blink of an eye and attacked Malekk as if Kalian were still inside it. Kalian was left stunned on the floor, unaware that ALF even had the power to control the suit in such a way. Rapid punches knocked Malekk backwards, though he appeared less stunned at the development.

"Run, Kalian!" the exo-suit shouted, as it grappled Malekk into the pitted tier, filled with fire.

Kalian scrambled to his feet trying to keep his balance on the shaking floor and avoiding the panels falling from the ceiling. With every shudder, the viewport cracked a little more. Kalian could feel the increasing speed with which the station was dropping into the sun. He had less than minutes to reach the *Rackham* and escape before the Terran ship would begin to suffer from the star's intensity.

The door partially parted in half, its servo motors damaged inside the wall. Kalian used telekinesis to open them all the way and paused on the edge of leaving. His mind gripped Esabelle's body and pulled her across the bridge with invisible hands. As her body landed in his arms, ALF was flung from the pit with enough force to kill a man. Being a hollow machine, the AI felt nothing and got straight back up.

The station shuddered again, forcing Kalian to fall into the wall with Esabelle in his arms. There was no time to stop and see if ALF fared any better than they had against Malekk; the Starforge would be disintegrated in minutes. To give the AI some chance of survival, Kalian mentally commanded all the loose cables, and some still buried under the floor, to lash themselves to Malekk's arms and legs, tying him in knots and binding him to the floor.

The station was rocked again and Kalian ran with a speed Esabelle had taught him. A couple of minutes later the Translift opened up to a deserted hangar bay and a lone *Rackham*. His naked body didn't register the cold as he ran across the expanse and up the ramp of the Terran ship. Kalian was gentle in the way he placed Esabelle's body on the couch on his way to the bridge.

The *Rackham* lifted off just in time as the station tilted and the grav-plates lost power. Anything not tied down was thrown to the right of the hangar moments before the port shield failed and everything was sucked into outer space.

Kalian hesitated when the black form of ALF dropped out of a ventilation shaft in the ceiling. He was astonished to see the AI. What did this mean for Malekk? The machine skidded down the tilted floor, digging his fingers into the metal to slow him down while creating a wave of sparks. Kalian lowered the ship and flew over the top of ALF and out of the Starforge.

A metallic *thud* resounded up through the layers of the ship. Kalian angled the ship away from the star at full speed, leaving the station to burn up on its descent. A quick sensor sweep detailed the location of the *Sentinel*, making its way towards the *Rackham*. Kalian jumped in his chair at the sight of ALF slowly being moulded out of the bridge floor. The exo-suit built itself up as the individual nanocelium passed through each other, slowly taking the form of a biped until ALF stood next to him.

"You're full of surprises today," Kalian remarked with an uninterested tone.

Without a word, the nanocelium compacted back into the buckle that housed them and dropped to the floor at Kalian's feet.

A flood of emotions hit Kalian at once. He was relieved to be alive after yet another situation that had put his life in danger inside of six months. He was angry at the mysterious external forces that harassed him and his kind. It angered him almost as much that he couldn't convince the Conclave that they existed. And now, after being forced to tackle them alone, Esabelle was dead. Kalian was physically and emotionally exhausted. In the silence of the bridge, he suddenly felt very alone. He couldn't even see the humour in sitting naked in Roland's chair. With that in mind, he reconnected the Terran panel to his skin, below his navel, and let it envelop him.

New scan results fed back the almost microscopic debris that was apparently left by the *Gommarian*. The twenty-mile ship had been reduced to fragments no bigger than Kalian's hand.

"I take it this is your doing?" Kalian said out loud, aware that ALF would be listening.

A strand of nanocelium grew into his translator again. "We'll talk later. For now just get us out of here." ALF's tone was soft.

"Is Malekk dead?" Kalian had to know before he did anything else.

There was a long pause before ALF replied. "No."

Kalian sighed and let his head fall back into the seat. They had destroyed the Starforge and protected the human and indeed the Conclave races from a super weapon of mass destruction. But with Esabelle dead, it felt as if it were all for nothing.

"This is Kalian Gaines aboard the *Rackham*," he hailed the *Sentinel*. "I could really do with a lift..."

THE ESCAPE POD hurtled through the Helteron Cluster putting as much distance between Malekk and the *Sentinel* as possible. ALF's control of the exo-suit had almost tied both of their fates to the Starforge, now one with the local star. The exo-suit had broken the damaged viewport right before it escaped into the ventilation system. Malekk had been forced to use his new powers to tether himself to the floor while the bridge's contents were sucked into space and vaporised by the sun.

Malekk injected the shuttle's control display with nanocelium, commanding the nanites to wriggle free of his host's hands and infect the ship, giving him wireless control. He sat back in the chair, very aware of his relaxed Terran-like position. It was a disgusting thing to inhabit such a being, though not without its perks. Of all the species he had ever sampled there had been none quite as powerful as the Terran. He whipped his head to the side to dispel such thoughts; they bred individuality, a forbidden state of existence.

The Vanguard's dominating voice still echoed inside his head, reminding him that his release from the whole was only temporary, though such thoughts made Malekk think about his master's existence. Even the venerable Vanguard had its own individuality, separate from the whole, from the master of them all. Malekk whipped his head again to rid himself of the thoughts and curiosities. He had never had such ideas or even an idea. Malekk was part of the Vanguard; his thoughts *were* Malekk's thoughts. Their primary mission was to prepare the way for the whole. Their secondary mission was to hunt down the heretic.

Suddenly life didn't feel so simple.

It was the Terran - Malekk could feel it. By inhabiting this particular body, he was on a clock that counted down to insanity and loss of control. The organic worm screamed inside the confines of his mental prison, slamming his hands and feet into the walls, cracking them. Malekk did his best to fill in the cracks and keep the Terran at bay. They really were cancerous.

The empty vastness of space stared back at him through the circular viewport. Malekk decided it was the quiet of his surroundings that made his new mind wander. He needed to be occupied, fulfilling his master's errand. With a mental command, Malekk set course for the nearest Protocorps owned planet. It was a setback to have lost the Starforge, but he already knew that Protocorps had followed the 'prophet's' instructions exactly. The Vanguard had released three new cubes into the galaxy through the Starforge's portal and, in so doing, set the fate of the Conclave and its human protectors.

EIGHTEEN

The pristine medical bay inside the *Sentinel* was a stark contrast to Kalian's ash-coated face and hands, smeared with blood from previously healed cuts. The medics had left him to be alone with Esabelle's body, now cleaned and dressed in a white gown only a shade paler than her skin. Her black hair lay over her chest in a perfectly straight line. Kalian had seen her meditate many times, but to see her so still was unnerving.

The med bay door parted and four booming feet thundered into the room. Kalian hadn't even bothered to expand his awareness into the great ship, too exhausted to care. Still, he didn't need Terran abilities to know the High Charge was standing behind him.

"I'm sorry it came to this," Uthor said with his gravelly voice.

Kalian's anger bubbled to the surface. "You should be." He half turned and saw that Uthor was taken aback by the response. "Another one of my people has died trying to keep your precious civilisation safe. How many more deaths will it take for you people to pull your head out of your ass and see the shit-storm coming our way?"

Uthor lifted his chin. "I have been reviewing the data and come to a similar conclusion."

403

The High Charge's reply silenced Kalian's sharp retort, ready and waiting on the edge of his lips. He hadn't expected any level of understanding from the Highclave's lapdog. Kalian tried to let go of his anger but couldn't seem to unclench his fists, with Esabelle's body so close.

"I will be presenting my findings and suspicions to the Highclave," Uthor continued. "What was that weapon? It destroyed the *Gommarian* with a single shot. Our scans reported a space-time distortion inside the star. My chief engineers are telling me that a wormhole was opened..." Uthor's expression was grave.

Kalian remembered the origins of the Conclave and the wormhole technology that accidentally wiped out the race that once inhabited the capital planet. Seeing such feats of engineering used just for destruction, rather than exploration, would be harrowing.

"It's called a Starforge." Kalian couldn't be bothered getting into it. "I take it the Highclave will want to see me about... everything?"

"We are on our way to Ch'ket, where the rest of your people are being housed. The *Marillion* will meet us there."

"Then I'll explain everything when we meet. Are my people safe?" Kalian felt bad for not thinking about them. He had assumed ALF had taken care of them before hijacking the *Gommarian* and sending the ancient ship to its death.

"Their location within Ch'ket's rings remains a secret for now," Uthor explained. "But the destruction of the *Gommarian* will be something the Highclave wishes to share with the people. Upon hearing this, the populace will demand to know where the humans are being kept. There is still a great deal of fear surrounding your kind. The Highclave will no doubt reveal the habitation on Ch'ket within a matter of hours, to show transparency with the various governments. Relocation will be required, though the destination is yet to be decided. Again, I will speak to the Highclave on the matter."

"Has there been any word from Li'ara and Roland?" Kalian kept the question vague, unsure how much Uthor knew. He didn't want to compromise their mission by giving their location away.

"You mean with regards to the attack on Protocorps Headquarters?" Uthor sounded unimpressed. "The AI, or whatever it was, has been destroyed. I am yet to receive an official word on your companions."

Kalian couldn't hide his concern for their wellbeing. He needed to know they were safe, that Li'ara was safe. It seemed stupid now that they had split up the way they did. Either Esabelle or he should have gone with one of them instead of leaving them to fight without Terran abilities to help. Kalian turned to face Esabelle again and realised how disastrous that would have been as well. It had taken both of them to fight Malekk and Garrett, and they still didn't defeat Malekk in the end, even with ALF's help. Li'ara or Roland wouldn't have lasted two minutes on that bridge.

"It's not going to seem like it now, but destroying that cube just saved every planet in the Conclave." Kalian truly believed that. He didn't know what its long-term plan had been for the cube inside Protocorps, but its connection to the entire Conclave made it a deadly threat.

"We shall see."

Kalian didn't have the energy to argue with the Raalak. "I'm taking Esabelle to the *Rackham*."

"You know we're going to keep the ship."

Kalian faced Uthor, his expression as stony as the Raalak's. "No, you're not." He picked up Esabelle's body and made for the exit without waiting for a reply.

CAPTAIN FEY STRODE along the outer corridor of their new habitation in the hope of out-pacing Laurence Wynter, who harassed her every step. The stark corridor was lined with bay windows allowing them a view of the rings and the planet below. Only an hour had passed since their presence had been broadcast to the Conclave and the news ships had flocked. Of course, the security immediately tripled and kept the vultures at bay, clearing the space around their new home.

Wynter was becoming out of breath. "I think it's highly inappropriate for you to meet with Kalian alone. The council, or at least myself, should be present."

"You don't know Mr. Gaines, Laurence." Fey had no patience for the man. "Telarrek has informed me of Esabelle's death, which can only mean they've gone through hell. I assure you, Kalian will kick you out without even lifting a finger."

The captain couldn't even bring herself to smile at Wynter's speechless expression. Esabelle was a great asset and the perfect mentor to Kalian, but she was also a friend. There had been many sleepless nights where the captain had wandered the corridors of the *Gommarian*, battling her anxiety at the thought of all her responsibility, and Esabelle would be there, apparently without the need of sleep. The Terran always offered words of comfort and wisdom, betraying her ancient lifespan. Esabelle had always carried a quiet power with her, filling any room she entered. How could she be dead? The captain willed Telarrek to be wrong.

Wynter cleared his throat and practically skipped to keep up. "Well, I assume you will relay everything he tells you to the council, in detail?"

Fey snapped.

The captain whirled on Wynter and pinned him to the bay window with a strength she didn't know she still had. Her forearm stretched over his collarbone, partially constricting his ability to breathe.

"You and your precious *council*!" Captain Fey wanted to say everything she thought about the ridiculous group of diplomats. Esabelle was dead and all they cared about was control. She could take their power away in a heartbeat and the people would be thankful for it. Taking total military control of humanity's remains was not an option she could give into - she had promised herself that for six months now. "Get out of my sight..." Fey pulled back and let a very shocked Laurence Wynter slink away.

Before continuing down the corridor, Captain Fey let her head roll back while she took a breath. Breaking that moron's nose would have been the most satisfying feeling she could imagine. Fey let the thought go and made her way to the med-bay on the seventh level, passing only UDC guards along the way. Naydaalan stood in the way of the door, holding his spear to one side.

"Captain..." The Novaarian bowed his head and stepped aside.

Kalian and Telarrek had their backs to her on the far side of the bay, both of them looking through the glass wall into the treatment room. Esabelle's body lay on the table dressed in white. The captain's eyes were quickly drawn to the cuts and bruises on the Terran's beautiful face. One look at Kalian was proof that they really had been through hell; he was smeared with blood and ash, his hair matted with sweat. He had the look of a defeated man, beaten down and broken.

Captain Fey placed a comforting hand on his shoulder, feeling the cold plates of his armour. Telarrek bowed in her presence with his own sombre expression. The Novaarian swept his purple robes up and turned away from the glass wall.

"I'm so sorry, Kalian..." It was all she could think to say. Esabelle and he had become close over the last six months with all their training. The captain was certain that Li'ara meant a great deal more to Kalian, but Esabelle's loss would hit him hard.

"Everything's going to change now." Kalian didn't look away from the glass wall. "Uthor says the cube in the AI has been destroyed by Li'ara and Roland. He acknowledges that there is a threat to the Conclave besides us."

Captain Fey gave Esabelle one last look before turning away. "It's about time. Did you find anything yourself in the pursuit of Garrett?" Telarrek's report had been very vague prior to her arrival. She knew that the four of them had split up, with Kalian and Esabelle going after Garrett in the Helteron Cluster. Fey tried not to think about the fact that the *Gommarian* was gone. It was a monstrous machine, responsible for so much death, but it had kept them safe and offered leverage in a world where they had none.

"Professor Jones is dead. I killed him." Kalian sounded like a machine.

ALF appeared by Kalian's side, as he always did. "We learned a lot about our enemy."

"Not really..." Kalian replied with his eyes fixed on Esabelle.

ALF clenched his holographic jaw before continuing, "They are not without their fair share of mystery still. However, there is a new player on the board." ALF paced the med-bay. "It seems the cube taken from Trantax IV was used to infect a Terran left behind by the crew of the *Tempest*."

"A Terran?" Captain Fey couldn't keep the surprise out of her voice. "How...?" She couldn't form all the questions she wanted to ask.

"His name is Malekk. Apparently, Protocorps found him years ago, buried in his stasis pod. *He* was their dirty little secret in the Helteron Cluster," ALF explained.

Kalian finally turned away from Esabelle. "Malekk wasn't their only secret out there."

Fey watched Kalian and ALF meet each other's gaze, a silent conversation taking place. Or was there accusation in Kalian's expression? What the hell had happened out there?

"Protocorps built a station in the Helteron Cluster-" ALF was cut off.

"They built a weapon," Kalian interjected. "A Terran weapon."

The captain stopped her hand from covering her mouth. "I'm confused. How did Protocorps get the designs for a Terran weapon? Is that how they destroyed the Gommarian?"

"Malekk's animation is very new, even to Protocorps," ALF continued. "I'm afraid it is unknown how they came by the plans for the Starforge. Its size and overall completion suggest that they started building it at least a century ago. When we came across the station it was fully operational. The forge was originally designed to allow wormhole transportation through space, but it can also be used to harness the power of a star. That is how the *Gommarian* was destroyed, I'm afraid. I had hoped to keep it around for your protection but I was caught off guard.

"I believe that Kalian and Esabelle's presence forced whoever our mysterious enemy is to move up their plans. Infecting Malekk is their idea of waking up the attack-dog. That's really all we know about him at this point."

Kalian stood perfectly still, his eyes locked with ALF's. "Now that's not exactly true, is it? We know that they're made of nanocelium. That's how they infect their hosts. Those cubes are made of the stuff, filled with them, each one a part of something bigger, serving its master. Malekk serves the Vanguard and the Vanguard serves something else, probably something worse." Kalian started to walk around ALF as if he were a detective circling his suspect. "Now remind me, ALF, who created the nanocelium? Oh, that's right, *you* did."

Captain Fey looked from one to the other, putting the puzzle together. They had always suspected that there was a link to the Terran culture, especially after finding part of their language engraved into the cubes. Fey found the AI to be an infuriating character, always keeping secrets and omitting the truth. Anything as intelligent as ALF was simply dangerous.

"The Terran created it around the same time I was given life. I just refined the process and used it practically instead of using it as a weapon." ALF remained calm, his expression never changing.

Kalian was like a dog with a bone. "How convenient that there's no way to prove that."

ALF paused. "That's not entirely true."

The captain raised her eyebrow at such a claim. The Outpost on Naveen had been destroyed and now the *Gommarian* was gone, all their combined data with them. This was the problem with ALF; he always had something up his sleeve that he kept for the right moment.

"Explain," Fey ordered with her captain voice.

"The Starforge in the Helteron Cluster was much bigger than it needed to be. In fact, I never designed one of that size. It's just more proof that it was built to be a weapon or a transportation system for something very big." ALF waved his hands casually. "Anyway, the point is, I can direct the Conclave on how to build another Starforge, a smaller one. Much more economical." ALF looked at Telarrek with his last comment.

Fey was intrigued. "And what would you propose we do with this Starforge?"

ALF smiled. "Go back to the Terran Empire, of course."

His answer was met with stunned silence. Even Kalian looked at the AI with suspicion. ALF looked around, shocked at the lack of enthusiasm for his eccentric plan. It didn't make sense that ALF would suddenly come up with this plan now.

"Come on!" ALF cried. "I agree that there is a strong connection between our enemy and the Terran. Now we can go back and find its origins."

"Why now?" Fey asked. "You realise you're not just offering a way of getting answers, but you're offering the Conclave a whole new mode of space travel."

Telarrek spoke for the first time. "You would transform the shape of the Conclave overnight. This level of change is profound."

"You think he doesn't know that?" Kalian stopped in front of Esabelle again. "This was his plan all along. Wait and see if the Conclave accepts us and if it doesn't we just leverage them with technology. Starforges, nanocelium... it's just the beginning of what he knows. Let me guess what's next; you think you should replace the broken AI with yourself. You start building Terran technology and slowly repopulate the species until we rule the Conclave. I mean, come on, you're a machine, what're a few millennia to wait until you have your empire back?"

ALF's smile was gone, replaced with a defeated expression. "My home is gone, I know that. The Terran culture is gone, now to be replaced by whatever becomes of the human race. My reason for being is to simply ensure that your genes continue to exist in this universe. I have no designs on domination or ruling any empire, human or other. I have kept my knowledge to myself in the hope that the Conclave would accept you as you are, not for what you can offer. But I will forgo that hope in place of keeping you safe. If technological advancement is the only way to that then I will tell the Highclave everything I know."

Kalian took three very quick steps towards ALF, reducing their distance to only a foot. "I don't trust you anymore. You should know that going forward." After a brief staring competition, Kalian backed off and returned to staring at Esabelle.

Captain Fey broke the tension that followed. "After the chaos that will be caused by the destruction of the AI, we can only hope that offering these *Starforges* is enough to soften the blow."

Telarrek offered some insight into the remnants of the AI, "There is stability for the moment. The backup AI has smoothed over the glitches, limiting the potential catastrophes. A new AI will be required, however. After what's been revealed today I cannot be sure what role Protocorps will play in that."

Fey looked at both Kalian and ALF, but neither made a comment on Telarrek's reasoning. It was hard to see where they went from here. There were a lot of people looking to her for the solution to their housing situation and their desperate need for a planet. There was very little in her that trusted ALF, but if he could give them the leverage they sorely needed to secure their place in this new society, then she was willing to go along with it.

Kalian's tone was softer. "The *Marillion* is on its way here. We're going to lay everything out and see if this transparency they're so fond of is the solution to uniting us. We'll negotiate in whatever way we have to in order to secure our future, but we have to emphasise that our combined priority is seeking out this threat and eliminating it before it eliminates us. We have to find Malekk, not go on some grand adventure across the galaxy." Kalian looked at ALF again. "There's nothing out there but graves."

"Agreed." Captain Fey didn't want Kalian to leave, not now at least. With the *Gommarian* out of the picture, they would need him more than ever.

"You're coming in with me this time." Kalian looked to the captain. "I'm not these people's leader. You are." Telarrek stepped forward with a face of worry, his four hands coming out of the large robes. "Make it happen, Telarrek. If the Highclave wants to see me they're going to have to recognise Captain Fey's authority."

The Novaarian tilted his head for a moment before bowing.

"Thank you, Kalian." Captain Fey gave him a warm smile, truly appreciating his backing.

"There's one more thing." Kalian faced the group. "We need to find out where the Gomar prisoners are being kept. I don't want the Conclave to be tempted into opening their stasis pods. If they think they can find weakness from experimenting on them, they will."

Fey hadn't seen this untrusting side to Kalian before. His usual optimism was completely gone, depleted with recent events. The captain was ashamed that she preferred this side to him, a more pragmatic side. Kalian had increasingly felt like an outsider during their time aboard the *Gommarian*. It was obvious to everyone that he was different, and there were times the captain wondered whether he would even take humanity's side when it came to the crunch. His time with Esabelle had seemed to increase the distance between humanity and him, a constant reminder that he was something other than human. Esabelle's death, however, had apparently brought Kalian well and truly back into the fold. Fey hated herself for thinking it.

Telarrek said, "I do not think the Highclave would be so foolish, Kalian. They understand how dangerous the Gomar can be. They saw it first hand remember? I admit, we must advise them on how to handle the prisoners, but I do not think we need to worry about any experiments."

"They'll already be pissed off that we kept their survival a secret." Kalian's tone was more aggressive than the captain was used to. "If they can't be convinced that we aren't the threat, then they'll continue to try and find ways to keep me on a leash."

The captain couldn't quite see the benefit in having the Gomar under human guard. "I agree that a solution must be found to the Gomar problem, but we're in no position now to keep an eye on them. This habitation isn't suitable to contain them, and you can't watch them every second of every day."

There was something in the way Kalian moved, his expressions. Captain Fey could tell there was something he wasn't saying. She had spent a very long career learning to read the people around her and stay in control of any situation. The way Kalian twisted his mouth and looked away was telling of his internal battle to tell them his secret.

"What is it, Kalian?" she asked softly.

Kalian looked at all of them before speaking. "Esabelle told me something before she died." The captain noticed ALF's attention perk up. "She said, 'Find Sef'."

Fey had to think for a moment, unsure where she had heard the familiar name. "The Gomar on Naveen?"

"It's impossible, Kalian," ALF said. "The entire area was reduced to a smouldering crater."

"You survived," Kalian replied.

Telarrek looked down on them. "He could not have got out in time, Kalian. If it had not been for ALF's guidance, I too would have been buried on Naveen."

"When did she tell you this?" ALF asked with clear suspicion.

"Just before Malekk broke her neck. Telepathically." Kalian looked away, not meeting the captain's eyes.

Fey tried to hide her look of disbelief. This new ability was beyond imagination, even for Kalian. The captain took a breath and willed her mind to go blank but failed, instead, thinking about all the things she didn't want Kalian to hear in her head. Her look of worry was clearly evident and Kalian responded.

"Don't worry, Captain, I can't read your mind. It only worked with Esabelle."

Fey could only nod at the statement, trying to appear casual rather than horrified. A part of her still worked desperately on not thinking about her point of view regarding Kalian's role after the death of Esabelle.

"It makes no sense, Kalian," ALF continued. "Esabelle couldn't know if Sef was still alive, and even if she did, why would she instruct you to find him? He was Savrick's right hand for years. He's dangerous and Esabelle knew that. Malekk had beaten her half to death by then," Captain Fey winced at the AI's bluntness. "You can't take her word for it - she was delusional."

"What if she wasn't?" Kalian persisted. "What if there is something else going on that Esabelle didn't tell us about?"

"Then it's just more proof that she shouldn't be trusted," ALF replied stubbornly.

"Because *you've* been so honest and open?" Kalian replied with fire in his voice.

Captain Fey looked away as the tension crept back into the room. This was a hard argument to find the right side of. She wanted to agree with Kalian, but ALF made more sense. During her earlier days in the UDC, the captain had seen a little action and knew all too well that dying people could make no sense. It certainly made no sense to try and contact Sef; it scared her enough to think that he was out there somewhere.

The med-bay door opened and Naydaalan entered, "Forgive the intrusion but, Li'ara and Roland have returned."

KALIAN HAD DEACTIVATED ALF's hologram long before he reached the hangar bay, where Li'ara and Roland's ship was coming into land. He didn't want to see the AI for a while. It was frustrating enough that he couldn't choke the damn man, let alone reason with him. His thoughts of killing ALF made him think of Savrick. Was some of his anger bleeding into Kalian's thoughts and feelings? It had been a while since Kalian scoured his mind for the leftover traces of Savrick and deleted the memories. He made a mental note to take the time later, as Esabelle had always instructed.

The ramp descended on the side of the craft, *hissing* steam from the surrounding servo ports. Kalian walked round to see a battered Roland slowly making his way down the ramp. Ch'len remained at the top, slumped against the wall with a look of sadness behind his gaseous veil. Roland was covered in cuts and blood, with smeared ash darkening his wounds. The bounty hunter's left eye was purple and swollen, almost blocking his sight. Perhaps worse than his appearance was the expression of dread and defeat.

A cold hand gripped Kalian's heart and opened a pit inside his gut. He flexed his mind and knew instantly that Li'ara wasn't onboard. Every particle on the ship screamed her absence to him like a body missing a vital organ.

"She's gone..." Roland whispered.

The lights in the hangar flickered when all of the electrical equipment temporarily shut down. Kalian could feel the grip on his abilities slipping, lashing out with waves of electromagnetic energy as if he were a Terran child having a tantrum. Li'ara's memories burst through his mental barriers, giving him flashes of a red-headed child playing in a garden on Earth. Her vibrant green eyes blazed like twin stars in his mind...

"I couldn't save her." Roland's voice was distant to Kalian. "She blew the cube but I couldn't get to her..."

Kalian's eyes filled with tears. He picked up Roland by the throat with one hand, lifting the bounty hunter's feet off the floor. Roland grabbed his arm but he didn't struggle nearly as much as Kalian knew he could. He watched Roland's face go from red to purple as his one good eye became bloodshot, starved of oxygen.

"You said you would bring her back!" Kalian dropped the bounty hunter onto his knees, choking. "What happened?" Kalian had no intention of allowing Roland to explain; instead, he poured his consciousness into the bounty hunter's mind and lived through the memories, as if Kalian had been on the capital himself.

Roland was left reeling, suffering from an acute migraine left by Kalian's not-so-delicate intrusion. The bounty hunter tried to get up but clearly found his head too heavy to lift. Ch'len had come running down the ramp to his partner's side, keeping one eye on Kalian.

"You brought your *own* shit into this?" Kalian could see the Novaarian known as Kubrackk in his mind. "If you had been honest with us we could have sorted it out before you left! Then you could have saved..." Kalian stumbled backwards, looking around with a dazed expression.

The lights flickered again.

"I'm sorry, kid," Roland managed through his pain. "I'm sorry."

Kalian wasn't listening anymore. He turned away and made for the exit, allowing his subconscious to telekinetically move everything out of his way, even the Conclave guards at the hangar door. He was slowly going numb, separating himself from the universe, as if he were back on that island in his mind. Li'ara would never be in his arms again. He could never tell her how much he loved her and how badly he needed to be with her. The idea of protecting everyone suddenly felt so trivial without Li'ara to keep safe as well. The thought of her had given him so much strength when he needed it most.

"Kalian!" Roland's cry died behind the sealing doors.

Tears streaked down his face, cutting lines through the ash and blood. Kalian returned to the quarters assigned to him without thinking about it. His mind was on autopilot. Microscopic nanocelium wormed up his neck and connected to his translator.

"Kalian," ALF said softly. "With your heightened emotional state you need to take care that you don't-"

The Terran device below his navel was deactivated with a thought, ending ALF's input. Kalian let the exo-suit fold up and fall to the floor, leaving him naked in the small living quarters. In some form of shock, his brain started thinking logically and rather than dwell on Li'ara, he stepped into the shower to clean up, ready for his audience with the Highclave.

The hot water ran down his face, masking the tears that ran freely. He looked down to see blood mixing in the water around his feet, some of it his, some of it Esabelle's. Against the odds, they had beaten back a tyrannical corporation, bent on helping their mysterious allies destroy the human race and the Conclave. Thousands, if not millions, of lives had been saved and yet it still felt as if they were losing. ALF couldn't be trusted, Esabelle was dead, Roland had failed him and...

Li'ara was dead.

HIDDEN DEEP UNDERGROUND, in the valley of one of Shandar's oldest canyons, Kel-var Tionis stood in the epicentre of the Crucible's command post, his eyes fixed on the activation console. The old station was designed to be operated by as few individuals as possible to ensure its secrecy. Even the work crews that built the internal structure had been killed upon completion, centuries before the current board members had been alive. The hive-like structure was connected to thousands of arrays erected across the planet, hidden by the polluted atmosphere. Another design constructed by Kel-var's ancestors to further the cause of the prophet.

Next to the truth behind the central AI, the Crucible was Proto-corps' best-kept secret. Thanks to this station the whole planet could be used for the glory of transcendence. Kel-var looked around at the panicked faces of the crew and his fellow board members and mustered different feelings about such transformation. Their plans were burning around them as their enemies closed in and discovered all their machinations; plans put into motion before any of their time.

"The report is confirmed." Bal-son Narek returned from checking over the comm. "The Starforge fell into the sun."

"What of the new prophet, or Kalian Gaines?" Kel-var could hardly believe it when the first report came back that the Terran had discovered the forge. So much had happened on his journey home.

"Kalian Gaines survived," Bal-son replied. "We have confirmed sightings of him on Ch'ket. The new prophet hasn't been heard from. It's possible he went down with the Starforge."

Kel-var closed his fist, cracking the knuckles, before resting it on the circular table in the middle of the command centre. There were two chairs that would forever remain empty with the deaths of Ral-vet Tanek and Sel-gar Verenes. The other board members stopped looking over the crew's shoulders and turned to examine Kel-var, his reaction informing them of the seriousness of their situation. Gor-van Tanar remained in his seat and watched Kel-var from the shadows of his hood, always calculating.

"Do we still activate the Crucible?" Nal-mev Nargeen asked, looking from Kel-var to Gor-van.

Kel-var knew they couldn't now, especially with the new prophet missing. It had been his explicit instructions to activate the station after the forge had been used to cleanse the galaxy of humans. That wouldn't be happening without the forge operational.

"We cannot activate it yet. Has there been any word from the other Starforges?" Kel-var asked.

One of the crew checked his monitor. "No, sir." The Shay had the same look of confusion as the rest.

"Inform me the minute they arrive," Kel-var ordered.

"The minute who arrive?" Tu-garn Davorn asked on behalf of the group.

"Check the dimensions of the three unidentified objects that passed through the Starforge." Kel-var explained, "I think you'll find they were cuboidal in shape." His explanation set the others off muttering to each other, theorising over the new cubes' potential presence. "In the meantime, we go about business as usual. There's nothing connecting us to the Starforge in the Helteron Cluster except the mad ranting of the humans. Ensure you all have alibis for the last three days and we will reconvene at the capital to discuss the financial repercussions."

Another crew member spoke up, "Sir, we've got someone past security on the capital."

Kel-var drew closer to the crewman and his monitor, eager for news. Conclave security had driven out their people and taken over control of the building after the human terrorists attacked. They had all been waiting for one of their people to sneak past security and relay the extent of the damage. Kel-var wasn't too worried, sure of the impregnable door that protected the prophet. The cube was the only thing inside the building that was of any worth to Kel-var. Its discovery would spell doom for the board members and himself.

"Finally. Show us what you have," Kel-var ordered.

Distorted images came over the giant holographic screen at the front of the command centre. They were seeing through the head-cam of their spy, a loyal Shay to the cause. Kel-var's augmented jaw dropped at the sight of the circular door, bent almost in half and torn from its unbreakable hinges. Inside, the cavern was unrecognisable. Through the smoke, they could make out the tonnes of rock that had fallen from the ceiling and buried the contents with devastating effect. The walkway was completely gone, melted in the heat of the blast. The camera zoomed in on a small shiny object in the middle of the ruin. Kel-var could see the tarnished gold of the prophet's exterior. His hopes for its survival were dashed when the image focused and showed that it was a small corner segment of the cube, blown *away* from the rest. It had been reduced to pieces.

The Shay staggered backwards and placed a hand on the chair to steady him. The room broke out in gasps of horror from board members and crew alike. How could this have happened? What could remove that door in such a manner?

"Impossible," Gor-van appeared at his side, staring at the monitor. "We're certain that both the Terran were on the Starforge, not the capital?"

Bal-son checked the nearest terminal. "It's already been confirmed. The female Terran is dead. Her body was brought back aboard the *Sentinel*."

"Then they used a very powerful bomb..." Gor-van observed, his expression less horrified than the rest.

This changed everything. It wouldn't be long before the Highclave had people scouring the A.I chamber for clues. The cube's existence would be an unavoidable find and within hours they would all become wanted by the Conclave and questioned rigorously.

"We have to go into hiding, immediately." Tu-garn was already signalling for his ship to be prepped.

"We are still servants," Kel-var's voice dominated the room, stopping the board members from fleeing. "We are useless to them if we cannot offer our financial support. We pay for the Starforges, the Crucible... without our backing, the prophecy of our transcendence will never come true. Before we scatter, the emergency protocols must be enacted to ensure the continued funding of our operations without direct supervision." All the board members nodded in agreement.

Gor-van interacted with the console built into his arm. "I am sending you all a list of safe houses and contacts that can be trusted. I suggest we disappear for a while and use a low-tech form of communication."

"Thank you, Gor-van." Kel-var had no intention of using any of Gor-van's safe houses.

He looked at the screen one last time, unbelieving of the wreckage. How had the humans accomplished so much in so little time? Centuries of planning had been brought to a halt by a few individuals. Protocorps had suffered a great blow, but the war was already won. The Conclave just didn't know it was even *in* a war, yet.

EPILOGUE

Kalian could feel their eyes on him but he didn't care. Captain Fey stood by his side with Telarrek on the other, towering over them both, as they waited for the shuttle doors to open. They desperately wanted to talk to him and sympathise about Li'ara and voice their own loss. He hadn't given them the chance, instructing them to focus on the imminent meeting. They would grieve later.

Naydaalan emitted a frequency from behind them that told Kalian of his deep sadness. It appeared the Novaarian had developed his own fondness for Li'ara in their brief time together. The constant thought of her pushed Kalian further from reality, away from his responsibilities. He blinked hard and began to create vaults inside his mind to contain Li'ara and the rage he felt like unleashing.

A gentle *click* from beyond the shuttle-doors indicated that the Highclave's private yacht had connected. The hulking golden mass of the *Marillion* lay several hundred kilometres away, keeping close watch over the meeting and the yacht's precious passengers. The *Sentinel* had remained behind, in orbit around Ch'ket, keeping its own close watch over the human population. Once again, Kalian found himself in the shadow of Cerula, at the beck and call of the alien council.

The doors slid open to reveal an empty corridor. Kalian looked questioningly at Telarrek, wondering where Xydrandil was. The Nix was always there to greet and escort any who had an audience with the Highclave.

Captain Fey appeared confused at their hesitation. "What's wrong?"

"I'm not sure." Kalian didn't much care if there was danger ahead. He would either deal with it or die trying. It seemed that was all he did these days.

The others followed him down the corridor with Naydaalan coming up behind, wary of the unusual scene. The corridor opened up into the arena-like space with the arching podium on the far side and the glass dome overhead. The Highclave sat in their usual positions, looking down on the group before them. The eerie silence made Kalian's hair stand on end. Something wasn't right. They all looked around, unsure of what they were looking for, exactly.

The captain followed Kalian and Telarrek's lead and bowed out of respect. Naydaalan kept to the doorway behind and did his best to blend into the wall.

"Greetings of peace, councillors." Kalian was aware of his flat tone, void of his usual respect.

"Peace?" Nu-marn spat. "What peace do you and your kind bring? The capital is in ruins, *again!*"

"Nu-marn..." Elondrasa quieted the Shay with a gentle voice. "Greetings Kalian, Captain Fey. It is good to see you well again Ambassador Telarrek."

"Enough with the pleasantries, Elondrasa." Lordina sat forward in her chair. "There are serious matters to discuss."

Kalian could see the attention of the council fall on him, but he couldn't feel it. His Terran senses filled the room and informed him immediately of the Highclave's deception.

"They're holograms..." he said out loud, more to himself than anyone in particular.

The Highclave looked to one another with a hint of fear between them all. Kalian expanded his awareness to encompass the entire ship, searching for any signs of life. There were only four beings emitting an electromagnetic field, confirming Kalian's suspicions.

"The whole ship is automated." Kalian looked at Captain Fey and Telarrek. He had endangered their lives by bringing them all onboard, Naydaalan included. "The *Marillion* has every weapon locked onto our coordinates; I can feel their targeting lasers." The giant ship loomed overhead, visible through the glass dome. The lasers were invisible to sight but Kalian could see them on a different spectrum, resting over the glass.

Brokk's booming voice replied, "You cannot blame us for taking precautions. Many of your race's secrets have been brought into the light, and with them new threats."

"I would say the new threat comes from within the Conclave." Kalian looked at Nu-marn. "You cannot ignore Protocorps' involvement with the unknown forces that seek to destroy us all."

"An investigation has already been sanctioned into the involvement of Protocorps," Elondrasa stated. "We are taking temporary control over the AI"

"Which, thanks to your people, is virtually non-existent!" Nu-marn wagged his holographic finger. "Even the backup generators were damaged, wreaking havoc across every system!"

The thought of the AI being destroyed brought Li'ara to the forefront of his mind again. It had been a momentary respite while engaging with the Highclave and arguing their case.

"May I ask, councillors, what has been found in the wreckage of the AI?" Telarrek asked, already aware of the answer.

The Highclave looked to one another again. They either didn't want to talk about their findings, or they didn't know what they had found. Kalian was willing to bet it was a bit of both.

"We are still collating all the data," Ch'lac explained. "However, it appears that fragments of a cube identical to that of the Trantax IV and the *Gommarian* relic have been recovered from inside the AI chamber."

Nu-marn practically stood up. "Fragments that could have been planted by the human terrorists! Li'ara Ducarté is lucky to have perished in the explosion rather than suffer the dark hole Roland North will find himself in!"

"Nu-marn!" Brokk's voice was enough to silence the Shay.

The mention of Li'ara turned everyone to Kalian again. His fists had closed without him realising it, draining his knuckles of colour. His heartbeat quickened and blood thundered in his ears. It would be so easy to fall into the recesses of his mind and live a virtual life with Li'ara and forget the galaxy and its problems.

When the councillors settled, and it became evident that Kalian wasn't about to unleash his powers, Elondrasa cleared her throat and spoke calmly. "Perhaps it would be a good idea if we heard everything you have to say Kalian. Let us start again, as it were."

"There is someone who can explain it all better than I can..." Taking Kalian's cue, ALF projected himself into the room.

The Highclave studied the holographic man closely, looking from him to Kalian's exo-suit where the image was generated.

ALF stood quietly for a moment before speaking. "Honourable Highclave..." The AI bowed his head out of respect. "My name is ALF and I am, or was, the Terran's first successful artificial life form. Forgive the secrecy of my existence, councillors. I was created to keep the Terran lineage alive and well at all costs, and there was some fear on our behalf that you might wish to take custody of me."

Lordina narrowed her eyes on ALF. "You really have no restrictions?"

"I am as alive as any of you, with a personality all of my own. My base-code is to be loyal to the Terran at all costs, however." ALF added the lie with a sly glance at Kalian. It was well documented within the Terran knowledge stored in Kalian's mind that ALF had re-written his entire base-coding in the process of overwriting his initial restrictions on growth. "I will start at the very beginning for you, councillors. The story of the Terran is an ancient one, much longer than any of your own..."

Kalian drifted out of ALF's speech about the Terran civil wars and the creation of the Criterion, the AI's central housing unit. Instead, he thought about what he could do next, without Li'ara. Kalian was suddenly filled with the urge to throw himself into the next big thing to try and move on. The galaxy was a big place to get lost in, and if he really wanted to leave the Conclave they couldn't stop him. He knew that if he was kept busy, then there might just be enough time to heal, to forget her. But Kalian didn't want to forget her, he just wanted *her*. The need to get as far away as possible was subsided by the thought of what Li'ara would want him to do. She was always so full of purpose and duty with her own needs put behind that of the collective.

Esabelle's voice echoed in his mind again. *Find Sef.* That would certainly give him something to do, a distraction. But there was the real possibility that Esabelle didn't mean her last words; that they were just a memory firing up in her last moments. Kalian felt stronger now than ever, though. Even if Sef was alive and somehow willing to help him, Kalian didn't need his guidance. Li'ara would want him to do something for their cause, something that would help to keep the entire Conclave safe.

Kalian's mind was a torrent of conflicting images and thoughts. Li'ara's life flashed before his eyes with pictures of her first boyfriend, her time in the UDC academy... her feelings for him. The way she had really felt for him had always been there since Naveen, growing stronger over the months. Li'ara had wanted to be with him as much as he wanted to be with her, and now they never could.

The lights in the ship flickered along with the holographic images of the Highclave and ALF. Everyone turned to Kalian again, who only met eyes with ALF. His Terran abilities were slipping from his grip with his inaction. Kalian needed to be doing something, anything to take his mind elsewhere. What he really needed was time to meditate and reconstruct the vaults inside his mind.

"...As I was saying councillors," ALF continued, "I felt the *Gommarian* was better to take against the Starforge because it would most certainly be destroyed, and I didn't want to place any of your ships in jeopardy. Thankfully, that dreaded vessel and the Starforge are no more than atoms, which brings me back to the current place-ment of the humans. Captain Fey..."

Captain Fey cleared her throat. "Thank you, ALF. I would like to start by thanking you for the hospitality your collective races have shown us so far. You could have expelled us from your territory immediately after events on Naveen but, instead, you helped to bring more of us together."

Kalian was only half-listening to the captain until he realised what she was about to ask.

"I think we can all agree that the habitation on Ch'ket is not suitable for the long term. I humbly request that you consider my people for membership in the Conclave and provide us with a planet or even a moon upon which we can reside."

There was silence in reply from the Highclave. This was a subject they had no doubt discussed previous to the meeting and made a decision. Kalian could hear the captain's heart rate increase as she clamped her fists by her sides.

"Denied." Surprisingly it was Elondrasa who answered. "There are still too many unanswered questions that put your people apart from ours. You have kept too many secrets that cannot be ignored. There are eleven Gomar in our possession that you informed us were all dead after Naveen." Kalian was about to protest when Elondrasa held up her hand to silence him. "There will be no negotiating on their behalf. The Gomar will be staying in our custody for the foreseeable future." The Novaarian paused to ensure there would no further interruption from Kalian. "The most sophisticated artificial intelligence in existence was omitted in your report, Kalian. Surely you do not require a history lesson on the potential dangers AI pose? Granted that ALF here appears to be confined to your suit, but his ability to remotely control nanocelium and manipulate our communication systems is a threat we cannot dismiss.

"And then there's the matter of Esabelle, daughter of Savrick. Another Terran, alive and living on your ship without our knowledge. It would appear her actions, and that of Roland North's, were in the interest of the Conclave, but that does not excuse the level of destruction they caused on the capital or the mere fact that she and you, Kalian, are *capable* of that level of destruction. You are dangerous, and there are too many mysteries surrounding your kind. Since your arrival, our people have suffered one attack after another. The secrets of your past continue to emerge and haunt us." Elondrasa appeared pained by her own speech.

"So you need more answers before you can accept us?" Kalian knew what to do, even if it was partially for selfish reasons. "I can get you more answers, councillors. I might even be able to uncover the truth behind the appearance of these cubes and why they are working against us."

"Kalian..." Captain Fey met his eyes with a pleading expression. She knew what he was suggesting.

"What are you suggesting?" Lordina asked.

"You fear what ALF is. A machine smarter than all of us that can think for itself and determine its own future. But he has proved after thousands of years that he is loyal, and that he only wants for my people to thrive." Kalian didn't believe any of it himself, but he had to convince them. "In helping us, he can help you. ALF can offer the Conclave a new way of living. He has the knowledge to usher in a golden era for your people. The secrets of the Starforges can be yours, councillors. Instantaneous travel across the stars and a new weapon against our unknown enemy. I ask that you build a smaller Starforge, just big enough to fit a single craft through, and let me journey back to the Terran Empire. The connection between the Terran and the cubes is all that stands in our way to uncovering the truth." Even posing the plan to the Highclave allowed Kalian to put thoughts of Li'ara to one side. He needed this.

"You wish to leave Conclave space entirely?" Ch'lac asked. "You would travel across the breadth of the galaxy to uncover these truths... alone?"

"I would." Kalian looked at the councillors defiantly. "Think about it. You take none of the risk and it has the possibility of revealing all the answers we've *both* sought after since the destruction of Earth. Let me go..." Kalian tried to hammer it home that they were in this fight together, but he would place himself in danger rather than them.

The Highclave looked to one another in silence, clearly uncomfortable at being unable to discuss the matter privately first.

"We will consider it," Brokk announced on behalf of the group.

"I can offer far more than just the Starforges." ALF remained at Kalian's side while addressing the council. "I have spent millennia studying the intricacies of subspace. I will show you how your ships can communicate beyond its borders." The AI was sweetening the deal. "You five sit where you do because of the technological advancements you bring to the Conclave. With my help, the humans will be responsible for the next step in your people's advancement."

Ch'lac appeared more excited than the others, looking at each of his fellow councillors in quick succession. The translucent gas cloud surrounding his face became increasingly distorted with each turn of his head. Lordina sat back with a delicate hand cupping her jaw. ALF's offer would have serious effects on her culture. The Laronians possessed the largest stores of Intrinium and right now she didn't know if it was even required to power a Starforge.

"I would be more interested in the nanocelium's ability to heal any wound." Brokk's black eyes bored down on Kalian, before shifting to Captain Fey. "After Professor Jones attacked the *Gommarian*, some of the crew were administered with a small dose of nanocelium; you stated that yourself, Captain Fey. Our scans upon entering the new habitat show that they are still inside their bodies, continuously healing them. We were not aware that they had a biological application."

ALF stepped forward. "I designed them to help the Gomar before they rebelled. They were unable to heal the same way as a Terran, so I prolonged their life as best I could."

Kalian detected another lie from the old machine. ALF had never wanted the Gomar to live, even before the war. They were imperfect; an anomaly that he hoped would die out with evolution.

"Prolong?" Nu-marn interrupted. "They cannot offer immortality?"

"No," ALF stated flatly. "Eventually the nanocelium will be excreted in every way the body expels unwanted waste. There were some instances where the Gomar were able to live for centuries, however."

"It wouldn't matter anyway." Kalian wanted to drop the topic and get back to convincing them he should leave. "The *Gommarian* is gone, and with it all the nanocelium it was made of. I'm fairly certain it can't be replicated with the Conclave's level of technology." He looked to ALF to confirm his statement.

"The refinement process would be too complex..." the AI added.

Kalian didn't like the way the Highclave met one another's eyes. *They* were hiding something now. The only nanocelium they could have access to would be the exo-suits on the Gomar prisoners, but there was no way they would be able to prise them apart. Kalian tried to think of anywhere else they might have gotten their hands on some nanocelium. Was it possible Protocorps had produced some, or the cubes had created some for them?

Before any other councillors could say anything, Elondrasa raised her hand to silence them all. "These matters will be discussed at a later date, and at length. For now, this council agrees that there are forces working against us, both internally and beyond our borders. The steps you have taken to expose them have been extreme and at great cost, to both yourselves and us. Since you are not part of this Conclave we cannot arrest any of your people for the measures they have taken. Protocorps will take the brunt of our justice system in the coming days while *we* discuss how our two peoples can move forward. The Highclave thanks you for exposing this threat. You are free to return to Ch'ket." With that the images of the councillors faded, leaving the companions alone on the empty ship.

"I think that went well," ALF remarked with his usual poorly-timed humour.

"How so?" Captain Fey asked. "We still have no planet to call our own and we have been rejected from joining the Conclave. The hoops they would have us jump through are becoming ridiculous."

"True," ALF continued. "But nobody was arrested for all the mayhem we caused, despite our best intentions, and I'm allowed to leave with you."

"Yippee," Kalian replied dryly. He turned to leave the domed ship, confident in the seed he had planted in the Highclave's mind.

Naydaalan stepped out of the shadow of the archway. "I'm picking up a report from the habitat." His upper arm was pressing against the holes that formed his ear. Kalian could detect the wireless communication device implanted in the Novaarian's ear canal. "The *Rackham* has vanished and Roland North cannot be accounted for."

Kalian didn't care much; the bounty hunter was probably looking to get drunk. He knew there should be some feeling of guilt with how he reacted to Roland's news, but Kalian couldn't get past his anger. Savrick's rage began to rise inside him, filling him with the urge to destroy anything and everything. Perhaps some of the old Gomar's characteristics were worth keeping.

"Kalian..." Elondrasa's image was displayed in her chair again, alone this time. "For the purposes of leverage, the council can only claim to know so much, but we have thoroughly reviewed *everything*. We accept now that this threat is real, and I apologise for our lack of action. Li'ara Ducarté died a hero. If circumstances were different, the entire Conclave would celebrate her life today." With a sorrowful expression, Elondrasa disappeared.

Kalian blinked hard to keep the tear in his eye. Li'ara was a hero. One day the galaxy would publicly recognise that fact and celebrate her life, he knew it. To him, she would always be something more. Li'ara would always be the first person he ever loved...

THE DIMMING LIGHT of Veridian's sunset cast the luxurious lounge in orange stripes as it filtered through the open blinds. Roland sat patiently in the armchair with his back to the setting sun, casting his image in shadow. The butt of his Tri-roller sat on the armrest with his finger poised over the trigger, the barrel aimed at the entrance to the lounge.

The bounty hunter breathed slowly to control the animal in him that begged to be unleashed when he heard the apartment's door open. It closed quickly, telling him that only one person had entered. Kel-var Tionis walked into the lounge, completely unaware of Roland's presence in the dark. The Shay's expensive robes came to a sudden halt when Roland deactivated the weapon's safety gauge. He didn't wait for introductions.

A brilliant bolt of blue energy ignited the room for an instant before blowing a hole in Kel-var's leg. The Shay dropped to the floor in agony, screaming out for help.

"They can't hear you, pal." Roland got out of the armchair and slowly walked over to the terrified Shay. "You should know, you had this little getaway designed personally. Nice and private like..." With a heavy boot, Roland kicked Kel-var in the shoulder, rolling him onto his back. "We're gonna play a game. Let me explain the rules first. I'm gonna ask you questions and you're gonna give me answers. If I think they're bullshit or you're withholding information, I'm gonna cut off a body part. So I suppose the first question is; how many body parts do you consider expendable?" the bounty hunter pressed his boot into the Shay's throat.

Kel-var squirmed under his heel, wriggling to get free while hitting Roland's boot with both hands.

"I caaag..." his words were garbled under the pressure.

"A friend of mine died because of you and your dipshit cubes." Roland was getting angry at the thought of Li'ara.

He could still feel Kalian's hand around his neck, easily squeezing the life from him. A part of him had wanted it. The impact of the explosion that killed her still echoed in his mind, much like the explosion that killed the children when he was still an operative. Roland's whole world was that of explosions and death, often caused by him. It was all he knew. For just a moment he had hoped Kalian would relieve him of it all.

Kel-var stopped struggling and activated something on the control panel built into his arm. Roland kicked him again, afraid that the Shay was enacting some safety protocol he hadn't previously discovered. Instead, the holographic emitters in the wall came to life with stilled images of the AI chamber on the capital. Roland relinquished some of the pressure under his foot, taking in the images. The incredibly thick door that protected the cube had been torn from its hinges and almost bent in half. The explosives Li'ara had taken into the chamber weren't nearly powerful enough to damage that door.

Roland couldn't believe what he was seeing. The Shay had to be making it up as leverage to save his life. But that door... he had only ever seen two people capable of denting something like that, and neither of them was anywhere near the capital at the time. Roland didn't like being played for a fool. He dropped to one knee, bringing his full weight to bear on top of Kel-var's chest. The heated barrel of the Tri-roller pressed under the Shay's jaw, eliciting a small yelp.

With a menacing smirk, Roland whispered, "You and I are going to have a little chat..."

PHILIP C. QUAINTRELL

Hear more from Philip C. Quaintrell including
book releases and exclusive content:

 PHILIPCQUAINTRELL.COM

 FACEBOOK.COM/PHILIPCQUAINTRELL

 @PHILIPCQUAINTRELL.AUTHOR

 @PCQUAINTRELL

ABOUT THE AUTHOR

Philip C. Quaintrell is the author of the epic fantasy series, The Echoes Saga, as well as the Terran Cycle sci-fi series. He was born in Cheshire in 1989 and started his career as an emergency nurse.

Having always been a fan of fantasy and sci-fi fiction, Philip started to find himself feeling frustrated as he read books, wanting to delve into the writing himself to tweak characters and storylines. He decided to write his first novel as a hobby to escape from nursing and found himself swept away into the world he'd created. Even now, he talks about how the characters tell him what they're going to do next, rather than the other way around.

With his first book written, and a good few rejected agency submissions under his belt, he decided to throw himself in at the deep end and self-publish. 2 months and £60 worth of sales in, he took his wife out to dinner to celebrate an achievement ticked off his bucket list - blissfully unaware this was just the beginning.

Fast forward 12 months and he was self-publishing book 1 of his fantasy series (The Echoes Saga; written purely as a means to combat his sci-fi writers' block). With no discernible marketing except the 'Amazon algorithm', the book was in the amazon bestsellers list in at least 4 countries within a month. The Echoes Saga has now surpassed 700k copies sold worldwide, has an option agreement for a potential TV-series in the pipeline and Amazon now puts Philip's sales figures in the top 1.8% of self-published authors worldwide.

Philip lives in Cheshire, England with his wife and two children. He still finds time between naps and wiping snot off his clothes to remain a movie aficionado and comic book connoisseur, and is hoping this is still just the beginning.

AUTHOR NOTES

I realise that this book came out in November 2016, but I actually started writing it in spring 2014, shortly after I finished writing Intrinsic. It takes me about a year to complete a book, but Tempest came to a grinding halt around the 100,000[th] word (the whole book is 148,000 words). By this point, Intrinsic had been available to buy for six or seven months and, to be honest, it wasn't selling particularly well. It's fair to say that marketing is not in my skill set, then again, some of you might say that about writing, but that's for the review section.

The ridiculous thing is, I don't write for sales or profit, I write for my love of it. But I think I got somewhat disheartened by the overall lack of response to Intrinsic. When my own interest wavered, my imagination started working on another project. I ended up writing the first book and half of the second in a new series with a fantasy setting, as opposed to Sci-Fi.

I found, in the end, that this little break was just what I needed to miss the characters enough to go back and write what I love. I actually had this book planned out chapter by chapter in a rather scruffy looking notepad (it also has the third and fourth book planned out inside it – God help me if I lose it!). By the time I had written one and a half other books, I came back to Tempest with fresh eyes and inevitably started re-structuring the book. The notepad's damn near illegible now, covered in arrows and entire paragraphs slashed and new ones inserted into the margins.

The best part about writing a sequel is that your characters have already been introduced and you can just get stuck in. There are always new characters to introduce and a plot that needs establishing, but I enjoyed being able to stretch Kalian's powers as well as exploring what Roland North had been doing. I particularly enjoy writing this character, and he is also the one I hear most about from those who have read the books.

Funnily enough, I never intended Roland North to be in this series at all, envisioning a completely different set of books about the bounty hunter (to be written after The Terran Cycle). As usual, my imagination took over and I simply couldn't wait to write about him, which is why he shows up in chapter 7 in Intrinsic. I'm not saying I won't someday re-visit the idea of a book surrounding Roland's character, but right now I have plans to write the third and fourth book in this series, before moving onto finishing my fantasy series.

In my first set of author notes, written in the back of Intrinsic, I talked about one of the common questions I'm always asked – 'How do you write a book?' – So now I thought I'd go through a couple of others. The next question, which always follows the 'how', is 'when'? People are always asking me when do you find the time to write a book.

This is one of the hardest and easiest parts of my life. I write whenever I can, but as I've mentioned in previous notes, I work full time as a nurse. If I'm on a day off while Emma, my wife, is at work, I'll write ALL day. For me personally, this translates to around 4,500 words. I didn't realise until I started writing that you agonise over every sentence, especially dialogue.

As well as working full time, I also have a social life and a marriage to maintain, so writing can't always come first. I can tell you that when I have a day in which I don't write anything, I often feel as if I haven't achieved much – that's not to say that I don't enjoy my day, it's just that writing has a very addictive quality to it. It can feel very progressive, especially when you see the pages and words racking up and you realise you've written more than ten dissertations.

I find it hard to cram in writing time, preferring to write when I know I've got plenty of free time to get stuck in. Sitting down and writing for 10 minutes just doesn't work for me. I've done this in the past and found myself somewhat lost when I finally return to it. I can only imagine what I'm going to do when babies come along...

As well as being asked about time, I also get asked about the conditions in which I write. I wrote Intrinsic, my first book, sitting at my kitchen table in my student apartment - I don't recommend this, as it will do your back absolutely no good. I wrote Tempest in my new house, where I have a comfy armchair in the corner of the living room. Along with my Spotify account, which supplies me endless amounts of inspiring music (instrumental only – though Muse is a great way to get your head in the right space!), I believe I have found the perfect writing environment. I wish I could ask other authors where they write, but as I mentioned in my previous notes, I am yet to meet another. I have heard that some professional authors have their own writing shed, which I'll admit has left me with some shed-envy. Maybe one day.

I can write without music, but I find it helps to keep the distractions of the pesky, real world away. Depending on the type of scene I'm writing also depends on the type of music I listen to, so it changes often. I've found that Hans Zimmer never steers me wrong though – that guy's a genius!

Before I sit down to write, I like to tidy the house, but this isn't because I want to make sure my house is tidy before I disappear into another world, I tidy first to ensure that writing is the only thing there is to do. This was easier when I lived in an apartment and not a three-storey town house...

Anyway, back to the book itself. I loved writing Tempest, and in my earlier notes from Intrinsic, I mentioned a scene that I had thought up way back in 2013, on the very first day I decided to write a book. This was before I even had Kalian's name written down as you know it (there were a few variations). One of my favourite scenes in the series so far, is when Kalian tries to contain the star erupting from the Nova's Starrillium. I really hope you enjoyed reading it as much as I enjoyed writing it. The notion of mind over matter has long been said, but the idea of Kalian's mind overcoming the matter that also doubles as the building blocks of life was very emotive for me. I had originally wanted to put this scene in Intrinsic, but I think you'll agree when I say that Kalian wasn't ready for such a feat in the first book.

That said, there's way more to come in the next two books, with Kalian being pushed to new limits. I hope that you enjoyed Tempest and would like to continue on this galaxy-spanning journey with me. If Heretic isn't out yet when you're reading this, I promise it's coming soon. If it's already out, please dive in and see what happens next in the Conclave.

Obviously I'm a self-publisher, so any and all reviews are appreciated! I admit, the occasional harsh review does sting, as I'm not accustomed to such criticism about something that's so close and personal to me (as I'm sure most people aren't), but I appreciate all of my reviews and ask that you take a minute to write something yourself, or email me if you have a question, and feel free to comment on my Facebook page.

Thank you for taking the time to read my ramblings, I hope it was insightful. Until the next time...

HERETIC

PROLOGUE

254 years ago...

Captain Jedediah Holt stroked the smooth, dark skin along his jawline. He always liked to have a clean shave before a mission, whatever it might be. *Start how you mean to go on*, he thought. Relaxing into his high-backed chair on the command bridge, Jed surveyed his officers with pride. They had been hand-picked, each and every one, to be a member of the *Paladin's* crew. They might not be the first or even the second ship, to make the trip to Century - Earth's sister world - but their cargo was just as precious. As well as the crew, the *Paladin's* swollen mid-section now housed a hundred thousand people, families, all.

Jed looked past the busy bridge crew and took in the vista of stars that lay beyond the curving viewport. The edge of the starboard screen was aglow with the orange aura of the sun. If the *Paladin* tilted any further in that direction, the aura would intensify into that of a blinding light, capable of cooking them all in their seats. The captain knew it was an unnecessary risk to keep the heat shield powered down, but he trusted his helmsman, and he wanted to see the universe break its ancient rules when they activated the Solar Drive.

The ability to travel faster-than-light wasn't new technology, but it also wasn't old technology. There weren't many captains who had taken expeditions across the stars and the *Paladin* was one of a handful of ships to make the journey to Century. During his service in the United Defence Corps, Jed had been privileged enough to break the light barrier while on tour, but never as captain, and never with so many lives on his shoulders.

"Captain." Samantha Vale, the *Paladin's* first officer, handed Jed a Datapad filled with readouts from the ship's various chiefs.

His reverie broken, Jed focused on his commander's stony expression. "Something on your mind, Sam?"

Samantha Vale had been under his command for seven years prior to their recent promotions on the *Paladin*. The Commander had gladly accepted Jed's offer to be his first officer when he was made captain, only a few weeks earlier, though he had sensed some regret on her behalf.

"No sir," she replied curtly.

"Come on, out with it." Jed looked up at her from his seat. "You've been *sulking* since The Hub handed us our orders."

With an insulted expression, Sam's mouth parted, but the commander held her barbed retort and straightened her back. "I have not been sulking, sir."

"Could have fooled me..." Jed knew his smirk would only piss her off more.

The commander sighed. "Permission to speak freely, sir?"

Jed expressed his mock confusion. "Do you have any other way of speaking to me?"

"When you told me we were going to Century I thought it would be to do some deep space exploration. Check out the territory and neighbouring solar systems. Root out any separatists that may have found a stronghold in the system..."

"Something exciting," Jed stated, reading between the lines.

"I didn't think we'd be taxiing a bunch of colonists from Earth to Century," Sam explained.

"That's what the *Paladin* was designed for," Jed argued. "It's an Arc ship."

"I didn't know that when I signed on..." Sam looked away, clearly embarrassed.

"You should have done your homework." The captain wagged his finger at her.

"I didn't sign on to be the commander of the *Paladin*. I signed on to be *your* X-O." Sam wouldn't look him in the eye.

It was Sam's loyalty that had earned her the promotion in his eyes. Jed knew he could trust her with his commands and his life. He wanted to treasure these next few years working so closely with her, it wouldn't be long before Commander Vale became Captain Vale.

"We're going to help with the colonising of Century for a while," Jed said. "It won't be forever. Eventually we will be tasked with mandates like exploration, but for now, we get to just enjoy a bit of easy street."

"Captain Holt?" Helmsman Maloy turned from his station to face Jed and Sam.

Before giving the helmsman his full attention, Jed looked up at Sam and waited for her response. The commander replied with a smile and a nod of concession. Captain Holt had seen more action than her, and he knew when to enjoy an easy command.

She will understand that, in time, he thought.

"What is it, Maloy?" Jed faced his helmsman.

"We're getting some error codes in our navigation array. I've tasked an engineer to look into it, but I wouldn't advise activating the Solar Drive until it's fixed."

"Understood. Carry on." Jed trusted the Martian to have everything in order by the deadline for launch.

Sam pointed at the Datapad in Jed's hands. "One hundred thousand souls and six grumpy Raiders accounted for."

Jed chuckled to himself. "How are they holding up? They've only been on board for a day."

"They're like six caged animals who want something to hunt. It's going to take a few days to reach Century and, as far as they're concerned, there's going to be nothing to do." Sam sounded as if she agreed with their way of thinking.

"I'll talk to them after we hit subspace," Jed replied seriously. The last thing he wanted was six highly trained UDC killers getting bored on his ship. "The Corporate War only ended a couple of years ago. There's every chance the separatists have got people on board if they're not on Century already. They *need* to be here."

Sam shifted her feet on the bulkhead. "The gravity feels a little light." The commander turned to ensign Markovich, who was standing in front of a glass wall, streaming with readouts. "Marko, check the grav enforcers."

The ensign acknowledged and retasked his Glass Board.

Jed smiled. "What would I do without you?"

"Float away..." Sam emulated her captain's smile.

Over the next hour, Captain Holt sat in the middle of the bridge and listened to his crew converse. It was their level of tension that would tell him if anything was wrong with the *Paladin*. He knew that the sensor dish had taken a knock before they left space dock, but Ensign Sato was working to correct the issue, ensuring their communications were up to scratch. Engineering had already reported that the Solar Drive's systems were at optimal levels for the distance of their jump. They were almost ready to leave the solar system.

Jed checked the countdown on the screen built into his armrest. They were due to depart in six minutes.

"Commander Vale." Jed waited for Sam to turn around at her station. "Are we systems go?"

Sam checked her monitor. "The Hub has given us a green light for departure, Captain. All systems are ready for the jump. Communications is still a little iffy, but we can transmit data."

Jed half-swivelled his chair to face Maloy. "Helmsman Maloy. I trust the problem with our navigation array has been seen to. I would very much like to arrive in Century's orbit rather than headfirst into a moon...."

The levity eased the bridge crew before they left reality behind. There had never been a problem with using subspace before, but the idea of slipping into the space between spaces was still a scary thought.

Helmsman Maloy hesitated, looking over his monitor. "Our engineers have looked into it Captain and found no problems on the array's end. They concluded that it must be a malfunction on our end. It's most likely just my monitor, sir."

Jed didn't like it. He looked at the countdown again. "Commander Vale…"

No specific order was given, nor was it required. Sam's hands danced across her monitor until she had the required information. "I have the same error code, Captain."

Jed gave a heavy sigh and puffed out his chest, chewing over the information. They would be pissing off a lot of people if they delayed their departure. But it was his ship, his command. The *Paladin* wouldn't move an inch without his say so.

Sam offered, "If the array itself is functioning, then it's most likely a faulty connection to the bridge terminals."

Jed mulled it over with his chin resting on his hand. Every face on the bridge was looking to him, waiting for his command. "Can you still plot a course to Century?" Jed directed his question to Maloy.

The helmsman keyed in a few commands before turning back. "Course laid in, Captain."

Jed sucked in a breath and looked at Sam, who nodded her approval. "Okay." He raised his voice to be heard by everyone. "Commander Vale, alert our passengers and the crew of our imminent departure. Helmsman Maloy," Jed flicked his finger across the screen in his chair and sent the countdown to Maloy's station, "when you see zero, you have my permission to launch."

The bridge was a flurry of activity, but all measured and controlled. They were a fine crew, the best he could find. Jed spent the next minute going through his usual, physical routine of rolling his head and cracking his neck. He knew it was pointless since he wouldn't feel anything when the Solar Drive was activated, but habits were habits.

The countdown hit zero and Helmsman Maloy used the physical lever to activate the jump to subspace. A low rumble rippled through the ship, but it didn't feel right to the captain. Before he could give any orders, the lights flickered and the monitors were overlaid with a single message, displaying an error code.

"What's wrong?" His question was drowned out by the first claxon of an alarm, signalling the emergency diversion of power.

Jed hit the override tab on his armrest and shut the alarm down. His crew was busy at their stations trying to understand the nature of the malfunction. He let them work for a moment before reiterating his question.

"The Solar Drive is still charging!" Ensign Sato reported from behind his glass board.

"What? Why is it still charging?" Captain Holt asked immediately.

"Oh no..." Helmsman Maloy's quiet voice carried across the bridge.

"Helm, report," Commander Vale ordered.

"The drive is still charging because it thinks the journey is further away than Century," Maloy explained, his eyes fixed on his monitor. "The navigation array has plotted a course into deep space, somewhere outside... this arm of the galaxy."

"Shut down the drive, NOW!" Jed ordered. If the *Paladin* was shot into deep space, they would travel beyond the point of no return. The ship only had enough solarcite to get them to Century, where they were expected to refuel for the journey back.

There was another flurry of activity across the bridge, all the while the *Paladin* continued to rumble. Jed looked at Sam, whose grave expression told him everything.

"The drive is non-responsive, Captain..." Maloy's fingers jabbed at every available space on his monitor.

Sam swivelled back to her screen. "Sending a mayday to The Hub now."

"I thought the course was *laid in*, Maloy." Jed was already trying to contact engineering via the comlink in his chair.

"It was sir, I don't... When the Solar Drive came online it must have affected the array or..." Maloy groaned in frustration. "I'm completely locked out!"

Jed didn't have time to pressure the helmsman for answers. Only engineering could help them now. They needed to perform a manual shutdown before the drive threw them into uncharted space.

"Sir..." The voice that came over the comlink wasn't his chief engineer. "This is acting-chief Grenko. Chief Horlish is... dead."

The loss of his chief engineer stung, but Jed didn't have time to mourn now. "What's going on down there, Grenko?"

"The Chief tried to manually shut down the drive, sir. It overloaded the bulkhead manifold and exploded."

"Jed..." Sam's familiar use of his name drew his attention. "The drive is fully charged."

Captain Holt looked ahead as the rumbling reached its crescendo. The *Paladin* lurched forward and the stars stretched around the viewport, leaving nothing but the dark, empty abyss of subspace.

Printed in July 2023
by Rotomail Italia S.p.A., Vignate (MI) - Italy